I AM
WATCHING

Emma
Kavanagh

KENSINGTON BOOKS
www.kensingtonbooks.com

ISBN-13: 978- 1-4967-1375-9
ISBN-10: 1-4967-1375-3
First Kensington Hardcover Edition: April 2019
First Kensington Trade Edition: July 2019
First Kensington Mass Market Edition: April 2020

ISBN-13: 978-1-4967-1376-6 (e-book)
ISBN-10: 1-4967-1376-1 (e-book)

10 9 8 7 6 5 4 3 2 1

Printed in the United States of America

Whoever fights monsters should see to it that in the process he does not become a monster. And when you look long into an abyss, the abyss also looks into you.

—NIETZSCHE

Do not be dismayed to learn there is a bit of the devil in you. There is a bit of the devil in us all.

—ARTHUR BYRON COVER

July 22, 1996

It began with the bodies.

They had been seated, backs propped against the tumbledown stones of Hadrian's Wall, faces a bitter white. Their heads were tilted forward, their jaws grazing their sternums. You might have thought that they were sleeping. But there was the color of them, the rigid emptiness of them, the first shadowy scent of decomposition riding on the promising heat of the day to come.

Fifteen-year-old Isla Bell felt the ground sway beneath her, the village and the moors retreating far, far away, so that it was just her and the dead. Her knees gave way. She sank down, her bare legs swallowed by wet grass. Her palms landed on an outcrop of rock, spikes of pain zinged through her hands, her stomach contracting, and she folded over, a dry heave, a merciless heat running through her.

They had been murdered. Isla was only fifteen, knew little of death, and yet even she had no doubt. Three people did not wander from their homes in the early morning and line up alongside one another in order to die. Not unless they had no choice.

A necklace of bruises ringed Kitty Lane's neck. Her hands had been folded into her lap, a knotted network of veins stark against the gray of them. She wore a fuchsia housecoat, bootie slippers lined with fur, her legs bare against the damp grass. Her head had begun to slip sideways, had drifted downward so that her tightly permed curls rested gently against the cheek of the corpse beside her.

Ben Flowers. Hadn't he got married recently? Rhian, Rachel, something like that? There was a line of blood, dried, along the side of his forehead. His arms, too, had been folded into his lap, but the left hung at an odd angle, as if he had been given an additional elbow midway along the radius. His jaw, that looked wrong, too, out of position somehow. And if you looked very closely, you could see the dark red bruise of finger marks on his neck.

And then there was Zach. Zach sat three seats across from her in English. Zach ate tuna sandwiches for lunch and hated spiders. Zach once broke his leg, trying to prove to his brothers that he was big enough to jump from a second-story window. Zach was quiet and kind and funny and, undeniably, dead.

She allowed her head to sink downward, looking at the blades of grass, the ant that hurried up her bare knee, and told herself to breathe. It had been a run. That was all. A day like any other, in which her eyes flickered open as the clocks rolled on to 6:00 a.m., the sunlight breaking through the chink in the curtains and her body thrilling with the fizz of contained energy. Her mother said that she was like a springer spaniel, needed a couple of good runs a day to be bearable. She had let herself out of the house, the clock reading 6:09. Through the garden and out onto the moor, vast in its rolling bleakness. Had paused for a moment, the cool air lapping at her skin. A kestrel had cruised above the scrubby moorland, dipped low over the curve of the Whin Sill, followed the arch of it as it clambered up into the amber dawn sky. Then she had pushed off, the sole of her foot shoving away the uneven ground below. She ran for the wall, the cold sharp in her chest, the barrenness pushing her to run faster, harder. A pull to the left, her running shoes followed the arc up the Whin Sill, her calves straining against the incline, breath coming hard and fast as she reached the height of it, balancing on the narrow ledge that abutted the stones of Hadrian's Wall. And then, after turning left, her feet worked to remain where they were on the slender pathway, running into the sunrise, so that its fingertips of red reached out to her, tugging her onward. The stones of the wall stretching out beside her like a column of marching ants.

She ran with a long, loping gait, fighting to keep

her balance on the sloping land, which seemed determined to tip her over. Perhaps that was why she ran it. Perhaps it was the bloody-mindedness of being where the land itself did not seem to want you. Or perhaps it was the wall. Because Hadrian's Wall was home to her. When she was a child and was asked where she lived, she would simply reply, "I live on the wall." The wall was what protected her from the moor, from the wildness beyond. It was that line of organization that cut across the moorland, suggesting that even this could be tamed by some stones and an abundance of will.

Then, as her lungs were straining and her heart was hammering and the outskirts of the village came into sight, she descended from the peak, a headlong dash down a wild slope, turning away from the cresting sun and the early morning mist that sat low across the horizon. Into Briganton itself, an oasis of civilization in a desert of green. The stone-built houses huddled together, immensely proud of their age and their neatness, the gardens put together with an excess of care, flower beds lush and organized with a precision even the Romans would have been proud of. It was still as she ran through the empty streets, a town frozen as it waited for the day to begin. She ran through the village, along the narrow pavements that graced just as narrow roads. Up past the primary school, past the tree that she had once got stuck in, up to the church, its heavy wood doors shut tight. Then at Bowman's Hill, the farthest reach of the village, once she had the Cheviot Hills in sight, looping left, back down and around until she reached the wall again. Running, her footsteps loud in her head;

thinking of little things, like exams and school and boys and the kind of things that you thought of when you were fifteen and alone; and then, as the landscape shifted and the moor flattened out beneath her, seeing something off in the distance that her mind simply could not explain.

Getting closer and closer and thinking that at any moment the scene would rearrange itself and then what was before her would make sense again. Because she was in Briganton, and in Briganton there were no dangers, and the world was small and orderly and safe. And so what she thought were dead bodies, well, that simply could not be.

Isla stared at the sharp-edged stone beneath her fingers. She didn't want to look anymore. She didn't want to see.

But then it was unlikely that Kitty or Ben or Zach wanted to be here either, so she forced her gaze upward, allowed it to rest on them. She needed to call for someone, needed to get help. Her father would be at home still, would not have left for his shift.

Isla pushed herself upright. Dad. He would know what to do, would be able to fix this, make it whole. But even as the thought formed, she could feel the lie of it. Nothing would make this whole. In an instant the world about her had changed. Nothing would ever turn it back to how it used to be.

That was when she heard the sound, a low moaning, like the wind that sometimes funneled its way down through the Cheviots, and a feeling of electrification raced across her skin, along with the knowledge that she was not alone.

Isla whipped around, expecting to see . . . what?

A killer waiting behind her? But there was nothing, just the moor and the sleepy village. And then again that sound. She wanted to run, could feel her entire body sparking with it, the need to escape. But she stayed, turning around, her gaze running along the clambering, dipping Whin Sill, past the stones of the ancient wall, the bodies before it, tracking past them even as they tried to stay her attention.

Then a flash of something, an unexpected shadow falling in just the wrong place. The slightest suggestion of movement.

He lay perhaps a hundred meters away, face-down in the grass. It looked as if he, too, had been positioned but had slumped down, the weight of his body tugging him down to the welcoming earth. Isla's breath became short again, a new horror plucking her from what was already horrific enough. She moved slowly, cautiously, toward the fourth dead.

The sound came again, and with the sound, the slightest twitch of movement.

Isla ran then, threw herself carelessly down into the grass beside the fourth victim. His eyes were closed; the hair on the back of his head was densely matted with blood.

"Oh God," she said. "It's okay, Ramsey. It's going to be okay."

Twenty Years Later:
Friday, October 21

The bogeyman – Isla

Monsters rarely look the way you expect. Isla watched Heath McGowan through the window. He lay prostrate, his head held in place with a cylindrical cage. He should have looked like the devil. And yet there he lay, all five feet nine inches of him, a thick frame supporting a square head, hair cut bluntly short, somehow smaller now than the last time she saw him. An ordinary man, a small pot of a belly beginning to form, nails bitten down to the quick. And yet it would be no lie to say that she had thought of him every night for twenty years, that every night, as her hand grazed the lamp switch, she had paused to drink in the last of the light and had thought of the killer on the wall.

She was a thirty-five-year-old woman, and she was afraid of the dark. Heath McGowan was the reason.

"You okay in there, Heath?" She leaned closer to the microphone, depressing the speaker button, keeping her voice light, friendly even. "We're going to get started in just a minute."

She watched him on the monitor, his eyes darting upward as they dissected her words. What was he looking for in there?

But Isla had done this kind of thing many times before, and she knew full well what Heath McGowan was hoping to find in her.

Weakness.

"You take your time, Professor." His voice was calm, almost relaxed, as if somehow he had made the coffin of the MRI scanner, the guards, and the shackles that waited for him disappear, and he was lying on a beach.

Isla released the button and glanced across at the prison guard. Steve? Stan? Attractive in an overmuscled way, he stood flush with the window that separated the control room from the scanner—separated him from his prisoner—his gaze locked on the machine and what could be seen of Heath McGowan's body. It was a strange sensation. To know that the room had been swept, that anything that could, even in the wildest of imaginings, be transformed into a weapon had been removed, that there was a guard here, one outside the door, another outside the door beyond that, and yet still to feel that your safety relied on the good grace of a monster.

"There's coffee there." Isla waved to the table

beside her. "And cake. You should make yourself at home. This will take a while."

The guard nodded, risking the briefest of glances in her direction. "I'm good. Thanks."

"MRI is ready." The radiographer was a small woman, neat and gray, unimpressed with the caliber of the patient. She drummed her fingernails on the desktop.

Isla depressed the button. "Okay, Heath. We're starting the structural scan now. This will take a few minutes."

"Yup."

It was a special kind of madness this, lunacy in the pursuit of science. To remove a man convicted of two or three or four or more murders from his prison cell, to place him into a transport, with guards who look at you like you have lost your mind. To bring him to a hospital, take him into a room in which you will have to remove his handcuffs, encourage him to lie down on a sliding table and be slotted into the clanging wildness of an MRI. All the while hoping against hope that whatever evil put him in prison can remain boxed away, at least for this little while.

And yet here they were.

"Lucky number thirteen." Connor leaned against the back wall, cradling a chipped mug.

"Lucky number thirteen," Isla agreed.

Thirteen serial killers. Thirteen times they had removed monsters from their cages, had peered into their brains, had felt their hot breath, their ice-cold smiles, and thirteen times, Isla had known that her survival depended on the good grace of the devil.

Isla watched Heath's feet, white sneakers slack against the table, and wondered what he was thinking. Of course, the real question was: Did any of the previous twelve count? Really, if she was being honest with herself, hadn't it always been about this moment and this man?

She had run across the moor on that July day twenty years ago, her heart beating hard, unsure whether she was running from or running to. Had flung herself through the back gate, past the gold-fish pond, screaming for her father like she was the one being murdered. She didn't know how she had made him understand, how she had put into words that which seemed so far beyond them, and yet somehow she had, and then she was running again, this time her father alongside her, pulling ahead of her, seeming to lead instead of follow. She had thought that Ramsey would be dead, that he couldn't possibly have survived the hours, years that it had taken her to call for help. And yet, miraculously, he was not, remained clinging to life, still facedown in the sodden grass. She had thrown herself down beside him, had clung to his hands, muttering comfort that she did not believe, while her father had stood and stared at the dead. Then a drowning cascade of sound, wailing sirens, blue lights thrown up against the stone walls of the nearby cottages, and people, everywhere, it had seemed.

More childhoods than hers had ended that day. Because it seemed now that all of Briganton had been experiencing a prolonged infancy, that it had been cradled by Hadrian's Wall and the Cheviots and the ocean of moorland, that the world had been kept at bay for longer than should have been possible. And then, on that July day, all that had been kept back came crashing in, and the faces that had before been creased up only with petty concerns now wore the telltale signs of terror. It seemed clear that whoever had done this was one of them. No one could quite put their finger on why this must be so. Perhaps it was because that was the worst they could imagine, and the entire village had suddenly realized that they were not immune to the worst, after all. There was no talking on street corners, no evenings in the local pub. The summer fete held three days after the deaths was attended by, at most, a dozen hardy individuals. Briganton had experienced real fear for the first time. Its response was to lock itself away. Isla's father vanished: Detective Sergeant Eric Bell was now needed far more elsewhere than he was in their little home. He became a ghost to them, a poltergeist leaving traces of bread crumbs on kitchen counters, creaking floorboards in the wee small hours as he returned for a few hours' sleep before beginning again.

Then, three weeks later, came the next one. The murder of nineteen-year-old Amelia West, a trainee nurse living two streets over from Isla's own home. And disbelief warped into blind panic. He, whoever he was, was not done. He was hunting.

Isla's parents began to talk about moving, about leaving the village that was in their blood, their bones. Her father, on the rare occasions she saw him, had grown older, more weighted down, either by the deaths or by his inability to solve them.

Two weeks after that came the murder of Leila

Doyle. Twenty-five years old. She had vanished while putting her washing out.

Isla stopped sleeping then, moved into her sister Emilia's room, where she would lie, staring into the lamp that remained steadfastly on as the night rolled around into morning. Waited each day, each night, for him to come for her.

And then, after six weeks of torment, there came a day on which her father was gone, for a day, a night, another day. She started to wonder if he, too, was dead, if her mother was simply afraid to tell them. Then the phone ringing late in the evening, her mother's hand shaking as she picked it up, silence and then her face changing transformed back to something that Isla had not seen in six long weeks. *He got him. Your father got him. His name is Heath McGowan.*

Heath McGowan had been arrested in a pub in Newcastle. He had gone there straight from the flat of his then girlfriend, Lucy Tuckwell. Eighteen years old and six months pregnant with their first child. When police—or, more specifically, her father—had arrived at the flat, they had found Lucy dead on the floor, the final victim of the series.

"Maybe we'll get a nice fat tumor pressing on the amygdala," Connor suggested. He sipped his coffee, watching the screen. "Love me a nice fat tumor."

Isla glanced back at him. Lanky and lean, hair cut short, but not short enough to prevent the ends of it from flicking up into those inexorable curls. It was different for him, she reminded herself. Some days, she felt she had known Connor her entire life, like he was a brother to her. But then she remembered that he had not been here back in the dark days, that he had not survived what they had survived, and so he would forever remain separate, able to know them only as one looking in through a window. They had worked together for six years, knew each other's rhythms and tastes. And yet, for Connor, what they did remained an adventure, a walk through a jungle on an organized tour, the simulation of danger, where the real threats had been filtered out, packaged away. Perhaps, thought Isla, that was why he always seemed so much younger than she, even though they were the same age. Perhaps it was the excitement in him, the thrill of academic exploration. For him, the horrors that they heard were little more than a scary story shared around a campfire. For her, they were her life and her home.

She shrugged. "You never know. Although, frankly, he's always been a prick."

The sounds began, thunderous bangs as the hydrogen atoms were shifted, realigned, shifted again. A rising harmony of beeps, one picture, two, three, four, a thousand. Isla leaned back in her chair, her eyes trained on the hands of the killer on the wall. They lay limp at his sides. Large, the fingers shorter than you would think, stubby. The hands that had wrapped themselves tight across the throats of Kitty Lane and Ben Flowers and Zach.

Isla had waited for this since she was fifteen years old.

They had said that she wouldn't get him, that Heath McGowan had built himself into a legend, that in twenty years he had not once spoken about the dead bodies he left seated against Hadrian's

Wall. Many had tried. For ten years following McGowan's arrest, Stephen Doyle, the husband of Leila, had written to him once a week, pleading for a meeting, begging to know what had happened to his wife in those last precious hours of her life, just how her end had come. "I just want to sit across from him," Stephen had said. "I just want to look into the eyes of the man who took Leila, so I can try to understand." But Stephen, like the journalists, the police officers, and the academics that followed him, had been met with a hefty wall of silence. McGowan, it seemed, would take his stories with him to the grave.

Isla, however, never afraid to tilt at a windmill, had written to him, pouring into the letter all the charm and the persuasion that she could muster. Had reminded him of their childhood connection, tenuous at best. And had promised to provide him with answers, to delve into the glorious mystery that was the McGowan brain and to lay the results before him.

To the amazement of all but Isla, he had written back.

It was a week ago that Isla Bell had first made the hour-long drive to Winterwell Prison, a fortress that stood alone on the edge of Kielder Forest, had watched as Heath McGowan was led into the room, seated at the desk before her, and had known that she had done what none had done before. She had got in.

"You look different." Heath McGowan had studied her with that spotlight focus that would have told her, had she not already known, that she was in the company of a psychopath.

"I'm older," Isla had replied coolly.

"Yeah." Heath had laughed, head dipping down, coquettish almost. "Aren't we all? But you . . . Age suits you. What are you? Thirty-four?"

"Thirty-five." Isla had sat at the desk, had watched Heath opposite her. Had felt her heart thundering. Had told herself that this was simply number thirteen. That she had done this many times before. That this was no different. Of course, all of that was a lie, wasn't it? Because this time, with this man, it wasn't about the stories, about victims who were simply names in a crime story. This time it was about the person who had left three dead for her to find. Who had tried to murder Ramsey and had failed. It was a feeling of the wind blowing as you stood on a cliff edge.

"Of course. Four years younger than me. I remember you from school, you know."

In her memory, Heath was a ghost in a ripped denim jacket, his lip curled into an ever-present snarl. One of them and yet not one of them. His mother a drinker, his father who knew where, he had landed on his grandmother's doorstep, would stay awhile, long enough to get himself a reputation as trouble, then would leave again each time his mother resolved to do better, to be stronger than her need for the alcohol. Yet weeks or months later, he would always return, each time angrier.

"I'm surprised you were there often enough to remember me," Isla said wryly. They were old acquaintances chatting about days past. They were neighbors sharing a history. They were a serial killer and the teenage girl who had found his first victims.

Heath gave another laugh. "Aye, well . . . had better things to be doing with my time. Your sister. Emily? Emilia? Now, she was always a looker. How is she?"

He was testing her, a great white nibbling around the edges of a cage to see if it really would protect the diver within. Isla looked at him, her gaze steady. Emilia had moved away from the village as soon as she was able to. She had married her first boyfriend, had three little boys, a detached house on a modern estate in Newcastle, and a rampant anxiety disorder—the last thanks to the man before her.

Isla smiled. "Emilia is fine. So, Heath, shall I tell you a little bit about our study? See if it's something you're interested in participating in?"

"Aye." He watched her, gaze hungry.

"I'm a professor of criminal psychology at the University of Northumberland. I specialize in brain function and its influences on criminal behavior." She slid into the speech like it was a comfortable pair of shoes. "I've worked on this with a number of other people in the past. What I'd like to do with you is have a bit of a chat, talk about some of your experiences, childhood, things like that, get you to take part in a few tests, and then, in a couple of weeks, we'll arrange for you to go through a functional MRI, magnetic resonance imaging, which will allow us to see how your brain is working, how it responds to stimulation, things like that."

Heath leaned forward, his forehead knitted in

a frown of concentration. "So . . . like, this functional . . . whatsit . . . does it, like, tell you why I do the stuff I do? I mean, will you be able to see if there's something wrong with my brain? If that's why?"

"It will certainly give us some indication, yes."

Heath sat up straighter then, and Isla knew. She had him.

A low buzz and Isla's head snapped around as she was pulled back to the present, the monster in the tube.

"Professor Bell?" The radiographer tapped some keys. "Structural scan is complete."

"Okay," said Isla. "Let's start with the moral decision–making task." She leaned forward, spoke into the microphone. "Heath? We've completed the structural scan. Now we're entering into the functional phase of the MRI. Keep looking at the screen in front of you. I'm going to present you with a series of choices. Use the button box I gave you to select one. You happy?"

"As a clam, Prof." His gaze on the monitor was flat, unmoving.

The guard snorted, rolling his eyes at Isla.

She pushed the microphone away, smiled. "Could be worse. The last guy we had in here decided to mark his territory by pissing on the floor."

"Charming."

Connor pulled out a chair beside her, lowered himself into it, one hand carefully grasping a cupcake. "Yeah, he was a beaut. Cupcake?"

Isla shook her head. "How the hell do you eat so much but stay so skinny?"

He grinned. "Good genes." He lowered his

voice. "How's Ramsey doing?" Nodded toward the scanner. "He, ah, he got any issues with this?"

"Why has McGowan agreed to do this?" Ramsey had asked. Her husband had put the pan on the stove harder than was strictly necessary, had lit a blue flame beneath it, had poured in a glug of oil.

Isla had kept her gaze averted, her full concentration directed to checking the tomatoes for inadequacies. "Ramsey, he's been in prison for twenty years. He's probably bored. The chance to have a nice day trip, even if it's just to an MRI scanner, probably seems like a pretty sweet deal." She had pushed closed the door to the fridge, expression effortfully light. Because it had seemed somehow crucial that she kept it hidden, how much this mattered to her, how great her own need was to sit across from the killer on the wall.

Ramsey nodded, the back of his blond head dipping up and down, just once. Swept the onions into the pan. Were his hands shaking?

"I just . . . I don't trust that guy." The rest was left unsaid. *Because he tried to murder me. Because he murdered my brother, five others besides.*

Isla turned, watched her husband's wide shoulders, the arch of his arms, quiet muscles beneath a plaid shirt. He still had nightmares that kept her awake into the small hours of the morning, her husband twisting and pulling at the sheets, his hands grasping at the pillow, at her, as in his dreams he attempted to save himself. To save his brother. And she would cradle him to her, mother to a small child.

It had become a rhythm in their marriage, calm waters shaken by something and by nothing, the swell of a wave, a crest, and then, from nowhere, calmness again. There would be long periods in which Ramsey slept peacefully, and then a change—restless nights leading into sallow mornings, quietness becoming a dense silence. His features gaining a sad slackness, a jumpiness, as if her husband had moved into a perpetual state of waiting, ready to leap at the closing of a door or the unexpected fall of a foot. The counselor had said that it would be like this, that there would be periods of peace laid alongside periods of unrest. Post-traumatic stress disorder coupled with relapsing/remitting depression. A diagnosis that Isla could have made herself. This period, these past five years, this had been the most peace they had known. Isla had begun to wonder if the storm had finally passed. If life could in fact be different. Then those words—"I'm going into the prison. I'm going to meet with Heath McGowan."

"If he's agreed to be a part of the study," Ramsey said, stirring the onions, the oil spitting, sizzling, "maybe it's because he knows who you are. You know what these guys are like, with their grandstanding. Wouldn't it just be the perfect twist of the knife to get to you? Your father's daughter. My wife?"

Isla dug the point of the knife into the tomato, and its "ripe to the point of bursting" skin ruptured beneath the pressure. She sliced with a fast sweep. Tried very hard not to feel that flush of anger. That she was by definition to be explained only by her relationship to someone else. To the men in her life. That she had got to Heath, had squeezed her way inside—had met with this success—only because of her father, the man who'd arrested Heath; and her husband, the man he had attempted to kill.

She let her knife race through the tomatoes, her heart beating fast. The trouble was, she wasn't at all sure he wasn't right.

Isla took a deep breath, her tread careful. This was, after all, her husband's story more than it was hers. She could bow out. Get Connor to do it. He was more than capable. And yet . . . Isla thought of that moment every single night, when, her hand on the light switch, she felt the fear race from her abdomen up to her mouth at the thought of the darkness about to come. She was not good with fear. Ramsey had caught her once, had come home late on a night when darkness had plummeted early, brought about by wild weather, had found her walking the blackened house, bare feet, wearing nothing but a camisole and absurdly short shorts. Had looked at her like she was insane. And she had never said it, had never explained to him that she had been pushing herself to the point of her greatest terror. With the darkness and the vulnerability of near nakedness, it had been like a private dare. *I bet you can't* . . . Isla had always been a sucker for dares.

"Well, I'm sure it will be fine. All the authorization is in place, so I don't really have much choice in the matter now," Isla lied. "Just . . . Look, these guys, they want something to fill their days in there. A study like this, it gets them interested. And they get to brag. You know, tell someone how clever they were, how they almost got away with it. I'm sure McGowan has no clue who I am."

Now Isla sipped her coffee, black, the bitterness of it making her wince. "Ramsey's fine. He gets that this is important. You finished up all the childhood stuff, right?"

They were two halves of a coin, she and Connor. He: developmental and environmental influences. She: cognition, genetic factors. Taken together, they could tell a story—how a serial killer became a serial killer. Because if you could tell that story, then maybe, just maybe, you could change it.

"Yeah. It's . . . not great. I mean, it's not as bad as some I've heard. Pavel Devreaux still gets to keep his 'worst childhood imaginable' crown."

Pavel Devreaux had killed eleven men, mostly homeless, helpless, in and around Calais in the late nineties. He had then eaten their internal organs.

"Heath's mother was an alcoholic, father erratic, but around just long enough to sexually abuse Heath from the ages of four to seven. Pretty vile stuff. The mother alternated between affection and fury, and it looks like little Heath had no way of predicting which way she would go. The most consistent presence seems to have been the grandmother. From what he says, she tried her best, but sounds like she was pretty overwhelmed by the whole thing. Heavily critical, not much in the way of affection. Would routinely tell him that he had been taken over by Satan."

"Well, she was right about that much," muttered the prison guard, keeping his stare on the unmoving feet of Heath McGowan.

Isla nodded, watching the screen where Heath's selections were flashing by. The test was coming to its conclusion. The attentional focusing one would begin shortly. She pulled a file closer, flipped the cover open. "I finished going through the PCL-R."

The Psychopathy Checklist—a measure of badness.

"And?"

She looked at him, her gaze flat. "Thirty-seven."

Thirty points would have indicated that he was a psychopath. Forty was the most extreme level of psychopath it was possible to measure.

Connor nodded. "Well, that's pretty definitive."

"Yes. Yes, it is."

Of course, thought Isla, sometimes you just knew. Even without a test. There was a certain feeling that occasionally came from sitting with a psychopath, that notion that your senses had been supplanted, that what you thought now, what you felt, came from him, this man in front of you, rather than from all that you knew to be true. It was like being bewitched and horrified at the same time, the watching of yourself from a great distance as you were led willingly into danger. Isla often thought of psychopaths as the anglerfish of the human race.

"I liked Briganton," Heath had said on that day, a week ago. He had leaned forward across the desk, his expression earnest, hands hooked together like those of a child at prayer. "I mean, my nan, she was all right. Lived there all her life. Course, you say that name now and all anyone ever thinks of is . . . you know."

You. The killer on the wall. There were coach tours now, organized excursions for the dark of mind, the opportunity for misery tourists to visit the famous murder sites in the North. Briganton was stop number three. Isla had stopped telling people where she was from, had grown weary of that look of almost recollection, of the dawning realization and, far too often, of excitement.

Then Heath had looked at her with the air of one who had recalled something. "How is your dad? I heard he became a superintendent. Superintendent Eric Bell. Has a nice ring to it. I always liked him. Gave me a hard time when I was pissing around as a kid, but he was all right. Course, I went off on him a bit when he arrested me." Something glimmered in his eyes. Amusement? "I heard that he became quite the celebrity. The great Eric Bell, the detective who brought down the killer on the wall. You know, he never even said thank you. I mean, that big old career of his, I did make it, after all." He had studied her critically. "You look just like him, you know?"

Isla had wondered faintly what it was that Heath was expecting. Did he expect her to cry? To rush from the room, a little girl pulled to pieces by the big bad wolf before her? Perhaps he did not yet understand just what he had done to her at the age of fifteen, how much he had changed her, and just how many wolves she had tamed since then.

"Yes. Yes, I do."

Fuck you.

Now the MRI thumped, beeped. Isla watched Heath's hands work the button box, the speed of them suggesting enjoyment.

"Professor? The structural scan has finished processing. It's ready to be viewed now if you want to see it." The radiographer didn't look at Isla, her gaze locked on her screen in an expression of rapt boredom.

Isla pushed her chair back and stood up. "Please."

She felt Connor behind her as the screen moved from black to gray and then an image filled it. She studied the screen, and despite herself, her heart sank.

"No gross abnormalities," she muttered.

Isla gazed at the brain of the killer on the wall, its swirls and ridges. There was no convenient tumor impacting on the amygdala that would explain the aggression, nothing that she could point to and say, "Here, here is where the evil lies." To all intents and purposes, they were looking at a perfectly normal brain. But then, wasn't that the thing with serial killers? Weren't they all, when you looked at them, perfectly normal? Right up until the monster in them was unleashed.

To stay or to go –
Ramsey

The rain poured down, a relentless barrage that made an almost night from what should have been an early afternoon sky. It turned the flat roof slick, and the wind that blew down from the Cheviots yanked at Ramsey, threatening to pull him over the side of it, send him tumbling down twenty stories onto the concrete below. He wiped his hands across his eyes, gritted his teeth, tried to sound calm. "It's okay."

"It's not okay." Stephen Doyle wasn't looking at him. Instead, his entire attention was directed downward, beyond the lip of the roof where he stood, to the empty air and the solid ground beneath. "It's not okay. It hasn't been okay since Leila . . . Do you know how hard it has been? Every day to get out of bed. Every day praying that something will happen, that I'll be hit by a bus, that I'll contract some horrible disease, anything, just so that it's over, so that I can see her again."

"Stephen . . ."

"Twenty years, Rams. Twenty years of what? This isn't life. It's torture." He leaned farther out, so far that it seemed inevitable that gravity or the howling wind would do what will had so far failed to do, would tug him outward, into the abyss.

Ramsey took one step forward, one back. Any closer and he might drive Stephen over, any farther and he wouldn't be close enough. His suit trousers clung to his legs; rain plastered the hair to his head.

Ramsey had been in Carlisle, covering a city council meeting, and had had a dull morning finishing up a dull article on truancy levels, their impact on crime statistics. One of those mornings that make you question your life choices, that make you think, *Surely there must be more than this.* And there was more, of course; there was Isla. And so he had left the city, had driven the short distance north, past the airport, the modest planes overhead ricocheting in the wind, and then on to the university campus. He would buy his wife lunch, perhaps persuade her to finish early for once, to allow herself to breathe.

And yet it had not worked out that way. He had slid his car into the parking lot, his gaze scanning left, right, for Isla's BMW. It was quiet here today, empty spaces filled with little but puddled water. Perhaps there were exams on, he thought. Perhaps it was the weather. He maneuvered the car into a space beneath the shadow of the tower block and twisted around in his seat. But no, there sat Isla's parking space, resolutely empty.

Ramsey sat for a moment, considered his options. He should go home. He had work to do, articles that were due in, and yet still he sat there, watching the rain batter against the windscreen. Then his gaze was caught by a loping figure emerging from the arts building. The man walked slowly in spite of the rain, and although he wore a coat, it hung unzipped, the sides flapping in the wind. Ramsey squinted through the rain, the man's movement triggering a memory. Stephen Doyle. He pushed open the car door, winced as the rain sparked against his face. "Stephen!"

But if the figure heard, he gave no sign of it, just continued on with his long stride, then disappeared into the psychology building. Ramsey sank back into his seat, considering. It must have been him. Although it had been a couple of months since he had seen him last, the memory of Stephen Doyle, his face seemingly tattooed with a grief that simply would not heal, was seared into his brain. He had heard Stephen had gone back to university. That he had begun a degree, although in what Ramsey would not have been able to say.

Ramsey was reaching for the ignition key when a car skidded into the parking lot, slid into the space beside Isla's. He grinned, pulled his hood up, and dived out into the rain.

"Connor!"

Connor spun round, arms filled with bags and

box files. "Rams." He blinked the rain from his eyes. "You looking for Isla? She's still out at the hospital. With McGowan, you know?"

It sent a prickle through Ramsey, the thought of that.

"She'll be a while yet." A heavy frown, his hair flopping into his eyes. "What the hell did you manage to do to your arm?"

"I slipped, jogging." Ramsey rolled his eyes, tucking his sling-held arm beneath his loosely draped coat. "Pain in the arse. Especially driving."

But Ramsey's attention drifted from Connor to a movement high up on the roof. He peered into the rain, straining to make sense of it. The dark sky, the never-ending rods of rain, the horizontal line of the roof that bisected his vision. And hovering on the edge of it a long, loping figure.

"Oh God."

Connor followed his gaze, head tilted backward, and his mouth grew slack with the realization of what they were witnessing. "Jesus . . . is that . . . ?"

"It's Stephen Doyle. He's going to jump." Ramsey took off running, footsteps light on the slick ground.

Now Ramsey stood on the rooftop and watched Stephen lean outward into the abyss, his coat flapping wildly. Stephen's face becoming slack, resignation setting in.

"I know, Stephen. I know," Ramsey said, blinking away the rain. "But you've lasted. You've made it this far. Don't throw it away now."

He sensed Connor behind him, moving around him, held out a hand. *Keep back.* A quick glance to his side, enough to ensure that they both understood: *This is close.*

"Throw it away?" Stephen gave a harsh laugh, which was tugged away by the wind. "Throw what away? That's what I'm trying to tell you. I have nothing. There is nothing to throw away. You know I lost my job? They said I was taking too many sick days . . . *Unreliable,* that was the word. You know I'm doing this damn degree?" He gave another harsh laugh. "My tutor just told me I'm failing. Failing. Something that any eighteen-year-old can do, I'm failing. I've even moved back in with my sister. Like a damn bum. Everything I had vanished with Leila on that day."

That day. It had been one of light and warmth and sunshine, when Leila Doyle had been hanging the washing out. A balmy summer's afternoon. When Stephen had gone looking for her, he had found her slippers, a basket of still wet washing tipped across the lawn. But of Leila there had been nothing. It had taken three days. For three days her absence had hovered over Briganton like a storm cloud. Then, on the fourth day, a police patrol had found her rapidly decaying body seated against the wall.

"I don't sleep. I haven't slept in years. Every time I close my eyes, I see her body, those"—his hands came up, fingers curving into a shape—"those fingers around her throat." Stephen shifted so that his right foot balanced half on, half off the roof.

Ramsey felt a prickling across the back of his neck. "I know."

Every night closing his eyes, every night promising himself that this night would be different. The darkness descending and then there they were again, the bodies, multiplied now into thousands, hundreds of thousands, each staring at him with empty eyes. Moving through them, searching, fear grappling with his insides, knowing what he would find, because it was the same every single night. Then seeing it, in among the mountain of death—Zachary, arms reaching out, lips moving. Leaning in so he could hear the last breath of voice. "Rams—"

He stood on the roof in the pouring rain, felt Connor moving alongside him, watching him, waiting for him to lead. The thing was, life for those living in the shadow of the killer on the wall was an uneven sort of dance, an unsteady jiggling motion designed to sidestep the past, while simultaneously keeping it in center focus. It was important people didn't forget. How often had he said that? And yet, when you couldn't forget, *you couldn't forget.* And so you became suspended in a kind of hinterland that was neither the past nor the present, but some heady, uncomfortable mixture of the two.

"We were trying for a family. Did I tell you that? Leila, she always wanted a big family, four, maybe five kids. She didn't want anything else. Just to be a mother, to be married to me. It was . . . it was such a good feeling to know that I was enough for her, that the idea of our family was all she dreamed of." Stephen wasn't looking at him, was leaning forward, looking down at the drop. "She would have been such a good mother. I think about that sometimes, about what it would have been like if we'd started already, if we'd had a kid. Thing is, I know it's selfish, but I just think it would have been better, you know, that I would have had a part of her still with me. That I would have had to have been normal."

What could be more natural? Ramsey had thought that too. *Isla, I think we should start trying. For a baby, I mean. I think I'm ready. Aren't you?* Ramsey had held it out to his wife, a gift or a burden, he wasn't sure, had offered it up like it was the most normal of normal things. And yet that wasn't why, was it? He wasn't just a man who had reached the age at which one started having children. He was a man who was stuck, who had become enmeshed in the past, and no matter how much he wriggled and squirmed, he had still not succeeded in releasing himself. But a baby . . . that was what normal people did. That was the shape of a normal life. It was a terrible thing, to want a child in order to save yourself, but if Ramsey dug deep, that was the truth of it. He wanted his child to set him free.

"I know what you mean," he told Stephen, but the wind had stepped up its efforts, the howling turning into a dull roar, as if an army marched across the moor. Ramsey's heart began to race as he saw Stephen swaying with the pressure of it, could feel Connor stepping closer, a low noise in his throat, almost a growl. "I want more than anything to be normal too."

Isla hadn't answered. She had opened her mouth, as if she would, and then, with the sense of a last-minute reprieve, the phone had rung, and she had hurried to answer it. They hadn't spoken of it since.

Connor touched Ramsey's elbow, making him jump. Eyes a question: *Shall we grab for him?*

The world had shifted, its focus narrowing onto this single point in time. Stephen Doyle; the position of his feet on the roof's edge; the slackness of his features, as if the life had already drained out of him; the angle of his body away from the building and out toward the tumbling ground below.

Stephen shook his head slowly, his gaze now on the ground. "It's better this way," he mumbled.

Ramsey felt Connor squeeze his arm, could see it as if it had already happened. That one short step—here safety, there oblivion.

Stephen was inhaling, a noticeable filling of the chest. Preparing.

"You know how I survive?" The words tumbled from Ramsey's mouth.

Time was suspended. Stephen, glancing back at him, frowned. It was a slight movement, small enough that you would miss it if your every sense wasn't trained upon it, but his body shifted, a small lean back toward the building.

"I refuse to let the monster win. I . . . I have dreams too. Nightmares. I see the bodies. Feel the fingers. But . . . I fight it. Because if I give in, if I give up, then he's won." He was aware that his voice was getting smaller. "I won't let him win." Ramsey glanced at Connor, a quick nod. "Stephen, I know it feels that this is your only option, but . . . you have survived. For twenty years, you have survived. I know it hasn't been easy. I know that you've . . . been tempted." An overdose had followed closely after Heath's trial and conviction.

Another one on the ten-year anniversary of Leila's murder. "I know there have been many times when you've wanted to end it. But you've survived. That in itself is an achievement."

Something was happening, a thought spreading across Stephen's face. Doubt, perhaps?

"This choice . . . ," Connor said quietly. "It can never be undone. And yet you have managed all these years without having to make it. Please, at least let us try getting you some more help. Let's see if we can make this bearable, at the very least. I have friends—they're the best people in the world to help trauma survivors. We can go downstairs now, make some calls, get you some help straight away."

Stephen stood, looking out into the gray night, and then leaned forward, peering down toward the ground. Then he was falling, tumbling, tumbling, body hitting the pavement with a crack. But no, he wasn't. He turned back, away from the abyss, reached a hand out to grip the wall, clung to it like a mother clung to a child, like he hadn't intended to throw himself to his death mere moments before. Ramsey felt Connor dart 'round him, unstuck at last, and saw him take a tight hold of Stephen's wrist, one hand on his shoulder, guide him back to the rooftop.

Ramsey simply stood, his head light.

"Come on. Let's get you inside." Connor's voice was now overlaid by fake joviality. "Rams? Shall we? Stephen, we'll give your sister a shout and then shove the kettle on. Nice cuppa, that's what we need."

"Yes," said Ramsey weakly. "That . . . yes."

Stephen, tucked between them now like an errant sheep between two dogs, nodded slowly, his voice low. "Aye. No, you're right. And if it doesn't work out, I can always kill myself another day."

The sense of being stared at – Mina

Detective Constable Mina Arian looked out into the world beyond. The rain had taken on a whole new force, the rising wind driving it sideways into the house, the open patio door. She felt it soaking into her trouser leg, turning the beige material brown. The wind pushing at her, driving her back, nature in charge. *You, inside. This evening is not for you.* She shivered, let her eyes track along the square paved garden path. Its sides were lined with flower beds, the low plants clinging to the ground, as if afraid they would be torn out, thrown into the night sky. Something moved in the distance, two lollipop bay trees bending and swaying with the wind. Three metalwork Mister Tumnus lampposts lined the central path, throwing out an orange light that moved and danced across the ground. And then, through the low wrought-iron gate, the wildness of the moor, all scrubby and dark. Hadrian's Wall was out there in the darkness, the stones of it sitting perhaps a hundred feet beyond the garden boundary.

"You're very exposed here." She squinted, trying to make out shapes in the shadowy light. "What's separating you from the moor? A hedge? How high is it?"

Victoria Prew tucked her cardigan tighter around her, shivered. All angles and edges, long deep red hair that hung around her shoulders. It looked like one good gust and she would be gone. "I don't know." The faint burr of a Scottish accent was just about discernible. "I guess five feet? I wanted to keep the view."

The call had come in at 6:00 p.m., just as they were packing up for the day, the shift skittering to an unremarkable end. The four of them in the criminal investigation department office had stood, their coats already on, bags slung over shoulders, and had stared at the ringing phone. Finally, Mina had sighed heavily, dumping her bag back on her desk, and had picked up the receiver.

"Possible break-in. Officers have attended, passed it on."

Of course they have, she muttered to herself. She glanced up at the other three detectives, farther from her now than they had begun, as each of them attempted to inch their way toward the door.

"We've got a call."

A loud shared groan, and then the mental calculations, the chess game beginning. *Well, I have to pick my kids up. Well, I worked late last night.*

Mina's gaze fell on Detective Constable Owen Darby, the only one who had not yet spoken, who stood, shuffling his feet like a schoolboy in trouble. He ducked his head, sheepish. "I've got a date."

Mina sighed heavily. "Fine. Whatever. I'll go on my own. But each and every one of you owe me!"

Mina looked at Victoria Prew now. She was, what? Forty? Make-up artfully applied, screaming money, lips pursed in a blatant red. You had to take your time with a red like that; you had to keep on top of it. It wasn't the kind of thing for someone chasing small kids around or mucking out animals. A bright white blouse tucked into a breathtakingly narrow pencil skirt. The cardigan—a rich gray cashmere—the only concession to the chill of the evening.

You could tell a lot about people by the way they dressed. Mina slipped her hands into her suit trouser pockets, feeling them tug against her thighs. Thunder Thighs. That was what they called her at work when they thought she couldn't hear them. She glanced again at Victoria Prew and her thin-as-a-pencil skirt and sighed inwardly.

"Mmm." Mina scanned left to right. The next house along had a high wall, seven foot at least, to separate it from the moor. She would be willing to bet her next pay packet that there would be no convenient gate built into it.

"How long have you been in Briganton?"

"Eighteen months."

Mina nodded. Six months longer than Mina herself.

The village of Briganton suffered from an extreme case of split personality. Proud of its history, continuously populated since the twelfth century, like stepping back in time and so on and so on. And yet simultaneously ashamed of what had come next. If you searched for Briganton on Google, what would come up would not be the history, at least not at first. No, to get to that, you first had to wade through the horror of the bodies left upon the wall. The villagers, the ones who had lived it, they kept it buried, weighting it down beneath the detritus of everyday life, and yet you could read it in their every move, in the way they walked, their gaze twisting this way and that, in the way they treated the moor.

She remembered Isla saying to her, late one evening, as they returned home together from the pub, solitary figures on desolate streets, that she couldn't possibly understand. That saying it would not equal living it.

Isla had waved expansively, had said, "The thing is, the new ones, they treat the moorland as if it were wallpaper, something put there to brighten up the view from their window. They don't understand. They haven't learned like the rest of us have. They always underestimate the wildness out there, the danger it can hide."

Mina had stopped mid-stride, had squinted at her still new friend. "Wait. What? You run along the wall every damn morning!"

Isla had grinned. "Aye, well. I've always been a fan of danger."

Mina watched Victoria shivering, slender arms wrapped tight around herself. "You settling in okay?"

In most places, eighteen months would have been sufficient, long enough to have left the "new" designation behind. But it was different here. Briganton was a place where people were born, where they stayed, each filling a specially carved niche within the village. Here you earned your place, and both Victoria Prew and Mina were some distance off that yet.

"It's okay. It's hard, you know. Everyone knows everyone here. So . . . it's fine."

That flash one. The one with that stupid glass house. Stuck up. Too fancy for these parts.

Mina nodded, schooling her face to stillness. It had seemed like such a good idea at the time, when the vacancies were announced—when London had become too much, too noisy, too breathless, too full—to escape north, away from the Met. "The money will go further," she had said as she rationalized to her parents, "and it'll be a break." She hadn't said that it would be a break from them, although the thought of that had been loud enough. And so she had taken the job, escaping across the North-South divide, thinking that it would be *Heartbeat* rather than *The Wire* and that life would become gentler.

Of course, she had given little consideration to the effects of moving to an eight-hundred-year-old village with a population of a thousand. Ninety-eight percent white. In which merely walking down the street in her Iraqi skin would become an exercise in exhibitionism. No matter that she had lived in London since she was four. No matter that her ac-

cent was laced with cockney. The heads turned all
the same. It had been explained to her once, a
"helpful" elderly neighbor putting into words that
which others only thought: "It's because you're
colored, see, love. I mean, not that I'm racist. But
see, people see you and they think of terrorists and
things, and, well, you can understand why they'd
be a bit funny about things like that. I mean, *I*
don't think like that, of course. *I* don't blame you
at all for wanting to get away from all the wars and
things, but people, they're not used to it around
here." It had seemed futile to point out that there
were few wars being fought in Blackheath. And
Mina had felt smaller and sadder and far more
alone than ever.

She looked out over the garden, thinking that,
in spite of their differences in skin color and style,
Victoria Prew was another hothouse plant that had
been transplanted into the English garden. The
one that everyone stopped to look at, comment
on. Not quite fitting and, because of that, fascinating to the eye.

Mina moved slightly farther out onto the patio,
so that the rain hit her jacket. Sometimes it was important to find the air, to gain for yourself room to
breathe.

"You're getting wet."

"Yes." Mina gestured at the outside lights. "Perhaps turning those off might be a good idea. Your
garden is acting like a lighthouse."

Victoria nodded. "Okay."

Mina moved inside, shivers running up and
down her arms. "When did you see the man last?"

Victoria stepped back from the doorway, as if re-

pelled by the thought. "Well . . . yesterday, I suppose. Only, the thing is, I've only ever seen a figure. He stands at the end of the garden, looking
in. I can't see his face, only the shape of him."

"How many times has this happened?"

Victoria shrugged, disappearing deeper inside
the wool. "Maybe a dozen. In the beginning, I didn't
think it was anything, just kids messing about. Trying to freak me out, you know?"

"Does it look like a kid?"

Another shrug. "I don't know. Not really."

"Have you ever approached him?" Mina thought
of the baseball bat she kept at the side of her own
bed.

Victoria bit her lip, the vivid red lipstick shocking against the snow white of her teeth. "No. I . . . I
didn't think it was anything, I really didn't. But
then, today happened."

"Show me."

They turned from the double-height windows.
Mina pulled the patio door closed behind her,
carefully slid the lock into place. Through the living
room, the white tiled floors only adding to the cold
in the air. The place was shockingly modern—
hideously uncomfortable-looking sofas, floor lamps
whose shape seemed to defy both logic and gravity.

Mina glanced back toward the windows. "You
might want to think about investing in some curtains."

Up the staircase—floating, naturally—its glass
sides leaving you feeling vulnerable, and then to
the landing. Mina stopped, looked out across the
expanse of the living room, the garden beyond. It
would be like a movie to someone standing out-

side. The house prided itself on style, casting aside privacy as an old-fashioned foible. It was, in essence, a Peeping Tom's dream.

"It's in here."

The bedroom was stark: white walls, white bedspread. Like sleeping in a lunatic asylum.

"I left the house at about seven this morning, got home about five, I guess," said Victoria. "And as soon as I walked in, I knew. I don't know what it was, I could just feel it, that someone had been in the house. I mean, at first I thought I must just be being paranoid, that it was all getting to me, making me jumpy, but then I came in here." She moved to the mirrored chest of drawers, slid open the top one. "See?"

Mina peered inside. The drawer was neatly subdivided into individual sections, a place for everything. To the left, a lined-up series of jewelry boxes.

"It's my locket. It's gone." Victoria gestured to a corner of the drawer.

"I don't—"

"It was here. Right here. When I came in, this drawer, it wasn't closed properly, and I knew I'd closed it this morning. I knew I had. When I checked, the locket was gone. It was shaped like a heart," Victoria added, her voice small. "My ex-husband bought it for me."

Mina nodded. Thinking that if someone came into her own house and took her sofa, it would take her a while to notice, what with the accumulated slurry surrounding it. "Is anything else missing?" she asked.

Victoria shook her head. "I don't think so. I just . . . I don't know how anyone could have got in. I used to keep a hidden key under a rock in the front yard, but once this all started, once this guy started watching me, I moved it. You know, just in case." She folded her arms tight around her. "Thing is, I was coping okay when it was just some pervert who liked to watch. I just . . . I kind of shrugged it off. But this, I mean, it's a whole different thing now. The thought that someone has been in my bedroom . . ."

A tear spilled down her cheek, bringing with it a dark line of mascara. Victoria wiped it away hurriedly.

Mina studied her. It had been hidden, beneath the make-up and the designer clothes. But she could see it now in this light, the dark circles beneath the eyes, the pull at the corner of the lips, the slenderness that was not slenderness at all, but grief and pain and loneliness.

Mina nodded slowly. "You're here alone?"

"My marriage . . . it broke down last year. Broke down. My husband broke it." Her fingers were moving against the wool, the coral nails clicking together in a hypnotic rhythm, and she smiled the kind of smile that no one really meant. "It was one of my closest friends. Turned out they'd been shagging for a year or more." She looked beyond Mina to the window, the rain. "It's . . . Even now I can't believe that it's come to this. I used to think we were so happy. He hates me now. He wants to marry her. I'm ruining that, because I won't bow down, agree to everything he wants." She shook her head. "Anyway, I moved here after. We didn't have any kids. It just, I guess, wasn't meant to be. So, it's only me."

A preternaturally silent house. *The feeling that your skin will slough off if someone, anyone, doesn't touch you soon. The words bubbling up inside, and your mouth opening, because for the briefest of moments, you have forgotten that you are alone.*

"I understand." Mina chose her words carefully. "Do you think . . . I mean, your ex-husband, could it be him? If you're having problems, I mean."

The woman paled. "No, I . . . no. I don't think so. No. He wouldn't do this . . ." She looked at Mina, pleading. "What do I do?"

Mina glanced around the bedroom, back down at the drawer. It was just a locket. Or was it even a locket? Victoria could be wrong. There was, after all, little evidence that anyone had been in here. It was entirely possible that her own fears had created a drama where none existed. That she had simply lost the necklace. Then she looked at the woman, her hands tumbling together inside one another, a pool of tears waiting to spill over. Mina looked back out through the window toward the wild moor beyond, the memory of the wall standing just beyond the light. Better perhaps to be safe than sorry.

"Okay," said Mina. "What I'm going to do is get one of our forensic guys to come in and sweep for fingerprints. Given that there has been a hidden key left outside, even for a short time, it wouldn't be a bad idea for you to get the locks changed, just to be on the safe side. The other thing that I think would be sensible is to install some discreetly placed CCTV cameras. Let's see if we can catch this Peeping Tom in the act and get him dealt with. I can give you some information about a guy I know who can install them. He'll make you a priority. The other thing—curtains. Get nice thick curtains, and make sure that when you are in the house and you have the lights on, you have the curtains closed. I'm going to go talk to some of your neighbors, find out if anyone else has seen anything suspicious, anyone hanging around."

Mina let her gaze rove across the bedroom as she spoke, and then, beneath the chest of drawers, something caught her eye, a shadow of dark against the bright white of the carpet. She sank down to the bedroom floor. What was that?

Then she saw it. A shoe print.

"Victoria? Have you seen this before?"

The woman crouched down beside her, let out a small noise that sounded like a kitten crying. "No."

"Okay. Okay, not to worry." Mina's heart was beating faster, and there was a ringing in her ears. "We'll get forensics to have a look at this." She glanced up at Victoria with a falsely bright smile. "It's fine. That's good. It gives us something to work with."

Victoria was still crouching, had curled herself up into the smallest of spaces. Now she looked up at her, her eyes wide. "What do I do?" Her voice quiet, little more than a whisper.

"Until we have the new security measures in place, do you have somewhere else you can stay?" asked Mina.

"My mother, she's just across the way in Eely."

Mina nodded, looking about the room. The

woman was right. Someone had been in here; someone had touched her bed and her clothes. Her stomach tightened. "I think," she said quietly, "that might be for the best. Just for a couple of days." She looked at Victoria, gave her a reassuring smile. "Go on. I'll wait while you get some stuff together. Don't worry, Victoria. We'll find him. Everything is going to be just fine."

Inside a killer – Isla

Isla watched the trees, the Sitka spruce and larch that ringed the campus, bending and swaying with the wind, the rain a steady drumbeat, and thought of forests and wolves and horrors that hid in the dark. The day had tumbled toward its end—8:45 p.m., a hard nighttime already fallen. Beyond the large office window, she could see only the whispers of branches, shadows dancing, the occasional light of a plane on its way out of the airport. In the daytime, this room was a sanctuary, warm and quiet. Her office was on the ground floor, larger than most, and sought after, with its view, not of students and cars and chaos, but of the trees and the countryside. In the winter, she could look through the skeleton tree trunks, down all the way to the lights of Carlisle. In the summer, she was ringed by a lush greenness.

Isla took a breath, telling herself that the feeling in the pit of her stomach, the knot of uneasiness, was simply excess adrenaline, the hangover from a stressful day.

She had waited for this day for twenty years. All that she had done before, she had done in order to bring herself to this point, this day, when she could place Heath McGowan into a scanner, reach inside his head, and finally attempt to answer the question that had pricked at her sleep each night for two decades. Why?

However, considering all that, the day had unfolded smoothly, unremarkably, even. Heath had completed the tasks required of him, had been polite and cordial, had caused no trouble, so that, in the end, she had had to remind herself who he was, what he had done. He had allowed himself to be taken from the scanner, to be led back into the control room, had held out his hands for the guard to cuff him, as docile as a lamb.

It should have been more dramatic than this, Isla thought. It should have been harder.

He had stood, unthinkably shorter than she by an inch, two perhaps, shuffling from foot to foot, seeming wrong somehow in the clean lines of the control room, and Isla had found herself feeling almost sorry for him, looking so uncomfortable and out of place. Then a wave of nausea had overtaken her, and she had returned to a bright summer morning on a limitless moor, to three dead bodies lined up in a row. Had taken a long swig of ice-cold coffee, the taste of it preferable to the memories. She had watched Heath watching the radiographer and Connor work, as if watching man prepare to land on the moon. But then, she had admitted, it probably felt like that after twenty years inside prison walls. She had watched him as he turned and his gaze snagged on the image of his own brain, brightly lit upon the screen. Heath had studied it with the intensity of a man examining a map of a distant planet.

"Is that me?"

What had that been in his voice? Wonder? Fear?

"It is," Isla said.

He shuffled closer, the prison guard watching his movements intently, eyeing Heath's distance from the equipment, which he could destroy, the utensils, which he could steal. But Heath McGowan simply stood there, attention focused on the image of his brain.

Then, in a voice approaching awe, "What does it mean?"

Isla paused, weighing her answers. What did it mean? That in structure, in appearance, Heath McGowan was no different from anyone else. That wherever his need to kill came from, it wasn't obvious simply by looking at the surface of him.

"It means that your brain looks perfectly healthy. All the structures of your brain are where they should be. There's nothing there that shouldn't be."

He hadn't taken his eyes from it yet. "Does it . . . does it tell you, you know, why?"

"Why?"

His gaze dipped down to his hands, the bright metal cuffs that locked them tight together. "Why . . . it happened?"

She watched him. *Why it happened.* Not *why I did it.* As if the murders were merely something that had happened to him, like catching the flu.

"No." She kept her voice gentle. "This looks only at the physiology of the brain. The functional MRI data will take a little time to process. We're going to run some analyses, compare your brain function with that of other people we've studied. Hopefully, once that's done, it should give us a better insight into how each area of your brain is working, whether some areas are underactive, others overactive." She nodded to the monitor, the image of the mysterious brain of Heath McGowan. "It will help us to understand why . . . why it happened."

"And when will that be?"

"Ah . . . tomorrow for the raw data? Maybe the day after. It will take a while to sort through, though. We did a lot of tests in there."

Heath nodded, shifted his gaze to her. He looked older, sadder. "Will you . . . When you find out . . . when you get your answers, will you tell me? Please?"

She found herself staring at him, taken aback by the question, the pleading in his voice. Again, the uncomfortable sensation of pity. "Yes," she said. "Yes, I'll tell you."

Isla rose to her feet now, studying the darkness beyond her office window. There was nothing out there. It was only her imagination. And, after all, it was the way of things after days like these. Sometimes, Isla thought, there were consequences of spending time in the presence of evil; even after you were free of it, its shadow remained. She turned her back on the window, her movements deliberate, and walked calmly away from the glass, the night outside, and tried to ignore the prickle up her spine.

Nestled between the spreading array of book-cases and the wall sat a circular mahogany table ringed with four narrow armchairs. They were not university issue. Isla had found them in a second-hand shop, had had them re-covered with a deep red fabric. She flung herself down into one, pulled her socked feet up onto the mahogany tabletop, and stared at the darkness, could see herself reflected in it. She was thirty-five but looked closer to twenty-five, the little make-up she wore serving only to make her look younger still. Isla gazed at her reflection, Little Red Riding Hood looking out at the forest. It was both a gift and a curse, this youthfulness. The men, the killers, they would look at her as a starving man would look at a steak, would misunderstand the innocence of her face for naïveté. Would tell her what they shouldn't, in the hope that it would impress, in the hope that she would fall to them, fall under their spell. They couldn't see beneath the surface of her. They couldn't see the iron fist within the silk glove. Had it always been this way? She studied her reflection. Little Red Riding Hood. Perhaps instead she was the wolf.

She pulled a box file from the shelf behind her, flipped open the lid of it, pulled a weight of paper from inside. There were manila folders, stacked one on top of the other. Isla arrayed them across the tabletop in front of her, leaving spaces between them, a dozen in all. Then she flipped open the cover of each, one after the other. A dozen men stared back at her. A dozen different photos tacked to the inside cover of the files.

Twelve men. Between them, they had murdered seventy-five people.

She studied their faces, as if there she would find some kind of physiognomic truth. The truth was they looked like twelve men, like any twelve men, some attractive, some not, some threatening, some nondescript.

If you wanted to find the commonalities within these men, she thought, you had to look deeper.

Isla turned a page, one for each file, so that before her lay twelve sheets, four images of the brain on each, each image taken at a different angle. There. There was what made these twelve men all the same. Splashes of bright blue in the amygdala, the anterior cingulate cortex, the parietal lobe. The riot of light indicating that these areas, so important in the ability to understand social situations, to process emotions, and to decide upon a course of action, were, in these men, failing. Then the same vivid blue in the orbital frontal cortex. *The area that helps us control our baser urges.* The entire paralimbic system standing proud, highlighted by its lowered density.

Isla studied the brain scans. These twelve men had been failed by their own biology. Their brains, while structurally perfect, did not work as they should, the entire paralimbic system, a network that ran throughout the brain, simply refusing to operate to its full potential. Like an ankle or a knee with an inherent weakness, so that its owner was limited in his or her ability to function in the world. But for these men . . . this dysfunction meant an awful lot more than the inability to run a marathon. Their failings and weaknesses changed the world around them, often bringing destruction, occasionally death. No one knew if the psychopathy—a complex, impenetrable personality disorder—was caused by the brain dysfunction or if the brain dysfunction was caused by the psychopathy. And yet, whichever way it fell, the results remained the same. Those suffering from a poorly functioning paralimbic system all showed the same basic traits— problems in feeling emotionally connected to others, a tendency toward being emotionally shallow, irresponsible, impulsive, and sometimes downright cruel.

Twelve men, all killers. All with the same fatal physiological flaws. Would Heath's scan show the same? It would be unscientific to jump to conclusions in the absence of evidence. But Isla would still be willing to bet her next month's salary that in Heath she would find an almost identical pattern.

Isla looked across the sea of psychopaths. It was an easy word to throw around—like being depressed when you are merely sad—and yet here before her were the true psychopaths. All scoring well into the thirties on the Psychopathy Checklist, all carrying with them that edge, the sense that you were little more than prey in the hands of a predator.

Isla leaned forward, her elbows on her knees,

chin resting on hands, and searched the images for a secret. Because these men, they didn't kill just once. They killed again and again, until they were stopped. And if she could find something, some unexpected area of blue hidden within their brains, that separated these twelve from the myriad run-of-the-mill psychopaths that stuffed the files in the bookcase behind her, then maybe she could use that to stop the next serial killer. Or the one after that.

A gust of wind tugged at the trees, battering branches against the window. Isla winced but refused to look up. A hundred and twenty people. She had scanned one hundred and twenty people so far. She had been scanned more times than she could remember. It was a long-standing family joke that it was always advisable to tell Isla what it was you wanted for Christmas, for birthdays, otherwise you would end up with a functional MRI image of your own brain, nicely framed. She had coaxed most of Briganton into an fMRI machine, including her mother, her father, her husband, and her sister. It was, she had told them, a gigantic adventure. After all, who could pass up the opportunity to see inside themselves? To drill right down to the heart of who you were?

One hundred and twenty people. Of those, forty-four met the criteria for psychopathy and had been imprisoned for various crimes, up to and including murder. Two control groups, then. The normals. The psychopaths.

Then the twelve serial killers. The ones for whom it wasn't simply a loss of control, a temper run amok, but rather a base urge, something that pushed them and pushed them until in the end they just couldn't stop killing.

She looked at the twelve. Her twelve. *What is it that makes you different? What pushes you beyond even the loose-limbed limits set by psychopathy as a whole?*

She reached down, pulled the Heath McGowan file free from her bag, and placed his photograph on the tabletop, beside the others.

Thought of his question. *Will you tell me why it happened?*

She studied his flat gaze staring back at her. Would she be able to? Could she find the answer?

A sharp rap on the door sent Isla's heart rate spiking. She sat up straight, rolling her eyes, angry with herself for the fear.

"Come in." It sounded harder than she intended it to, a bark that she didn't mean.

"Don't shoot!" Ramsey's head peered around the door; his hands were raised in front of him. "Good day, then?"

Isla grinned, shrugged. "I like to sound mean. It keeps the students away. What are you doing here?"

Her husband slipped into the room, pressed the door firmly shut behind him. "I had to go pick some stuff up for Stephen Doyle. Thought I'd call in on you and see if you ever plan on coming home."

Isla smiled, studied him, the way she sometimes did when he came upon her unexpectedly. Tall, six feet two on a good day; broad shouldered; and blond. Looking at him made her heart skip a beat. Isla was pretty sure she wasn't alone in thinking her husband was devastatingly handsome. She was observant enough, had seen enough heads turn in his presence to know that it was a generally accepted conclusion. Ramsey was hot. It hadn't happened between them straight away, after Zach, after Ramsey's attack, and the killer on the wall. While the village fought to understand itself and Ramsey's family grieved, there were other concerns than romance. And then, suddenly, it was past and Heath was arrested and they were safe again, no matter how unsafe they continued to feel.

And then Ramsey was gone. Escaping Briganton and all the dark memories that it carried, for a journalism degree. For ten years, Rámsey Aiken was little more than a memory of a dream, and when she thought of him, it was facedown in damp grass, an inch from the door of death. Then, one night with Emilia in the Aubrey Arms, two glasses of wine down and heading for the bottle, the door swung open, bringing with it a chill breeze and the transformed figure of Ramsey. *They say time stands still in moments like these.* Isla was no romantic, and yet even for her, that much was true. She watched him survey the pub—searching for his brother Cain, she would later discover. Then his gaze swung closer and closer, until it was on her, and a wide smile broke across his features.

They had been together ever since.

He kissed her on the forehead. "You know you have odd socks on, right?"

Isla looked at her feet, one yellow, one blue. Shrugged. "I couldn't find a pair. Then I realized I didn't care."

"So?" He sank into the adjacent chair, carefully

shifting his injured arm. "How was it? The scan, I mean." He said it lightly, and if you didn't know him, you might be fooled, but Isla could see it, the crease around his eyes, hear the catch in his voice.

"It was fine." Isla kept her gaze steady, her voice even. "He was very well behaved. Did the tests properly. There was no issue with too much movement, so we should get some good data out of it."

She had answered, and yet the truth was, that wasn't the question, was it? He wasn't asking her about her study; he was asking about her experience of sitting across from the man who had tried to kill him.

She opened her mouth. Closed it again. "He wasn't what I expected," she added quietly.

Ramsey nodded slowly. He picked up Heath's picture, studied it, was quiet for a very long time. Then he asked, "So . . . has he said anything about . . . you know?"

Three dead bodies sitting on the wall.

Three more to follow.

"No. Nothing," Isla said, leaning her head back, suddenly exhausted. "It's not unusual. The information has value. Heath knows that. When all their power has been removed, men like this, they like to keep what they have, the truth of what they did, guard it, in case one day it will be of use to them. Heath knows that we want him to talk about what he did. He's getting pleasure from depriving us of the answers we need."

Ramsey nodded slowly, plucking at a thread that had worked its way free from the seam of his trousers. "I know." Then he sighed. "So, I had a different day . . ."

"Yeah?"

"Stephen Doyle attempted to jump off the roof of your building."

Isla stared at him, and Ramsey held up his hands. "He's okay. He didn't, obviously. But he's in a bit of a rough spot. I took him to his sister's, said I'd come back here and get his things. Connor is going to arrange some counseling for him. Well, some more counseling." He shook his head. "This thing just never ends, does it?"

"No," said Isla softly. "No, it does not."

Saturday, October 22

"It'll be okay" – Mina

It began with a distant figure running.

There should have been nothing to that, nothing at all. But in the murky early morning light, something about the movement made the hairs on the back of her neck stand on end. Mina slowed the car, the Ford Focus's engine groaning, leaned forward across the steering wheel.

Mina peered through the spotting rain at the shape, willing it to coalesce into something that would begin to make sense. A long khaki coat, mud-soaked Wellington boots, a rain hat wedged firmly down so that the face was all but obscured. A lolloping, uncomfortable run, long looks thrown back over her shoulder. A dog, a dark-haired cairn terrier, towed behind, short legs a blur of movement.

Yvette Goulding.

Mina flipped her turn signal on, pulled the car up on the curb, shoved the door open. A gust of wind snatched it from her, forcing it to strain at its hinges.

"Yvette?"

The wind tugged at the response, pulling it from Yvette's mouth and throwing it away toward the moors, until only a whisper remained. "Help. Help me."

"Yvette." Mina hurried toward her, the wind yanking at her coat, at her hair. "What—"

And Yvette, with her steel-rod back, her glowering menace, the iron librarian, as the children called her, sank to her knees on the rain-soaked pavement, gripping Mina's hands. A noise breaking free from her that sounded like keening.

"What is it?" Mina held on to her, allowing herself to be pulled down so that at last they were both kneeling on the ground in the rain and the wind.

Yvette looked at her, tears flooding her cheeks, whispering, "It's happened again."

Perhaps somewhere else, that would not have been enough. Perhaps in another place, it would not have felt like the intervening twenty years had been simply an exercise in waiting, the silence between notes.

But it was not another place. It was Briganton, and even Mina had been here long enough to understand the way things worked. Time stilled, and the rain stopped.

"Where?"

The dog had pushed its way in between them

now, was burying its nose in Yvette's neck, whimpering. The elderly woman pulled the little dog closer to her, words directed into its fur. "At the end of Dray Lane."

Mina stood up, leaving Yvette Goulding and Jackson, the dog, sitting on the ground, and began to run. Water threw itself up from the lake-deep puddles. Round the corner and into the heart of a hurricane. The wind funneled through the narrow passageway, shoving her backward. *Don't come this way. You don't want to see this.*

But there was no choice.

From tarmac to slick mud, which threatened to throw her from her feet with each step, the uneven ground straining her calves, her thighs. Not looking up, because somewhere inside, she already knew what it was she would see.

And then looking up, because ultimately you had to, didn't you?

She stopped dead in her tracks.

She had googled Briganton after the real estate agent had offered her the house. And what had appeared first was not about its history or its scenery or its people. Instead, there was a picture in a newspaper, a woman, propped against the wall, dead. It had been taken by an enterprising journalist with a long-angled lens, had made the front page of every newspaper. There was a flurry of complaints in the comment section, about the media failing to allow for dignity in death, but what good did that do? The picture had been taken. The memory formed.

And now it was here again.

Only . . .

Mina stepped forward, recognition tugging at her.

Red hair. A single Christian Louboutin shoe. A woman standing at her floor-to-ceiling windows, telling Mina that she liked the view. And Mina telling her that she would be safe. That it would be okay.

Victoria Prew.

The body on the wall – Mina

Victoria sat, her back pressed against Hadrian's Wall. Her red hair hung in rat's tails, wet against the slack gray of her cheeks. A vivid red line of finger-marks ringed her throat. Her hands were folded into her lap, and a dark swath of mud ran up her back, coloring her blue coat black. There could be little doubt that Victoria Prew was dead.

Mina stared at the body, felt a tremble begin just above her right knee, a sense of heat rising through her cheeks. It wasn't the deadness of Victoria that did it. In ten years in the Met, Mina had seen plenty of deaths. It was the grass beneath her, the way it bent and leaned, muddy pools blossoming beneath her thighs. It was the aged gray of the stone wall that pressed up against the peacock blue of her coat.

It was the sense of a legend being catapulted back into life.

"Mina?" said Owen. "Are you okay?"

Mina stared at the body. "Yes," she lied.

The CSIs moved around the body, the wrinkling of their plastic suits creating an uneven harmony against the inevitable thrumming of the rain on the roof of the hastily erected tent. Mina folded her arms across her own forensic suit, drew in a couple of low breaths.

"This was her? Last night's call?" Owen kept his voice pointlessly low. As if there could be any secrets in such a small space.

"Yes."

I told her it would be okay. I told her she would be safe.

Mina's vision was dancing, shifting back and forth between Victoria Prew, alive and vivid, and Victoria Prew, dead. It was dizzying, like a film that flickered between black and white and glorious Technicolor.

"Poor thing," said Owen softly.

"Excuse us, guys," said a CSI. "I need to get around you."

Mina made an effort to smile. "Sorry, Zoe. I'll give you some room. I'm going down to the house. I just . . ." But the words failed her, falling away, and, in lieu of them, she ducked beneath the tent flap out into the mercifully cold air. She breathed deeply, the chill grazing her throat, and tried to push away the memory of the woman's slack face, limp hands.

A small knot of people had formed at the cordon, set up where the boggy moor gave way to pavement at the boundary between the wilds and the village. Brightly colored umbrellas punched holes in the dull day. A police community support officer stood guarding the entry to the site, looking thrilled and terrified in equal measure. Mina scanned the crowd, careful to avoid eye contact with any one person. She counted one, two reporters. Could pick them out in their North Face jackets, their inappropriate shoes. The rest, they were Briganton people. Her gaze landed on diminutive Maggie Heron, standing among the crowd, with well-worn boots, a coat thrown over a nightgown, long gray hair braided down her back, her face heavy with resignation. For people like her, for the ones who had lived through the killings, this would be as the reawakening of a dream.

Mina turned away, suddenly aware of the cameras, the swing of their lenses toward her, and looked along the wall. You could see little beyond it this morning, a heavy mist sitting low across the undulating hills. It had stopped raining, and yet the moisture still sat heavy in the air. Waiting.

Then a sound behind her, the rustle of the tent, Owen ducking awkwardly beneath the low door. "Getting a bit warm in there. You're going down to the house?"

Mina nodded.

"I'll come with you."

They walked in silence, the only sounds the distant murmur of the gathered crowd and the schlep of their boots through the mud. Mina kept her gaze on the houses that sat perhaps a hundred meters along from where the body had been left. Large homes, high hedges fencing them off from the wall. And there, four houses along, stood Victoria Prew's, with its boxlike face and indecently low gated hedge. It was a dull day, visibility terrible, the mist making everything soft at the edges, and yet even now, Victoria's house stood out like a beacon.

Mina walked steadily toward it, wondering if the murderer had stepped where she was stepping now. Had he felt his foot jar against this rocky outcrop? Had he felt the wind that worked its way up across the moor strike his face?

She slowed her step, approaching the rear of the house with an overabundance of care, her gaze fixed now, not on the house itself, but on the ground. He had stood here, watching, Victoria had said so herself. That is, she allowed, if the murderer and the stalker were in fact one and the same.

Mina studied the ground, the oozing mud, the white flecks of rock, the grass still gleaming with rain. Nearer to the rear of Victoria's home, the mud eased off, leaving behind only gray stone, the occasional patch of grass. Nothing in which to leave a print. Mina stood for a moment, then turned around in a slow circle.

"Anything?" asked Owen.

"No footprints. Can you see anything? Drag marks? Based on the mud on her, he pulled her some distance."

Owen pursed his lips. "I'm going to look closer down toward the wall. It's boggier there. Maybe we'll get lucky."

Mina nodded. She didn't say that lucky days generally did not begin with a dead woman left sitting at a wall. She looked up toward the house again, the vast expanse of the bedroom window now looking for all the world like a cinema screen. I stood in there last night. Was he here? Was he watching us? she wondered.

She felt her breath begin to quicken, a feeling akin to panic beginning to flutter around the edges of her awareness.

Focus.

Whatever had happened, it'd happened quickly. The first team at the scene had found Victoria's car waiting for her in the driveway. Inside the driver's footwell, a single shoe left sad and alone, lying on its side. It was as if she had made it into the car, with one foot at least, and then had been dragged back out of it. An umbrella had been found caught on a hedge, its frame twisted about by the force of the wind or by something else. The attack on her, when it had come, had come quickly, filling little more than the time it took for her to open the car door and climb in. Less. He had waited until she was distracted, fumbling with her keys, perhaps folding up that umbrella that had got so wildly out of hand. And when she was vulnerable, because of the dark and the distraction and the weather, he had pounced.

Why was Victoria here? Why had she come back? Mina had watched her drive away, and so she should not have been there, on her driveway, waiting to die. And yet here they were.

Mina crouched down to study the ground that lay immediately beyond the back gate.

"I've got some drag marks," Owen called, "a little farther down that way." He gestured toward

Hadrian's Wall, back in the direction of the tent. "It would have been a fair task getting her that far. I mean, she wasn't big by any stretch, but still . . . I wouldn't fancy it."

Mina stood up and stared in the direction he indicated. A flash of yellow marked the spot, the evidence marker waiting where Owen had left it.

"The thing I don't get," said Mina quietly, "is why move her at all? If you want to kill her, why not just kill her where she was originally attacked? Why not leave her there? I mean, it's not like he was trying to hide her. Why go to all that effort?"

Owen bit his lip.

"What?"

"Maybe . . . I mean, the killer on the wall."

Mina frowned. "You're kidding, right? You think Heath McGowan broke out of prison, came to kill her, put her on the wall, and then broke back in."

He shook his head. "I don't mean that. I mean, this village. It's lived with what happened for twenty years. To have something like this, it's going to be terrifying for them."

"Okay?"

Owen shrugged. "I don't know. I'm just saying that it's a pretty good way to distract people from your real reason for wanting her dead."

Mina looked back toward the house. "She did say her divorce had got nasty. She seemed pretty sure that the stalker wasn't her ex, but still . . . how often do you hear that? Oh, he'd never do that." She let her gaze track along the wall to the tent. "Maybe you're onto something."

There was a sudden movement at the cordon, the parting of the crowd, a flurry of voices. A stooped figure in a large overcoat broke free, ducking with an awkward stride beneath the yellow tape, out toward the body. Detective Superintendent Eric Bell.

It had been a deciding factor for her, when the job had been advertised, a vacancy in the Northern force. When her family had gasped in horror at the thought of her crossing the great North-South divide, trekking into the unknown, she had held him out to them as a balm. *But I'll be working with Eric Bell. You know the one. He solved the killer on the wall case. Remember?*

Eric Bell had been the one to make the link with McGowan, a little spot of that charm he kept in special reserve poured into the ear of McGowan's grandmother. It was enough that she voiced her own doubts about the boy, mentioned that he'd been asking questions about the habits of her neighbor, Kitty Lane, that he had a quick temper and a nasty little drug problem. Told Bell where he could find him, with that girlfriend of his. Of course, by the time Bell got there, the girlfriend had become the next victim. And then the arrest and the whole world throwing itself at Eric Bell's feet, the detective who had caught the killer on the wall. He became a celebrity, for a while at least, the darling of the media. Mina had seen him in more than one documentary about the case. "He even wrote a book about it," she had said to her mother. "Think of the opportunity."

The truth was, it was Eric Bell that had drawn her to policing in the beginning. Those stoic images of a hero policeman that had filled her teenage years, his legend sufficient that he was no longer a Briganton commodity but one cherished by the whole world. Or so it had seemed to Mina, anyway. Imagine being that, being the person who could end a reign of terror, who could bring safety and justice.

And yet it had turned out that it was not always wise to meet your idols in the flesh, that few illusions were allowed to survive the scrutiny that came with close contact.

She had introduced herself back when she first arrived, a long and, in retrospect, frankly embarrassing speech about the extent to which he had inspired her. She had got perhaps two-thirds of the way through it when Detective Superintendent Bell had simply turned on his heel and walked away.

Thinking back on it now, Mina couldn't really blame him.

She watched him march toward the tent, the determination marred only by the limp, a hiccup in his movement. "God, it's like the arrival of Madonna," she muttered.

"Yeah, well, the great Eric Bell. What do you expect? The entire village is probably ready to conduct human sacrifices if it'll help him close this thing down like he did last time." Owen shook his head. "Come on, we'd better get back. You know, pay homage."

"Yeah," she said. "Just a second."

Mina peered over the gate into Victoria's garden.

"What?"

"No, I just want to see." She hooked the catch with her finger, pushed the gate open, the metal screeching against the path. "The lights." She gestured to the narrow lampposts. "They were on last night. I left the house at the same time as Victoria. I don't remember her turning them off."

"Maybe she did it when she came back?"

Mina moved carefully from lamppost to lamppost and stood on tiptoe.

"What is it?"

An uneasy feeling settled on her. "The lightbulbs have been unscrewed. Look. You can see where they're coming away from the base." Mina looked back down the path toward the gate that connected front garden to back. "Before he moved her body, he made sure the garden was in darkness so if anyone looked out of their windows, they wouldn't see."

She felt cold now, suppressed a shiver.

He had stood here, where she stood. Had stretched up, calmly extinguished the lights. Mina looked down at her feet, still resolutely on the paved path. And there, in the sodden grass right before her, was a shape. She ducked down.

"Owen, I've got a footprint."

Beginning again – Isla

The water was so hot, it scalded her. Isla moved, positioning her face into the stream, a thousand pinpricks against her cheeks, as if this would wash it away. A body at the wall. A body at the wall. She swiveled the dial, turning the heat up. She couldn't see, the water beating too hard for that. And so her back prickled with the sense of being stared at, her hands moving up to wipe her eyes, evolution taking over where common sense had left off. *It's okay. It's okay. It's just your imagination.* But her hands moving, anyway, clearing her vision, her heart thumping with the need to know that he wasn't here, that she wasn't the next one dead.

She blinked into the light. The bathroom was

empty, save for the dense clouds of steam. She closed her eyes, hung her head, and stepped back beneath the water.

She had run this morning, as she did every morning. Every single morning, she laced up her shoes, slipped the catch on the back door, and slid out into the darkness. Every morning, that same shoot of fear up her back. Pushing off, her heart beating out of proportion to the level of strain, and telling herself that it would be okay, because it was just fear, and fear could be conquered. Out the back door and down Dray Lane and then through the field, until finally she reached the wall. Running, the wall at her right, because here she felt like something bigger than herself, that she was a part of what had gone before, perhaps tracing footsteps left across the centuries, and that thought made her feel bigger and smaller both.

Or perhaps she ran the wall for the other reason, for the fear itself. Daring herself to repeat that run of twenty years ago, to face it, every single morning. To lay footstep after footstep past the place where she'd found the bodies, simply to prove to herself that she could. That she would not be beaten.

But today, with the thundering rain, the ground so soft it seemed that it would swallow you whole, today she had done something different. Had run down Dray Lane, had paused in the early morning darkness. She could feel the wall somewhere beyond, waiting. But it was wet and the ground was saturated and she had pulled her hamstring only a few days ago, so if she overdid it now, she could be out for weeks. Instead, she had reversed herself, back up Dray Lane, sticking to pavements, had run up past the church, the florist, had circled out of Briganton, up onto the country roads, had swooped back down, the village laid out before her.

Had she gone the other way . . .

Isla dumped the shampoo in her hands, more than was strictly necessary, let it flood into her eyes, where it stung.

She had been on her way back home—had started thinking about hot coffee and a shower, hotter still—when she saw the crowd that had gathered at the edge of the moor. And in spite of the impossibility of it all, she had known. Had begun to run harder, hamstring be damned, and had snaked her way through the elbows and the umbrellas until she drew level with the cordon. Then the tent, and, emerging from it, alien in his forensic suit, her father.

"Dad!"

She felt the crowd pull back from her, driven by the force of her bellow, felt the PCSO twist to stare at her, inappropriately dressed in Lycra, wet hair plastered to her head. And her father. He pulled up short, his shoulders settling in what, even at that great distance, appeared to be resignation. He gestured to her, a quick flick of his fingers, an order that had to be obeyed, and Isla followed, sliding across the cordon to the far side, where the prying eyes were fewer. They were still watching, though; she could feel the weight of their gaze on her back.

"Isla," said her father. "You're soaking."

Isla stared at him, assessing whether he had had a stroke, then glanced down at her running clothes, back at the tent behind him. "I . . . yes . . . Okay, never mind about that. What the hell is going on?"

"Nothing. It's nothing. Go home."

"Don't give me *nothing*. That's a forensic tent. Is there . . . Dad, is someone dead?"

Her father looked away, and it seemed to Isla as if he was trying to find a way to flee from this conversation, as if some particularly witty conversational gambit would make her forget about the police and the forensic tent and the descending sense of the inevitable having come to pass.

"Dad! Please . . ."

"Yes, Isla," her father snapped. "Yes, there's been a murder. A woman is dead at the wall."

The shampoo now ran into her mouth, the taste acrid. A body at the wall. A woman murdered and left for the world to find her in the historic stomping ground of a serial killer. What did that mean? A copycat? Someone looking to walk in the footsteps of Heath McGowan, continue his good work? Or something else, a single solitary violent act, hidden in the history of a serial killer?

Ramsey had been cooking when she got back, had been preparing the pancake batter for Emilia and her boys. A family breakfast, one that Isla had played along with, pretending that she didn't know what they were trying to do. That her sister would walk into the house, would hand the baby to Isla—Isaac, six months old—wrapped up in his fluffy bear suit, his skin peach soft, smile like a thousand-watt bulb. That Emilia and Ramsey would smile and say that Isla was a natural, and oh, didn't Isaac just adore his auntie Isla? It had become a long-running dance. And Isla would smile, too, and would pretend that her husband hadn't co-opted her sister into this endless war to reproduce.

She had stood at the kitchen door, had watched her husband as he hummed along with the radio, the whisk hitting the sides of the bowl in time to the music, balancing the bowl on the countertop, awkward with his one good arm. Had felt a lightness in her head and a hollowness in her stomach. She'd watched her husband, felt a wash of guilt, then another wash, more familiar—that fear again. She had hung in the doorway for an absurdly long time, unable to move, forward or back. Had started to say it. Once. Twice. But always the fear, the words ending before they had begun.

And then he had turned, had seen her, the whisk stopping mid-rhythm, had known without her saying that something was wrong.

Isla had opened her mouth, not knowing what would come out of it until it came. "There's been another murder."

Isla scrubbed at her hair, nails scraping against her scalp. Eyes shut tight as the shampoo leached into them. The burning not enough to drive away the image of her husband's face growing slack, the lightness becoming fixed, color slipping away as he made sense of her words. Not Ramsey the man now, but Ramsey the teenager, the only survivor. The radio still trilling, oblivious, the clank of the whisk hitting the side of the bowl.

Thoughts fluttered and collided. They needed organizing. But for now, all she could think was that it had happened again.

Isla snapped the shower off and grabbed for a towel, suddenly aware that her hands were shaking. Wrapped it around her, tight, her insides liquid. She stared at her reflection in the mirror. "Breathe," she said to the woman. "Just breathe."

The fear growled.

Isla slipped out of the bathroom, padded across the landing in bare feet. She knew where Ramsey would be.

The file was spread out before him across the habitual orderliness of his desk. The newspaper articles, the pictures. He sat, slumped back in the desk chair, staring at it.

"You okay?"

Ramsey nodded, an acknowledgment of her presence rather than an answer in the affirmative. "It never goes away, does it?"

Isla moved closer, slid into his lap. Feeling his breath on her bare shoulder, she rested her wet head against his cheek. "It'll be okay."

Because what else did you say? When it seemed that life had moved on finally, had allowed you to leave a serial killer, a dead brother, in the years long past. When you finally, finally, started looking to the future, started to make plans that did not involve murder, and then this. It was as if they had been playing make-believe all these years; as if their lives, their plans, all of it was simply a game of dress-up, a diversion to fill time until the real nub of their lives would return.

Ramsey kissed her on the shoulder, his arms moving around her.

"My dad, he said that the victim was in the middle of a nasty divorce," said Isla. "That she'd moved here to get away from him."

Isla felt Ramsey shift beneath her. "So . . . you

think that's what it is? Someone using the whole killer on the wall thing to throw the police off?"

Did she think that? Who the hell knew? The truth was that right now, Isla would say anything to make her husband feel safe again. And that lie, it was as good as any other.

"Could be. I think it's certainly something worth considering."

He sighed, and she could feel the relief in it. That whatever this latest horror turned out to be, it would not be the horror from twenty years ago. Best to forget that, whichever way it went, a woman had been murdered.

A sound downstairs, footsteps, then a trill of voices. "Isla? Rams? You here?"

Isla looked at her husband. His expression changing to a smile. "Circus is in town." He kissed her on the nose, shifted her to standing. "You dress. I'll go prevent the monkeys from running amok."

Isla stood where he had left her, listening to his quick tread on the stair, the faux-angry "Who's making all this noise?" roar, the cascade of boyish laughter that followed. They adored him, the boys—Noah, six, and Elijah, three, baby Isaac. She tucked the towel tighter around her, listening to their shouts. Ramsey would be such a good father.

But then, inevitably, her gaze fell to the newspaper cuttings that remained splayed across the desk, and her insides tumbled.

She shook her head, took a deep breath, and slipped into their bedroom, dressed quickly, not bothering with make-up. She took the stairs slowly and, as she walked, tried to push away the fear.

Her sister stood in the living room, laughing, her children clambering across their uncle's broad back, the baby somehow miraculously sleeping soundly in his car seat. Emilia was beautiful, had always been so, right from childhood. Golden blond curls that framed her face, pronounced cheekbones, soft where Isla was hard. Then, in the periphery of her vision, Emilia noticed her sister, the laughter slipping away.

What?

It was a question unframed, but they had lived life long enough together that most things did not need to be said. Isla nodded toward the kitchen, felt her sister slipping into line behind her.

It smelled of coffee and of pancakes. It smelled of life. As if this room had failed to note what was going on around it. Isla closed the door tight behind them.

"What's going on?" Emilia's forehead furrowed. Based on the look of her sister, she was expecting to hear of some marital argument, an issue with work.

"Something happened this morning, Em. They . . . they found a body on the wall."

Her sister's hand flew out, gripped the corner of the oak table. "A . . ."

"She was murdered."

Tears sprang quickly. Isla had always envied her sister this, the emotions that lay there, right at the surface, not buried down so deep that it would take a mining crew to unearth them.

"Oh God."

"It's okay, Em . . ."

"No. The boys. I have to get them home." Her

sister was looking around the kitchen, gaze wild. "We . . . I have to get out of here."

Suddenly they were teenagers again, two crushed into one bed, afraid to sleep alone. Long night hours in the glaring light, as if daytime was something you could hang on to, carry with you. For Emilia, the horror had been too much. She had run from the monsters that Isla had turned to hunt.

"Em, Em . . . it's okay. It's not that."

"No, Isl. He's coming back. He's coming back." The tears spilled down her cheeks, hands grasping at her sister's. "I have to go . . ."

"Em." Isla cupped her sister's face in her hands. "No. He's not coming back. Heath McGowan is in prison. I know. I've seen him there. This—it's something else. Dad will figure it out."

"I just . . . my boys . . ."

"I know, Em." Isla pulled her sister into a hug. "I know."

Briganton below – Ramsey

He walked. Footsteps thudding against tarmac, blood pounding in his head. *I have to get out, Isl. I have to get away.* Thick soles hit the pavement in a rhythmic tread, *thump, thump*, fast enough that it was a run in all but the name of it. His sling bouncing against his chest, awkward, pointless. Breaths coming in quick, hard, steady intervals. Down the hill, onto Beacon Road, police cars in the distance, that damn crowd still there, waiting for . . . what? What could they possibly hope might happen now? Ramsey turned sharply, away from the village, following the road as it wrapped around the outer edges of Briganton, and tried to ignore the cars that slowed down, rubberneckers drinking in the misery. Past the primary school, its windows festooned with pumpkins and witches riding on broomsticks, yard eerie in its silence.

He walked because it was better than sitting, watching Isla watching him like he was some kind of unexploded bomb, waiting to see what the damage would be. The phone ringing again and again. *I just heard. How is Ramsey?* Until eventually, it seemed as if the whole of Briganton had encircled him, waiting to see just what he would do.

How was Ramsey?

Ramsey shook his head, pushing himself harder along the rain-soaked pavement. *How the hell should I know?*

"It's a domestic. I mean, it has to be. You said she was in the middle of a bad divorce, right? It has to be that. The husband has gone after her and has put her . . . there to throw police off, to get people frightened." They had sat around the dining table, Isla, Emilia, and the three boys all watching as Ramsey had turned his perfectly portioned squares of pancakes over and over, occasionally raising the fork to his lips, then lowering it again. "I mean, it makes sense, right?"

"Rams," Isla had said softly, "the children."

The boys had watched him, eyes as big as saucers.

"It's all right, Aunt Isl. We know all about the bad man," offered Noah cheerfully. "Tom from year two said that the bad man nearly killed his nan, only she was lucky and went to bingo that night. He said that his dad said that they should have lit the bastard up like Vegas."

"Noah! Language!" said Emilia, looking close to tears.

"Sorry. But he is a bastard, though. That's what Tom's dad said. That he'd have carried on killing people if our granddad hadn't stopped him." Then a thoughtful pause. "What's Vegas?"

Emilia hadn't stayed long after that, had offered a limp excuse about shoe shopping for the boys, that Adam would be back from football, even though they all knew that Adam's Saturday morning football had an unfortunate habit of drifting from morning to afternoon and then right back to morning again. Ramsey had helped her load the kids in the car and had wondered if perhaps he should have left, too, years ago. If life would have been easier had he followed his sister-in-law's example, got the hell out of Dodge.

He took a sharp right, a narrow footpath that climbed precipitously skyward, feeling the strain in his lower back. It didn't matter. All that mattered were the overhanging branches, the trees that encircled him, so that it seemed he was climbing through the center of an artery. The crack of twigs beneath his feet. His own breath, in, out, proof positive that he was alive.

That's it. Just concentrate on that. On the breaths and the footsteps. Don't think of anything else. That's enough.

Only it could never be enough, could it?

That insidious mind of his. Thinking of Isla's face and Emilia's fear and the phone ringing and ringing. They had put his photo on the news. The only known survivor. One of the initial victims. How could he be here again? Twenty years of trying so hard to be something different, someone else, and yet still catapulted back in time, right back to the beginning of it all.

Victoria Prew. The name was circling, had become like birdsong. He could taste the bitterness of it and so pushed harder, until his thighs screamed, traction becoming slick on the leaf-covered incline.

An editor had called. A major London newspaper. *Hey, Rams. Long time no see. Hey, fancy doing a bit more freelancing for us? This murder thing, up there in Briganton. Fancy writing a piece on it for us? I mean, you have a unique perspective on the whole thing. It would be a kind of "Is this the next victim of the killer on the wall?" thing.*

He should have hung the phone up on him.

But he hadn't, had he? He had breathed deeply and smiled politely and said yes. He was, after all, a journalist. That was what he was supposed to do.

The tunnel became narrower and narrower, the spindly trees pressing down on him until it seemed that they would crush him alive. And then, a reprieve. He broke through, the dark of the sky replacing the dark of the trees, tarmac turning to scrubby grass beneath his feet. Bowman's Hill curved ahead of him, dull green meeting dull gray. He walked on, until he ran out of ground, and stopped at the peak of the hill. He looked up at the sky, at the heavy clouds that sat overhead, unshed raindrops prickling at his skin.

Breathe. Just breathe.

Hands on his hips, Ramsey paced, circling the top of the hill. Looking at the sky, at his feet, and yet there it remained. Briganton spread beneath him.

He closed his eyes, opened them again.

The village sat in an ocean of cloud, Brigadoon appearing from the mists. The edges of it ill defined, as though someone had spilled water across a painting of it, smearing the lines. Ramsey stood and stared. He could just about make out his street. Where Isla would be. Waiting. *We should have moved away. We should have done it a long time ago.* Isla not saying anything, because what was there to say? That their entire lives had become an exercise in waiting—waiting to move, promising themselves that they would, that one day they would break free, but somehow never quite getting that momentum. Waiting for children, because it wasn't quite the time yet, because things weren't quite perfect. Waiting for the deaths to begin again.

Ramsey moved his gaze, following their street down to the crossroads, taking a right, a right again. Camberwell Street. Three houses from the end. That was where Amelia West had lived. The last but one victim.

They had found her key in the front door, still jammed in the lock outside. Had found her handbag on the pavement. "The thing with Amelia, she was stubborn," her mother had said. "We told her it was dangerous, that someone was out there hurting people, but she just pooh-poohed it. 'It'll never happen to me.'" She had been found the following morning, sitting at the wall. Strangled.

Ramsey moved, returning to his pacing. His eyes on the church now, its spire lost in cloud.

That was where they had had Leila's funeral. A bright Indian summer day. A shining mahogany coffin. Stephen folding himself up on the doorstep of the church, wailing a cry that should have woken the dead.

It didn't.

Down beyond the church, lost to the cloud, was the wall. Ramsey crouched down, could feel the long grass graze his bare legs, rested his good elbow on his knees, head in his hands. *Look away, because then you won't think about it. Look away, because then it won't be there.*

It was always there.

That day, twenty years ago, had begun with the sound of the front door closing. Eighteen-year-old Ramsey had lain in his bed, watching the first chinks of light work their way around the curtains. Five a.m. or thereabout. Had listened to his brother's step past the bedroom window. How long had he lain there considering sleep? It couldn't have been long, because by the time Zach came back past the house, this time loaded with a thick strapped bag, sentinel rows of newspapers, he was already up and dressed and waiting for his brother. *Come on. I'm awake. I'll give you a hand.* How many times had they done that? Too many to count. Ramsey remembered his own fifteen-year-old days, his own paper route, and twelve-year-old Zachary, up and dressed at the arse end of dawn. *I'm coming with you. 'Kay?*

Ramsey dug his fists into his eyes, willing away the image. Zach's dark curls, which came up to Ramsey's shoulders. The leanness of the boy, like someone had taken all his limbs and stretched them out. The sprinkle of acne across his cheeks, the adolescent unfinishedness of him. His gentleness. His laugh.

And then, that morning, the sun just beginning to break across the horizon. The streets deathly quiet. The kind of cold that hinted of a heat to come. The whisper of newspapers against the bag. Zach telling him a story about . . . what? It seemed now that there were no words to it, only overlarge teenage gestures and the trill of a laugh.

Then a rush of footsteps. Zach's scream. A sharp pain in the back of his head. The blackness.

Ramsey felt his body sob, pushed it back down.

That feeling of floating, of being carried. The voices and the sirens. After forcing his eyes to open onto the painfully bright day, he had looked up at the sky. *Don't worry. You're going to be okay.*

Then more footsteps and knowing these ones without ever seeing the stepper. His mother breaking through the crowd and shoving paramedics away and saying, "That's my boy. That's Ramsey. Oh my God, oh my God. Is he okay? Are you? What happened . . . ?" Then seeing . . . what? Something that tugged at her, that made her realize there was more. "Where's Zach?" A rising panic, her voice getting shrill with fear. "Ramsey. Where is he? Where's your brother?"

Did they tell her? For the life of him, Ramsey couldn't remember. Or maybe she had just known, mother's intuition. She had sunk to the pavement beside the stretcher, one hand holding tight to her middle son, the other hand waving wildly, as if to catch hold of the one that she had lost. Screaming his brother's name, as though that way she could bring him back, as if through sheer force of will, she could make him return to her. A flock of birds bursting from the trees, spiraling skyward.

Ramsey let himself sink to the sodden ground. The hospital, the whole world watching him like he was a species of thing they'd never seen before.

His mother in that damn chair, not eating, not sleeping, just sitting there, guarding her precious surviving child. And then, after days that felt like weeks, being released and returning home to a home that was no more. His father lost inside a prison of his own making. His older brother, Cain, hovering over them all, trying to repair the irreparable. And his mother smiling a painful smile and kissing him and retiring to a bed that she remained in. She died two years later, the effort of surviving her youngest child finally becoming too much to bear. The doctors said it was her heart. That she had been killed by a massive myocardial infarction. To Ramsey that seemed like an extremely complicated way of describing a broken heart.

He stood up, stretching his legs until they hurt. Specks of rain began to peck at his skin, and he turned his face toward them. Thought of Victoria Prew slumped dead against the wall. Below, a police car drove a slow, winding path through the center of Briganton. Ramsey wiped the rain from his eyes and watched its steady trail, a feeling settling like a boulder in his stomach. It wasn't over. It had only just begun.

The price of fear – Mina

Mina could hear the voices, a flock of starlings startled by a sheepdog. She heard bags being dropped onto tables, the melody of computers being turned on. Moving day. The major incident room was filling with people, as they all prepared to begin. They sounded like children returning from a long summer holiday, a feigned weariness, the thrill poking at the edges of the words. It wasn't surprising, Mina supposed. The killer on the wall. A bedtime story for sleepovers and nightmares, one that you told your friends to thrill them, or so you pretended, but really you said it so that the words would no longer circle, lost and alone in your own mind, as if reducing it to cheap gaudiness would make it less terrifying when you were alone at night.

"So what, then?" Detective Superintendent Eric Bell leaned back in his chair, his arms folded across the bulge of his belly, straining at the buttons of the striped shirt, dark hairs escaping through the gaps. He studied her, as though she was a particularly fascinating breed of insect.

"I . . ." Mina righted herself, attempting to keep her gaze steady. "I saw Ms. Prew to her car. I made sure that the front door was locked behind her." She looked down, her voice petering away under the force of that gaze. "I . . . I made sure that she was safe."

Victoria Prew walking, three feet in front of her, her head ducked from the rain. The sound of her quick footsteps on the graveled drive. A suitcase, tugged along behind her. A walk like she was on a catwalk, in spite of it all. Mina had her hood pulled up so that she was looking at the world through a tunnel, but still the raindrops worked their way into her eyes, turned her hair lank. Watching Victoria, the dark hedges, the suffocating skies. Victoria sliding the suitcase into the waiting trunk, the trunk closing, swallowing it whole. Climbing into the car. Closing the door. Smiling at Mina as the window slid down. *Thank you for everything*.

Superintendent Bell nodded slowly, thoughtfully. His lips pursed.

But she wasn't safe, was she?

He didn't say it, didn't shape the words, and yet there they were, nonetheless. Victoria Prew wasn't safe.

Mina's vision shifted, warping now from the superintendent, with his cold stare, to Victoria sitting propped against Hadrian's Wall, fingerprints ringing her lily-white throat, long red hair hanging down in a curtain.

Mina chewed at the fingernail of her index finger, the edges of it grating at her tongue. "I don't . . . I don't know why she went back there. I really don't, sir. She was afraid. I told her to go to her mother's, until we had the house secure. I don't know why she went back." Her voice was climbing, an edge of panic to it, and Mina dipped her head, cursing herself.

"Her mother said that she spoke to her," said the superintendent quietly. "That she'd forgotten some work files. Said she was just popping back to pick them up." He bounced a pen in the palm of his hand. "What did you do after she left?"

Was there an edge to his voice? Was she hearing that, or was she simply imposing judgment where there was none? Mina shifted on her seat, an attempt to sit at attention.

"I searched the immediate area, sir. I wanted to make doubly sure there was no one in the vicinity."

The Land Rover Discovery pulled out of the drive, its wheels gobbling up the gravel. Then Mina, alone in the puddled darkness, feeling something run up and down her spine: the sense of being stared at. Turning sharply, her hood flying backward, so that the rain battered against her face and she had to squint to make out the shapes beyond it. The hedges leering over her, dense with shadows. Running her flashlight across them, the white circle of light bouncing as a gust of wind pulled at it. She'd thought it was nothing, just the darkness and the wind that made her feel uneasy, like prey. Then a sound. A crack, like a foot pressed onto a twig. Her heartbeat climbing, the flashlight beam becoming less steady, and her mind screaming at her to step back, to run. But she didn't run. Instead, she stepped forward, closer to the hedge and the shadows, one hand reaching for her ASP, the extendable baton cold in her fingers.

And then . . .

A movement pressed against her thigh, making her insides leap and her ASP swing wildly. The slow unfurling realization that it was the ringing of her phone, set to vibrate. Her breath steadying, the sound of her heartbeat deafening in her ears. Swinging the flashlight across the hedge again, stepping closer, she felt the phone stop its vibrations. Reaching her hand out, pushing the branches aside, crouching so that she could see through the leafy tunnel of them, peering inside, the nightmares in her head, expecting to see eyes staring back. But there was nothing, only the wind and the rain.

Then her mobile, the ringing starting up again.

Mina pulling it from her pocket, gaze still tight on the hedge and the shadows. "Yeah?"

"Where are you?" The words making little sense to her at first, the meaning of them drowned out by the anger that flavored them.

"I . . ." Darting the flashlight beam across the shadows . . . Was that another crack? Or was it simply the movement of the leaves in the wind, her own vivid imagination. "I'm working, Mum."

"I've been calling and calling, and you haven't answered."

A quick memory of her coat slung across a chair in the immaculately styled living room of Victoria Prew. A wash of relief at her own carelessness, quickly followed by its regular companion, guilt. "I'm sorry, Mum. I—"

"This job of yours. Always this job. What about your family, huh? What about your life? Have you told them you need time off to visit us?" And on and on it went, a song so familiar that Mina could have sung it without her mother's aid.

Little point in arguing. It had always been this way. Mothers and daughters, so very complicated. The problem, Mina supposed, was that the life she wanted, the life she had chosen, had turned out to be very different from that of her mother. The fact that she had not wanted a marriage or children, when those were the very foundations on which her mother's life was built. Mina would have struggled to insult her mother more.

Mina turned in the darkness, allowing the flashlight to skitter across the front of the house, sweeping it in an arc toward the road, and tried not to allow the guilt traction. *It's an opportunity. A chance to make my mark somewhere new.* But that had been a lie, hadn't it? Mina had run from her world, had run to Northumberland, had made good her escape.

"Did you do a house-to-house?" Detective Superintendent Bell leaned forward in his chair, his fingers steepled together, Solomon preparing to give judgment. His forehead had creased into a frown.

"Yes, sir." Mina looked down again. "I secured the scene and went door-to-door within the immediate vicinity. I knocked on your door, sir." Three doors down from Victoria Prew, a double-fronted cottage with a rose-covered trellis and two expensive cars in the drive. "There was no answer," she added unnecessarily.

The superintendent pursed his lips, nodded slowly.

"The next-door neighbor, Mr. . . ."

"Lewisham."

"Lewisham," Mina agreed. "He said that he had seen someone inside the house earlier in the day." She glanced down at her notes. "His estimation was that it would have been between two and two thirty. He didn't think much of it. Assumed it was a boyfriend, someone staying with her. Mr. Lewisham explained that he'd never actually had a conversation with Victoria Prew, that he spoke to her once to tell her that she needed to keep her bins on her side of the property line, but other than that . . ."

There was no reaction from Eric Bell other than an empty stare. Mina felt color flush her cheeks.

"Anyway," she continued, "yes, so we can confirm from the footprint, the missing locket, and Mr. Lewisham's statement that the intruder was inside the property around two o'clock yesterday. No one else saw anything. Most people were out at work at that time."

The superintendent had picked up a pen, was batting it gently against the edge of the desk. "The coroner has indicated a time of death somewhere between seven p.m. and ten p.m. Where were you when Ms. Prew was being murdered?"

Mina shifted, the tone setting her teeth on edge. "I . . . I left Ms. Prew at approximately seven o'clock. I did the house-to-house until . . . nine? Maybe a little later."

"You didn't return to the Prew house?"

It was an innocent enough question. And yet Mina felt a prickle up her spine. "Sir, no. I understood Ms. Prew to be safely on her way to her mother's, and I knew the house to be secured . . ."

"So you didn't bother?"

Mina opened her mouth, closed it again. Eric Bell was studying her, and for a brief moment, she wondered if he was trying to get to her. She shifted.

"Well, Ms. Arian, it is a real shame, that. I mean, we have to be realistic here. In all likelihood, Ms. Prew was murdered in her own drive while you were drinking tea and eating biscuits in her neighbor's house. Perhaps if you'd been a little more thorough . . ."

It felt like a body blow, and Mina's gut twisted with the rank unfairness of it all.

"But there's no use crying over spilled milk." The superintendent turned back toward his computer, waved a hand, apparently done with her. "You can go."

A policy of murder –
Mina

Mina slipped into the bathroom, eased the door closed behind her. Nodded to the woman who stood at the sink, a quick half smile, before tucking herself into the bathroom stall, sliding the lock carefully closed. She stood, listening to the woman wash her hands. She was humming, a song that Mina couldn't identify. The squeal of the tap turning, the gurgle of the sink. A swoosh as paper towels were pulled from the dispenser, and then the grating of the door on the linoleum. Mina waited as the sounds of the office beyond filtered through, as the door swung shut, sealing her in silence again.

Then she kicked the door of the bathroom stall. Hard.

There were tears building up behind her eyes, just waiting for her to give in to them. It was . . . unfair. That was what it was. She had done all that she could do. She had dotted the i's, had crossed the t's, and so for Bell to blame her, to tell her that had she done more . . . No. Mina brushed at her eyes with her hands. No. This was bullshit. This was shoveling the responsibility onto her. She had done everything she could.

Had she?

Mina sank onto the closed toilet seat, her head in her hands. She heard a sound, like an exhalation of breath. That damned scent dispenser filling the room with the throat-clutching smell of violets. She hated violets.

Was he right? Could she have done more? If she had gone back to the house again, if she had turned left instead of right, or right instead of left, would Victoria Prew be alive now?

Nausea threaded itself through that god-awful artificial smell, and for a moment Mina felt her stomach dip and brought her hand to her mouth. What if she had actually driven Victoria to her mother's? What if she hadn't left her alone?

What was it Mina's mother had said? That she was good at running away, leaving people to deal with their problems alone. And it was hardly a lie, was it? Wasn't that what she had done with her own family, after all? Escaped north, sought out a place where she could be herself, where she could breathe.

Eric Bell's words raced around inside her skull. *Perhaps if you'd been a little more thorough . . .*

Mina put her head in her hands. *Stop. Think.*
She thought of Victoria hefting her suitcase into
the trunk of the car, and of her smile. *No,* thought
Mina. *He's wrong.* There had been no reason to believe that Victoria was in imminent danger. She
had never reported being followed or seeing anyone anywhere other than at the house. And she
was leaving the house. Mina knew that; she waited,
watched her go, the brake lights growing dimmer
and dimmer in the pouring rain. Mina had secured the house. She had asked the questions.

I could not have seen this coming.

She let out a breath, allowing her head to bounce
gently against her hands, as if that way the words
would enmesh themselves with her thoughts. *I could
not have seen this coming. This was not my fault.*

She thought of the super and sighed, running
her hands through her hair. He was angry; that
much was clear. The McGowan case, that was his
finest hour, the foundation on which his career
had been built. This, the murder of Victoria Prew,
would have the effect of an earthquake rattling
that foundation. Perhaps it seemed to the superintendent that his mythical early work was being
questioned now, found wanting.

Mina shook herself, stretched out her arms
against the narrow reaches of the stall. *Pull it together now.* She turned in a tight circle and released
the catch on the door. It was fine. She was fine.
She had done all she could.

She studied herself in the mirror. There were
dark circles under her eyes that no amount of con-
cealer would cover. Her fingertips pulled at the
lines that had begun to form in the corners, across

her forehead, and she felt more tired still. Mina looked at her watch and sighed—10:00 p.m. and no sign of the day ending yet. She breathed out slowly, squared her shoulders, and let herself back out into the melee.

The incident room thrummed with the trill of voices, the odd burst of laughter. They twisted around in their seats, enjoying the freedom away from a teacher. There were perhaps forty of them in all. Tomorrow there would be more. More still the day after that. But today there were only forty. They had divided themselves into two distinct groups. The young ones, those too new to remember the first time. They were the ones with the light faces, voices high with excitement, whose fingers danced with adrenaline, who were bursting to get out there to catch themselves a serial killer. Then there were the old-timers. Mina counted three, four of them, the ones who sat, head down, arms folded, as if at a funeral. They knew what was coming.

She sought out Cain Aiken. He had positioned himself off to one side, had pulled away from the others. He leaned forward, elbows on his knees, fingers interlocked as if in prayer. But then, Mina allowed, he had lost one brother, had almost lost a second. Perhaps he was praying.

Mina slid into an empty seat positioned between the two camps. She was new. She was young, or youngish at the very least. And yet a woman she had spoken to yesterday was now dead, and so, she thought, that aged her, separated her from the pack. She looked up as Owen took a seat beside her.

"You see this?" he asked, gesturing at the television screens.

There were three in all, each tuned to a different news channel. Each one of them showing stone cottages and rolling hills, a wide-reaching moor and Hadrian's Wall. And there, a pimple on a perfect face, the forensic tent. The sound had been turned down low, so the words were lost in the tumult of the room, and yet you could feel it in the perfectly appointed frowns of the reporters, the horror of it, the tragedy. And something else, in the movements that were a little too quick, the eyes that sparkled a little too much—the message that this, right here, was a really good story.

"The place is crawling with them," muttered Owen. "Apparently, they're knocking on every door in Briganton, trying to get quotes. Not just local papers either. All the nationals are here. There's a bunch of them camped downstairs. I had to use the back door when I came in."

"Great," said Mina. "That should make life easier, then." She shook her head. "I never did ask . . . How was your date the other night?"

Owen's thin cheeks colored. "She canceled. Said she had gastroenteritis."

Mina looked at him, sympathetic. "Well, people get stomach bugs."

He snorted. "Yeah. They don't usually go clubbing with their friends then." A glance at her. "Facebook is a terrible thing for liars."

Mina smiled, patted him distantly on the arm. "Never mind. I'm sure love will find a way."

The voices sputtered into silence as the door to

the major incident room opened, admitting Superintendent Bell, followed closely by his boss, Detective Chief Superintendent Byron Clee, a short man built like a bulldog, coming up hard on fifty and looking more like a criminal than a man charged with catching them.

Forty heads turned to watch them march across the room, Eric Bell limping ever so slightly, a struggle he did his best to hide. Bell looked up at the television screens and scowled.

"Right then," he said, taking up position at the front of the room. "Listen up, please." He waved behind him to a picture that had been tacked to the whiteboard at the front of the room. "Ladies and gentlemen, this is Victoria Prew. She was thirty-nine years old, an accountant with Whitney-Stone in Carlisle. Originally from Edinburgh."

Mina studied the photograph. The woman it depicted looked different from the woman she had met, her face fuller, eyes brighter, caught in a laugh. It must, she thought, have been taken before the divorce. Before her world fell apart.

"Next of kin, her mother, has been informed and is currently being supported by an FLO," continued Bell. "She informs us that Ms. Prew was going through a rather nasty divorce."

Victoria had said that her ex-husband was angry with her, that she was ruining his plans for a new life. Mina's gaze shifted to the other picture, which had been placed beside the first, that of the dead body of Victoria Prew, her gaze vacant, skin ashen. And in among the rhythm of the superintendent's words, something scratched at her. The ex was angry. Mina forced herself to stare at the dead body. The question, though, was whether this was a murder committed by an angry man.

"A team of officers is currently out in Edinburgh, looking for the ex-husband. So far they have been unsuccessful."

Victoria's death, the strangulation itself, it would have taken, what? Three, four minutes? It was the result of a determined, concentrated effort. Mina squinted, bringing into focus the bruise of finger-marks on her neck. But angry? There had been no beating, no stabbing, little of the physicality that might have provided a vent for the fury of a ruined life. In essence, the murder of Victoria Prew was clean. Businesslike.

"I cannot emphasize enough," said Superintendent Bell, "how important it is that Mr. Prew is located in a timely manner."

And what about the display? The positioning of the body on the wall? Was that the behavior of an angry man?

Mina looked back at the television nearest her, now showing the face of Heath McGowan. The scrolling feed at the bottom of the screen read *Another body in the killer on the wall case?* And that was it, wasn't it? Little matter that the deaths were separated by twenty years. Little matter that the murderer was behind bars. Little matter that the case of the killer on the wall was closed.

She stared at the picture of Heath McGowan.

"Now, given the proximity of the two events . . ." Superintendent Bell's voice came back into focus. "It is, of course, of primary interest to us to locate the individual who broke into Ms. Prew's house and who, we believe, has been stalking her. I also need to point out that, given Briganton's history, there is likely to be a substantial amount of concern from the public. We want to get this thing resolved as quickly as possible, with as little drama as possible. To be clear, my policy for this investigation is that the matter should be treated as entirely independent of the original Heath McGowan case. While I recognize that there are similarities in the body placement, it is my opinion that this has been done in order to throw off investigators. This case is therefore to be treated as a stand-alone, rather than to be considered in any way related to the original murder series."

Mina looked at Cain Aiken, his gaze still on his fingers, his lips pursed. She could see the sideways glances from the others, hear the odd mutter. She felt her heart begin to beat faster.

"Is there some problem in the room?" asked the superintendent.

The mutters dropped away; gazes tilted downward.

"Thank you. Right, where's my outside action team?"

A wave of hands from the far right corner, a low "Here, boss."

"I need you to canvass the neighborhood. See if anyone in the vicinity heard anything, saw anything. Check around the village. I believe the Aubrey Arms has CCTV. See if they picked anything up on that. The church also has CCTV. They had some problems with vandals a couple of years back. Dan?" Eric Bell looked out, attempting to locate a face. "Yes, Dan, I need you to go to Whitney-Stone, talk to her colleagues. Heather? Heather, you're with the family."

He looked out over the array of faces. "We're going to be putting in some long hours here. Tell your families not to expect to see much of you for a while."

Then, to Mina's own surprise, she felt her hand snaking its way up, heads swiveling toward her.

"Sir?"

The superintendent's look had become hard. "Yes, DC Arian."

"Sir, I'm sorry, but I . . . I was just wondering . . . So, just to be clear, you said that your policy is that this has nothing to do with the killings on the wall?"

Surrounding heads swiveled from Mina to Bell, then back again. Chief Superintendent Clee folded his arms across his chest, waiting for what would come next.

"The killer on the wall is in prison," said Superintendent Bell.

"Yes, but given the similarities—"

"Let me be clear, DC Arian. All we know at this stage is that a woman is dead. Those early murders were extremely well publicized. A number of books have been written, documentaries made, in the intervening years, detailing the murders, the MO. As such, it would be no great stretch for someone with sufficient motivation to replicate the body placement, the cause of death, with this particular murder in order to skew the investigation. I must emphasize that this does not mean we have a serial killer on the loose."

"But it is true that some serial killers work with partners? I was just wondering, given what's happened, whether we would be considering the possibility that there was an accomplice that was not found in the original investigation." Mina felt her voice become smaller, as if it could barely believe that it was escaping her.

Superintendent Bell studied her for long moments. "No, Ms. Arian. No, we will not."

Sunday, October 23

An exercise in death – Isla

Isla drove slowly. The narrow roads were empty of traffic, but their sides were lined with parked cars, the entire world once again descending on Briganton to look in on a murder. The rain had abated, the promise of it still heavy in the air, in the low-slung clouds, and Isla shivered, fingers moving, turning the heating up to full. Slow out of her street, down the hill, left at the corner. Past the Aubrey Arms, the smokers spilling out onto the street, their heads tucked together in gripping conversation. It didn't take a detective to figure out what they were talking about. Isla could see it, in the tightness of their backs, the tension in their shoulders. She passed the florist, closed today, but

Moira was on the doorstep, anyway, deep in conversation with Mrs. Patterson from the big house. Moira looked like she had been crying, Mrs. Patterson's hand resting on her forearm, head dipped close.

Isla breathed out, a long, controlled breath. A right turn, as she headed toward her parents' house, but it was the police vans she saw first, the vivid yellow tape cutting through the gray day. The house of Victoria Prew. Had Isla known who she was before yesterday? Would she have recognized her, had she passed her in the street? A forensic officer trudged across the gravel drive, hefting a case in one hand, head down, presumably so she didn't have to look at the knotted journalists leaning across the cordon. It happened so quickly, Isla thought. Yesterday the house was a home, severe in its glass and steel. Today, a crime scene. And Victoria Prew? Who had she been before this? Although the sad truth would be that it did not really matter, not to the world at large, anyway. Because with her death, she had been reborn as something different. The victim of a murderer.

Then Isla's parents' house. This one far more traditional, with its wide bay windows, rose-covered trellis, the porch with the twin potted bay trees, looking for all the world like it was empty, locked up for the winter. But Isla had spoken to her mother that morning, had been swamped with faux good cheer. *Your father said it was the ex-husband, that it's nothing for us to worry about. It's not like last time, not at all.* Her father, predictably, had been nowhere to be seen.

Then she was out of the village, a cloak thrown off her. The cloistered roads, with their overhanging trees, gave way to wide-open spaces running across the countryside like arteries through a heart. Isla put her foot down, driving far too fast and yet needing that speed, as if with it she could outrun the village and everything contained in it.

"Why don't you come for lunch?" her mother had asked. "Don't go into work. It's a Sunday. Who goes into work on a Sunday? Especially this Sunday." And yet, when Isla had suggested it softly to Ramsey, he had shaken his head. No, he wasn't up to a family gathering. Yes, he'd rather be on his own, did she mind? He would go for a walk, just him in the cold, damp air. Maybe give his brother a call. "After all," he had said, shaking his head, "this affects Cain as much as it affects me."

The university parking lot was empty. Isla pulled into her usual bay, turned the engine off, and sat for a minute, perhaps two, gathering herself. Then she blew out a breath and concentrated on the movement of her fingers, lifting them, one by one, from the steering wheel. The ringing of the phone cut in, its suddenness startling her. But it was only a phone, after all. Nothing to worry about. She pulled it free from her handbag, glanced at the caller ID.

"Connor, hi."

"So, I'm sitting in my office, going through the fMRI results, and I'm thinking to myself, *Who the hell would be daft enough to come into work on a Sunday?* And then I look out of my window, and what do you think I see?"

Isla laughed, giddy with relief. "Put the kettle on. I'm gagging for a cuppa."

"Will do."

The rain had begun again. Isla took another breath and then shoved at her door, weighted her umbrella in her hand, carefully locked the car door behind her. She held the umbrella at her side like a truncheon, scanning the empty tarmac. Her eyes lingered on the tree line as she calculated the distance from the car to the door. Then she moved, her walk slow, measured, heart screaming at her to run, run like the wind. But no. Isla walked as if she had all the time in the world, entered her code into the keypad with deliberate care. Still, only when she was inside the cavernous lobby, the door shut tight behind her, did her breath return.

"Tea, one sugar. And a chocolate biscuit, because it's a Sunday and what the hell."

Connor was wearing tracksuit bottoms, a long-sleeved T-shirt with a stain on the shoulder, his hair standing up in chaotic fashion.

"Are you . . . Dude, are those your pajamas?"

"Hey. Don't judge me. It's all about the looks with you, isn't it?"

Isla grinned, took two of the chocolate biscuits, and sank into the armchair tucked into the corner of Connor's office. Smaller than hers, the room had vanished under the weight of the chaos within it. Stacks of folders vied for supremacy, ringing the walls, until it appeared certain that Connor spent his days building paper forts. There was a desk— Isla was relatively confident on that score. And yet all that was visible to the naked eye was paper, drifts of it that clambered up the sides of the computer monitor, threatening to bury it alive.

Isla took a sip of the tea. "You know, I have a feeling that when Armageddon comes, it's going to look a hell of a lot like this office."

"Yeah, well." He sat opposite her, lifting his bare feet onto a pile of books. "It's the sign of an active mind."

"It's the sign of an active psychosis."

Connor bit a biscuit in half. "So, ah, you okay? I heard about that woman. The murder."

"Ah, just peachy, you know me." Isla sighed. "You can't move for the bloody media, though. I've had to leave the curtains closed throughout the house. Caught a reporter looking in the kitchen window earlier."

"Jesus. Tough on Rams."

She shrugged. "He actually handles them far better than I do. You know how he is. Everyone's best friend."

"Are you suggesting you are not equally delightful?" Connor adopted a mock-shock expression. "Surely not."

"Bite me."

"See? There it is."

"So, you have McGowan's scan results or no?"

Connor nodded. He pulled a file from the top of a tower beside him and laid the photographs out across his knees. "It's the same."

A sequence of blue running right throughout the paralimbic system. The function of the entire system compromised. The face of psychopathy.

Isla leaned closer, ran her finger across the top of the colors. "Well, it's what we were expecting."

"The physiology of psychopathy is pretty definitive. But as to the rest of it . . . I don't know. I feel we're missing something."

The rest of it. That driving force that turned a psychopath into a serial killer.

Isla stared at the images, now not seeing them. Instead seeing Victoria Prew's house, its wide windows framing the moorland beyond as if it was a picture. But the trouble was that windows worked both ways. On the tail of that came a murky memory, one she had almost forgotten, of her early morning runs, soles landing hard on the uneven ground that surrounded Hadrian's Wall. And then, looming large in the gloom, a square of light that punched across the moor like a lighthouse. And Isla's gaze irretrievably pulled from the sinuous ground on which she ran to the house and the bedroom and the figure moving inside it. She would not have known Victoria Prew had she bumped into her on the street. But she knew that house and that bedroom. If you were someone with that hunger, that need you were fighting against, and you were out walking the wall, maybe walking a dog, maybe simply trying to escape yourself, and you saw that light and that room and that woman . . .

What would you do then?

Isla stared at the pictures of Heath McGowan's brain. If you were someone like Heath, you might watch Victoria Prew. And perhaps you would imagine what you could do to her in the darkness of night, when she was unsuspecting, unprotected.

And for a while that imagining would be enough to sate the need. Then one day, maybe when you were tired or angry or stressed, and those controls, those high walls that you had built to separate the public you from the real you, maybe they sank a little, the exhaustion or the stress or the rage shifting the focus so that everything felt a little more blurry, a little less clear. Maybe on that day the imagining of your hands on her neck would no longer be sufficient. Maybe on that day it had to be something more, the feel of the woman's skin beneath your fingers, the gasp of her final breaths, her body going limp beneath you.

"What?" asked Connor.

"I . . ." Isla stopped, her thoughts racing. Then she pushed herself up, grabbed the phone on Connor's desk, dialed the number quickly, half not expecting an answer. One ring, two, three. Then—

"Hello?" Her father sounded irritated. A drumming of noise in the background. "Who's this?"

"Dad. It's me."

"Oh, Isl. Hi. Love, I'm a bit busy . . ."

"No, I know. I just . . . I needed to ask you something. Just quickly. Dad, did Victoria Prew have any issues with a Peeping Tom? In the past couple of weeks. Months, maybe?"

A long pause. Then, "Yes, she did. Why?"

"No. It's nothing, just an academic question. You, ah, you find the ex-husband yet?"

Her father snorted. "Guy's missing. Neighbors said they think he's gone on holidays. Holidays. Yeah. I'm telling you, it's the ex that did it."

Isla bit her lip. "Okay, well, I'll let you get back to it. Thanks, Dad." She replaced the phone quickly, cutting off the inevitable questions that would follow.

"What was that?" asked Connor, frowning.

"The murder, the one in Briganton."

"Yes."

"I'm just . . . Look, hear me out here. Let's call it a mental exercise." Isla leaned back against the desk.

Connor grinned, cracked his knuckles. "I could use a workout. Go for it."

"Right. My dad, he thinks . . ." Then Isla stopped herself. "Okay, he *says* his money is on Victoria Prew's husband. They were going through a nasty divorce. But . . . the murder . . . it was a blitz attack. Whoever this was, he came from nowhere and took her down in the amount of time it took to get from her front door to her car. Less than that, even. Forensics found her shoe inside the car. So she'd made it. Whoever killed her, he did it fast. He had to have been waiting for her, seen the opportunity and taken it. But then . . ."

"Why move her?"

"Why move her? It makes no sense. It dramatically increases your time with the body, which means you are increasing the risk of someone seeing you, not to mention the additional chance that you will be leaving hair, fibers . . . Why do that? Why expose yourself like that?"

"Well, say it was the ex-husband, maybe he doesn't realize all this. I mean, to be fair, we're coming at it from a fairly experienced perspective."

Isla looked at him flatly. "The ex is a barrister. I looked him up. He defends criminal cases. Probably knows more than we do." She pushed herself up again, paced in the small empty square of floor between the two chairs. "Whichever way you slice it, the advantages you gain from briefly fooling the investigators into thinking it's something to do with the killer on the wall are nothing compared to the additional risks you take on by moving the body to the wall."

"Unless you have to."

"Unless you have to," agreed Isla. "Unless the murder isn't enough, but the compulsion comes from the scene itself, the arrangement of the body, replicating, as close as you can, the original murder series."

"So . . . ," said Connor, "a copycat?"

"Okay," said Isla. "Let's say it is a copycat . . ."

"Okay. Let's say that it is."

"The first crime in the killer on the wall series was a spectacular." The word stuck in her throat, the memory of three dead bodies, her own husband almost dead. "Three victims, should have been four. It was as if Heath wanted to begin with a bang, show the world just how bad he could be. So why didn't this one do the same?"

"He's inexperienced. Taking four people down, that's a big job. Maybe he's psychologically not ready for that."

"Right. It's almost like it was an urge that simply overwhelmed him. The crime itself, it was opportunistic, as if the chance simply presented itself to him and he grabbed at it. Victoria Prew, her house, it has these big wide windows, no curtains, nothing to stop anyone from looking in, and when you're out at the wall, you can see everything . . ."

"The perfect victim for someone who is building up to a murder."

"How many times have we seen that before? Edward Frey? Remember? He watched those teenagers for months before he went after them." Five teenage boys, in and around Hackney. When he was finally arrested, police found a shrine to each and every one of his victims, photographs dating over months, all taken without the boys' knowledge. Isla sat back down, her knees bouncing. "So, let's say it is that. That this is someone who has lived with the legend of the killer on the wall, what he did to the community, how he became famous for those murders. He has this curiosity . . . What would it be like to kill someone? And he sees Victoria Prew through her window, so the thought, it just grows and grows, until in the end it's no longer just a curiosity. Now it's a need. The question then becomes, what comes next? He's broken the seal. That urge he's been keeping at bay, he's given in to it now, which means it's a damn sight harder not to give in the next time."

Connor was watching her. "Which means he's going to kill again," he said, his voice soft.

Isla nodded slowly. "He's going to kill again." The world bucked and swayed. "I need to call my father." Isla pushed herself up, reached for the phone.

"Superintendent Bell?" This time he sounded extremely irritated.

"Dad. It's me again."

"Jes . . . Isla, I'm extremely busy here."

"I know. I just . . . Dad, I've been thinking about this, about the murder. And the thing is, I don't think that this lines up with it being the ex-husband. Not at all. Dad, I think you've got a copycat on your hands. And—"

"Isla. Can you prove it?"

"Um . . . no."

A heavy sigh. "Love, I understand what you're saying. But I have to work with the evidence. And right now, the evidence is telling me to take a good, hard look at Mr. Prew."

Isla turned, studied the rain as it bounced from the windows. "I get that, Dad. But . . . I have a really bad feeling about this. And if this is a copycat . . . he's going to kill again."

A silence at the other end of the line. Then her father said, "Okay. I'll look into it." And just like that, he was gone.

Isla stood for a moment, cradling the phone, a sound that made little sense cutting into the edge of her awareness. Then the scene shifted, and she located the sound. "My office phone," she said, hurrying to the door. "It's ringing."

A couple of quick steps across the silent hallway, a quick tug at the handle, the sound of ringing deafening now in the empty room.

Isla grabbed for the phone. "Professor Bell."

There was a click and then another click.

The voice, when it came, catapulted her back twenty years, then forward to an MRI scanner. Isla gripped the edge of the table.

"Professor Bell? It's Heath."

Isla struggled to bring her thoughts together. "Heath? What . . . what can I do for you?"

"No, see, thing is, I heard about what happened. There in Briganton. And . . . you know, nasty stuff. Just thought I'd give you a call to check that you're okay."

Isla's mouth opened, closed again.

"So, are you? Okay, I mean?"

The next step – Ramsey

Dusk had begun to fall, a relentless march of twilight beating its way through a sky that had failed to muster much in the way of light, anyway. The two men stood in the kitchen, watching the darkening sky. There was talk of a storm coming, another one, of rising waters and savage winds. It seemed appropriate, thought Ramsey. Pathetic fallacy at its finest.

"You want to go?" Cain squinted out the window, expression doubtful. "It looks like rain."

"It always looks like rain," replied Ramsey. "Yeah, come on. This house, it's starting to close in on me now."

Still, his brother hung around, teeth gnawing at

his lip. Older by two years, Cain was bigger, taller, broader, his hair shaved down to his scalp, good looking, but in a hard kind of way. They had handled it differently, Zach's death, Ramsey's attack. Ramsey had poured himself into his words, making a name as a journalist who put the victims, the victims' families, front and center. It was full immersion, saturation in tales of grief and pain. "I don't know how you stand it," Cain had said time and time again. "All that sadness." For Cain, healing had come through the chase. He had put in an application for the police force a week after Zachary's death, had been successful a year later, had swiftly moved through uniform, into CID, where he had remained. *I like it there. There, I'm not one of the hunted. There, I'm the hunter.*

"What?" asked Ramsey.

"No, it's just . . ." Cain pulled a face. "The Aubrey Arms, you know there are going to be people there, right?"

"In a pub? *No!*"

Cain rolled his eyes. "I meant they're going to be all over us, Rams. You know how it can be around here. Especially for 'the only survivor.' "

Ramsey shrugged, pulling a dark red sweater over his head. "They don't mean any harm. They care about us, that's all."

His brother looked unconvinced. "I don't know how you stand it, the incestuousness of this place. It's as if people don't get that there is a whole entire world beyond the borders of Briganton."

"Some of them don't. Some of them have literally never been as far as Carlisle." Ramsey stuffed his feet into hiking boots. "I like it. It feels . . . I don't know, like family, I guess. I like being surrounded by people I've known all my life. I like knowing how they're going to feel about things, what they're going to say."

Cain studied him. "It doesn't make you feel suffocated?"

Ramsey grinned. "Not really. You really are antisocial, aren't you?"

In truth, Ramsey craved the sound of it, the rumbling roar of chatter beyond the thick pub door, the way it built in a wave, reached a crest as you pulled the door open. He needed that roar now, other voices to take the place of the ones that chased one another round inside his own head. He needed a pint, coal-black Guinness with a snow-white top, the cold of the glass against his hand. Perhaps, after two pints, maybe three, a quick cigarette, the heat of it filling up his lungs, he would feel then that he was still alive. That this thing that had taken over his world again had not killed him. Not yet, anyway.

"Come on, then," muttered Cain. "Best go if we're going."

They slipped out the back door into the burgeoning night. A bitter wind had whipped up and now snaked its way beneath Ramsey's coat, and he entertained the brief thought of turning back, that his brother was right, that they were better off keeping to themselves, that a pint at the kitchen table would serve just as well. But still he kept on, tucking his head deeper inside his jacket. It wasn't just the drink he needed, but the life surrounding it.

"Must be bloody mad." The wind tugged at Cain's voice and flung it away from them. He pulled at the low garden gate, held it open for his brother. "Where's Isla this fine evening, anyway?"

"Work. Studying monsters. You know how she is."

Ramsey felt his brother watching him, could sense the words arranging and rearranging themselves behind closed lips.

"She . . ." Cain pulled the gate closed tight behind them. "She works long hours, doesn't she?"

Ramsey nodded. If you concentrated hard enough, sometimes you could take words at their face value, could ignore the layers of meaning stacked beneath them. "She's good at what she does."

"You, ah . . . you guys never think of having kids?" The question had the flavor of one long marinated.

Ramsey glanced at Cain. He was looking down, watching his feet brush through the tumbledown autumn leaves. Cain had married just a little bit before Ramsey himself, but unlike for Ramsey, shortly after the marriage had come a little girl, Kayla. And shortly after that had come a divorce. Cain, it transpired, was not really the marrying type. Or, to put it bluntly, not the monogamous type. His ex-wife had caught him in bed with their neighbor. It had not gone down well.

The tremulous fingers of a yew tree scraped Ramsey's cheek, and he brushed the branch aside carefully. Of course he thought about having children. Of creating another person, a tiny shining package, all soft skin and rounded flesh. Of eyes gazing into his own with endless wonderment, knowing beyond all doubt that, whatever had gone before, for this person he was not "one of the Aiken family" or "the only survivor"; he was simply Daddy. Of the quiet of the house punctured by childish wails and high-pitched laughter, and the very immediateness of that need pushing away all else until it became a distant memory. Of life taking the place of death.

Yes. He thought of it.

"Maybe," Ramsey replied. "One day."

"Ah." His brother nodded sagely. "Not quite ready, is it?"

Why not, Isla? Why not do it? We're not getting any younger, and if we leave it any longer, maybe it won't ever happen.

And Isla looking at him, but not at him in that way she did when she had retreated entirely inside herself. *I don't know. It's just . . . it's such a big thing, Rams. And what if . . .*

What if what?

Nothing. Nothing. Let's just give it a bit more time? Yes?

Ramsey pulled his zipper up to his chin. "Plenty of time for grown-up stuff like that." *Plenty of time.* It was a mantra and a prayer. That the sand would not escape from the hourglass, leaving them standing there with nothing.

"How's work going?" asked Cain. A big brother checking in. "You writing anything now?"

"Couple of articles. I've been approached about writing a piece about the murder—you know the drill—from the 'survivor's' perspective. Kind of an inside look into what it's like to be a victim." He shrugged. "Feels a bit like I'm cashing in. I don't know. That said, I think it's an important message, that the effects of something like this, they don't just end when the killings end. They go on and on."

Cain nodded. "Get what you can out of it, is what I say. You've been through enough. You've earned it."

Ramsey scuffed his boots as he walked. "I went to see Stephen Doyle earlier. Wanted to make sure he was coping okay, you know, with the murder and everything. It brings stuff back."

"Yeah," Cain agreed quietly. "And is he? Okay?"

Ramsey blew out a breath. "What can I say? He's as okay as he can be. Pretty much just sat there the entire time. Barely said a word. Sister is worried to death about him."

A right at the bottom of the hill, and the two brothers walked on, tucked in tight against the hedges, in the vain hope that they would find some protection from the wind.

"Maggie. Maggie."

On the corner of Camberwell Street, an elderly man stood in the garden that wrapped around three sides of a semi-detached house. He wore pajamas—plaid—leather shoes, a dressing gown, its tie open and waving out behind him like a tail.

Ramsey frowned, squinting into the gloom. "Ted? You okay?"

Ted Heron spun on his heel, his dressing gown flying outward. "Who . . . Ramsey?"

A quick glance at his brother and Ramsey hopped the wall, landed lightly on boggy grass. "What is it, Ted? What's up?"

The man looked at him, seemed to be shuffling through his thoughts, trying to get them to line up in order. He had been a police officer once, back

before his first stroke. Now at eighty-five, he mostly
followed along behind his wife, waiting for her to
guide him, make sense of a world that was becoming increasingly nonsensical.

"I can't find Maggie," he muttered. "I . . . She
came out to find the cat. But . . . that was . . . I
don't know . . . I forget things, see, lose track." A
tortoiseshell cat butted its head against Ramsey's
leg, purring like a drill. "Now I can't find her."

The brothers looked at one another.

"Okay, Ted," said Cain, his voice unnaturally
light. "No problem. So . . . she was here, yes?
When you saw her last?"

"I think so," moaned Ted, his head swinging left
to right, as if somehow Maggie might have miraculously appeared on the lawn before them. "That
was what she said, anyway. Or . . . I mean, I think
that's what she said. Have you seen her?"

Ramsey drew in a deep breath. "Cain, why don't
you take him inside? Ted, go on. You look freez-
ing, mate. You go with Cain and let him ask you
some questions." A swift nod from his brother.
"And I'll go and knock next door. I bet you anything that's where she's gone. I'm always seeing
Maggie and Lillian chatting when I'm out on my
runs." The lies dripped from his tongue like
honey. But was a lie really a lie when it was what
the other person wanted so badly to hear? "She'll
be in there, I bet you anything." He nodded, smiling brightly, a brief shared glance with his brother,
the moment containing twenty years' worth of
fear, and then he turned, walked briskly across the
lawn to the bright red door of the adjacent house.
Three loud knocks and Ramsey realized that his

hands were shaking. He tucked them inside his pockets, telling himself that it was the wind, that was all.

A single figure moved behind the swirled glass, movements careful.

Hurry up.

"Who is it?"

"It's Ramsey Aiken."

The clatter of a chain being slid, the door creaking inward. Lillian peered out at him from beneath a vivid bush of garish red hair. "Hello, love. You coming in?"

"No, Lillian. I . . . Have you seen Maggie? Is she here?"

"No, love. I heard her calling for Mitzy, ooh, must have been well over an hour ago now, but I was watching *Songs of Praise*, see, so I didn't . . ." She pushed the door open wider, and Ramsey felt the inescapable sense of cards slotting into place. "Why? What's wrong?"

Ramsey looked up the street and down, then back at Lillian as she knotted her fingers together.

"Lillian, I think we may have a problem."

Family connections – Mina

The elderly man sat on the abundantly flowered sofa, pajama legs hitched up, exposing a pair of pallid legs that ended in vivid red socks with the distorted woolen face of Homer Simpson etched into them. Mina sat perched on the edge of a scuffed leather armchair, her notepad balanced on her knees, and tried to concentrate on the page, on her writing, and yet time and time again, her gaze kept coming back to those legs and those socks. The image had the shape of a memory as it was being etched, and Mina knew that, for years to come, whenever she thought back to this night, she would think of those socks.

"I just don't understand it. I mean, she only

went out to call Mitzy." Ted shook his head. His hand shook, too, as he ran it across the back of the offending cat. She arched her back, reaching up into the touch, apparently oblivious to the trouble she had caused. "That was . . . How long ago was it now, Ramsey?"

Ramsey Aiken sat beside him, his hands folded in his lap, his only concession to fear the one foot that he drummed against the floor. "Well," he said softly, "I wasn't here then, remember?"

"No. No. That's right." Ted looked around the small living room. "Maybe your brother would know?"

Ramsey caught Mina's eye in a moment of silent communication. Ted's confusion was getting worse. Twice he had stood up to go and call Maggie, saying that she must not have heard them arriving, that she must be getting ready still. Twice they had had to remind him that his wife had vanished.

Mina looked at her watch. The call had come in to the station forty-five minutes ago. She had been going through CCTV footage, a pursuit quickly abandoned when the shout went up. Twenty minutes after that, she had arrived at the scene. Which meant that Maggie had been missing for at least an hour, quite possibly a lot more than that. She glanced through the window, at the shape of Cain beyond, his head dipped away from the driving rain, the phone to his ear as he briefed Superintendent Eric Bell. Mina felt a flush rise through her at the thought of the superintendent, at that slowly nodding head, the lips puckered in disdain.

"So, Ted . . ." She spoke carefully, the words wanting to take the shape of those addressed to a child, but then that would be patronizing. He wasn't a child. She coughed, tried again. "Ted, what time did you say you saw her last?"

He paused, hand held high in mid-stroke, much to the irritation of the cat, who looked up at him with a low mewl of protest. "I . . . Did I say? I don't know."

Ramsey leaned forward, blond hair catching the light from the standard lamp behind him. "What were you watching on TV, Ted? When she said she was going outside. Do you remember that?"

Ted shifted, his gaze falling on the dark television set, as if the motion would tumble him back in time and he would see Maggie once more standing before him. "Was it . . . no . . . it could have been . . . no. Well." He shook his head. "I just can't remember."

"Okay, Ted," said Mina lightly. "No problem. We'll figure it all out."

Police teams were searching along Hadrian's Wall.

It was Cain who had made the call. *A Briganton resident has vanished.* The air in the major incident room had stilled; forty people had held their breath. Then, the wave of it crashing onto the shore. *Someone find Superintendent Bell. We need to brief him.* A flurry of activity, then Chief Superintendent Clee stepping in. *Right, listen up, chaps.* Chaps? *We need a team out searching the wall. Now.* A unifying thought flying through forty minds. That it was happening again. *I need someone to meet Cain at the scene and free him up, interview the missing woman's husband.* Clee had given a vague squint around the room as he fought to remember a single one of their names. Mina had raised her hand. *I'll do it*. They had poured out of the station together, Mina to a car, others to vans, had left the station in a convoy, sirens wailing.

Mina had wanted to believe that it was nothing. That the hysteria shaken loose by the death of Victoria Prew would account for it. That the elderly woman—she was eighty-two, remember—had simply wandered away, got chatting to a friend, gone for a walk without telling anyone. And yet . . . as she watched a van peel away, take a hard right down toward the wall, Mina had known somewhere hard in her chest what it was they would find there.

"What was Maggie wearing, Ted?" Mina asked quietly.

"A . . . a long whatsit. Skirt. Was it . . . gray, maybe? Or brown? And a sweater. With red roses on it. I remember that." He looked sideways at Ramsey. "Loves roses, docs our Maggie. Always know what to do if she gets a bit cross with me. Nice bunch of roses does the trick." He prodded Ramsey in the thigh. "You need to remember that, lad, what with that missus of yours. Always appreciate roses, they do."

Ramsey smiled. "Thanks, Ted. I'll remember that." He looked at Mina, smiled, and she felt herself flush, instantly cursed the heat as it hit her cheeks. But then, she reasoned, it was to be expected. Ramsey was a celebrity of sorts or, at the very least, the most like a celebrity a little place like Briganton could produce.

"Mina?"

She looked up. Owen Darby hung in the door-

way of the living room, long and lean and rain
soaked. "Can I have a quick word?"

"Would you excuse me for just a moment?" Mina
said, pushing herself up to standing.

Ted's gaze followed her, his eyes widening.

"So, Ted," said Ramsey. "How old is Mitzy? She's
a lovely looking thing."

Mina slipped into the kitchen, pushed the door
closed behind her. "What's up?"

Owen folded his arms across his chest, feet shifting. "I've done the entire street. No one saw anything. Most people, they had their curtains closed,
lights on. No one saw Maggie outside. No one saw
her leave."

Mina sighed. "Shit."

"Yeah."

"Anything from the search teams?"

He shook his head. "Nothing yet. They've gone
over the wall that runs behind the village, and it's
clear." He shrugged. "Maybe it is nothing. Or, I
mean, not nothing. Maybe it's not *that*. Maybe she
wandered off, has had a fall. They're extending
the search area now. Heading farther out east and
west along the wall. A separate team is heading up
to Bowman's Hill."

Mina nodded absently. "Okay. Well, maybe you're
right. I mean, God, let's hope you're right." She
stood staring at the Formica countertops. "Do me a
favor. Let me know if they find anything?"

He studied her, then nodded. "Of course."

Mina let herself back into the living room. Ted was
talking in wandering, stop-start sentences. Would
they have to get some kind of carer in? she wondered.

Was he safe to be left alone? There was a daughter, living up in Glasgow. She should call her.

Mina opened her mouth to ask for the number and then closed it again.

Ted had stopped talking, was staring at the blank television screen, frowning.

"Ted? What is it?"

"I . . . a car."

"Sorry?"

"I heard a car."

Mina and Ramsey shared a look.

"What car, Ted?"

"Well, it was . . . Let me think now . . . What was on? It was . . . the news. That's what it was. I was watching the news, and I remember because at first I thought it was on the TV and that's where I'd heard it. But no, it wasn't. It was outside."

"Okay, great. What exactly did you hear?"

"I heard a car door. But not a car door. More like . . ." He gestured, lifting his hands up into the air and bringing them down. "More like a trunk being closed. Then I heard a car door. Then the car drove off. And it was when the news was on."

"And this was after Maggie had gone outside?"

"Yes," he said triumphantly. "And I know it was, because I went to say to her, 'Who on earth is that out on a night like this?' And she wasn't there. And I was going to go and look for her, but then I remembered, she was getting the cat in. So . . . does that help?" he added anxiously.

Mina smiled. "That's a great help. So, let's think. What time is the news on?"

Ramsey didn't look at her, was looking down at

his hands. His voice low, he said, "Seven. The news is on at seven."

And her insides turned as the mathematics of it all worked itself out. That it was now coming on to ten. That Maggie had been gone for almost three hours.

"Okay . . . I . . ."

"I just worry about her, you know. She's been so upset."

"What do you mean? You mean about the murder?"

"Aye, well. It hits home, see. Ramsey here, he knows what I'm talking about, don't you, lad? When you've lost someone like that, and then to have it happen again."

"I . . ." Mina cast back in her memory, looking for some hook to hang the conversation on. "I'm confused."

Ramsey's voice was low. "Maggie is Kitty Lane's cousin."

Mina stared at him, the pieces shifting into a new shape.

"Let me just pop outside and see if there are any updates." It wasn't news she needed, but air. Mina ducked out the front door, grabbing her coat as she went, sucked in the coldness of the night. The wind was cruel now, and thin drops of rain had begun to fall. Mina looked up into them.

Shit.

The world was moving beneath her feet, and she put out a hand to the low stone garden wall, steadying herself. Maggie was Kitty Lane's cousin. And two days after a woman was murdered, her body abandoned on the wall, Maggie had vanished. Bile eased its way up her throat; heat rushed to her face.

Shit.

Mina pulled her mobile phone from her pocket, dialed quickly.

"Major incident room."

"It's Mina Arian. I need to speak to the SIO."

A muttered conversation, dull sounds, which to her mind seemed to carry irritation within them. But then, that was probably just her. The rain had soaked into her hair, plastering it in spindly rivulets to her face, and she swept them from her cheeks.

"This is Bell." Did he sound angry? Or was that simply the way he always sounded?

"Sir, it's Mina Arian. Sorry to bother you, but there's something I think you should hear." The words rolled, a snowball tumbling downhill. "Maggie, the woman who's missing. There's a link between her and one of the victims from the original series. Kitty Lane. They were cousins. And, sir, we've worked it out. She's been gone for nearly three hours now. It's another one, sir. I'm sure of it."

There was a long silence on the line. "Yes," said the superintendent. "Yes, I know they're cousins." Another silence. Then, "Firstly, I think it's important you calm down. Don't forget that you are currently Ted's contact with this investigation, and the way in which you handle yourself will reflect on all of us. Secondly, I take on board what you're saying, but frankly, Mina, Maggie is getting on in years. She's been looking after Ted single-handedly.

And yes, this thing with Ms. Prew, it's bound to upset her. Like as not, she's gone off on her own for a bit."

"Sir, with respect, I disagree. I think we need to start considering that this is a second series—"

A heavy sigh. "Yes, Mina, I am already in the process of expanding my policy to include the possibility of this being a copycat. But, frankly, the search teams have not found anything that would suggest this is anything other than a coincidence."

She was pushing it, and she knew she was pushing it. And yet still Mina closed her eyes and pushed. "Sir, my question is, what if it isn't a copycat? What if it is an accomplice? Someone who was involved in the first series of murders, who has returned to start again?"

The silence had a different texture this time.

"Ms. Arian, are you suggesting that I somehow failed to do my job appropriately in the first killer-on-the-wall investigation?"

"No, sir. I'm just saying, Heath McGowan has never been willing to talk about the murders, not to anyone. We always thought that was a power play, but what if it wasn't? What if he wouldn't talk, because he was protecting someone? Someone nobody connected with the murders at all?"

"Ms. Arian . . ."

"Sir, I really—"

"That will do. How about you let me set policy, while you get on and do your own job? Yes? Right. Now, until we have any information indicating otherwise, this remains a missing person case. Until we have any further information, the original killer-on-the-wall case remains closed, with the solitary murderer involved behind bars. Now, if you don't mind, I am extremely busy. Thank you."

Then nothing but silence against the drip, drip, drip of the rain.

Another one? – Mina

Mina held the phone limply in her fingers. The rain had begun to bounce, a thrumming rhythm against the pavement. It soaked the screen, making her fingers feel brittle with the chill of it. She would have thrown the damn phone were it not for the fact that she would then have to pay for a new one. She stared at the swirling blue lights, the sheeting rain smudging the edges of them. She could cry now. The tears would mingle with the raindrops, and no one would ever know. And yet, ironically, tears were the furthest thing from her mind.

A steady heat had begun to build inside her, a rolling anger. The great Eric Bell was not interested in solving this case. The great Eric Bell was interested only in himself and how their findings would reflect upon him.

Mina stood in the bouncing rain and considered. *There are moments where life bifurcates, in which the crucial choices that define an existence are made.* She could go back inside. Be the good little girl. Do what she had been told to do. Or she could do what needed to be done instead.

With firm steps, Mina opened the front door, the heat shocking against her skin. From inside the living room she could hear Ramsey's tones, low, reassuring. She walked quietly past the living room door, along the corridor that ran the length of the house, to the rear of it, all the while imagining Maggie's cautious steps preceding hers, her slippered feet noiseless in the deep-pile carpet.

She had gone out to call the cat.

Mina reached the back door and stopped, slipped a pair of plastic gloves on. Then she carefully pressed down on the handle, and the door slid open without complaint. She stopped, looking about her for footprints, for any sign that Maggie had perhaps not even made it out of her own door before disaster came. But there was nothing. Just a concrete step and an ocean of lawn, made loose by the pouring rain.

Maggie Heron is Kitty Lane's cousin.

Mina stepped out onto the grass, and the sudden shock of the cold made her shiver. Where would Maggie have stood?

She surveyed the swath of garden, a green lawn that tucked around the house, the rear and right-hand side of it bordered by trees. Took one step, two. Would this be it? Where you would stop to call for an errant cat? It seemed to Mina that she could hear Maggie's voice. She looked down again, studied the ground, letting her gaze roam about the garden. Her attention snagged on the tree line, on the shape of the trunks toward the rear of the garden, the way they twisted away from one another, almost forming a tunnel. She walked closer, peering through the rain into the kaleidoscope of branches. See, the rest of the garden, you could see that from the road. But here, in this little copse, the trees cradled you, shielding you from view. If you wanted to take someone from this garden, this would be the place.

Mina pulled her flashlight out, ran it across the branches, through to the other side. What was that back there? A road? As she began to pull back, something caught her attention. A twist of material, the edge of a red rose. She stooped down, her heart thumping. This was what she was wearing. Maggie came this way.

She tagged the evidence, then played the beam of light across the trees and the ground beneath them.

Then Mina quickly turned, ran back the way she had come, her footing slick on the sodden grass. There was no care this time, just speed. She hurried out through the front door, hooked a sharp left onto the pavement, and followed the tree line. She passed Owen, watching her with a frown, but did not stop, following the arc of the trees until the street behind her had vanished from view. And there behind the house was a lane. It was narrow, unpaved, but wide enough, just about, to get a car through. She let the flashlight dance across the ground, all stones and ruts and mud, until she reached the copse and that almost hidden tunnel that had formed itself within it.

Mina stopped and crouched down, gaze hooked on the ground.

A tire track.

"I need CSI here," Mina bellowed.

The sound of footsteps behind her, but she didn't look up, all her attention stuck on what was before her. The sinking knowledge that Maggie Heron would not be coming back.

"What is it?" Owen sounded out of breath.

"Call CSI. I have a piece of Maggie's sweater on a branch on the other side of these trees, and I have a tire track."

Owen stood beside her, silently surveying the scene. "Oh God."

"Yeah."

"I'll call—"

But before he could call anyone, his radio sparked to life, a musical tone breaking into the quiet, and Owen pulled the Airwave radio from his belt, slid the volume up.

"We've found her."

It took some moments for Mina to process it, to pick the words from their tinny background and piece them together into something that made sense.

It took even more time for the tone of them to register, the meaning of them to take its fullest shape.

"She has been left at the wall, half a mile east of Briganton. Forensic teams to attend, please."

It was a dream. That could be the only logical

explanation. The dipping of Owen's head, the way
the ground shimmied beneath her feet, all of that
made it clear that this could not possibly be the
way her life was meant to go. The lifetime of moments standing there in the rain, cold gone now,
washed away when the world flipped itself on its
head. Then turning her back on Owen, being
pulled by something beyond herself, forcing her
reluctant feet to move, lifting one and then the
other in an ungainly robotic dance. The heat of
the house was jarring, so that she felt she could
not breathe. Staring at a picture hanging in the
hallway, of Maggie and Ted, seventy years and a
murder ago. Forcing her feet to move, her hand to
push at the living-room door, and then the voices,
first Ramsey's, then Ted's, and then, as they saw
her, the expectant, terrible silence. Framing the
words and still not framing them, for it seemed
that they had been there the whole time, simply
waiting for her to say them. *They've found her. I'm
sorry, Ted.*

Ramsey covering his face, his one good hand flying to Ted's shoulder, and waiting for the tears, for
Ted to fold himself to the floor, for his heart to
stop, and for him to drop dead in front of them.
But instead, the old man sitting there, staring at
her, his lips moving with words that would not
break free. Crouching on the floor before him,
her hand upon his knee, and being able to see
only those damn socks with their gaping Homer
Simpson, who stared at her and stared at her. *Do
you understand, Ted? I'm sorry, but Maggie is dead.*
Shaping it into inevitability, so that there would be

no room for him to bargain or to deal or to pretend that what was happening wasn't. *She's dead.*

And still Ted sitting, shaking his head, and saying, "But she only went out to look for Mitzy. That's all."

The family liaison officer arriving, the call to the daughter. The wailing screech of tears magnified by the phone line. Ramsey taking the phone from her, telling Ted's daughter, Ellie, that it would be okay, that he was here, that he would stay with her father until she came. Tears rolling down his cheeks and landing with a splash on the table below.

Then out into the breathless air, the rain hammering, and willing it to wash everything away. Knocking on door after door after door, seeking answers that did not come.

There was no doubt about it now, if there had ever been at all. Superintendent Bell was wrong. Whatever had happened in that investigation twenty years ago, something had been missed, a vital piece. And now that loose end was flying free.

Monday, October 24

Bringing in an expert – Isla

They stood as if at a funeral, fluorescent jackets harsh against the rain-filled sky, the bleakness of the moor. One of the police officers recognized Isla, afforded her the silent nod, which was all he could muster right now. She stood at the cordon, her hood pulled up so that the world appeared to be coming down a long tunnel, and felt the rain and the lack of sleep marry together to bludgeon her.

"Isla." Her father's voice was hoarse with tiredness; his face slick with rain. "Come through." He lifted the police tape, ignoring the pair of officers that guarded it, and waited while she ducked under. "It's a little bit of a walk." He turned, not waiting for her, his Wellington boots pulling at the sodden ground.

Isla tucked her hands into her pockets, feeling her own boots being sucked downward into the remorseless mud. "Where are we going, Dad?"

But her father hadn't heard her or, if he had, was choosing to ignore her. She kept her head down, driving into the rain across the uneven ground, and felt the fear wrap itself tight around her. She wanted to trot forward, grip hold of her father's hand, a little girl again, but she wasn't a little girl, was she? So she pushed the fear back and trod onward as the moor rose, watching the wall snake up it toward the shimmering gray sky. And then she saw it. White shapes sharp against the gray. They stood beside the wall, moving in an uncoordinated dance, and a memory trickled back to her of the time before.

"This is where Leila Doyle was left."

Her father kept walking, just a grunt of agreement to show that he had heard. Isla hurried to catch up, a seed of suspicion sprouting in her insides. They followed the course of the wall as it began to climb, the white shapes coalescing into the forensic team and, just beyond them, a slumped figure.

"Oh God." Isla stopped, her hand to her mouth.

Maggie Heron looked narrower in death, her face slack, eyes open and empty. Nausea rose in Isla again, and she pushed it back, wanting nothing more than to sink into the sodden grass. "I . . . oh my God . . ." She could feel the heat racing to her cheeks, the world lurching treacherously.

Her father stood some distance off, his gaze hooked on the dead woman.

Isla wanted to reach for him, the child in her seeking comfort. But then, comfort had rarely been her father's strong suit. *No. Steady.* She breathed in through thin lips, the scent of death lingering on the air. *Courage.* She forced herself to take small, steady breaths. *This is work. This is not real. This is work. This is not real.*

"See," said her father, finally. "I was afraid of this right from the start. When that Victoria Prew was killed. I thought, *This doesn't feel right. Doesn't make sense that this would be a domestic.*"

I'm telling you, it's the ex that did it.

Isla glanced at her father, then away. Her hands were shaking. She stuffed them into her pockets again.

Her father turned away from the body, nodding toward the emptiness of the moor beyond. "Let's take a walk."

After one last look at the forlorn shape of Maggie Heron, she turned and followed her father. A sense of unreality hung across the moor. That they could be here again. Had she expected this? She had said it, that he would kill again, had offered the words up to her father like the answer to some Mensa puzzle. And yet the essence of it, the whole thing beginning again—that had felt far removed from her, a psychological exercise rather than the truth of her existence. She felt her left foot sinking into the mud and pulled it upward, throwing her balance off, and her arms flailed as she tried to correct it. But it didn't matter, did it? What she had said. What she had calculated. None of it made any difference now, with two bodies left on the wall.

The truth of it settled on her, heavy and inevitable. It had begun again.

"Ramsey okay?" Her father's voice seemed to come from far away, and she picked up her pace, matching his long stride.

"He's still at Maggie and Ted's." Except it wasn't now, was it? Now it was merely Ted's. "Says he's going to stay there until their daughter arrives."

"He's a good lad."

"Yes. Yes, he is."

Isla hadn't known. As she walked along behind her father, she cast her mind back. She had stayed in the office late, far later than she should, she reflected. She'd sat at her desk as the dim light fell and night overtook day, as the wind picked up and the branches of a lone tree scraped against the window, setting her nerves on edge. She hadn't called home, had intended to, but had gotten lost in an internal physiological control analysis, poring over Heath's results, comparing them to those of the control subjects, the ones with no signs of psychopathy. Why hadn't she called? Was it simply that she had been too busy? Or was it something darker, her own fear perhaps? It was, undeniably, safer living in her own head, the harsh reality of the world kept at bay by the sheen of brain tissue analysis. Or perhaps she had been afraid of what she would hear in her husband's voice, that sense of despair, the distance that spoke of a boat slipping its moorings, as he drifted off to where she could not follow.

Isla set off from the university late, a little after

eleven, the results still rotating in her mind, so much so that at first, she didn't notice the police lights. Then, of course, once she did, it seemed that she had known all along that they would be there, that this was why she had delayed and delayed until homecoming was unavoidable. Two streets from their home, half a dozen police cars. Those were numbers no one wanted to see.

She stopped the car, jumped out. Her eyes searched the crowd for a familiar face. But it seemed that their tiny village had become a cosmopolitan hub, littered with hard-faced strangers. Then, through the crowd, a small figure swathed in an overlarge coat.

"Mina."

At first Mina didn't hear her, stood and swayed, looking like she was about to cry. Then she turned. Their gazes locked, and a look of something flitted across Mina's features.

Relief?

"It's bad, Isla. It's so bad."

"Who?"

Didn't she know then that the victim could be anyone? That it could be her mother, her father, her sister. Her husband.

"Who, Mina?"

Mina looked down at her feet and said, her voice bubbling in that way that spoke of unshed tears, "Maggie Heron."

Maggie, who had been the lollipop woman, who had kept candy in her pockets to distribute to her favorite children or to those that had done well in school or those that just really looked like they could use a treat. Maggie, who never could seem to remember whether she was Isla or whether she was Emilia, and who always told her the story about that time when they were both little and climbed her apple tree and got stuck, so that Ted had to go up after them, coax them down with chocolate drops and licorice.

Her first thought after that was that she had been right—Victoria Prew had not been a one-off. Her second, that she had never hated being right more. Her third, that she had to go home, that she had to break it to Ramsey.

Then Mina, wiping her eyes, said, "Ramsey is inside. He's looking after Ted."

Later Isla would reflect that she shouldn't have been surprised. That was, after all, what Rams did. He cared for people. He looked after them. When someone fell, he caught them.

The house was stiflingly warm; the bars of the electric fire were orange. Ted was sitting in the window, peering out into the darkened night, body stretched tall in anticipation. He was, Isla realized, waiting for Maggie to return. Ramsey stood up as soon as he saw her, wrapped her in an embrace that might have been for her but in truth seemed to be mostly for him. He clung to her, breathing in the scent of her, his body shaken by one single intake of breath that, had he allowed it to, could have become a sob. Isla gripped his broad back, his wide arms, closed her eyes and breathed thanks that it wasn't him, that she wasn't Ted—that she wasn't sitting at a window, waiting for her dead husband to return.

And so the night unfolded, the two of them sitting side by side on that terrible flower-ridden sofa, while Ted sat. Waiting. Ramsey eventually fell into an uneven sleep sometime around four, his cheeks pressed against a knitted throw, his forehead creasing, fingers flickering as his dreams chased around inside his head. And Isla, she simply sat, watching Ted, watching her husband, and trying to puncture the dizzying sense of disbelief that had taken hold of her.

"Dad?" Their steps had now fallen into sync on the uneven ground, and Isla glanced across at her father, his face half buried within his hood. "Why did you ask me to come here?"

His stride shortened. "I thought you could help."

"Help?"

He coughed, a rattle that made Isla wince. "Say it is a copycat. What's that about, then?"

"How do you mean?"

"Well, are they nuts, or what?"

Isla grinned in spite of herself. "That's not the technical term for it, no."

"Okay." He shook his head, and a shower of raindrops flew about his head like a halo. "So, what's the point of it?"

Isla kept her gaze on the mud-pooled ground. "Some people simply can't help themselves. They need to kill like we need family, comfort. It's an itch they just can't shake. For people like that, when they see someone like Heath McGowan on the news, on the front of newspapers, there's an appeal in that. They think that if they emulate them, if they do the same thing, then they will achieve the same result."

"Celebrity?"

Isla shrugged. "Sometimes. Or, if not celebrity, then notoriety at least." She paused, turned back toward the wall, the distant signs of police movement and the memory of the body hidden in among it all.

Her father pulled up short alongside her, followed her gaze. "Bet McGowan is loving every damn minute of this."

She glanced at him. Thought of Heath's phone call, her stomach shifting with the memory of it. *Just thought I'd give you a call to check that you're okay.* What would her father say if she told him that? Or her husband? Isla watched the distant figure of Maggie Heron. No. In this case, silence was best.

"I'm sure Heath is getting something out of it." Not a lie either. Isla had no illusions that the call had been prompted by concern. Psychopaths were not known for their empathy. He had called her to insert himself into the events in Briganton. He had called her in the hope of knocking her off balance, of hearing her fear. For Heath, these murders would be the stuff of dreams. "He wouldn't be the first. Ted Bundy coached a fellow prisoner, taught him how to gain easy access to victims using personal ads." She stubbed her toe against a rock. "They call it a murder mentor. Someone who inspires a copycat."

Her father turned to her, his face darkening. "You think McGowan is involved?"

Did she? "I don't know. I can . . . I mean, I'm sure that the power of feeding something like this would appeal to him."

The wind tugged at her clothes, whipped her hair so that it beat against her cheeks, sending little electrical sparks across her skin. She watched her father and wondered, *How does he stand there, so together, so collected, when the world is falling apart around him?* She saw him shift, his hand moving to his knee of its own accord, the merest hint of a wince crossing his features. He'd injured it playing rugby sometime in his thirties. It had ended his playing career, wounded his pride more.

Perhaps, she thought, it was all a charade. This togetherness, this equanimity. The coldness a work tool. After all, didn't she do the same? Best not to allow yourself to feel the true horror of what your research subjects had done, because if you did, the only rational course of action would be to run from them, screaming. Best to shut all that away in a room of its own, else how would you move forward? It was, thought Isla, a skill she had inherited from her father.

"I'll go and see him." The wind tore the words from her, throwing them away into the wilds.

Her father frowned. "What?"

"McGowan. I'll go and see him. If he's involved . . . if he's controlling this, then maybe he can stop it."

Eric Bell turned, facing into the wind now, so that the little hair that still remained to him flew backward like a train. "I'll go with you."

It was not a question.

Isla glanced down, looked at the boots, which once were black, now speckled with the mud of the moor. She was a child again, asking her father if she could walk to school alone, being told no. *Maybe when you're bigger.* Her left foot began to sink, the liquid earth beneath it shifting into a dark wave that lapped at the sides of her boot. She moved, pulled it free with a squelch. Opened her mouth to speak and found no words. What was it about parents? Even when you were thirty-five and married, and even though you lived your life right up against the most dangerous men the world had to offer, one word and you could be catapulted backward in time, until you were small, vulnerable again. The fear lurched, making her feel light-headed.

"The thing is, Dad . . . I don't think that would be a good idea." She did not look at him as she spoke, twisting away, ostensibly from the wind, but really from his steady gaze. She fixed her eyes on the village behind him, on the stone houses, the tall steeple, Bowman's Hill beyond. The sky had begun to darken overhead, steel-gray mounds of cumulonimbus clouds, trouble brewing. Isla studied the village. If she looked hard enough, she could see her house, the place where her husband was, the place where she was a grown-up. Isla selected her words. "I have a certain rapport with Heath. It's essential for the research we do that they are able to talk to us. I think that bringing in you, the man who ended his killings, I think that's likely to shut him down." It sounded like a question, the way she said it, and Isla cursed the doubtfulness in her voice.

Eric watched her, seemed to be considering, and then nodded, just once. "Fine. Do what you think is best," he said. "So what else?"

"What do you mean?"

"Well, all this. I want your opinion."

She looked at the wall. "Okay, well, in the original series of murders, the victims selected didn't seem to have any particular characteristics linking them. Instead, it appears that McGowan used a hunting-ground technique. So victims were chosen based on their availability to him and their mere presence within Briganton."

"But not this time."

Isla shrugged. "Well, it's hard to say. I mean, Maggie is related to one of the original victims. But then, Victoria Prew . . . she's new here, doesn't have family in the village. She's . . . different."

"So . . ."

"So, I don't know. It's possible that Victoria was the straw that broke the camel's back. That her house, its openness, its obviousness, perhaps that was what started the ball rolling. Pushed him to take that first step into killing."

"And now?"

"He's had a little more time to consider just what it is he wants to achieve. Maybe he is merely evolving his strategy. Maybe he's gone from that one initial impulse that led him to kill Victoria Prew to a more considered selection of victims. Or then again, maybe Maggie was just there. A victim of circumstance."

Her father turned, looked toward the village of Briganton. "Then the next victim could be anyone."

"You said Victoria Prew had reported a break-in. What about Maggie? Had she had anything taken? Reported being watched?"

"I don't know. Ted's not the most reliable of witnesses," said Eric.

"Also, I'd keep an eye out for anyone trying to get too chummy with the police. It's not uncommon for these guys to try to insert themselves into the investigation. Also, the families . . . the ones who lost people last time. I'd look out for anyone who has recently got friendly with them, or is especially curious about them and their background."

Isla watched her father as he nodded slowly, his gaze pulling back from the village and landing on her, his expression grim.

"What?"

"If he's going after the families of the original victims . . ."

"Yes?"

He looked away across the moor. "That's you, Isla."

The arrival of
a letter – Ramsey

He would have to go home some time. Ramsey poured boiling water into a bulbous teapot, watched the level rise until it threatened to overflow. He had been in the Heron house for eighteen hours now. Eighteen hours in which the world had changed. Had he closed his eyes once last night? It hadn't seemed so. Ted had remained sitting in the armchair by the window, waiting. Ramsey had suggested to him that he go to bed, that some rest would be good for him, that he needed to take a break, but Ted had simply shaken his head, given him a small smile. *If I go to bed, I might miss her coming home, mightn't I?*

Ramsey stared at the cups, bone china with a pink trim. Imagined Maggie washing them the morning before, running the tea cloth round inside them, without any thought that it would be the last time she would do it. His head was aching; the lack of sleep had built up into a low, throbbing headache pulled taut across his forehead. He weighted the teapot carefully in his hands, allowed it to tip forward so that the steady stream splashed into the cups. He had learned many years ago, when the darkness threatened, to focus on the small things. The steam rising from hot tea. The smell of bread. The sound of rain against a window. When the large things in life were simply too large to bear, it was the small things that could save him. He unwrapped a packet of chocolate biscuits, the sound deafeningly loud.

A woman's voice crept beneath the kitchen door, high and loud. "How could it have happened? But why? I mean, are they sure?"

Ellie had arrived just a little while ago, a round woman with a screaming shock of orange hair. She had entered cautiously, as if it wasn't her parents' home anymore, as if the loss of one of them had taken away her surety, and now she simply wasn't certain how one walked or spoke or thought. She had had the lost, vacant look of one whose world had suddenly become entirely alien, had clutched Ramsey's hand, a familiar face on a distant planet, hadn't cried, instead whispering, over and over again, "But how? But why?"

Of course there had been no answers to give. Why? Because the monster had wanted her. There was little more to understand.

Ramsey reached into the fridge, poured 2 percent milk from a plastic bottle into a dwarfish milk jug, trying to breathe, watching as it splashed over the sides onto the dark oak tray, and all the time thinking of hands around Isla's throat, her body propped against Hadrian's Wall.

He should go home. At some point he would have to. But then there would be nothing but a swamping silence and the choking terror of what was to come. Ramsey put the milk back into the fridge and closed the door softly. No, he was better here, being of use, keeping busy, even if all he was capable of was spilling milk on a tray.

He picked up the tray, balanced it carefully with his one good arm, pushed open the kitchen door with his back. Ellie was sitting on the sofa now, riotous hair in her hands, the heave of her shoulders suggesting tears. The family liaison officer, Holly, a pleasant young woman who spoke in studiously soft tones, sat beside her, hand upon her shoulder. And Ted: he remained at the window, waiting still.

Holly watched as he placed the tray on the coffee table and said in a low voice, "I've called the doctor. I thought perhaps a sedative . . ." A glance across at Ted, oblivious to their presence. "Maybe the way to go."

A sedative. Yes. That would be the thing. A single tablet, the yawning embrace of sleep, enforced forgetting. But then, after the forgetting would come the remembering. And that for Ramsey had been the worst of all times, for years and years following Zach's death. Sleep would dance around him, now drawing closer, now pulling away, tempting, teasing, until finally wrapping him in a relentless embrace, and he would fall into her, drowning.

And, if he was lucky, he would forget, would escape to a gentler life in his dreams. Then would come the waking, the soft climb, as of one forcing his way from a hot bath, then the shock of the bitter cold air as the remembering would hit.

"It's going to take some time for him," offered Ramsey, "to come to terms with things. He's in shock now."

A low moan escaped from Ellie, startling him momentarily with the realization that he had forgotten she was there. "I should have come home more. I promised I would. And then, what with work, I didn't and now . . ." A choking sob.

"Hey." Ramsey sat on the arm of the sofa, he and the FLO bookending the weeping woman. "She was so proud of you. Do you know, I'd see her most mornings, when I was out on my runs, and she would talk about you so much? My brilliant daughter, the teacher. Don't you dare allow yourself to think that you let her down, not for a minute." He watched as the lie settled in, as her back straightened by a degree, as blissful relief passed across her face. Because the truth was, sometimes you had to lie. To tell the truth—that the only time he had ever heard Maggie mention her daughter was in complaint, about her lack of visits, about her inability to marry—the truth would be cruel. Whereas the lie—the lie was kind.

A sound broke into the following silence, a cheerful chirrup that seemed entirely out of place in the grieving house.

"Sorry," said Holly. "That's me." She shifted, pulled her phone free, frowned as she read. Then she leaned forward, looking toward Ted. "Ted?"

For a moment it seemed that the old man hadn't heard her, but then he shifted, dragged his gaze reluctantly from the window, took in Ellie, Ramsey, Holly, somehow seeming surprised that he was not alone, after all. "Hmmm?"

"Ted, I needed to ask you . . . You haven't had any break-ins recently, have you? Found anything missing?"

He frowned at her, a teacher looking at an errant student. "Well, she couldn't find the cat. Remember?"

"No, Ted. I mean . . . Well, did either you or Maggie ever have the sense that you were being watched?"

He stared at her, but the light in his eyes had faded, the conversation swerving perilously close to a cliff edge he was not prepared to acknowledge.

"Ted?" interjected Ramsey. "Can you think of anything? It could be really useful."

Ted sat, rubbing his fingers together, and then finally sighed and shook his head. "I don't know. You're going to have to ask Maggie."

How long could he keep this up? wondered Ramsey. How long could he protect himself with this fictional reality? He realized with a sinking sensation that he envied Ted and his opaque world.

"I remember something." Ellie's voice was quiet, painfully uneven. "She . . . a couple of weeks ago, two, three at the most. Mum, she'd gone to put flowers on Aunt Kitty's grave. She did that every week, always on a Friday. Only, she said that this time when she went, she was, you know, clearing out the old flowers, wiping the gravestone down, she said she kept feeling that someone was watching her."

"Did she see anyone?" asked Holly.

Ellie shook her head, a faint smile appearing. "Mum, she reckoned it was Kitty watching over her. She's like that. Anyway, she left, went to the bakery to get some bread and stuff, and on her way back, she had to pass the graveyard again."

"Okay?"

"Well, thing is, the fresh flowers, the ones she had put on Kitty's grave, they were gone. The grave was empty. I was pretty upset about that, thought it was local kids messing about. But Mum, she said that it was a miracle, a sign that Kitty was still with us, because she had always loved flowers in life."

"Roses."

"Sorry, Ted?"

"No, I was just saying *roses*. Maggie loves roses, she does." He stopped, clipping the words off abruptly, and for a moment seemed to be on the edge of a realization. Then he shook his head. "Her and her roses, eh?"

"So . . ." Holly looked back at Ellie. "This was how long ago?"

"Ah . . . two . . . No, it was three weeks ago, because I'd just gone home after a visit. So yes, three weeks."

Somehow, Holly managed to nod. She managed to make it appear that this information was useful, yes, interesting, yes, and yet hide the shift that it brought. That while for them this had only just begun, for the killer the journey had started weeks ago. She smiled at Ellie, muttered something about that being very helpful, and then, and only then, glanced at Ramsey, her eyes round with alarm.

"Excuse me a second. I should just call this in."

They sat there, the three of them, as Ramsey thought about what he had been doing three weeks ago, about how the world on the surface of it had looked perfectly ordinary back then, about how much had changed since.

Finally, Holly returned, her mouth a straight line. "It's fine," she lied, with an unconvincing smile. She studied him. "Ramsey, why don't you head off, get some sleep? You look done in."

"I'm okay." His tongue felt thick, words unwieldy with exhaustion.

"Seriously, Rams. I'm here. I have this covered. Go. Get some sleep."

He looked from Ted at the window to Ellie, who was slumped back against the sofa now, her gaze far away. He had always known that he couldn't stay here forever, keeping busy, being useful, that sooner or later life would have to be faced. "I do have an article to write. Maybe I'll pop home, try to get some words down. Will you call? If they need anything?"

He was ushered out, with profound thanks and tearful gratitude, into the cold autumn air, which bit into his lungs, slapped him awake. The rain had slowed, a meager drizzle now, although the pavements remained littered with standing puddles, debris tugged there by the wind. One foot, then another. That was all there was to it. He felt the tarmac hard under his soles, the cold wind lick against his collar. Just one step and then another.

His mobile buzzed in his pocket, and Ramsey

paused, pulling it free. The text message was from his editor. **Heard about old woman's murder. Horrible. Hope you're doing okay. Thinking it would be a good idea for you to expand your article. Not just about Prew, but old woman, too, and any other victims. Whole "what it's like to live under the threat of a serial killer" angle. Do you have access to Heron family?**

Ramsey stood in the cold, staring at the text, and for the briefest of moments considered throwing his phone, dashing it to pieces right there on the pavement.

Instead, he typed a reply. **Fine.**

It was a sad truth that, in spite of all else, there remained bills to pay.

He pushed at the metalwork front gate, its yawning screech loud against the wind. Felt for his keys, carefully selected the one that would fit the Yale lock. Ran his finger along the edge of it, trying to ignore the sense of a limitless darkness below, of the creeping familiar numbness, all the familiarity of an old friend returning for yet one more unexpected visit. Slid the key into the lock.

The door opened with a groan, and a wave of tiredness washed across him. Ramsey was suddenly aware of the stickiness of his skin, the bitter tang in his mouth, the billowing edges of the world. He stepped inside. *Sleep. Sleep would help.* And the remembering that would come when he awoke? Well, he would simply have to handle that then. He had, after all, done it before.

As he stepped to close the door, his foot lost traction, slipped on something that lay on the hardwood floor, sending his heart rate spiking.

Ramsey looked down to see the letter beneath his foot. Slowly, he bent to pick it up. Block letters sprawled across the front of it. TO MR. R. AKEN. His name spelled wrong. Carefully, he opened the envelope and pulled free a photograph.

He and Isla kissing on their front step yesterday morning.

And on the reverse, a single sentence in block letters. I'LL BE SEEING YOU SOON.

The pen pal – Isla

"But surely," said the young woman, "psychopathy is simply a way of approaching the world. I mean, we all exist on a spectrum, right? Like, some of us are emotional, and some aren't. Aren't psychopaths just that? A group of people who operate on the low empathy end of the spectrum?" She leaned forward, elbows resting on impossibly narrow legs, skin a sun-kissed beige, blond hair streaked with blue. If you looked close enough, you could make out a mottling in the crease of her arm, on the knees, which poked through the strategically ripped jeans. Sun kissed from a bottle, then.

Isla nodded as she tried to remember a time

when she had given a shit about such things as a year-round tan, ripped jeans. Was there ever one? God, she was tired. She still had not warmed up from her early morning walk across the moor. She swallowed, her vision swimming. Nausea rising again. "The difficulty we encounter when looking at psychopaths is that many studies have shown that their ability to assess the emotional state of others can be extremely well developed. They can be very good at identifying how others are feeling." She glanced around the tutorial group, the four youngsters nodding solemnly. Was the office getting warmer, or was it her?

"So," said Parker, the sole boy in the group, "it's not an empathy problem, then. Not if they can recognize what other people are feeling. Is it . . . Is the problem that they don't respond to the emotions of other people? So, like, if I was a psychopath, I might know that you were upset, but that wouldn't bother me, make me concerned." He delivered the words carefully, quietly, his eyes flitting between Isla and Scarlett—she of the ripped jeans and fake tan—looking for approval, acknowledgment.

Isla smiled at him, watched his shoulders sink by a fraction. It was getting warmer. Her head swam. She needed to lie down. She needed to sleep. Had she eaten today? She couldn't remember. Her stomach twisted painfully. No. No, she hadn't eaten.

"But they are responding," protested Scarlett. "They are just responding differently from most people. Like a predator responding to prey," she said brightly, finding the world such a fascinating place.

Forgotten in their debate, Isla watched them. To these not yet adults, this was an experiment of the imagination. It was like a ride on a roller coaster, a horror movie watched with the lights off. For them, none of this was real. Even the newspaper stories, the knowledge that death was stalking just a little over fifteen miles from here, none of it mattered, not really. Because they were safe and whole, and the horrors of this world had not reached them. Not yet.

Isla took a sip of water, trying to pull her mind back, trying to concentrate. She hadn't slept. Had attempted an hour, letting her head fall back against the high back of the armchair in the corner of her office, wishing for a reprieve, but eventually, she had given it up. With her eyes closed, the world about her gone, all she could see were the dead bodies of Maggie Heron and Victoria Prew.

"I think," interjected another girl, Ursula, a fledgling thing who looked far too young to be allowed out into the big bad world alone, "that the thing I find most fascinating is the ability of psychopaths to disguise themselves. I mean, think about it. Anyone could be one!" Her expression bright, she looked at Isla.

Did she understand the weight of it? Did she understand the measure of her words? That there were those who brought death, and that they were able to hide beneath a mask of civility. A predator hiding in plain sight.

"That can certainly be true," interjected Isla. "But often what you see is that a psychopath will give himself away to the people nearby, that their tendency toward impulsiveness, recklessness, will lead to seepage, their family, friends recognizing that something is just a little 'off' about them."

Isla held it up before her, a defense against the worst of it. It comforted her, this thought that if you were smart enough, if you knew enough, then the signs of a psychopath, the signs of a serial killer, would be there, if only you were brave enough to look. How many times had she heard it? Stephen Beaumont killed seven people across the state of Georgia, a massacre spread over ten years. And his daughter, in the weary aftermath, looking at Isla, tears running down her cheeks, said, "He had a temper, that was all. How could we possibly have imagined it would go this far?"

Sometimes it occurred to Isla that she had chosen this career as a shield. That she would cloak herself in knowledge, and in that way she would be safe.

The ringing of the office phone fractured the conversation, and, for a brief moment, Isla considered waving it away, ignoring it, because she was in a tutorial, and she didn't answer the phone in tutorials. Then the fear, creeping, inevitable.

"I'm sorry, guys. Just a second." She pushed herself up, grabbed the phone from the receiver, praying for nonsense, for admin. Hell, for a call center chasing payment protection insurance.

"Isla? It's me."

Isla blew out a slow breath, the knowledge that her husband rarely called her at the office settling on her.

"What is it? What's wrong?"

A meaty silence as Ramsey parsed the words, trying to figure out a method of delivery. "Everyone's okay. It's okay. Just . . . I really think it would be a good idea if you came home."

Later on, she would not remember the excuses she made to her students. She would not remember whether she locked her office door. There would be a dim recollection of passing Connor, of his reaching out for her, his "Isla? What's wrong?" and of running, of barely acknowledging his existence. The little she would remember of the drive was that it was too fast, too reckless, and yet, perhaps thanks to an intercession from a God who had done little in the way of protecting recently, she made it home alive.

They were waiting in the living room. Someone had lit a fire, wood logs in the open hearth. Her father stood beside the window—it seemed to her that he was half in, half out, as if he would fly away if only he could. Her mother, on the sofa, arms wrapped around the middle of her. Isla's gaze flew around the room, fear suddenly making her breathless. Then she found Ramsey, in the armchair. His head was in his hands.

"Baby? What is it?" Isla squatted beside him, pulling his hand into hers. "What happened? Are you okay?"

Her husband looked at her, placed his palm against her cheek, and gave her a small smile. Then he gestured toward the coffee table.

It had been placed in a plastic evidence bag, the image made iridescent by the sheen of it. Isla stood over it without touching, stared at it. It must have been taken yesterday or the day before. There was too much noise in her brain now, too many screams, for her to remember things exactly as they had been. They had been leaving for work when Ramsey had pulled her back to him, had kissed her deeply, and she had thought of the vanishingness of life and had gripped hold of him as if for the last time. She remembered the smell of him, the sound of the rain hitting the porch roof, the pressure of his lips against hers.

She felt herself sway. No. She would not give in. She stared at the color of the leaves, of the dim light, trying to orient, trying to focus. Around the edges of the image was a smattering of leaves, framing it as if it had been an artistic choice. Perhaps it had. It had been taken through the hedge. It had been taken from perhaps ten meters away.

Isla tried to relocate that morning, tried to dig out a sense of being stared at. Because you would know, right? If someone was standing ten meters away from you, watching you? Surely you should know? But there, in the recollection of that morning, there was nothing but the smell of her husband and the sensation of his kiss.

She looked at him. "Did you hear anything? That morning . . . did you . . . ?"

Ramsey shook his head, expression grim.

"Jesus."

She sank down onto the arm of the chair, her legs pressing against his, comforted somehow by the weight of them. He reached across and turned the picture over, so that she could see the words printed carefully on the back.

I'LL BE SEEING YOU SOON.

"It's a warning," said her father quietly. "He's coming for you."

Isla felt a weight of tears building up, snaked her fingers through her husband's. One word circling through her brain over and over. *No. No, no, no, no, no, no, no.*

"We need to get you two somewhere safe."

Isla looked up at her father, his face hidden in shadow.

"He's clearly got you in his sights. Let's get you two set up in a hotel somewhere, a nice long way away. Just until we've caught him. Until this is all over."

"No," Isla said quietly.

She felt her husband looking at her, and then a squeeze, the pressure of his hand in hers.

"Isla . . ." Her father's voice held a warning.

"We can't run, Dad. That way, it will never end." She spoke to her father but looked at Ramsey, who studied her, his gaze running across her face, as if he, too, was trying to understand. Then another squeeze of her fingers, and a short, sharp nod.

"Isla's right," he said quietly. "I'm tired of being a victim."

"But, Isla, Rams, love . . . ," interjected her mother. "Think, now. There's no shame in leaving. Don't you think—"

"No," said Ramsey quietly. "Bonnie, I'm sorry. I know you are both trying to protect us. But Isla is right. We're staying."

Her father moved closer, his hands sliding onto his hips as he prepared for war. She could see it as if it had already happened, the argument, the thrown accusation.

"You understand the danger you are both in?" Her father was not her father now. It had happened but rarely during her childhood, yet each occasion stood bright against a dim background of recollection. Now he had the hard edges on him, the barely held back anger, which made her stomach flip. It was, her mother said, his policeman voice, designed to dominate, to be obeyed. "You understand what you are saying? That you have been identified as a target? That so far, whoever this is has had no difficulties whatsoever in killing whomever he sets his sights on?"

Eric wasn't looking at Ramsey, but at Isla, words hard, eyes pleading. Isla felt a tumble of guilt with the crashing awareness that it wasn't just herself she was risking. She looked at Ramsey, met his gaze, his hand tightening on hers. The silent conversation.

We stand our ground. Agreed?

Agreed.

"We're not leaving, Dad."

The fire crackled, popping in the hearth; a flurry of wind threw tree branches against the window. In the room, silence. Isla had shifted her gaze, was no longer looking at her father but at the fingers of her husband, interwoven with hers. They would stay. They would not run. They would catch him.

"Well, then." Bonnie's voice seemed to come from a great distance. The sofa creaked as she pushed herself to standing. "What about I make us a little something to eat? I think we could all use some lunch. Some soup? Isl?"

Isla looked up at her mother and smiled. "That would be great, Mum. Thank you."

"I'll pop the kettle on too. I think we could all

use a nice cup of tea, don't you? Eric, love, you're staying?" There was an uptick on the end of her words, words hopeful and doubtful all at once.

"No." Her father was watching them, face dense with storm clouds. "No. I'm going back to work."

What was that expression as he looked at Isla? Disappointment? Irritation?

"Isla," said Eric. "That thing we talked about earlier . . ."

Visiting Heath McGowan.

"Yes?"

"Don't do it. Understand?" Her father fixed her with a look, one that was meant to be obeyed.

Isla opened her mouth to object, but her father was already gone. Her parents had slid from the living room, and the low thrum of their conversation now eased its way back under the poorly fitted door, so that the words vanished in the crackle of the fire and the whirring of the wind, and yet the anger remained.

"Well, that went well," said Ramsey softly.

She leaned forward, rested her head against his. "We're going to be okay."

Did she mean it? Or was it little more than a useless platitude, a reassurance in the face of certain doom? What were they doing? What was she doing? Ethan Charles, Albany, New York, murdered six women by slitting their throats ear to ear. When they found him, he was carrying in his pocket the tongue of one of his victims. Stephen Vincent, killed three in Birmingham—two women and a man. Before their deaths, he raped and sodomized each of his victims repeatedly.

What the fuck was she doing?

"I just need to pop to the loo, okay? Could you see if my mum can find everything?"

The hallway was empty now, but the anger seemed to hang in the air, the ghost of an outrage lingering behind. Isla took the stairs quickly, let herself into the bathroom and closed the door behind her, slid the thick metal bolt into place.

Then she vomited into the toilet bowl.

Stephen Vincent had kept his victims alive for more than a week, chained in the basement beneath his house. Had abused them, tortured them, over and over again. He hadn't removed the earlier victims, had chained his latter ones up beside what little remained of their predecessors as a potent warning of what was to come.

Isla sank to her knees, feeling the heat rush through her, another round of nausea hitting.

What was she doing?

They should run. Her father was right. They should run and run and get the hell away from here, and what was she thinking, taking this stand? Reckless, that was what her father had called her more than once. *You're cavalier about your own safety, Isla.* And she was, wasn't she? Careless and selfish and seemingly unable to remember that she was not the only one at risk here.

She wiped her mouth with the back of her hand, flushed the evidence of her fear away. Rinsed water from cheek to cheek, thinking of a locked drawer and envelope upon envelope.

There were voices coming from the kitchen, the soft thrum of music, the smell of soup beginning to wind its way up the stairs. Isla walked with soft steps to the study and eased open the door. The filing cabinet sat in the back right-hand corner. She reached for a cup that sat on a high shelf of the bookcase beside it, retrieved a small silver key, then sank to her knees, carefully and quietly unlocked the bottom drawer, and pulled out a box file.

Deep breath.

Isla sat down on the floor, her back against the wall, legs crossed, and flipped open the lid of the box file. Inside, the papers formed a weighty pile. After sliding her fingers underneath, she pulled the papers free, separated them into four piles, the way she had so many times before. Four piles, arranged left to right in a row before her.

Isla closed her eyes briefly, then opened them again, drew the first pile closer. A sheaf of white paper, lined, its roughened edges torn from a notebook. She read the top one, its words as familiar as a lullaby.

> *Dear Prof,*
> *I hope you are keeping well. Things are the same here. I'm taking art classes. Will have to send you a picture next time, ha-ha. I read your recent paper re brain stuff but didn't get most of it. Maybe you can explain it to me next time I see you. Glad to see you won that award. Telling all the boys about it. When are you coming to see me again?*
> *Yours,*
> *Stephen*
>
> *P.S. One of these days I'm going to come to your house in the dark and fuck you until you want to die.*

There were more than a dozen of these, a one-sided correspondence that had started about a week after she first interviewed Stephen Vincent. She followed the thread of the uneasy letters, picturing his stick-thin arms, his narrow fingers. They came to the office. Every couple of months there would be one waiting for her in her cubbyhole. Unpleasant, and yet what he knew about her, those nuggets of her life that he referenced, all of it was easily available. She breathed out carefully, laid the sheet back down.

The second pile consisted of a sheaf of folded A4 paper, each sheet bearing a picture sketched in pencil in quick, sure strokes. Isla picked up the top one, a Madonna and Child, the mother's eyes closed, her cheek resting peacefully on her child's head, blissful in its serenity. Inside the makeshift card, a message in beautiful cursive script.

I'm going to slice you open from your pussy to your throat.

Every Christmas another card would appear in her cubbyhole at the university, stamped and postmarked. Isla studied the picture, feeling nausea rise again. She had never been able to identify the artist, although she had narrowed it down to two possibilities. A wannabe serial killer foiled before he could really explore his talents, Duncan Lea met a middle-aged woman through an online dating service, took her out for two extremely romantic dates, and then, on the third date, took her back to his apartment, where he had prepared a meal of duck with pomegranate, her portion generously laced with Rohypnol. After eating, he slit her throat open. Her badly mutilated body was discovered by his landlord two weeks later, after neighboring residents began to complain about the smell. Or Lionel Allen, a highly charming and educated man, a schoolteacher specializing in mathematics, who murdered nine young men across the West Midlands.

Isla replaced the Christmas card on top of the pile; then her fingers moved to the next stack—the one-hit wonders pile. A delirious assortment of charm, vile threats, and the promise of worse to follow. Some sourced, identified; others a mystery.

When had it come to this? she wondered. When did receiving letters like these become a normal part of life?

She told herself that she didn't think about them, that it was just part of the job, that you couldn't let it get to you. And yet that wasn't true, was it? Because there they were, every time the mailbox clattered. You didn't think of them, and yet there they were, anyway, right beneath your skin.

Isla let her head rest back against the wall, the bitter taste of bile still fresh in her mouth, and let her gaze spool across the first three piles. They were a reminder that she could handle this. That whatever was to come, she had been there before. She had survived. She would survive again.

Creaking floorboards, footsteps coming closer, and Isla considered standing up, grabbing the piles of paper, and stuffing them away. But then, she reflected, the time for hiding was at last over.

"Isl? You okay?"

Ramsey looked drained, emptied out. He let himself into the room, closed the door tight behind him. "Look, love. If you want to go, do as your dad says, then we'll go. It's no problem. All I care about is that you're okay, so if you want us to leave, we leave."

Isla smiled and reached out a hand for him. "I'm okay. And no. I'm not going anywhere. Let's stay and see this through."

Her husband lowered himself to the floor beside her, studied the piles of paper. "What is this?"

Isla pulled her knees up. Didn't look at him. "They're death threats."

"What?"

"Well," she corrected, "mostly death threats. Some of them are just offers to fuck me."

"Are . . . You're kidding, right?"

That guilt again, that she had kept this from him, had buried it—one more in a line of too many secrets. Isla opened her mouth, then closed it again.

"Why didn't you tell me?"

"I didn't want to worry you." It wasn't an excuse, and they both knew it.

"Worry me? Jesus, Isl. See, this is what I'm talking about. You, everyone here, you treat me like I'm made of glass. What happened, happened. And, I might add, I survived, so this whole victim treatment . . . Frankly, it gets really old."

Isla placed her hand on his arm. "I know. I'm sorry. If . . . if it makes you feel any better, we all get these, all of us who do what I do. Connor is gutted that I have more than him."

"Well," said Ramsey, looking at the piles. "Have you shown them to your father?"

Isla snorted. "The great Eric Bell? Are you high?" She sighed heavily. "Look, these first three, they're just your run-of-the-mill kind of threats. Some are nasty, but it's just the usual crap. They don't bother me."

"Okay," said Ramsey. "And this one?" He nudged the fourth pile with his foot.

Isla rested her chin back on her knee, didn't answer her husband, the words there but her mouth unwilling to say them. Then, finally, she reached out, pulled the top sheet off the pile, and handed it to him. She looked away. After all, she knew the words by heart now.

> *Dear Isla,*
> *I continue to watch your career with fascination. Your ability to delve into the dark workings of the criminal mind is truly remarkable. I wonder if you would have been able to save me before it was too late. Or do you restrict your talents to those already captured by the law? Perhaps your abilities lie in analysis rather than detection. A shame if that is the case. The latter of those skills would surely be of greater assistance to you in the time that is to come. Nonetheless, I continue to watch you with admiration and affection. To that end, I must mention how beautiful you looked last Friday. Green really is your color.*
> *I will see you very soon.*
> *Affectionate regards,*
> *x*

Ramsey frowned, looked at her. "Last Friday?"

Isla pulled in a breath. "It was two weeks ago. I was at the prison with Heath McGowan. I was wearing a green blouse."

"So . . ." Ramsey looked from the letter to her, then back again. "So McGowan, then?"

Isla leaned forward, sifted through the pile, and pulled out an envelope. She handed it to Ramsey.

"Okay?"

"It was hand delivered, Ramsey. It was hand delivered here. To our home."

He stared at her. "What?"

"Everything else, all the other letters I've ever had, they've come to the university. The stuff they say, all of it is public knowledge, things anyone with a computer could get online. But this one . . . Whoever this is, they know things. Things that they shouldn't know. Unless they had been watching me."

Ramsey's face grew ashen. "Isla . . . the photograph. I . . . I assumed it was about me. That that was what it meant. But it's not, is it? It's not me he's after. It's you."

A cold case – Mina

Mina stood looking out across Briganton. The village spread beneath her, following the curve of Bowman's Hill, a chocolate box scene. She could just about make out the primary school from here, could hear the incongruous sounds of children laughing, the odd shriek breaking free of the cacophony. She tucked her coat tighter around herself. Did they sense it, the village's children? Did they understand what had happened here? Although, Mina allowed, whether they sensed it or not, it would change them in some fundamental way, would alter who they grew up to be. The world swam. She could no longer remember how long it had been since she'd slept, and a pronounced nausea was beginning to build in the back of her throat. She turned slightly, following the rooftops, which seemed to pave the hill beneath her all the way down to the moor, and her gaze snagged on the dark line of Hadrian's Wall.

And she found herself wondering who would be next.

"I got you this."

Mina started, pulled from her reverie by the thin paper cup that Owen thrust into her hands.

"It looks like crap," he said apologetically, "but better than nothing."

She studied the murky gray liquid that smelled vaguely of coffee. "Where the hell did you get this?"

Owen sipped his own and winced. "Gah. That's . . . urgh. Oh, some particularly enterprising guy has set up a table outside the church. Trying to cash in on the sudden influx of visitors. Seriously, I won't be offended if you don't drink it. It tastes like he washed his pants in it first."

Mina glanced up at Owen. How could he look so well put together? So well rested? With an effort, she gave a smile and tried to forget that the little make-up she wore when she began work—whenever the hell that was—had skidded away under the relentless battering of the weather, that she had tugged her hair up into a rough bun and, quite possibly, had left a pen in there somewhere. Then she turned her attention to the cup, and she deliberated whether to dump it, contents and all, into the bin but finally settled for downing it in one gulp. Caffeine was caffeine, after all.

Owen watched her gag and grinned. "I did warn you."

Mina shrugged. "I thought it was probably preferable to speed. Anyway, anything from number three?" She nodded back toward the row of houses.

"Nothing. They didn't see anyone unusual. I quote, 'Thing is, if I saw someone carrying a dead body on his back, I'd've called you, wouldn't I?' "

"One would hope." Mina stuffed the empty cup into her bag. "Come on. Let's do it."

They walked side by side, rounded the corner onto a street of squat terraced cottages, their facades screaming of age and steadfastness. Mina quickened her pace, ignoring the first house they passed and the second and the third, and finally came to a stop before the fourth. Kitty Lane's house.

The terraced house, low and aged, sat alongside a crop of its like. Mina remembered this house from the crime scene photos of the original murders: the cherry tree that stood in its front garden, its blossoms like candy floss on a stick, the winding cobbled path that dipped and dived between roses and freesia, leading up to a door, a rich royal blue. Of course, that was all a very long time ago. Now the cherry blossoms were gone, and the cobbled path had vanished beneath a gravel overlay that formed a hastily assembled driveway. A lonely bay tree stood in a tub beside a doorway that was no longer blue but a sorry white plastic.

They stood together before the sad gravel drive and looked up at where it had all begun.

"You know," said Owen, "I remember her so

well. Kitty, I mean. She used to . . . She was kind of bent over by age, so I used to think that she looked like a walking question mark. She was always out. Every time you went outside, you'd see her. Always walking. I remember asking my mother where she could possibly be walking to. My mum, she said that it was because she was lonely. That she walked so she could talk to people."

Owen's voice had become low and distant. "I remember once, when I was a kid, my mum had taken me to the corner shop, and Kitty was in there. She was talking and talking and talking. In the end, Mr. Mullens went into the back room—I'm sure just to get away from her—and so Kitty, quick as a snake, reaches out, steals a handful of sweets, and shoves them in her pocket. I remember being horrified and weirdly impressed that this little old woman could do something so . . . naughty."

Mina glanced up at him, curious. "Did you tell your mother?"

"No," he said, thoughtful. "I think Kitty kind of expected me to. She knew I'd seen. But I just stood there. And as she was leaving, she patted me on the head—her hands were all twisted up from arthritis, I remember—and slipped me a penny sweet."

Mina laughed. "She bought your silence, you mean?"

Owen grinned. "I'm telling you, I've got a dark edge."

"I can tell." Mina studied the house. "Come on, then." Her feet crunched across the gravel, and she knocked on the door, quick and loud.

"Sure, but we haven't done the first houses yet," protested Owen.

"Uh-huh." Mina didn't look at him, her focus on the door before her, and on the murky opaque shape that was drifting into view. Footsteps on a linoleum floor, then the door swinging inward, a young woman—midtwenties, perhaps—a baby on her hip.

"I'm DC Arian," Mina said, smiling. "We're making enquiries about the murder of Maggie Heron."

She watched the baby watching her. A single bubble of yellow snot protruded from its left nostril, growing and shrinking with its breath.

"Oh," said the woman. "Okay, sure. I mean, I don't know anything, but . . ."

"Can we come in?" asked Mina brightly. "Thanks." She surged inside the house without waiting for a reply.

The door opened onto a living room, or the memory of one. Now it was only a box, with off-white walls, biscuit trim, a fireplace surrounded by empty space. A large baby bouncer spilled awkwardly outward from a corner, making the room feel smaller still.

Mina stood, useless. A feeling of being catapulted back to a time in which she had never been. She thought of the crime scene photos again, could feel the weight of them in her bag, and she turned, looked about the room, and saw it as it had once been: The carpet a conflagration of color, pinks and purples and mauves battling it out against the orange of the wall. A different fireplace, its tiles chipped and stained with cigarette smoke, wrapped round a coal fire.

At the time of the original murders, investigators found Kitty's living room undisturbed. When officers attended the scene, scant minutes after the body of Kitty Lane had been found, they discovered the television on, the back door wide open. Maggie reported to police that her cousin was relatively well off, and that she made it a habit to keep cash in a tin on the mantelpiece. When police found the tin, it was empty.

"Is everything okay?" The young woman shifted the baby on her hip, looking nervously from Mina to Owen. "I mean, you could sit—"

"Can I see the kitchen?" The words tumbled from Mina before she could stop them, and as she felt Owen's gaze lock on her, a flush rose in her cheeks at being found out. "If that's okay, I mean."

"I . . ." The woman frowned. "I guess . . . but . . ."

And then fate intervened, and the baby, under whose gaze Mina had started to feel uncomfortable, gave a small hiccup, a look of surprise, and then vomited copiously, coating itself, its mother, and a good portion of the floor. The child let out a searing wail.

"Oh, I don't believe it. Did she get you? No? Okay, look . . . I . . . I'm really sorry, but I'm going to have to go and change her." The mother looked down at her blue sweater, now richly adorned with what presumably had once been carrots. "And me," she added. "Do you mind?"

Mina smiled brightly. "Of course not. Take your time."

She stepped back quietly, closer now to the kitchen, watched as the pair hurried up the narrow staircase and out of sight, the baby's wails diminishing and finally sputtering out.

"Okay, what was that?" asked Owen.

"What was what?" Mina asked innocently. She turned and slipped into the kitchen. A small room that smelled of fresh paint, the cramped space breathlessly full of cheap units and rough-edged counters. She stood for a moment, then pulled the crime scene photos from her bag, flipped through to the photograph of the kitchen, and studied it.

The back door stood full open. A chair lay on its side, and on the tiled floor, a narrow swipe of blood.

"Are those . . . Where did you get those? We're not supposed to be doing this! Superintendent Bell—"

"Superintendent Bell is wrong," returned Mina shortly. "Look, the quicker we do this, the quicker we can get the hell out of here." She held out the photograph to him. "It was here. It was here that she was attacked. You see the blood?"

Owen scowled at her, then peered closely at the photograph. "Kitty's?"

She nodded. "Yes. And on the door, here, just above the handle, they found McGowan's prints."

Mina turned in a circle in the narrow space, then opened the back door, slipped outside into the cold.

"The file says that they think he got Kitty's body out this way," she said, Owen inches behind her. "See the back gate? It opens onto a lane. It's quiet, but wide enough to get a car down." Mina looked about the garden: no sign here now of what had gone before. "The mud was disturbed right there inside the back gate. The team concluded it was due to her body being dragged. There should be a picture . . ." Mina flicked through the photographs. There it was, the back gate, a flower bed beside it, grass flattened down, a drag mark that sliced through the earth like a scar. Déjà vu circled her. She wasn't at Kitty Lane's, but at Maggie Heron's. The narrow lane conveniently placed behind the house. A car waiting. "If that was it, if he had a car there, then it's the same MO. Same as with Maggie."

"So, whoever's doing this, he's doing his damnedest to replicate what happened last time."

Mina didn't answer, had ducked her head. After raising the photograph closer, she studied the earth, the drag mark.

"Is that a footprint?" asked Owen, peering over her shoulder at the photograph. "Look, there. Right by the gate."

Mina studied the notes. "Yeah, hang on . . . Oh, here it is. They took impressions of it but could never match it to anyone." She looked up at him. "Including Heath. Wrong size. They ultimately concluded that it must not have been related to the murder."

Owen was watching her. "Mina, why are you doing this? Going all Nancy Drew, I mean. If Bell finds out . . ."

Mina looked back down at the photograph, although she wasn't really seeing it. "I . . . I don't know. I just can't shake the feeling that if the original investigation . . . if it had been done properly, then this wouldn't be happening. We have so many resources deployed, looking at what's happening right now, but maybe the answer isn't there at all. Maybe it's right here, in what happened twenty years ago."

Owen looked along the length of the garden, now nothing but an overgrown lawn. "What about witnesses? It was a warm night. People would have had windows open. Did no one hear anything?"

Mina shook her head. "According to this, the neighbors next door were having a barbecue. They were in the garden throughout the afternoon and into the evening, then moved into the kitchen as it got later. Reported they had the door open the entire time, didn't close it until maybe midnight."

"And the pathologist said she was killed . . ."

"Sometime between five p.m. and nine p.m." Mina shrugged. "Neighbors said they didn't hear a thing."

"Can we talk to them?"

"They both died ten years ago."

"The Billingses, of course they did. Bugger." Owen folded his arms, looked at the high fence, let his gaze swing over toward the back gate. "So, we have early evening, a warm night, a party right on the other side of the fence, but no one hears a thing." He shook his head. "Well, he may have been indiscreet when it came to prints, but I'll give him one thing—he was fast. To have got into the garden, to have overpowered her before she could make a sound."

Mina looked back down at the crime scene photo, at the flower bed and the faint outline of a shoe. "Unless . . ."

"What?"

"The shoe," she said, flicking through the notes. "It was . . . it was a man's size eleven." She stopped, a cold prickle running down her spine. "Owen, that's the same size as the shoe print I found in Victoria Prew's house."

"I . . ." He shrugged. "Okay?"

Mina stared down the path toward the back gate. "Owen, the shoe print, the one they found here . . . What if it *was* related to the case?"

Owen frowned. "How do you mean?"

"I mean, what if the original crime series didn't have just one killer? What if there were two?"

Those with experience – Isla

Heath was waiting for her, his hands folded neatly on the desk before him, his features calm. Had he been told she was coming? As the guard closed the door behind her, Isla stepped aside and studied him. Yes. His features were carefully composed. His gaze settled on her, seeming to punch straight through to the heart of her. Just the vaguest hint of a smile. Yes, he knew.

"Professor Bell. I wasn't expecting to see you again so soon." There was self-satisfaction in the way that he drew out the words. "Please, have a seat."

He believed that he had drawn her here, that the phone call had been enough to get inside her head. Isla slipped into the opposite seat as Heath leaned backward in the manner of a puppeteer who had pulled all the right strings. Isla thought about the photograph. About the letters. *Was it you?* Perhaps she had in fact been pulled here. Perhaps what she thought of as free will was merely the effect of walking in the thrall of a psychopath.

Isla felt the yawning of unease.

"Oh," she said, "you didn't know?" The tone she affected was one of easy surprise.

A shift, the sense that the puppet had gone rogue. "Know?"

"Well, the tests. The fMRI scans. We always come back in after they are completed. It's nothing to worry about, honestly." Her best reassuring smile. "It's just a mop-up, a chance to run through what we've done. Let you know what we've found and see how you're doing now." She watched him lean backward, then forward, a dozen calculations flashing across his face at once. "Is that okay?"

"Ah . . . yeah. Sure."

Isla set her briefcase on the desk between her and Heath and popped the clasps. "So, we've completed the scans." She slid the scan photos out, placed them carefully before him. "What we do is we compare the way your brain functions to that of the general population—those who did not score within the psychopath range on the Psychopathy Checklist. We then compare your results with those of the other people we've studied who have been identified as showing psychopathy. Now"— she pulled a pen from her case, running the cap of it across the shape of the brain on the top scan — "you see this here? This is the paralimbic system. It covers a number of brain areas that deal with things like emotional processing, our ability to govern our own behaviors and to motivate ourselves, and our ability to control ourselves. Can you see that this is showing up in a different color from the rest of your brain? Yes? Okay, what that tells us is that this whole area is functioning differently than we would usually expect."

"Differently?"

Isla looked up, gave Heath her gentlest smile. "It's underperforming, meaning that the things this area is supposed to do are much harder for you than they would be for other people."

He was leaning over the scans, letting his finger run across the surface of them, the stubby tip of it charting the wash of blue. "So . . . ," he said slowly, "there is something wrong with me." He said it as a revelation—"There *is* something wrong with me." His shoulders sagged.

Isla watched him. "You seem relieved, almost."

Heath didn't answer, and Isla wasn't entirely sure whether he had even heard or whether he was lost now within the map of his own brain. Then he glanced up, and she realized that what he was actually doing was debating—to lie or not to lie.

She cocked her head. "Why not try the truth? You never know, you may get a taste for it."

Heath started, then flung back his head and laughed. "Yeah, fair enough, fair enough. All right, Prof, here it is. Thing is, I've always known I'm not like other people. Didn't take a scan to tell me that. But seeing this here"—he jabbed at the blue with his thumb—"it's . . . I don't know. I guess it makes more sense now. What's different about me, I mean." He stopped, considered. "Can I ask you something, Prof?"

"Of course."

"Why? Why did this happen to me? All this blue in my brain. Why is it like that?"

"Well," said Isla, "that's what we're trying to fig-ure out. You know those interviews that Connor has been doing with you? The stuff about your childhood, what it was like growing up. That's so we can try to figure out what it is that makes some-one's brain develop in this way." Isla hesitated, bal-ancing. "And we can then try to figure out what makes them kill."

Heath looked up at her, his expression shifting to . . . what? "So you can stop people like me, you mean?"

It was like sitting beneath a microscope. It was like a school assembly where you sat onstage and you had turned up naked.

"Yes, Heath. So I can stop people from being killed."

The temperature had dropped; the air had be-come thick and tense. Isla heard the guard shift and suddenly realized she had forgotten he was there. Heath had leaned back in his chair, had folded his arms, and was gazing at her from be-neath lowered lids.

"Yeah," he said slowly, "what's going on in Brig-anton . . . nasty stuff." It was a challenge, a game.

Isla simply sat.

"You know," said Heath, "I've got a theory."

"I'd love to hear it."

"This one, you know, who's killing these people . . . I reckon he's doing it because he wants to be like me. You know, famous."

She could hear it in his tone. The low-level thrill. Isla watched him, thinking of her father, of his confidence that McGowan was involved. Was fueling the latest tragedy to befall them. *Then what?* Isla had thought. *How? Say he is. Say Heath is knowingly serving as a murder mentor. How would that work? Would it be someone he has served time with, someone around him long enough to become enchanted by the legend of the killer on the wall, who has decided that he wants his own shot at infamy? There would be plenty of options, certainly. So someone who has served with him has now been released to carry on the good work. Would he maintain contact? Would he need to? Or has he, whoever he is, gone dark?*

Or then there's the other option—that this is nothing to do with Heath at all.

"Perhaps," said Isla carefully.

Heath shook his head. "I'm telling you, Prof," he said, "you better catch this guy quick. He's not going to stop unless you stop him."

Careful.

"And how do you know that, Heath?"

He dipped his head, the faintest trace of a smile; it had gone when he looked back up. "Call it experience." He shook his head. "Funny, though, don't you think?"

"What is?"

"Funny that he's decided to do this now."

"I'm not following."

"Come on, Prof. All these years, the killer on the wall has been in prison. All these years when Briganton has been safe. Then you come to see me, you start your little experiments, and now . . . well, you'd almost wonder if the two were related."

Isla felt her pulse quicken, the nibbling edges of fear. "Are you saying that this is happening because of the research I'm doing with you?"

Heath shrugged expansively. "Hey, I'm just a common criminal, me. I don't know. Look, all I'm saying is, why now? Maybe you should be asking yourself that."

Isla attempted to catch her thoughts as they skittered off in a myriad of directions.

"You know," she said, "that's a really interesting point. I mean, this is the thing we have that no one else does—your experience. I think you're right. I think this guy is trying to be you. So we have a huge advantage here, because no one knows what happened back then, twenty years ago, better than you do. Heath . . . you could crack this."

But Heath simply smiled. "Oh no," he said, "not yet. I'm having far too much fun."

An opportunity – Mina

Mina stood alone in the empty street, the cold night air pricking at her fingers, her face. The cloud cover was complete now; the threat of rain sitting just beyond the horizon. It felt as if she was wrapped in cotton wool, clouds pressing down on her from above. Down the hill and in the near distance, the moor was lost to a heavy mist.

She looked at the front door of her tiny terraced cottage. Her skin felt sticky with exhaustion; the need to take a shower, to climb into a freshly made bed was almost palpable. And yet still she stood there. It was, Mina was prepared to admit, perhaps not the wisest of moves, given the current climate.

She turned and began walking slowly away from

the safety of her own front door and the small comfort of simply being able to stop. She couldn't stop. It wasn't over.

She walked past the church, took a left, around the florist's, down the hill past the now empty primary school, with its dark stone, high turreted towers, down and down until the mist that sat on the moor seemed to reach out to her, filling her lungs. She took a right along a narrow side street containing terraced houses larger than hers and yet small for all that.

She walked and walked, number twelve, number thirteen. Number fourteen. There Mina stopped.

The Aiken house. Or what had been the Aiken house, at least.

The house nestled within a row of like-minded houses. They had been added to the ancient village maybe forty or so years ago, when it had finally become apparent to Briganton that expansion was the only path to survival. Three bedrooms, according to the files, hardly sufficient room to house three growing boys, and yet house them it had. At least until one of them had been murdered, another escaping by the skin of his teeth. From there it had been a steep slope of decay. The mother dead within two years, the father resolved seemingly to drink himself into oblivion. Cain and Ramsey moving out, away, and then, as all things seemed to do in Briganton, ricocheting back again to settle, seemingly pulled by a past that would not let them go.

Mina studied the house. It had been tarted up, a double extension added to the back of it, a new gravel driveway laid at the front. Simply looking at it, you would never know what had happened there, would never sense the tragedy that had unfolded.

That was the front door. That was the path down which they had walked.

Mina looked at her feet, puddled in the orange glow of a streetlamp. They would have stood here, not knowing what was to come. Then they would have walked along this road, Zach delivering papers to house after house, then a left, then a right.

Mina turned and began to walk, the first whispers of rain pricking at her skin.

The mist was denser here, the moor just a house width away. Mina's breath sounded loud to her. If it happened here, if there was a sudden rush of footsteps, hands raised in attack, would she hear it in time? Would she be able to defend herself? Strange to walk on, that thought in mind, and not to really care.

Mina walked until she reached Dray Lane.

She stopped.

It was like a tunnel into a tomb, a narrow channel of semi-light looking on to the pitch black of the moor. The wall was somewhere down there, the memory of too many bodies. And here, on this narrow inlet, was where it had happened. Where Ramsey and Zach were taken.

Mina stuffed her hands in her pockets and shivered as the lane tugged the wind toward her, thin raindrops spiraling into her face. How did McGowan do it? She looked about her. The moor was close, it was true. It would have been a fairly quick trip to drag the bodies to their dumping ground.

Yet still. Kitty Lane was one thing. Small, bird boned. But two teenage boys, one a man in all but name? If you were going to do it, what would you do? How would you control them?

She thought of the statements made twenty years ago, sitting now in the trunk of her car. Mc-Gowan had attacked Ramsey first, had rushed him from behind, beaten him about the head with an object, never identified. And that made sense, when you thought about it. Take out the older boy. The greater threat.

But then . . .

Mina turned on the spot, considered the scene. McGowan would have had to leave one of them here. He was strong, but even the strongest of people would not have been able to drag two bodies at once out to the wall. Which meant one of them must have been left behind in Dray Lane, a matter of meters from the road and houses, in the early morning of a burgeoning day. Anyone could have come across him. Anyone could have seen.

Unless . . .

Mina looked down the long tunnel to the moor beyond. Unless McGowan wasn't alone. Unless there were two.

A shiver raced along her spine, up into her hairline, and in spite of herself, she turned, checked behind her, just in case. But there was nothing, only the rapidly plunging night and the wind. She should go home. It was almost ten, and work would begin early tomorrow. And . . .

Mina wrapped her hand around her ASP. Just in case. Began the slow walk back home.

She had only just left Dray Lane, however, when

the beam of headlights broke through the darkness, grew brighter, brighter, and a car skidded to a hard stop beside her. Mina whipped about, raising her ASP slightly from the side of her body, a certain sense of inevitability settling on her.

"Mina, what the hell are you doing out here on a night like this?" Isla had wound the passenger window down, was leaning across the seat and frowning. "Dear God, are you trying to get yourself killed?"

Mina grinned, ducking her head down level with the opening. "I'm trying to tempt him out of hiding. It's not going well."

"Get in." Isla rolled her eyes. "I'll take you home."

Mina slid into the car, the reminder of what warmth felt like making her suddenly cold. She shivered. "You just now finishing work?"

Isla steered the car back out into the road. "Yeah. I was out at the prison. Bloody accident on the road, so it's taken me a good two hours to get back."

"McGowan?"

Isla pulled a face. "Yeah. For all the good it did me."

Mina sat, feeling the heat begin to filter through her. "Can I ask you something, Isl? As a psychologist? The wall. Why there? Why move the bodies at all? If it's the kill he's after, why bother with that?"

Isla slowed as she passed the primary school, drummed her fingers against the steering wheel. "That's a hard question to answer. Mostly because we don't really know which 'he' we're talking about. This one, the one who killed Victoria Prew,

Maggie Heron, he's following on from where Heath left off. So the wall, that's pretty much integral to the process. Otherwise he's just some guy killing people. That's not what he wants. He wants to be the killer on the wall."

"Okay then," said Mina, "what about McGowan? Why did he do it?"

Isla blew out a breath. "There's been a lot of debate about that. Of course, Heath entirely refuses to comment, thus ensuring that the debate continues. There are a number of things we can take from it." She signaled right into Mina's street, slowed to navigate the narrow byway. "They were fully clothed. All of them. That suggests it's not about sex for him. It's something different. The fact that they were all left in a more or less natural position, so sitting up . . . some people think that indicates a level of remorse on the part of the killer. That he's somehow trying to undo what he's done."

"Really?" asked Mina, frowning.

Isla shrugged, pulling the car to a stop beside Mina's cottage. "It's certainly an option. But the wall, the fact that he left them there, where it was inevitable they would be found and in reasonably short order . . . Hadrian's Wall is Briganton. It makes this place what it is. A child of Briganton is a child of the wall. By placing them there, Heath was essentially flipping the bird to the entire village. It is about fear. It is about using your kills to create the maximum level of impact. In Heath's case, his target audience was all of Briganton."

Mina sat for a moment, thinking about Dray Lane, the darkness, the whipping wind coming off the moor, and suddenly, here in the safety of Isla's car, she felt afraid. "This is . . . shit," she said quietly.

"Yes." Isla leaned back in the driver's seat, closed her eyes. "Yes, it is."

"You okay?"

Isla opened her eyes, peered at the dashboard. "Well, it's nine fifty-six p.m., and I'm still alive. So we're going to call this a good day."

Mina snorted. "Tell me about it." The rain had begun to work itself up now, hitting the windscreen in large drops. "I'll let you get off. Thanks for the lift."

"Yeah, well, don't do that again, eh?" said Isla. "My nerves can't take another one."

Mina grinned. "Yes, Professor." Then, with her hand on the handle, Mina stopped. "Hey, just one more thing. From what you said, whoever's doing it this time will have to move the bodies. That's a critical part of being the killer on the wall."

"Yeah?"

"Well," said Mina, "I'm just thinking . . . Is there any way we can use that?"

Isla frowned. "Well . . . I mean, it's an extra process. He's placing himself with the bodies for longer than he needs to be. He has to somehow transport them and position them." She shrugged. "I mean, think about it. He strikes quickly, apparently from nowhere. But then he has this whole length of time in which he *has* to be near to the body. I would say that what you have there is a vulnerability for him. And, maybe, an opportunity for you."

Tuesday, October 25

The journey of
the dead – Mina

A fog lay across the city, most of Carlisle still enjoying the privilege of sleep. Mina shivered, staring out the office window into the opaque dawn. It seemed that shapes were coalescing there, forming, falling, re-forming. It felt like a hangover, this level of tiredness. She raised the mug, downed another slug of bitter black coffee, and prayed for it to take effect. She had finally reached home a little after midnight, had stripped off her clothes, leaving them in a puddle on the floor, then had climbed into bed naked, not caring about the chill in the air, safe in the knowledge that from this much exhaustion would come sleep. And it had, in a fashion. A clumsy, ineffectual sleep, littered with wakings and fallings, with the feel of rain on her skin, with dead bodies lined up, one after the other, along the wall. And Ted, cradling the cat, saying that he couldn't understand it, that Maggie had gone out only to find Mitzy, after all.

Mina felt eyes on her and glanced sideways at Owen, one of the few others who had made it in at this early hour. The room itself seemed to be holding its breath, as if it, too, knew that in a matter of minutes, the door would open and detective after detective would flood in, settle into seats, prepare for the next briefing with various degrees of enthusiasm.

"What?"

"Nothing." Owen blushed and shifted his focus back to his computer screen. "Just . . . you look tired."

Tired. Her alarm had roused her at 5:31 a.m. A psychological ploy, kidding her brain that she had slept past 5:30, so evidence of a reasonable night's sleep. She had stood in the shower, letting the water thunder over her upturned face, had dressed in the previous day's clothes, tugged her still wet hair into a rough plait. She looked like a stinking pile of garbage, and she knew it.

Mina returned her gaze to the window. A car passed on the street below, its headlights puncturing the early morning dark. She watched as it rolled slowly past, a flicker of orange, its left turn signal flashing. And she thought of Isla's words. *What you have there is a vulnerability for him.* She watched the car making its steady turn, watched until the red of the brake lights vanished from view. They were all talking about the murders. About his need to kill.

But what about this other need of his—to display the bodies, seating each and every one of them against the wall? What if that was the way in?

Mina took another sip of her coffee, turned and pulled her chair over to her computer, then flipped her notebook open.

Okay, the transportation phase. The point at which our killer puts himself with the body for an extended period of time. What had that looked like for Victoria Prew? Mina tapped her pen on the page, allowing the flash of memory to roll over her. Of Victoria, her cardigan wrapped around her, vivid in the hard white of her living room. Of Victoria dead against the wall.

She was attacked on the driveway.

So, forget the kill for a moment. Think about what comes next.

Victoria inert, crumpled to the ground, a deadweight in the most literal of senses. *And if you were to move her, if you* had *to move her? What would that look like? Would you tuck your hands beneath her armpits, drag her across the rough stone of the gravel driveway?*

She flipped through her notes.

There were no drag marks left on the drive.

Mina pursed her lips. *Okay. So, it's gravel. You know that the weight of the body will leave an indentation. So, what? You sweep the marks away with . . . what? Your foot?*

"Owen?"

"Yeah?"

"Do you have the crime scene photographs from Victoria Prew's? I'm looking for the outside ones . . ."

He glanced up, seemed to be working to piece her words together, then a slight shake of his head. "Sorry. Yeah. Ah, hang on." Owen pushed himself up, fingers scrabbling through the tray of papers that sat on his desk. "I . . . Here they are. You want . . . ?"

"Yeah, I'll just take the lot. Cheers."

Mina pulled the glossy pages out of the envelope, selected the ones that showed the outside of the house, and spread them across the desk. There was the car, still parked on the driveway. There was the garden, the indentations in the mud. She frowned. *Right, somewhere there should be . . . There.* The side passage that led from the front to the back. It was closed off by a high wooden gate. No lock, just a latch.

Had they . . . ? Yes. They'd checked the gate for prints, the hinges for fibers. They'd come back empty.

Another picture, this one of the narrow passage itself. Pushed up against the wall of the house was a cavernous wheelie bin. Beside it, two large plastic boxes for recycling. And beside that . . .

"Bingo," muttered Mina.

"What?"

She waved the photograph at Owen. "Why were there no drag marks on the driveway? It's a pretty safe assumption that he moved her across the gravel. We already found drag marks at the rear of the house, so we know he was dragging her . . . so why none in the gravel out front?"

"I'm guessing this is a rhetorical question . . ."

"The sweeping brush. See? It's tucked beside

the wheelie bin. He covered his tracks. Just like he must have closed the car door after he'd killed her."

"The shoe . . ."

Mina shrugged. "Maybe he missed it? It was gray. The interior was gray. Dark night."

"Okay," said Owen, frowning, "so he killed her and then tidied up after himself. Any prints on the brush?"

"Ah . . . I can't see anything that says it was examined. Do me a favor. Could you call downstairs for me? See if someone can go back out to the house and check it out?"

As Owen picked up the phone and dialed quickly, Mina flipped through the pages of her notebook. *Okay. We know he dragged Victoria out to position her. But Maggie, that was too far. No way could he have done that. So then, the tire track.*

She pulled her keyboard closer, typed hurriedly. The CCTV from the Aubrey Arms had been examined. If you were going to drive through the village from Maggie's to the wall, you'd have to pass by there. She ran quickly through the report, then blew out a breath. Nothing. Three cars passed in the relevant time period. One, a young mother with three children in the backseat. Two, a group of four hikers, who actually stopped in the Aubrey Arms for food. Three, a man in his mideighties. None of them fitting the profile of the murderer.

Mina leaned back in her chair, her eyes fixed on the screen, her mind elsewhere. There was a tire track at the rear of Maggie's house. He must have driven her. Nothing else made sense. She moved the mouse, pulling up an aerial map of Briganton.

If he had driven out of the lane, hooked a quick left . . . he'd have risked being seen immediately outside the house, but other than that . . . he could have driven north, heading toward Bowman's Hill, then taken another left, come out of the village on country roads, and then ducked back around toward the wall, all the while avoiding CCTV, ANPR. Which suggested that this guy, whoever he was, he knew Briganton well.

"God." Mina scrubbed at her eyes, unsure whether what she needed was to sleep or to cry.

"Someone's going out to the Prew house now," said Owen, placing the phone back down. "Did you know that Chief Super Clee ordered a forensic reexamination of everything from the McGowan murders?"

"You're kidding?"

"Nuh-uh. Zoe just said." He gestured to the phone. "Maybe the bosses have as many questions about Superintendent Bell as we do."

"Interesting . . ." Mina stared at the map, then sat up a little straighter. Victoria Prew was dragged. Maggie Heron driven. But what about the original victims? She let her finger trace across the screen. The first bodies—of Kitty and Ben and Zach—they were left on the section of wall that ran immediately behind Briganton, just a hundred meters from maybe a dozen houses. The problem was that there was a time lapse between the murder of Kitty Lane and Ben Flowers and the display of their bodies. Witnesses at the time testified to passing that section of the wall—dog walkers, joggers and, much to their intense mortification, one couple who had been using the wall as an alfresco romance point, unbeknownst to their respective spouses. All of them reported nothing out of the ordinary. The evidence was clear that the bodies were not left there much before 4:00 a.m. So where were they kept in the meantime? The original investigation had never been able to pin that down, and Mc-Gowan had remained as silent on that score as he had on so many other things.

Mina traced the line of houses, identical then as now, with one notable exception. Where Victoria Prew's house now stood there had been a ramshackle building, at odds with the grander designs around it.

"Owen," she said, "what's this?"

"What?" He wheeled his chair closer, squinted at the screen. "The bungalow? That was Mr. Minnaker's. Grumpy old sod. Died when I was, I don't know, thirteen?"

"So before the original murders?"

"Oh yeah. Maybe . . . three years before. The house was in a bad way when he was alive. Once he died, it pretty much fell apart. Stayed like that for . . . God, years and years, until the developer that built the Prew house bought it and knocked it down."

Mina was no longer paying attention. She was looking at the shape of the parcel of land, the small square house that sat in the center of it, the way the rear of it opened onto the moor, only a low hedge separating garden from wilderness. She studied the trees that ringed the front of it, dense and overgrown, creating a private oasis, where one could hide pretty much anything. Even a car.

"The house," she said. "Was it well secured?"

"Secured?" Owen snorted. "No. Kids were always breaking in there. I remember when I was fifteen, we had this party there and . . . well . . ." His voice skittered away; color rushed to his cheeks. "No," he finished limply. "No, it wasn't secured."

Mina felt the room shift. "Owen," she said, "what if that was where the bodies were stored? In the original murder series. What if that's where McGowan and whoever he was working with . . . if they left them where Victoria's house is now until it was time to move them to the wall?"

Owen seemed to freeze in time. "I . . ."

"That would mean," continued Mina, "that Victoria was connected to the original murder series, just like Maggie was."

"I'm not following."

Mina jabbed her finger at the map and the tumbledown house. "Maggie, she was the cousin of an original victim. But Victoria, apparently, had nothing to do with the original series, because she wasn't here. But maybe Victoria wasn't murdered because of who she was, but because of where she lived."

The victim – Ramsey

Ramsey stared at the computer monitor, trying to concentrate on the lines of text.

> *The village had shifted, now no longer safe and quiet, now a place that death stalked.*

He rested his fingers on the keyboard, feeling the shape of the keys, the ridges and the valleys between them. *Concentrate.*

Ramsey leaned forward, put his head in his hands. He kept seeing Isla's face, the raw, unadulterated fear on it when he had said the words—*It's not me he's after. It's you.* It was an alien feeling when what you were used to seeing in your wife was a fighting-back attitude, flashes of fear snatched away by steely resolve. It was the hallmark of their life together, that refusal of hers to be weak, to be vulnerable.

He thought of the letters, with their quiet, un-expressed threat, of the picture of the two of them, the words printed on its back.

Isla had simply shaken her head, unwilling to see that this was anything other than a side effect of her job. Ramsey had done what he knew he shouldn't. When Isla had left to return to work, he had picked up the phone and called her father. Along with Bonnie, Eric had been waiting for her late last night, and upon her return, she'd been met with a storm of righteous indignation and fatherly fear.

"I need to see these letters. Jesus, Isla, where's your sense? Why didn't you bring them to me as soon as you got them?" Eric had snatched the letters from Isla's unwilling hands, had read them rapidly, his face paling. "Isla . . . you know what this means, right? You understand what is going on here?"

"Eric . . ." Bonnie, her voice oil on a storm-tossed sea.

"No, Bonnie. She has to start thinking. This"—he held the letters up in front of Isla's face—"it's McGowan. You said these started after she first went to see him, yes, Ramsey?"

Ramsey looked from the contained fury of his wife's gaze to the less contained fury of his father-in-law's and chose his side. "Yes."

Isla stared at him, a look that said in no uncertain terms that he had made the wrong choice.

"It's him. It's bloody him."

"Dad." Isla's voice was like ice.

"You know that you probably started this. Yes? You get that?"

Isla froze. "What? Started what?"

"You don't think it's a coincidence? That you start to do your little experiments with Heath Mc-Gowan and suddenly the killings on the wall begin again? You've rubbed his nose in it, Isla. The fact that we survived, that he's in prison. And now he's found some damned wicked lackey to finish off what he started."

Ramsey, expecting his wife to fight back, took one inadvertent step away in anticipation of the war to follow. And yet she did not say a word. Simply turned, walked out of the room, slammed the door behind her. Eric left eventually, blowing out on a gust of fury, the letters sealed tight in an evidence bag, words such as *irresponsible* and *cavalier* thrown behind him for good measure.

Isla had not spoken to Ramsey since. She had slept in the spare room, had left the house before he woke.

Outside his study window, the sun had broken through the clouds for the first time in what felt like weeks. Ramsey looked up, watched its pale light, the faintest trace of blue sky beyond the gray. That, he supposed, was the point of it all, wasn't it? That the blue sky remained beyond the black. It had stopped raining; the wind had dropped. Perhaps it was a sign that somehow life could return to what it had once been.

Ramsey closed the window of his document, pulled up Safari. The news pages were still there, where he had left them, tab after tab opened side

by side. THE KILLER ON THE WALL STALKS BRIGANTON
ONCE MORE. On each page, pictures of the victims,
of Zach in his schoolboy finest, his hair split into
awkward curtains, his smile tentative, embarrassed.
And another picture—Ramsey in a former life, one
filled with teenage acne and angst. The tagline "The
only survivor of the killer on the wall."

He shoved himself away from the computer,
walked with long, loping strides to the door, out
into the hallway, down the stairs. The day outside
was colder than it had been, the parting of the
clouds bringing with it an ice-cold wind. Perhaps it
would snow. Ramsey climbed into the car, thinking
that snow would be nice.

The streets were quiet, the country roads qui-
eter still, and he arrived at the university more
quickly than he had anticipated. He parked the
car in the visitors' parking lot and hurried away
from it, passing small huddles of people, students,
and staff, whose heads turned to follow him. Their
gazes dipped as he met them, the watchers deny-
ing to themselves who they were—voyeurs caught
up in the latest chapter of a sensational story. He
walked quickly through the lobby and pulled open
the door on the right, to a long corridor that led
to a series of offices. And Isla's.

Isla's door stood firmly shut, the drifting sounds
of a keyboard easing from behind it. Ramsey
found himself pausing, overtaken now by a craving
to see his wife, to feel her hand on his cheek, to
have her center him, bring him back to the middle
ground. And yet the door was closed so firmly. He
raised his hand, then dropped it again, sighing
heavily.

Ramsey carried on down the corridor, two, three doors, to where Connor's door stood propped open. Through the narrow slit he could just make out the edge of him, of his dark sweatshirt, his wild hair. He tapped lightly on the door, watched as Connor twisted in his chair, recognized him, his face hurrying through a race of emotions.

Then, "Ramsey. Come on in."

It was . . . chaos. Few other words would work. He closed the door behind him, picked his way around towers of papers that appeared to have been dumped randomly on the office floor. "Hey, sorry to disturb."

"Nah. Take a seat."

Ramsey looked from left to right, searching for the proffered seat.

"Yeah, just whack those journals on the floor. There you go." Connor had swiveled in his chair and was watching him closely. "So, how you doing?"

Ramsey sank into the chair, shrugged. "You know. Fun and games. I went out to see Victoria Prew's mother yesterday." He looked at Connor and winced. "This bloody article I'm writing. They wanted me to get her reaction to what happened. Jesus. Imagine it. What do you suppose her reaction would be?"

Connor was studying him. "How was she?"

"She was actually very nice. Said she wanted to talk about Victoria, wanted people to see her as more than just a victim. But the grief, you could smell it, you know?"

"Yeah, mate. I just, I can't imagine it." His expression had become grim "It's . . . I mean, you.

To go through it once is bad. Twice, it's just unbelievable. You, are you doing okay?"

Connor leaned forward now, a priest ready to take confession, and suddenly Ramsey felt absurdly like laughing. *Okay?* He could barely remember what okay felt like. He shook his head. "I . . ." Stopped, drew in a breath. "Zach's picture. It's everywhere." He gave a little laugh. "My picture is everywhere. You have any idea how shit I looked as a teenager? Now it's all I see."

Connor was watching him, gaze intent.

"You know, I knew Heath," offered Ramsey. "Before, I mean. It's a small village. Not too many people you don't get to know in a village like this. He was . . . You could tell he had issues, if you know what I mean. Just looked like the kind of guy that was destined for trouble. Of course, no one had any clue just how bad things would go." The words were coming now, spilling out in an irresistible wave. "The thing is, the thing that I keep thinking about, is that I saw him a couple of days before the murders. It was early, like, really early, and Zach, he'd gone in to get his newspapers for his round. I was helping him, see. Because, I don't know . . . I sometimes wonder if it was because I got this sense from him, you know, that he wouldn't be around long, so I was trying to get as much time with him as I could. But honestly, I think at the time it was just because I liked hanging out with him. He was a good kid."

An image of Zach flashed before his eyes, of his hair roughened from sleep, the newspaper sack slung across his shoulder, of his bouncing, exuberant gait.

"Heath, he'd been drinking. I mean, you could smell it on him from a mile away. Was on his way back to his grandmother's after a night out. But, you know, he was pleasant enough, so you don't . . . you just don't think. He asked me what I was doing up so early, and I told him about Zach and his paper round. I said that he did it every morning." Ramsey rubbed his hand across his face. "Thing is, now I don't know . . . Was that why? Was that why he went after Zach and me? Because I told him where we'd be?"

Connor bit his lip, seemed to be picking his way carefully through his words. "Rams, guys like this, when they find a target, they go after the target. Honestly, I don't think there's anything you could have done about it. You and Zach, you were just unlucky that it was that day, that you happened to be there when he needed victims."

Ramsey wiped his eyes, sitting up straighter, pushing away that image of Zach walking in front of him. "I . . . Look, this isn't why I came. I'm sorry. It's . . . Right, I needed to talk to you about Isla."

"Okay?" Connor frowned.

"She's been getting death threats." Ramsey watched as Connor's eyes darted around as he tried to think up some covering lie. "She showed them to me, Con."

"Oh, okay, yeah." He coughed, running his hands through his hair. "Well, yeah, it happens. I mean, it happens to me too. Not as much as to Isla, but it's kind of part of the job."

"And did she tell you that letters have been coming to the house?"

Connor paled. "What? No. Jesus."

"Look, I'm worried. The murders, these letters. I mean, the kind of people she deals with, you both deal with, what if it's made her a target? Her father, he's freaking out about that, and maybe he's got a point. Everyone is thinking that these killings are about what happened in Briganton the last time, that that's the motivation, but what if it's something different? What if whoever it is has come to Briganton because of Isla? What if they're using the village's history, playing to the media, the local fears?"

"So, what?" asked Connor. "You think this is someone we've dealt with in the past? Someone we've studied?"

Ramsey sighed. "I don't know, Con. Maybe it's just my paranoia. I just . . . if anything ever happened to her."

Connor looked down at his hands. "Yeah. I know. Look, I'll go through all my old records, see if I can find anything that rings a bell. And as for Isla, I'll keep an eye on her, make sure she's safe."

Ramsey nodded. "I'd really appreciate it."

The knock on the door startled him and Connor both, its three quick raps pulling him back into the world.

Connor rolled his eyes, pulled a face at him. "Come in."

The door eased open. A young woman, achingly thin, with dense make-up, blond hair streaked with blue, smiled brightly at Connor, then Ramsey. "Hey. I have my assignment."

"Oh, Scarlett, excellent. You're the first one to the finish line."

"I do like to win." The girl gave a tinkling water-fall of a laugh and pushed the door open farther, and they saw a narrow young man hanging in the hallway behind her. His gaze flicked up to them and then away again, but his hair was brushed forward so far that it was astonishing he could see anything at all.

"Hi, Parker," offered Connor. "You have your assignment too?"

The boy looked up at him, his cheeks flaming red, then darted his gaze back down. "No, I, I forgot to bring it in. I can go get it." He glanced down at his watch. "Is that okay? I mean, I can be back here by five . . ."

Connor looked at Ramsey, gave him a quick grin, then turned back to the students. "I'm here all day, Parker."

The girl was watching Ramsey now. He looked down, picked at the fabric of his trouser leg. Almost wished that she would just come right out and say it, the way some did: "You're that guy, aren't you? The *victim*?" But then it seemed her gaze was torn away, pulled by something outside the room, and she stepped back, shifting her attention elsewhere.

"Hi." Parker wasn't speaking to them but had colored. His gaze dropping, he looked like he regretted speaking.

"Hey, Parker, Scarlett." Isla's voice came like a cold drink on a hot day. "You okay?"

"Fine," chirruped Scarlett. "Just dropping off an assignment."

She backed out of the room, allowing Isla to take her place. The sounds of her and Parker's footsteps, their low murmurs echoed down the quiet corridor.

Isla frowned at Ramsey. He watched her, waiting to see whether the storm had passed.

She gave him a half smile. "Do you work here now?" Detente.

He grinned, suddenly able to again. "Yeah, Connor has hired me as a cleaner. He needs someone to sort out this shit hole."

"Hey!" protested Connor. "I'm sitting right here."

Isla smiled, hefting a briefcase from hand to hand. "Dude, seriously. My husband's going to need a tetanus shot now. Right. I'm off."

It was something in the way she said it. The way the words were formed, defiantly almost, the way her eyes darted down, brushing the edge of his gaze.

"Where are you going?" asked Ramsey. His heart had begun to beat a little faster.

"I have some more tests to run."

It was the way Connor shifted, pushing himself upright, the look of alarm that flashed across his face.

"Isla," said Ramsey quietly. "Where are you going?"

She wouldn't look at him, and then she did, a square look, one that dared him to press her, all trace of the frightened girl vanished. "I'm going out to the prison again. I'm going to continue the tests with Heath McGowan."

Perhaps the room suddenly became silent, or perhaps the air had been sucked from it. It was difficult for Ramsey to tell. "You . . ." His heart was thundering now. "Isla, are you insane?"

She didn't answer, just looked at him.

"I . . . I don't know what more proof you need. Whoever is doing this, they have you in their sights."

"Yes," replied Isla calmly. "And Heath is in prison. So it's not him. Therefore, I'm going to continue my research."

Ramsey could feel the swell of anger rising up as he pushed himself to his feet, could tell the words that would come would be hard as nails. "Jesus Christ, Isla. How much more? How much more do you need to do to prove yourself? Yes. You're not afraid. We all know that. Only I bloody am. And that man"—he was shouting now—"that man killed my brother. That man almost killed me. That man is dangerous, Isla. He is so dangerous, and you have brought yourself to his attention. Every day. You are visiting him every day. What do you think that means to him? What do you think he's going to do with that? You're making this worse, Isla."

She looked from him to Connor, her head lowered, jaw tight. "What would you have me do, Ramsey? Run away? Hide? Well, guess what? This is who I am. This is what I do. And I'll be buggered if this bastard is going to stop me."

"And if he's controlling it? If it's Heath who is running this, from inside his prison cell?"

Her color was high now; voice cold. "Then someone had better figure that out. And if you'll excuse me, that is just what I intend to do."

Dying flowers – Mina

Mina's calves ached. The wind had picked up, was hurling itself into their faces as if it wanted nothing more than to drive them backward, indoors, where they belonged. She and Owen rounded the corner of Dray Lane and stood looking down toward the wall.

"Well, that went well." Owen shivered.

They had walked the route, two miles from the lane that ran behind Maggie's house, up toward Bowman's Hill, out of the village on winding country roads, and then back down until they reached the wall. Mina wasn't sure exactly what they had been looking for. Anything really. And yet here they were.

"It was worth a shot," she offered.

Owen grunted. "Would have liked to have seen the super do that."

Mina grinned, thinking of Eric Bell, with his burgeoning potbelly and his almost hidden limp. "You think the great Eric Bell couldn't have whipped our arses on that?"

Owen snorted. "We heading back?" Then, seeing her expression, he frowned. "What? Oh God, what now?"

Mina shrugged, the hood of her coat brushing against her ears. "Thought maybe we could just pop along and visit the scene of Ben Flowers's attack. You know, seeing as we're here."

"Min . . . you're going to get us fired."

Mina wrinkled her nose. "I know. I'm sorry. Look, you head back and tell the super, I don't know, that I've got period cramps or something."

"Period cramps? Really?" Owen rolled his eyes. "Dear God. Come on."

They retraced their steps, walking quickly through the village, past the Aubrey Arms, a right at the church, down the hill, the cold wind scrubbing at their cheeks. The Dog & Bone sat about a third of the way down the hill, its placard swinging wildly in the bitter cold wind—a bloodhound gnawing on a bone. With its tattered notice boards and scuffed paintwork, it had a rougher feel to it than the Aubrey Arms. There was rarely trouble in the village, but when there was, it usually came from here. It also had the rather dubious distinction of being the last place that Ben Flowers was seen alive.

"So," said Mina, flipping through a file as the

wind tugged and pulled at the pages. "Ben Flowers, twenty-six years old, ran his own gardening business. Which is . . . yeah." She held up a photograph, faded with time. "Did you know him?"

Owen shook his head. "I heard the stories, after. But no, I don't remember him." He leaned closer in to Mina and the file. "He wasn't a small man."

It had been taken in the church grounds, that photograph. It showed Ben, lost in concentration, working on the grounds, a shovel in hand, his thick arms taut, flexing into deeply curved muscles, a wide chest.

"He was married, no kids. Wife was a Rachel Flowers. On that night, that last night, he'd come here"—Mina waved toward the Dog & Bone—"with his friends. The investigation dug up more than a dozen people who remembered seeing him. Reports were that he was quite drunk."

"Quite?"

"Steaming," amended Mina. "He stayed here until late, about one fifty a.m."

A lock-in.

"He finally left," said Mina, "apparently barely able to walk. A friend of his, Toby Benedict, was with him. Reports indicate he was also pretty drunk. What happened next is less clear. Toby, in his interview, said that they walked together down the hill"—she gestured at the sloping pavement that led down into the heart of the village—"but that he, Toby, that is, turned off along Wiseman's Lane. Last he saw of Ben, he was still ambling downhill."

Mina sighed, took another pull of coffee from her thermos, letting her gaze trail across the pub door, seeing a staggering, useless behemoth of a man, buffeted by the night air, making an unsteady turn down toward the village. She moved away from Owen, calculating the proceedings. You could just about make out the church off there in the distance. To the right, a couple of streets connected with this road, leading to homes and people, but on the hill itself, there was little to break the silence. A little farther down, a new housing estate had sprung up on the left as you descended, well embedded now, with its box houses and self-consciously manicured lawns. But twenty years ago, a walk down this hill would have involved nothing but you and the moors.

"It would have been pretty isolated back then. Not a bad spot to make a kill."

"So, no one saw Ben after he left Toby Benedict?" Owen asked.

Mina shook her head. "Not until his body was found the following morning."

Owen looked back at her. "That's interesting."

"The original investigating team certainly thought so. In the original case, Toby was earmarked as a possible suspect. Until they found Heath McGowan, of course." Mina walked back toward Owen.

"Okay," he said, "so let's think this through. Do we have a time of death on Ben Flowers?"

"Ah." Mina leafed through pages. "Between one fifty and three a.m."

"And Kitty was five p.m. until eight p.m., yeah?"

Mina nodded. "Okay . . . so Kitty first. Then Ben. So based on our theory, McGowan, and . . . whoever else, took both victims to the derelict bungalow that stood where Victoria Prew's house is now.

They leave them there until the early hours of the morning. Then move them to the wall." Mina drained the coffee, her insides growling. She wished she had thought to bring food with her. "Okay, so according to Ben Flowers's postmortem, Flowers received several blows to the head with a large, flat object, consistent with, say, a plank of wood. Some were glancing. Others were enough to have knocked him out. Grazes on his elbow, his knee, suggest that at some point during the evening, he had fallen, perhaps against the curb."

Mina nodded, thought of . . . *What's her name? Eve?* A detective she had never met before this case. "Hey," she had said, "did you know they took fingernail scrapings from all the original victims?" They couldn't get anything from them back then, but it might be worth pursuing.

Mina stared up at the wavering sign. Perhaps, in the end, it would all come down to science, after all.

The sound of voices shattered the quiet. Two little girls emerged from the new estate, dressed in thick pink parka coats, their hair pulled into high ponytails. They walked on either side of their mother, both chattering loudly. Mina watched them, their laughter gripped by the wind and thrown at her. Amazing, somehow, that innocence could remain even in the light of so much death.

"You said he was married? Ben, I mean."

"Rachel Flowers," agreed Mina. "She's . . . ah, lives in Braith, so not too far. She's a nurse now." She grinned at Owen. "Fancy popping in for a visit?"

Owen groaned. "You are going to get us in so much trouble. Fine. Fine. Let's do it."

* * *

A hamlet with little more than a dozen houses nestled up against Kielder Forest, Braith sat perhaps ten miles from Briganton. Mina drove the shimmeringly wet country roads with care.

"I never did hear back from that girl," offered Owen. "The one who stood me up."

Mina eased her foot off the accelerator and nodded slowly. "Probably for the best. Sounds like a flake."

"Yeah." Owen sighed.

Mina glanced at the clock. She had had four missed calls from her mother overnight, had called her back on her way into work. Her mother had had a nightmare. Had seen Mina throttled by the killer on the wall. *I want you to come home. I want you to leave there, come here where it's safe.* That bubble of something hard had formed in Mina's belly again. Was it anger? Resentment? That she had run so far, and yet it still was not far enough? *Really, Mina, if only you would come home. That's what I really need.* And Mina had felt that old familiar sinking sensation, heard the sound of the only door sliding closed. "No, Mama," she had said, slipping her foot into the gap. "I can't do that."

She and Owen spoke little as the remaining miles slipped by, Mina looking out across the vast emptiness of the moor. Some people called it lonely, but for Mina the undulating scrub represented freedom. Eventually, as a pallid sun broke through the dense clouds, Mina pulled the car up outside a small detached house with a trailing ivy clambering up its frontage, the trees shielding it from the world outside. A pink child's bike sat outside the front door, a bubblegum helmet hanging from one handlebar.

What had she expected? That twenty years on, Ben Flowers's widow would still be drawing her curtains and wearing black? She released her seat belt slowly and climbed from the car, dense with the unsettling sense of abandonment, the forgotten dead. And yet, that was how it was, wasn't it? How it had to be. That people died, were mourned, and then left behind.

She followed Owen slowly along a stone-covered drive, waited while he drummed politely on the door. The sound of hurrying footsteps, and then the door swung open. Rachel Flowers was in her forties now, and there was no other word to describe her than *beautiful*, with large brown eyes, full lips, make-up careful and discreet. She was also bald.

"Oh, hi. Sorry. I . . . Mornings are crazy here. I haven't even put my hair on yet."

Owen stuck out his hand, face stoic. "I'm DC Owen Darby. I called from the car? This is DC Mina Arian."

"Of course. Come in. Come in. I've made coffee. Can I get you anything to eat? Some toast? The kids are in the living room, eating their breakfast, so perhaps best if you come through to the kitchen."

They followed her down the long hallway, into a brightly lit kitchen.

Rachel poured coffee into three large mugs. "Terrible for you, of course, but frankly, I wouldn't get out of bed without it. Was it a yes on the toast?"

"No," said Mina, stomach growling. "Please don't go to any trouble. Coffee is fine."

"Pish. It's no trouble. Have a muffin, then. Blueberry, so I hope that's okay?" Rachel shoved a plate of muffins toward them, slid onto the bench seat beside Mina, then dumped two heaped spoonfuls of sugar into her coffee. She ran her palm across the smooth stretch of her scalp. "Excuse the dazzle of light hitting my scalp. I have wigs, which I tend to wear if I'm out and about, but my God, they're uncomfortable. Still, one always feels that one should warn people so as not to shock them. Bald lady inside. Beware."

"Are you . . ."

"Sick? No. Well . . . alopecia. It hit just after Ben . . . Stress, I imagine. Shocking at the time, of course, although somewhat less shocking than your husband being killed by a serial killer, so, you know, perspective. Still, it's been a long time now. It's amazing what you can adapt to." She moved the muffins to beneath Mina's nose. "Please, take one. So, you wanted to ask me about Ben?"

"Yes." Mina's fingers had gripped the muffin without her fully intending them to, were clutching it tight, with little apparent intention of letting go. "I'm so sorry if this brings up painful memories for you."

Rachel waved her apologies away. "That's the thing about grief, about losing someone like that. It never really leaves you, anyway. It creeps under your skin. Sometimes, I'll be doing something silly, like sitting in traffic or weeding—weeding is a good one—and I'll hear Ben's voice. *Don't do it that way. Do it this way.* And, do you know, even after

twenty years and a second marriage to a man whom
I love more than life itself, still, in those times, I'll
miss Ben so much that it physically hurts."

"I'm sorry," repeated Mina.

"It's life," replied Rachel, breaking a muffin
apart with her fingers. "You survive. Not too much
choice, really. And honestly, I don't know how
things would have been, had he lived, I mean. We
were very young. And Ben, he still wasn't ready,
not really, to be a husband, a father. Of course, you
couldn't have told me that at the time, but in hind-
sight . . . Still, to have that happen. It changes you
as a person, you know?"

"Can you tell us a little about that night?" Asked
Mina.

Rachel didn't look up, dug her finger into the
cake, breaking a blueberry free. "He'd gone out
drinking. Ben liked a drink. Not that I'm saying he
had a problem or anything, because he didn't. Just
liked socializing, you know? I mean, me, I'm a lot
more . . . I like my own space. I'll be honest, I wasn't
happy with him. He'd been doing it a lot, leaving
me to it, you know? Going out with the lads. So,
that night . . . I was less than impressed. I went to
bed at, I don't know, ten, but I couldn't sleep.
Never could until I knew he was in, safe and
sound. So, you end up clock-watching, waiting for
the sound of the key in the door. By about one
thirty, I was livid. The waiting and waiting, it wears
you down. He'd said he wouldn't be late, so of
course that made it much worse. I got up, threw a
coat on over my pajamas, and stormed out, thinking, I don't know, that I'd drag him out of the
damn pub if need be. But when I got there, they

all told me he'd left. And . . . well, you know what came next."

"Rachel, which way did you walk?" Asked Mina.

"Up Hill Road."

"And you didn't see anything, anyone?"

She shook her head slowly. "I saw . . . A car passed me just when I got onto Hill Road, and I remember because it was so late, and I was thinking, *God, did they see me in my pajamas?* I didn't see anything but headlights. But other than that, nothing." She sat for a moment, quiet. "When it all came out in court about where he'd been attacked . . . I have to tell you, I didn't sleep for weeks. If I'd been a few minutes earlier, I'd have found him. Maybe it wouldn't have happened. To think that I walked right by the spot from which he'd been taken maybe a minute, two minutes after it happened . . . It's the worst thing in the world."

Mina nodded. Placed a piece of muffin in her mouth. Sweet cake, the pop of sour blueberry.

A stampede of feet, the kitchen door swinging open, a little boy, four, perhaps five, with a shock of bright blond curls, careening through it, throwing himself onto his mother's lap.

"Mummy, Sophia shouted at me."

Rachel ran her fingers through the boy's hair, rolling her eyes at Mina. "Why did she shout at you, Henry? Did you do something to her?"

"No. I just told her she was a stinky, fat bum, that's all."

Mina suppressed a smile.

"Jake? Sorry, guys. Just a second. Jake! I don't know where he . . ."

The boy was perhaps twenty, tall and handsome

enough to make Mina blush. She caught Owen's eye, and his grin made her blush further.

"Sorry, Rach. I tried to keep him in the living room, but he got away from me. Come on, trouble. Leave Mummy to talk to these nice people."

Rachel watched them leave. "Oh, that's not my boy toy. My boy toy is a forty-nine-year-old dentist, bless him. I'm sorry you didn't get to meet Charlie, but he's up and out early. No, that's my nephew Jake. He's at the University of Northumberland. He's studying engineering. Lovely lad. Stays with us in term time to save a bit of money. Of course, he's good with the kids, so I'm glad to have him. Look . . ." She leaned closer, lowered her voice. "I need to ask you something. The photograph, did you ever find out where it came from?"

Mina swallowed hard, glanced at Owen. "The photograph?"

"Yes, the . . . you know." Rachel gestured, her fingers moving rapidly. "I just, I never heard back. And I called and called and left so many messages. In the end I think he got sick of me. Maybe that's why he didn't reply."

"I'm sorry, Rachel." Owen had leaned in and had lowered his voice to match hers. "What are we talking about?"

"The photograph."

Mina frowned. "What photograph?"

Rachel looked down at her fingers. "It was a photo of Ben, sitting up against Hadrian's Wall." Her voice dipped. "He was dead. You could see that clearly. I gave it to Eric Bell. He promised he was going to look into it. That he'd let me know what he found out. Only I never heard from him again."

Was it in the file? Had they missed it? Mina glanced at Owen, who shrugged in return. "I . . . I'm sorry, Rachel. We must have missed it in the file. So this was . . . what? Just after Ben's death?"

Rachel knotted her fingers together tight, her lips compressing. "No. It came in the post. About a year after Heath McGowan went to prison."

Loose lips sink ships – Mina

It was a little after three by the time they returned to the office. The room itself met her with a wall of sound, of voices and the clacking of keys and ringing phones. She stood there for a moment, allowing the tide of it to wash over her, drowning her thoughts. The sky beyond the window had turned a steely gray; a sheet of hard rain had turned the world opaque.

Mina slipped into her seat with a vague attempt at keeping her expression nonchalant, as if she had been only where she was supposed to be, nowhere else. She logged in to her computer and all the while thought of Rachel Flowers, with her smooth scalp, her vivid smile.

How did you do that? How did you survive when your husband was murdered by a serial killer? It seemed . . . wrong, almost. Then a second voice chimed in, criticizing the choice of words. *How could it be wrong? What was the woman supposed to do? Lie down and die along with her husband?*

Mina watched the computer flicker into life. And yet the question was how. How was it possible that Rachel Flowers had battled through, battled on, begun again, in spite of all that had gone before? Imagine the courage in that, the resilience that would lead you to keep showing up in life, day after day, even knowing what the worst of it could bring. Then, thought Mina, there was her. She was thirty-one years old and had never had a boyfriend of more than a fortnight. And she could call it bad luck, poor destiny, fate, whatever the hell she liked, but the truth, when she plucked up the courage to look at it, was that it felt safer that way. Because it seemed that all of life was a battle to be who she was, a fight against the people who loved her most to stand her ground, and that she simply did not have the energy to fight one more person. That it was safer to be alone and at least that way to live, rather than risk opening her life up to one more person who would try to build a prison around her.

So there she was, alone and lonely, frightened and running. And there was Rachel Flowers, with her house with the climbing ivy, and her husband and her two children and her nephew, the triumvirate of voices high and excitable, surrounded by so much life that the thought of it was suffocating almost. Mina's anger shifted, grew. Because who the hell was she to give up the way she had when this woman, this widow, had continued to fight on?

"Ah, good of you to come in, Mina."

She had, it seemed, slipped into some kind of reverie akin to sleep. Mina set her hands flat on the desk, attempting to ground herself, and looked up. Superintendent Bell stood in the periphery of her vision, his face hard, arms folded.

"Sir, I . . ."

I what? I have been chasing leads, trying to prove your investigation wrong? The words disintegrated in Mina's mouth, and instead of speaking, she merely sat there, her mouth agape.

The superintendent frowned at her. "I need you to chase up forensics on that photograph sent to Professor Bell."

It took Mina a moment to figure out who he was talking about. Because Professor Bell was Isla, with her quick wit, her long stride, and her steady gaze. Then it took her another minute to add in the photograph, to separate it out from the one that had been sent to Rachel Flowers. The words floated up to the roof of her mouth that it was ironic that he was chasing one photograph, yet when Rachel had begged and begged him, he had refused to chase another.

Of course, she said none of this. "Of course."

"Quickly, please."

The superintendent turned and walked away, his progress interrupted only by the limp, which he worked so hard to control. An old rugby injury, that was what Isla had said, something that flared up when the weather was bad or life was particularly tough. Mina sat watching him for a moment.

He didn't like her. That much was pretty clear. Was it that she was a woman, perhaps? Or was it merely that she was—as her mother would say—difficult?

But then, reflected Mina, had she not been difficult, she would still be living in London, three doors down from her mother, married to some nice man who made her want to stab herself in the eye with a fork, and with two kids, on her way to three. Difficult could be an advantage sometimes.

She picked up the handset and dialed. The phone began to ring.

"Okay . . . yes. Okay, thanks. No, I will." Said Owen.

Mina twisted in her chair, watched Owen hang up his phone, scrub his palms across his face. "What?" she said.

He sighed loudly, leaned back in his chair, his legs out in front of him in one long catlike stretch. "I need a beer. That was Winterwell Prison. The super"—he glanced around, lowered his voice—"he's got this idea that McGowan could be coaching his copycat."

Mina rolled her eyes, transferring the phone from one ear to the other. "Which is obviously the simplest explanation."

"Indeed," said Owen. "Anyway, I had them look into Heath's contacts over the past couple of years. I mean, if he's involved in these killings, he had to have been in touch with his guy on the outside. Wouldn't you think?"

"Okay?"

"So, they went back through their records." He took a deep breath, ready for the grand finale. "Turns out McGowan hasn't had a single visitor since his grandmother died eight years ago. Well, apart from the superintendent's daughter. Professor Isla Bell, her colleague Connor Leary, they've so far visited him five times as a part of their research. Other than that, nothing."

Mina pursed her lips. The sound of the phone ringing in her ear faded now into the drumbeat of the room. "What about calls?"

Owen grinned. "Nope. McGowan hasn't made any calls in about two years—and the ones before that were sporadic and brief. Mostly to his mother. Once they stopped . . . Oh, he called Professor Bell a couple of days ago, but that's it." He shook his head. "Of course, there's always the possibility of contraband mobiles. I mean, they're rife in there. Or if it was someone who'd served time with him . . . If that's the case, then whoever the killer is, he's gone dark."

Mina shifted the phone, smiling. "Gone dark? Okay, Mr. Bond."

Owen gave a little laugh, which petered out as he appeared to consider something. He opened his mouth.

"Hello? CSI, Zoe Miller," said a female voice.

Mina started, had forgotten about the phone she held, about the long, long ringing tone. "Oh, hi. Yes, DC Mina Arian from—"

"Dear God, are you psychic or what?"

"Am I . . . ?"

"I was just about to ring up with what we've got. You ready?"

"I . . . sure."

"Righto, team going through Victoria Prew's house got something. It looks like someone jimmied the window in the downstairs laundry room, broke the lock, so that it looks like it's shut up tight, but all you'd have to do is lift the window and you'd be in." Zoe's words tumbled out quickly, an edge of thrill to them. "I mean, she thought she had the house all safe. Turns out he could have gone in and out whenever the hell he felt like it. No wonder she was freaking out." There was a pause. "Thing is, I don't get it. Why he didn't kill her in the house, I mean. Why do it outside, where anyone could see?"

Mina had twisted in her seat, was staring at the clouds, thinking of Victoria Prew standing in her bedroom. How many times had he been in there? Had he been there while she was home? While she was asleep? "Maybe watching was enough. For a while at least. Maybe the thrill of being there, of being near her, without her knowing . . . maybe it was enough."

"Until . . ."

"Until it wasn't," Mina said quietly.

"Well," said Zoe, "while he was using that window as his own personal cat flap, he made a mistake."

Mina's mouth fell open. "What?"

"They found fibers, trapped in the latch."

"Okay." Mina nodded slowly. "So . . . when we find him, we have something to connect back to him. Good, yes, that's good . . ."

"There's more," said Zoe in the manner of one who was enjoying drawing out a reveal. "They also found a hair, trapped in the frame of the window. And it had a root. Which means . . ."

"Which means DNA," finished Mina.

"Yes, DC Arian. Yes, it does."

"How long?" Mina's pulse sounded in her ears. Her entire body tingled.

"The lab knows to rush it. They're starting on it right now. As soon as they've developed a profile, we'll be able to run it through the system. You'll pass all this on to the super, yeah?"

Was her voice coming from far away, or did it just seem like that to Mina? "Yes, of course. Yes."

She slid the phone into its cradle and stood, felt the floor bucking beneath her feet. They were almost there. It was almost over. They could stop this before it got any worse. Two deaths, they were bad enough, but any more—that was just unthinkable. Here, they could finish it here. She walked, her legs feeling as if they no longer belonged to her, to the superintendent's office, raised her hand to tap on the already ajar door.

"Joyce, how are you?" His voice rolled from inside, a barely contained thunder.

Mina took a step forward, one back, her hand hanging uselessly in midair. She peered through the gap, could make out the super sitting at his desk. He looked up, frowned, but waved her in, anyway, one finger to his lips.

"Eric." A woman's voice floated from the speakerphone. "I'm bloody soaking. How the devil are you?"

"I'm good, thanks. Not the day to be outside, is it? Joyce, you know that Chief Inspector Hale is handling the media on this."

Joyce Beale. Reporter with the *Northern Standard*. Mina bit her lip.

"Jesus, Eric. He's a child. I keep wanting to ask if his mother knows he's out."

"Well, what are you going to do? They're all children these days."

Mina wondered briefly if the super had forgotten she was there. She shifted in place and was rewarded with a heavy scowl.

"Isn't that the truth? Honestly, Eric, don't make me jump through hoops, there's a good lad. You just tell me what I need to know, and I can go sit down and have a nice G&T."

"Well"—Eric Bell leaned his head back in his chair—"you know, Joyce, we're getting there. We really are. My officers are working extremely hard and are chasing down all possible leads. We have every confidence that this will be solved quickly."

Did they give you a course on this? Mina wondered. *When you become a super, do you have lessons on how to bullshit the media? Or is it simply that Eric Bell is very good at bullshit?*

"Okay, yes, but of course, each day that this case continues unsolved, there is a very real danger to the residents of Briganton. Is that not the case?"

"Well, you know, Joyce, you're right. It is currently a dangerous time. And I would advise people within the locale, most especially female residents, to take care, be aware of going outside alone, of putting yourself in a position in which you are isolated or vulnerable."

There was a long silence, then, *"Especially female, Eric? Is this you being a misogynistic dinosaur?"*

Mina felt herself moving forward, her feet dragging her against her will, one hand going up, as if with it, she could stop the train that had just slipped its brakes. And yet it wasn't enough, was never going to be enough, and the train plowed on regardless.

"Well, Joyce," said the superintendent, "based on what we've seen so far, it would certainly appear that whoever is responsible for these killings is targeting females."

Wednesday, October 26

Through the eyes of the victims – Isla

Isla laid the photographs out across her desk. Not brain images this time, not murderers either. Victims. She laid out the A4 color copies she had printed out, one beside the other, so that when she was done, she was looking down at Kitty and Ben and Zach and Amelia and Leila and Victoria and Maggie. And, of course, Ramsey.

She looked down at the array. The radio hummed softly in the background, some jaunty tune entirely at odds with the early hour and the dark, dark day. She felt her breathing steady, her back straighten. Because the rest, it was all bullshit really, when you came down to it. This was the why, the people before her. And if it took her surviving some nasty little love letters to figure it out, then so be it.

It was early; the university was empty save for her. Isla glanced up at the ring of trees that surrounded her and spared a quick thought for what could be hidden in the early morning gloom, then turned her back on the broad window, focused once again on the dead.

Help me.

She picked up the first photo in the line, that of Kitty Lane. Eighty-two years old, twisted with arthritis, her entire frame seeming to wrap about itself. The evidence suggested that Kitty was the first to die. A small, narrow woman who lived alone—an easy first target, a gentle start to the game.

She placed Kitty down, picked up the next picture along.

But then, what about Ben? Ben was a large man, strong, capable. So not vulnerable, although at the time it had been suggested he was drinking. Nonetheless, the leap from Kitty to Ben seemed akin to climbing Bowman's Hill and believing yourself ready to ascend Everest. And from there to Zach and to Ramsey. Two at once, the ultimate test.

Isla ran her finger along the next image, tracing her husband's jawline. Was that why he survived? Because Heath had simply bitten off more than he could chew?

Then, for three merciful weeks, nothing. A stultifying silence, which to some had seemed like the end, the danger over, the monster fled.

She picked up the next pair of photographs. Amelia, five feet five, a thinness that looked painful. Leila, five feet two, little more than a wisp.

She set them back down.

So there was logic, a rational progression of thoughts. Too much, too fast, and so a scaling back, approaching targets of more manageable proportions. And then Lucy. Poor pregnant Lucy Tuckwell. For Heath, the most personal of all the murders. But then, perhaps you could not group Lucy with the rest. The MO this time did not match: not strangulation here, but rather a relentless cascade of fists that had pummeled the girl into bloody oblivion. No display here either. Indicators that, for Heath, Lucy had marked a loss of control, an impulse kill that went beyond what he was prepared to deal with.

Isla stepped back, studied the original victims. Heard a creak beyond her door, someone else in early, and, in spite of herself, glanced up, checked to see that the door was locked. Another creak, whoever it was trailing off along the corridor. Isla shook her head: the fear was starting to get to her. She slid her gaze across to the two photos that sat separately, Victoria Prew and Maggie Heron. Again, the victims were both women, both thin, and although Victoria had some height to her, Isla could imagine that if you had enough stature and strength, she would pose little challenge.

And their murders had been conducted out of doors, in the darkness or the failing light, both committed while the women were distracted—Victoria Prew by the rain, the opening of the car door, Maggie Heron by her tendency to deafness, her focus on the missing cat.

But then . . .

Isla pulled her chair closer, sank into it. Her elbows on her knees, she stared at the photographs. This wasn't a case of killing on impulse. In Victoria's case, he had been watching her, and he had gone into her house at least once that they knew of. Whether he had been in Maggie's . . . that was a question that her father was still trying to get Ted to answer. His rote response had become, "I don't know. You'd better ask Maggie." They were talking about getting social services involved. So, had the killer been in Maggie's home? No one knew. But, her father had said, what they did know was that he had followed her, had removed the flowers she had left on Kitty's grave.

Isla felt cold. So they had both been preselected. He had picked them, had researched them, and then had killed them. She thought of the photograph of her and Ramsey kissing, of the letters dropping through her front door. Was Ramsey right? Was her father right? Had she been preselected too? She was taller than the other women and perhaps slightly stronger, but in real terms, it seemed unlikely that would make too much of a difference. Especially now that he'd gotten a taste for it, built his confidence up.

The music she had been dimly aware of sputtered out, a woman's voice taking its place. From the low thrum of words came the one Isla had been waiting for. *Briganton.* She leaned across to the radio, twisted the dial up.

"Investigations are still under way into the two murders that have taken place in the village of

Briganton. While police say that the case is progressing, there are those in the media who cannot help but draw links with the killer on the wall—Heath McGowan—currently serving time in Winterwell Prison for his crimes. Police Superintendent Eric Bell issued a warning late last night, telling all women within the village of Briganton to be aware that they may be at risk from this predator." Then a grating jangle of music, the country's attention now shifting away from the distasteful talk of death.

Isla's insides flipped. "Oh God."

She pushed herself up from her chair and began to pace futilely, her fingers dancing. That . . . what her father had said. It was a challenge, the throwing down of a gauntlet. Words like that, especially from the great Eric Bell, they would be sufficient to rig the game. It seemed to her like the spiraling of a roulette wheel, the ball heading for one pocket, aiming straight at her, and then a jostle or a shove and suddenly it had moved, heading now in an entirely new direction. *Tag, you're it.*

It would be a man. The next one. It would be a man.

Isla grabbed for the phone and dialed her father's number. He had to know. Had to warn the village that his words, they had changed the game. But all she got was an empty ringing, a wary answering machine. She hung up, dumped the phone into its cradle with greater force than she should.

Okay. She paced back toward the window, beyond which a thin sort of rain had begun. *So the*

*killer, he'll be hunting again. A man now. Based on
what we've seen so far, distraction is his friend. He'll be
looking for someone not paying attention. Maybe playing
on a phone, maybe listening to music on headphones.*

But where? Because the thing was, Briganton as
a hunting ground had now become far, far harder.
The police presence was intense, fanning out and
seeming to fill every corner of the small village.
So, if it was her, if she was looking for her next kill,
she would adapt her approach, would spread her
net wider in the hope of catching an unsuspecting
victim. She would go somewhere where there were
a lot of people, where there remained a sense of
safety. Somewhere like the university. Her heart
thrummed faster at the notion. But when you
thought about it, it made sense. Here the students
and staff moved as if they were in a bubble, as if
what was going on was a world away rather than a
mere twenty miles. Here people were not afraid—
not yet, at least. They were still prone to distraction—and wasn't that his home run swing?

She stepped close to the window, cardigan tight
around her, and for the first time allowed herself
to feel the danger, the fear that raced hard on the
heels of it. She studied the shapes of the trees, of
the waving branches, shadows that danced with
the wind. Was he out there now? Her head began
to swim the way it had so often lately, and she
leaned against the window, her gaze still on those
trees.

Are you coming?

The sharp trilling of the phone broke into the
silence, an electric shock across her skin. Isla felt a

wave of nausea and closed her eyes briefly, trying to pull it all back together, telling herself that she was fine, trying to ignore the lie of it. She grabbed the handset.

"Isla Bell."

And there he was again, that voice with the roughened edges, the rolling middle notes. "Hello, Professor. How are you?"

Isla straightened, stepped back from the window so that she was hidden by the wall, struggling to get her mouth to work, her tongue to obey. "Heath . . ."

"I'm sorry to disturb you. I thought that perhaps you would be in to see me later, but I couldn't be sure of it. And, I thought we should talk."

Isla pulled her chair up, sat carefully on the edge of it. "Okay?"

"I just heard your father on the news. The great Eric Bell seems to be losing his touch. Suggesting that your guy is going after just women. That seems . . . silly."

Isla worked to balance her voice, to not let the edges in her words seep out. "Silly?"

"Oh, come on, Prof. You know what this means."

"You tell me."

A quick laugh. "Fine. I'll play. Your father has told the world that only women are targets. Serial killers, well, we're contrary sorts. Not keen on being told what we're going to do. Yeah? So, the obvious answer? He's going to knock off a couple of guys. Just to put your father in his place."

Isla's gaze fell on the photos, on the array of people dead because of the man on the other end of the phone. Her fingers slid up, gripped the edge of the desk, and she blew out a slow breath. "Heath," she said, "tell me how to stop him."

Another laugh. "I can't do that. But I will tell you one thing—and I say this only because I like you. Your father has an uncanny knack for pissing people off. And you, Prof, you're a very public, very obvious way for someone to make your father pay. I'd watch your back."

The truth of it? – Isla

The prison guard tugged her bag open, a wide, yawning abyss of papers and detritus. He looked up at Isla and smiled. "You're here more often than I am these days."

She smiled back. "Part of the job," she lied.

They had called her full of herself back in the provincial days of comprehensive school, when your value was rated by the lushness of your hair, your ability to sashay and to flirt with boys. They had said that she was odd, with her eternal stream of books, her fierce need for knowledge, that she thought she was better than they. At the time, she had believed them to be wrong. Isla watched the prison guard open the side pocket, the one where she kept pens, her mobile phone, and, for perhaps the first time in her life, admitted that perhaps her school-mates had in fact been right. Perhaps she did think she was better than anyone else. What other explanation could there be for standing here, for putting herself inside this prison, a place where she had no need to be? It was hubris. The belief that she alone could achieve what others could not. That with her scientific mind, with her under-standing of the monsters that dwelled in the dark, she could tease out the answers. That, in spite of his steadfast refusal to speak to the police, Heath McGowan would talk to her.

She watched the guard, thought of Heath's phone call. *I'd watch your back.* She could get to him. With the right leverage, the pressure in the right place. She could get him to tell her what he knew about these new murders.

"You're going to need to leave your phone," said the guard apologetically.

"Of course." Isla slid it out of the bag and tried not to see the five missed calls from her husband. She passed it across the table, pushing back the jab of guilt.

She could make this work. She had tools no one else had. She had experience that was lacking in others. She could get him to talk.

"Right, then. You want to follow me?"

Isla hitched her bag onto her shoulder and smoothed down her blouse. She followed the guard, working through the numbers in her mind. A score of thirty-seven on the PCL-R—highly psychopathic.

An IQ score of eighty-one—intelligence on the low side of moderate. There was no easy formula. Nothing one could tap into when talking to a psychopath. There were so many gradations, so many variations. But the constant was that to them, this would all be a game. *Move. Countermove. You have to know your opponent.* Heath McGowan, aged thirty-nine. Murdered five people using manual strangulation. Risked exposure by transporting their bodies to a display position. Reckless. Was captured when he murdered his girlfriend during the course of an argument. So, prone to impulsiveness, a tendency to use violence, not just for the thrill of it, but also as a response to frustration.

The guard tugged open a door, waited as Isla followed him through, pulled it tightly closed behind them. But that wasn't it, was it? That wasn't how she reached him. That was the route tried by detectives, and it had been met with nothing but a smile and empty air.

The door clanged, sealing them into the cocoon of the prison. Isla thought about Heath, the boy. About that lurking, doubtful character who hung around on the playground, who always had a story to tell, of bold moves, daring escapes. Thought of his mother, turning up every now and again, heroin thin, her gaze unfocused and unnatural, seeming to skitter right across her son. She thought of how Heath would move, how he would position himself time and again, make a desperate effort to catch his unreliable mother's gaze, then the anger in him when he failed. She thought of his grandmother, a dictator in miniature, her forehead knotted in a permanent line of tension. Remembered the sound of their front door banging, Heath stalking away, tight with anger, his grandmother's words flying loose into the Briganton air: *You're a waste of space.* The battery of tests that Isla herself had put him through, the way he watched her face, searching for micro-expressions: *Is that right? Did I do it okay?*

"He's waiting for you," said the guard, pointing her toward an interview room. "I'll come in and keep watch."

"Thank you." That was the way in. That was the path. All those years of looking for approval, only to be met by stony silence. Heath was a man starving, his need to be the one others looked up to gone unmet for so long.

Heath was sitting beside a table. Was looking at his hands. Didn't look up when she walked in. Isla's stomach contracted, and another wave of nausea threatened to fell her. Heath's guard was up. She could see it in the set of his shoulders, in the slight smirk that raised the edges of his mouth.

She affixed a smile to her face, slid into the seat opposite him. "Hello, Heath."

He didn't look at her right away. One beat. Two. Long enough to establish that he was in charge. Then his eyes moved upward. "Professor Bell. Couldn't stay away, I see."

"How are you, Heath?" Her voice was molten chocolate.

"Popular, so it would seem."

Isla shuffled through her options. There was play ignorant, pretend she didn't know about the police visits, three so far. All resolutely unsuccessful. That strategy would have the advantage of creating some distance between Isla and the law. But Heath was watching her now, searching her features, waiting for the lie. "I heard the police have been to see you."

Heath smiled slowly. "They send you in? See if you can do any better?"

"No."

The smile broadened, stretching out to the ends of the earth. The triumph of one who believed he had caught a lie. Heath leaned back, head cocked to one side and a shutter sliding down over his features, as it all started to slip away before it had even begun.

"I just . . ." Isla began to flounder. A sudden thought—*I shouldn't be here.* And then, whether by accident or design, she didn't know, a tear slid down her cheek.

It was like an explosion contained in a small room. The guard standing at the door shuffled his feet, one step forward, one step back, as he raced desperately to figure out what he should do next. Heath's brow furrowed; he sat up straighter, leaned closer. Trying to read her, trying to understand.

"I'm going to be honest with you, Heath." Her voice was quiet, on the verge of inaudible. "I shouldn't be here. If my father knew . . ." The great Eric Bell. His daughter breaking rank, turning to Heath in defiance of his orders. "I know that you have enough on your plate, being here, dealing with all this." Isla waved about the room. "But the thing is, what you said, about me being in danger. I think you're right. Whoever is doing this, I think he's coming after me. There have been letters through my front door. He knows where I live. He's watching me, waiting. And my dad, he's trying, of course, but really, there's just nothing he can do. He can't protect me."

He watched her, intent. "What is it you think I can do? Stuck in here?"

It was a test, a challenge thrown down. One wrong move in either direction and she was done.

"I . . ." Isla looked down, took a deep breath. "Look, I'm going to tell you what I think is happening. I think that these killings, that they're being done by someone who was inspired by you. I think that this person, whoever he is, he looks at your fame and what a well-known figure you have become, and I think he wants to be like you." Too much? Had she overdone it? But then she saw it, that almost infinitesimal straightening of his posture, that slight elevation of his chin. *That's it.* "I don't know who else to turn to for advice. I think that he's going after people who were in some way connected with the original killings. But there doesn't seem to be any way to get out in front of him. But you, you know more about that original series than anyone else does. Maybe, with your knowledge, you could help me."

She sat, waiting, telling herself she was a victim, that only the man before her could help her. Because there, right beneath those thoughts, sat the truth, and if she allowed that in, if a micro-expression of that should cross her face, then all of this would be over. He was watching her, his eyes flitting across her face, plumbing it for information. Isla's heart beat faster still as she balanced on the edge of the knife.

Then he leaned back again, folding his arms across his chest.

Shit.

Breathe. Just breathe. She looked down into her lap, allowed the tears to build up in her eyes. There was one more piece. One more card. But if she played it . . . Isla thought of Ramsey. There was little doubt that it would be a betrayal, to have held this in so close and so long and then to finally release it here, to this man. And then, in the periphery of her vision, she saw him give a slight shake of his head, and the decision slotted into place. Because she was here, and she was so close, and she had to solve this, so that it was solved and they were all safe.

"The thing is, Heath, I'm pregnant."

His gaze snapped back to her, became laser focused. She heard the guard's quick intake of breath and his attempt to disguise it as a cough. Heath had never shown any remorse for his actions, had sat through an entire trial, listening to evidence on the murder of six people, without once reacting. And yet, her father had said, when they showed the scan photo of his unborn child, he had put his hands over his face and cried.

"Are you really?" There was something strange in his voice, sounding like hope almost, and Isla's stomach flipped again at the thought of what she had done.

"I am. I'm eight weeks along." The words felt unwieldy, as if they simply didn't belong, coming from her mouth. And yet there seemed to be a lightening, as if her spine was unfurling with the release of them. *Yes*, thought Isla. *I, Isla Bell, am eight weeks pregnant. I, Isla Bell, am going to be a mother.*

"Ah, Professor Bell . . ." The guard had ceased his dance and now stepped forward, the look on his face one of frank alarm.

Isla looked up at him and smiled. "It's okay. I don't mind Heath knowing." She wanted to telegraph a message, *I know what I'm doing*, but still Heath was watching her, always watching, so instead she looked back at him, gave a little laugh. "You know you're the first person I've told?"

Heath shifted in his chair, leaned in again, his gaze intent. "You know my girlfriend was six months pregnant?" he said quietly.

Isla felt a rush of nausea that had nothing to do with morning sickness. Had she blown it? Had she pushed too hard? Gone too far? Betrayed Ramsey for nothing?

He looked down at his close-bitten fingernails. "Sometimes I wonder why it happened. With Lucy, you know? I mean, I loved her." He stopped, considered. "At least, I think I did. I mean, she did things for me, had sex with me. But if I did—love her, that is—I wouldn't have done what I did, would I?"

Isla didn't answer, her senses drowned by the hammering of her heart.

"Maybe she was just a habit," he said. "I mean,

she was the first person, the only person, really, to treat me like a human. Maybe that's why I think that I loved her, because I kept going back for her to be good to me. She made me . . . normal, I guess. And I needed that. But I sometimes think that if I had loved her, I mean really loved her, I would have felt it in here." He tapped his fingers against his chest. "Wouldn't you think so?"

Isla chose her words carefully. "It's not uncommon for people who have your pattern of brain function to report the same thing."

Heath stopped, thought for a moment. "Answer me something, Prof. This has been bothering me for a very long time." He looked up at her. "Am I capable of love? I mean, really?"

Softly now. "I think that you are capable of forming attachments, with people that you like to be around. Whether that is the same thing as love, who can tell? It's like someone who is color blind talking about the color blue. They can act like they know what blue looks like and even think that they do know what blue looks like, but their blue may be entirely different from everyone else's. I certainly think you were attached to her. And based on the work we've done together, we know that you have some problems appreciating other people's feelings, that you struggle to control your temper. I think perhaps those things together can explain what happened with Lucy."

Heath sat, silent. Isla suddenly became aware of the unnatural heat in the room, the closeness of it. Or maybe that was just her?

Then, "Look, Prof . . . Isla. Can I call you Isla?"

She had started this. She was the one who had disturbed the dynamic of their interaction. Isla smiled. "Of course."

"Look, Isla, I'm going to be honest with you. I like you. You come here. You talk to me as if I'm an actual person. That means something, especially in this place. And"—he let out a bark of a laugh—"you took me on a road trip. I got to see the sky because of you. So, I think you're all right." He leaned closer. "I want to help you. Because this guy, if he kills you, who the hell is going to visit me, hey?"

A sense of inevitability now, of rolling toward a preordained conclusion. She had done it. She was there. Isla could feel the guard, his attention straining, a dog on a leash, because he, too, knew that what had happened here was something special, that she had broken down a twenty-year wall. Without really meaning to, she splayed her hand out flat across her belly. *It's almost over. We're almost done.*

Heath fixed his gaze on hers. "This guy. The one who's doing it. You need to find him. Because, believe me, I've seen some bad, bad men in here over the years. He ain't stopping until you stop him."

"Can you give me anything, Heath? Anything that can help me find him?" She was pleading now, but she no longer cared.

Heath sighed. "It's been twenty years, Isla. Twenty years I've lived this life. Being the killer on the wall, it gives you something in a place like this. It means they're careful about fucking with you.

You get respect . . ." He snorted. "Never thought I'd end up having a conversation like this."

It seemed to Isla that all the air had fled from the room, that time had suspended itself, that the universe had shrunk down into these four walls, this moment.

Heath reached out, took her hand in his. "Isla," he said softly, "I didn't do it. I'm not the killer on the wall."

Buried treasure – Mina

Mina stared at the computer screen, watching as the lines danced and shimmied. It would be here somewhere, a single point of light in among a sea of stars. She scrolled the mouse, rolling the screen back up to where it began, sighed, and tried to focus. *Where the hell are you?*

The pizza beside her had begun to congeal, a single sad slice of pepperoni. It had slid its way down onto the plastic plate, and then a puddle of grease had blossomed out beneath it. She should eat. She glanced at it, felt her lip tug into a grimace. *Never mind.* Mina tucked her chin into the dense wool of her roll-neck sweater and tried to ignore the acerbic whistle of the wind that had begun to creep its way around the office windows.

"Anything?" Owen leaned over from the seat beside hers, stared at the screen.

"Nothing." Mina rolled the screen down. "I'm on my fourth pass through It's not there."

Owen studied her, frowning. "You mean . . ."

"I mean Superintendent Bell never entered into evidence the photograph sent to Rachel Flowers." Mina shoved the mouse away from her, the early blossom of anger building in her.

"Well . . ." He was about to argue with her, was lining his words up to be as reasonable as he could while still informing her that she was wrong.

The anger solidified, tightening her chest.

"Perhaps the logging team just missed it." He stood up and said, "Come on. We can go through the evidence boxes."

Mina watched him and sighed. But she pushed herself up, nonetheless, the thought of Rachel Flowers, with her smooth scalp, her calm, graceful air of endurance, propelling her forward. She followed him out of the bustling room, into the corridor, down a flight of stairs and then another. The evidence room was in the basement, a corner room that seemed to contain more space than was possible. They walked the length of it, until they reached the boxes linked to the Heath McGowan series, a wall made out of memorabilia of murder. Two dozen boxes, perhaps more.

"Jesus," muttered Mina. She followed Owen to the farthest end of this wall and shook her head. "Jesus," she said again. "Okay." A deep breath. "Owen, do you want to start at that end, and I'll start at this?" She glanced at him, generating a smile that felt somewhat alien. "And . . . go."

Mina knelt on the chill floor, pulled the first box toward her. It would be here somewhere. It was the only thing that made sense. That it had been missed, had never been logged. She flipped through package after package. One box and then another and then another.

"Did Zoe find anything on the broom handle? The one from Victoria Prew's house?" asked Owen, his voice muffled by the *shush, shush, shush* of flicking paper.

Mina pulled a face. "I rang down this morning. Kind of got the feeling that they're at breaking point down there. When I asked about the broom, she yelled at me. Said it's on the list."

"Well . . . they've got a lot to process, I suppose."

The floorboards above them creaked, moaning through the basement office, and after a while the sound began to take on the tone of a lullaby, soporific and soothing. Finally, Mina reached the middle. The last box. Owen finished searching the box adjacent to hers, looked up, shook his head. Her belly flipped, the anger morphing into something else. Fear.

She eased the lid off the final box, scanned the gathering of plastic bags inside. She worked her way slowly, methodically. It would be in here. It had to be in here.

It was not.

As she ran her fingers across the bottom of the box, her gaze moved up to Owen.

"It's not here, is it?"

She shook her head. "No, it's not."

He sat there on the thin carpet for a moment, biting his lip. "So . . . what are we thinking?"

The fear growled. "Well," she said, "the way I see it, there are two options. Either he actioned it, without keeping any written evidence of having done so, investigated it, and forgot to report back to Rachel . . ."

"Okay . . . His case notes were pretty comprehensive, though. From what I've seen so far, he wrote down everything, right up to what time he took a dump."

"Agreed. Also, thanks for that mental image. And Rachel said that she tried ringing him repeatedly, only he never got back to her. Which suggests avoidance rather than forgetting."

"Which leaves us with . . ."

"Which leaves us with option B. That he buried it."

Owen whistled. "That's a big accusation."

"What, bigger than 'We think you did a shit investigation, so we're going to reinvestigate behind your back'?"

He grinned. "Okay, maybe it's not that big. So, come on, explain your reasoning. Why would Superintendent Bell bury this?"

"Look . . ." Mina suddenly became aware that they were whispering. "This case, it made him. The media coverage, the reputation. All of it came from the fact that he pretty much single-handedly investigated and solved the killer on the wall murders. I mean, think about it. If you wanted a case, a *big* case, that got tied up in a pretty pink bow, this would be that case. The evidence was inescapable. The conclusions unavoidable."

"But . . ."

"But then, a year after Heath's conviction, a letter arrives at the house of a victim's widow, containing a photograph of the victim's body. I mean, that, it muddies the waters, don't you think? Your nice clean case is suddenly a lot messier. And . . ." Mina rocked back on her heels, warming to her subject. "What makes it worse, I don't see how one can avoid the conclusion that Heath McGowan had help. No matter which way you slice it, someone else was involved. Someone that the great Eric Bell never caught." She shook her head. "I can see plenty of motive for making this letter disappear."

Owen watched her carefully and then, finally, nodded slowly. "It's a big accusation." No judgment, merely a statement of fact.

"Yes," agreed Mina.

They tucked the boxes away in silence, both of them soaking in the implications. Then Owen stood and looked down at her. "What are we going to do with this?"

Mina pushed herself to her feet and shook her head. "I . . . I just don't know."

They walked slowly up one flight of stairs, two.

"Look," said Mina, "if you want to back off a bit, I'll understand. This . . . it was my idea. You shouldn't have to deal with this."

Owen walked beside her, his shoulders up high, hands tucked into his trouser pockets. "Ah well. I'm in it now." He grinned briefly. "Let's just say you owe me a pint when all this is done."

Mina felt a brief flutter in her insides.

Then there came the sound of heavy footsteps down the corridor. Superintendent Eric Bell walked slowly toward them. He looked weary, his face ashen, and it was long moments before he raised his head and noticed them standing there.

"Well?" he said, voice ragged. "Inside, if you don't mind."

He looked, Mina thought, like he was about to cry. The future pulled itself into sharp focus. Another body. Another death. She moved through the door without realizing what she was doing.

The super followed her in, gestured her to the conference table. "Everyone." His voice came out as a thin approximation of itself, and he coughed, tried it again. "Ladies and gentlemen, your attention, please." The susurration of voices stopped as heads turned to him. "Can I have you all gathered around the conference table? Quick as you can."

The scrape of chairs, the floor shifting under the weight of moving feet, and then they were all sitting, waiting for what now seemed inevitable. Mina took a seat beside Owen, shared a quick frown with him before turning her attention back to Eric Bell. He had elected to remain standing, was bouncing on the balls of his feet with nerves or simply excess energy. His gaze swiveled around the crowd. His eyes pausing briefly on Mina, he gave a quick nod.

"Right. I know you've been working hard. I know these conditions"—he waved about the ungainly room—"are not ideal. Now, to keep you informed . . . there has been a development."

Who would it be this time? Someone she knew? Someone she passed in the street every day?

"Following on from the murder of Maggie Heron, I ordered that any forensic evidence found in the original murder series be resubmitted for examination."

Mina watched him. *He? He had ordered?*

"Twenty years ago there was nothing that could be done with what we had, but given the developments in DNA testing, I thought it was worth a shot now."

Mina folded her arms, a bubble of irritation forming.

"We are still waiting for most of it, but they have finished looking at the fingernail clippings that were taken from the original victims. The new tests have revealed DNA underneath the fingernails of both Zachary Aiken and Amelia West."

A low murmur filled the room.

"The lab has been able to establish a DNA profile."

The murmur became a rumble.

"Just a second, please, people. You need to hear this." The super looked down, appeared to be steadying himself, then up again. "The lab has determined beyond all reasonable doubt that the DNA found under the fingernails of Zachary Aiken and Amelia West does not match that of Heath McGowan—"

"Wait," interrupted Owen. "So, what does that mean?"

Mina spoke softly. "It means that Heath McGowan wasn't the one who killed them."

And so it goes – Ramsey

Ramsey walked the university corridors, a careful, measured pace, heel, toe, heel, toe. He walked calmly, because then he was merely walking, not pacing. That the route he had chosen took him along Isla's corridor and past her locked door, well, that was merely a happy coincidence. Ramsey's head swam. He had spent the day interviewing students, trying to get the perspective of those who had not been around for the original murders, for whom it was a story, nothing more. These new killings, did they change things at the university? Or did the students remain within that permanent bubble?

"Thing is," a boy, maybe eighteen, maybe a little older, had said, "we're okay here. It's only Briganton, isn't it? And I mean, I'm not worried for me. Although maybe if I was a girl, I'd be a little more concerned."

"Are you taking precautions?" Ramsey had asked. "Walking in pairs, avoiding isolated spots, that kind of thing?"

The kid had laughed. "Nah, mate." Then, sensing that perhaps he had crossed some kind of line, he had assumed a thoughtful expression. "We're watching out for the girls, though. You know, walking them home, that kind of thing."

Ramsey had nodded and scribbled in his cryptic shorthand, and had wondered what it must be like to be young and bulletproof.

Then, after an interview or twelve, he had set himself up in the library. The librarian, recognizing him, taking pity on Professor Bell's abandoned husband, had installed him at a desk, pointed out the power outlet for his laptop, left him to it. He'd finished the article—"Inside a Village under Siege"— had sent it to the editor of the *Journal*. Then he had walked slowly through the university grounds, back down Isla's corridor, back past her closed door.

Now he moved on toward Connor's office, where a layer of light seeped out from beneath the door. He gave two sharp taps and let himself in without waiting for acknowledgment.

At first, Ramsey could not identify what he was seeing. Then his eyes adjusted to the dim lamplight, and his brain sorted through the chaos of papers and debris to pick out Connor, sitting on the floor, knees pulled up to his chest, back resting against the desk.

"Connor? What the hell are you doing?"

In his hand, the other man held a sheaf of papers. He looked up at Ramsey, waved it at him. "Join me. I'm journeying to hell." His voice was rasping, as if he had just been awoken from a deep sleep; his expression, flat.

"Well, with an offer like that . . ." Ramsey closed the door behind him and picked his way through the detritus. "What is that?" He took the proffered papers and flicked through them.

dear conor Im fucking coming for u don't sleep coz then u wont see me your going to die.

"That's . . . charming."

"You want more? I've got tons," Connor said flatly. "Gummy bear?"

Ramsey frowned, shook his head. "No, thanks. Why are you going through these?"

"I don't know." Connor carefully placed a gummy bear in his mouth, rolled it around. "I just thought . . . maybe whoever's sending the threats to your house . . . I thought maybe something I had might link up with it. Give us some connection."

"Anything hopeful?"

Connor snorted. "Not unless you call threatening to cut my penis off and feed it to me anything hopeful."

Ramsey lifted a pile of papers from a chair and sat down. "Christ. And I complain about having to write about county fairs for the thousandth time."

"Yeah, well"—Connor's voice was thick with the candy—"let me tell you, this is no county fair."

Ramsey looked down at his hands. "You heard from Isla?" There was probably a subtler way he could have eased the conversation around to its real point, but he was tired and his patience was limited.

Connor studied him from beneath a chaotic crown of hair. "No. I'm assuming she's still out at the prison. Did you call her? Maybe she's stuck in traffic?"

"Phone's off."

"Well, she'd have had to leave the phone in a locker. Probably she's forgotten to turn it back on." Connor glanced at the clock on the back wall, which had, predictably, run out of batteries, then down at his watch. He frowned briefly. "She'll be back soon." He glanced about the room, striving for a subject change. "Want to go for a pint?"

"Nah. Not really in the mood." It was a lie. A pint sounded like an extremely good idea. And yet Ramsey didn't want to leave the building or the hallway. He was, he reflected, like a Labrador retriever that sat inside the front door and waited for its master to return from work, afraid to leave in case somehow it missed the moment of reunion.

"So, what's your father-in-law saying? About the murders, I mean. They must have some idea by now, right?" Connor leaned his head back against the desk.

"Not that I know of," said Ramsey. "Then, Eric isn't the most communicative of men. But far as I know, they're still bumbling around in the dark."

Connor nodded slowly. "It's mad. That someone can do this again and again and get away with it. I mean, you guys, you've lived it for all this time. I remember Briganton before this happened. You know my aunt and cousins used to live here? They moved after . . . what happened. I used to visit them when I was a teenager. And this place, it was . . . well, I don't want to say dull, but . . ."

Ramsey grinned. "But dull."

"Yeah. Dull. Then the killings started. My aunt, she just couldn't bear to be here anymore, said that all the things, they just changed how she felt about the village. I mean, I know things like this, they happen, but you just don't expect them here, in a place like this." Connor sat for a moment, silent. "Whoever this is, I bet you anything he's basking in what he's done to this place. How he's made people afraid."

Ramsey rubbed his hands through his hair. "Do you think . . . I mean, maybe he'll stop. Maybe he'll get tired of all of this. There's a lot of pressure on him now. A lot of people watching. You think he might decide that he doesn't need to do this anymore?"

Connor ran his index finger across a letter that sat in his lap, tracing an unknown shape. "I wish I could say yes, Rams. I really do. But, these guys . . . It's rare that they stop. They may manage to control it for a while—months, years, even. But once they've got a taste for it, that doesn't tend to change." He picked the papers up, shuffled them into a perfect pile. "It's not uncommon, when you have a serial killer, to see things go quiet, for law enforcement to think, *Oh, great. It's over.* Honestly, though, it's hardly ever about that. More likely, whoever did it was picked up, arrested on some other charge. Maybe they died. Or maybe they moved on, went somewhere else. But wherever they go, they're always the same. And as long as they are alive and free, the killings just keep coming. So often they crave the fear, that sense of terror that their crimes mean for everyone else."

Ramsey sat up a little straighter in the chair, heart beating faster, an idea forming. "I . . ." *No. Yes.* "Connor, how do we know that this is where the recent spate of killings began?"

"What are you saying?"

"I'm saying, What if this isn't the beginning of a chain, but a continuation?"

Connor stared at him—or not at him, but through him—his face dark with calculations. "It . . . no . . . Well, I don't know. You'd need the police records . . ."

"I'll call Eric." Ramsey stood up, could feel his head swimming. He slipped out the door into the empty corridor, pulled his phone from his pocket, and dialed quickly. Eric answered on the first ring.

"Ramsey. What's wrong? Where's Isla?"

"She's . . ." *Don't say, 'At the prison.' Don't say, 'At the prison.'* "She's fine. She's at work."

He could hear his father-in-law sigh. "Okay, right. So? What is it? Called to tell me you've brought her to her senses?"

And he was back to pacing again, a dozen steps this way, a dozen steps that. "I was just talking to Connor. You know, works with Isla?"

"Right?"

"And, look, we were just thinking, Eric, what if the murders didn't begin here? How do we know that the killer hasn't been working elsewhere, that he's just arrived?"

The wind screeched.

"Well . . . ," began Eric.

But no, it wasn't the wind, was it? It was something else.

"Jesus, Eric, someone's screaming."

Ramsey took off at a run; Connor's door flew open as he reached it; Connor took off for the exit doors ahead of him. Far away he could hear his father-in-law's voice, now all but forgotten, the phone hanging uselessly in his hands as Ramsey raced after Connor's rapidly disappearing figure, through the doors, out into the bleak black night. The wind whipped around them, tearing at their clothes; a puddle of orange light extended meters beyond the university and vanished into a pool of blackness.

Connor was spinning rapidly in a circle, shouting, "Where was it? Where did it come from?"

Then movement, a shifting of the blackness, and in the wind, a kind of moaning—and they were off running again, picking their way through undergrowth and over rain-laden grass to a figure slumped on the ground. Ramsey dimly made out long hair, a slender figure. Then a movement, the scene changed again, and the slender figure with the long hair was pulling backward and away, was pushing up to stand, grabbing hold of Connor's hands. It seemed that she would collapse without his body holding her up. He knew her, Ramsey realized with a start, had seen her before, earlier that day, when she had come to hand her homework in.

Her words were indistinct and hard to follow, littered as they were with sobs. "I found him," Scarlett said. "He's dead."

Ramsey stepped closer.

In the darkness, what was hidden in shadows became clear. The body of a young man propped against the trunk of a tree, his head lolling forward, his hands folded in his lap.

"Jesus," said Connor. "Parker."

First the one – Mina

Mina pulled up alongside a marked police car, its driver's door hanging open. The university was a sea of lights, the blackness of the countryside punctured by red and blue. *Here we go again.* She breathed in deeply, could just about make out a small crowd gathered behind the cordon, and Ramsey, his head in his hands. Mina squinted, trying to find the shape of Isla among the figures, but the rest were mere silhouettes. She sat for just a second, trying to calm herself, to find a center ground in which there was not a dead body sitting, in which all that they had known for twenty years had not just been proven a lie.

Mina climbed out hurriedly and pushed the car door closed harder than she had intended, the slam of it startling her, and saw Ramsey look around, his attention drawn by the sound. Mina raised her hand in a grim variant of a wave, moving straight toward the tree and the lights and the latest in a line of deaths.

The boy remained where he had been found, sitting half sunken in the rain-sodden grass, his back resting against the aged trunk of an oak tree. He looked breathtakingly young, boy-band hair flopping forward so that it covered his eyes. No color remained in his face, skin the gray of day-old snow. A circlet of fingermarks ringed his neck. He was, what, eighteen? Nineteen at the most?

Mina stood and stared at him and suddenly, for perhaps the first time, felt old.

"Mina. Hi." A uniformed officer, who looked little older than the dead boy before him, appeared at her elbow, his face grim. "Parker MacDonald. He was nineteen years old. He was last seen by his friends at lunchtime today. Failed to turn up to a seminar at four. Scarlett Lee"—he indicated the cordon line, where a narrow, weeping girl stood folded in on herself—"she found him about thirty minutes ago."

Mina nodded, because what was there to say? They were all becoming uncomfortably proficient at this game. She stepped aside to allow room for the inevitable flow of forensics in their white suits, passing through the inner cordon, approaching the dead boy. It seemed to her that she had exhausted her reservoir of responses and was now simply running through the motions. *Another corpse? Ah well.* The PC at the cordon lifted the police tape up, allowing her to pass beneath.

"Ramsey?" she called.

He looked pale, had little more color to him than the dead boy. "I can't believe this," he muttered quietly.

There was the sound of weeping off to Mina's left. The slip of a girl, her head in her hands, was weeping with so much force that Mina found herself wondering if it was genuine or perhaps part of a show. A maneuver to bring herself closer to the heart of the action? She shook herself slightly. When had she become this cynical? An uncomfortable-looking man stood beside the girl, every now and again patting her arm in the thinnest version of sympathy.

Ramsey followed her gaze. "That's Connor. Isla's colleague."

"Where is Isla?"

His eyes darted away, then settled back on her. He gave a sigh and a half smile. "I'm not sure, to be honest. She was out at the prison, but I had expected her back by now."

Cold prickles raced along Mina's spine as a new scenario played itself out for her. It did not, however, have long to solidify, for moments later, there came the roar of an engine, the screeching of tires, and a car door slamming. Mina did not have to look to identify the running footsteps as those of Ramsey's wife.

"What's going on?" Isla's hair flew out behind her, disorganized and wild. She grabbed Ramsey's arm as if to stabilize herself. "Mina, what are you—"

Then, unwilling to wait for answers to be handed to her, Isla peered around, squinted toward the body of Parker MacDonald. "Oh my God. That's Parker." Isla's hand flew to her mouth as tears sprang to her eyes.

"You know him?" asked Mina.

"He's . . ." Isla breathed deeply, sliding her hand into her husband's and leaning into him. "He's in my tutorial group. Is it . . ." There was no need to finish the sentence. Or even to begin it.

"Yes," said Mina. "Yes, it's the same."

Isla's head dipped, and she squeezed her husband's hand tighter as he rested his head on hers. "Oh God."

Precisely.

Mina opened her mouth, searching for something to say. But all she could see was that dead boy, the fingermarks on his throat, the inexorable knowledge that for all her digging, for everything they had done, the sum total of what they knew was less now than when this had all begun.

They knew that it was not Heath, that it had never been Heath.

And they knew that whoever this was, he was not done.

Then, from her pocket, came the merciful ringing of her mobile phone, and Mina's stomach flipped. Wondering just what was coming next, she said, "Just a second," turned her back on Isla and Ramsey, and moved farther into the parking lot. "Hello?"

"Mina, hey, sorry. I know you're at the scene," Owen said. "Only, she's rung four times, and she really wants to speak to you. Thing is, I don't really get what she's on about. Something about a letter and a nephew . . ."

"Wait, stop. Who's ringing you?"

"Rachel Flowers. No, Rachel . . . Gilbert. Said she's had some letter . . ."

Mina watched the forensic team begin to set up as the crowd that surrounded the dead body of Parker MacDonald grew. Where were they all coming from? How did they know?

"Fine," said Mina. "Patch her through." There was a click and then a muffled sound on the line. Was it crying? "Rachel? Rachel, are you okay?"

"Mina, it's my nephew." Her words were like a spear through a gazelle.

"Your nephew?" Mina's insides sank. "I'm sorry . . ." She looked back at the boy on the ground. "Do you mean Parker?"

A silence. "What? No. My nephew's name is Jake. You met him. Remember?"

A flash of a handsome young man hoisting a little boy up on his hip, a wide grin.

"Yes. Sorry . . . I . . ."

"Mina, I can't find him. He never came home last night. And when I went to the door just now, there was an envelope. It was addressed to me."

It was the day before, and they were discussing her husband. It was now, and they were discussing her nephew. Sometimes the conclusions are inevitable.

"There was a picture inside." Rachel's voice was rising now, flecks of panic tinging it. "I think he's dead."

Mina couldn't breathe. She couldn't breathe. "Rachel, I'm on my way."

She did not say goodbye to Isla or to Ramsey. In truth, Mina had forgotten their existence. All that mattered was to get into the car, was to drive, drive, drive, as if she could drive fast enough to outrun this nightmare that was chasing them.

Thinking more than once that this could be how her life would end, Mina weaved through narrow country lanes, the car feeling light on the wet surface. And yet, in spite of that, it did not, and after minutes or hours, she arrived at Rachel Gilbert's door, her nerves in shreds, but other than that, mostly in one piece. Rachel was waiting for her as Mina opened the garden gate, was standing in the brightly lit hallway, in a pair of leggings, an oversize jumper, her scalp smooth.

"Mina," Rachel said shortly. "Here it is."

She thrust the plastic bag into Mina's hands before she had even stepped across the threshold or had time to register the sound of water running, the childish shrieks that came from up above them. Mina glanced up, disconcerted suddenly.

"My husband is bathing the children. I don't want them around for this."

"Yes," Mina breathed. "Of course." Rachel Flowers—Gilbert—had not moved from the hallway, with its wooden floor and its art deco lamp on a dense oak dresser. She folded her arms across her chest. In the light, it was clear that she had been crying. But in spite of that, her chin was up.

"I put it in a plastic bag," Rachel said. "To protect any evidence."

"Right. Yes. Good idea." Mina's vision was swimming. She frowned, attempting to bring the photograph into focus through its clear plastic cover.

Green, an endless stretch of it. The suggestion of the arc of a hill. The figure of a young man seated in among the green. "When did you see him last, Rachel?"

"Last night. He went out to meet some friends, and I haven't seen him since. But he's not a child. And I wasn't worried . . . and then . . ." Her voice cracked, broke. "Is he dead?"

Mina didn't look at her, looked instead at the photograph, and the position of the head and the position of the hands, and that faint mark around the lad's neck.

"I . . ." It was a roller coaster, another dip down into a precipice. "Look, Rachel, I'll get some teams out looking for him. If he's injured, we need to get to him as quickly as we can." But she was lying, and she knew that she was lying. "Just give me a second." Mina dug her phone from her pocket and stepped back into the chill wind, the promise of rain. Dialed quickly, walking with calm, measured steps down the path, away from the house. One ring, two rings, three rings. *Answer the bloody phone.*

"Owen Darby." He sounded flustered, breathless.

"It's me. I need a search team." She hadn't slipped the latch back on the garden gate, and the wind had taken it, was banging it again and again against its frame.

"Okay . . . yeah, they're already en route . . . Ah, they should be getting to the university any minute now."

The wind snatched at her face, forcing tears into her eyes. "No, Owen. Not to the university."

"What?"

Mina glanced back at the house, where Rachel stood in the doorway, watching her. She turned her back on her, dropped her voice. "I think we have another one."

A long silence and then, "Oh my God." There was a sound that made Mina wonder if he was crying. "Where? Where is it?"

"I . . ." Mina squinted down at the photograph, the formless shapes in the bleak light. She moved closer to the house, holding the photograph up to her face. "I think it's Vindolanda. The hill just beyond it. Tell them to start there."

"I'll get a team out as fast as I can." Owen didn't even bother saying goodbye.

Mina stood on the path, watching the gate slam open and shut, open and shut, thinking of the dead and those who killed them. Then she sighed in lieu of crying and turned back toward the house.

Rachel's face had slid into flat resignation. "So . . ."

"A team will go out looking."

"He's dead, isn't he?"

Mina opened her mouth, intending to lie to her. But something in Rachel's gaze stopped her in her tracks. "Yes, Rachel. Yes, I think he probably is."

Rachel began to cry then, fat tears rolling down her smooth cheeks. And yet not once breaking her gaze from Mina's.

"You know it's his fault, right? Eric Bell. You know that this has happened because of what he said," she accused.

Mina shifted. *Whoever is responsible for these killings is targeting females.*

"This guy, whoever's doing this, he's trying to prove Bell wrong, isn't he?" said Rachel, brushing her palms roughly across her cheeks. She waved her hand. "You can't say, I understand that. But the thing is, I know Bell of old. If he had listened back when I got that photograph . . . maybe this wouldn't be happening now. But he didn't care then, and he doesn't care now." She folded her arms tight across her chest, keeping her gaze on Mina. "My nephew is dead, Mina, and it's Eric Bell's fault."

The shadow within –
Isla

It was a waking nightmare, one filled with the yowling wind, the laden skies, the swirl of blue lights, and the body of a boy sitting propped against a tree.

I'm not the killer on the wall.

For Isla, it seemed that the whole world had turned into a repugnant farce. That death could follow death, one after another after another, mocking her belief that she had ever known enough to solve this unanswerable riddle. As she'd stood at the police cordon, her husband's arm tight around her, the sobbing of Scarlett a sound track to an unending movie, it had suddenly become clear just how naive she had been. Twenty years. Twenty years of chasing monsters, of fighting to understand the worst of the worst, and yet she knew nothing. She was a child playing doctor, telling herself that she had the tools to keep the world around her safe, if only she could look at it from the right direction, turn the prism in just the right way so that the light split just so. She had stood at the police cordon, watching as the forensic team swarmed across Parker's body like locusts, and there it had become clear. She knew nothing at all.

I'm not the killer on the wall.

How long had they stood there? Here, now, in the soft warmth of her own bedroom, it was no longer clear. It had been long enough for the tent to be erected, long enough for her father to appear, walking the scene with his stiff back, his immovable face, commanding his forces, doing something real, something that mattered. It had been long enough for her fingers to turn stiff with the cold, for her cheeks to begin to burn, and her back to ache.

Now the bed cradled her, coaxed her: *Lie down. It's okay. I will make everything better if you simply lie down and sleep.* But Isla sat on the edge of it, still wrapped in the denseness of her bathrobe, and stared at her reflection in the dark window. With her wet hair, her face free of make-up, she had aged, had skated through a decade in the past day. She put her hand to her belly, or rather to the thick fabric that lay across it, and imagined that she could hear the heartbeat of the child within. Had she done this before? Probably not. Because, in truth, the four weeks that had followed that strangely empty day—when she had run back and forth to the toilet a myriad of times, waiting and waiting and thinking, *This time, this time it will be there*, and yet each time had come away balanced on a knife edge, fear on one side, elation the other— And for days after, the same. The waiting, telling herself that she was busy, she was under stress, that this would account for it. Knowing she could simply take a test and then she'd know, but not taking that test, because she was simply too frightened to see the results. The nausea gripping her—not in the morning, so where did that term come from?—but all day, every day, a relentless delirium that made the world uneven and jagged edged.

It was another three weeks before she finally took a test. In the bathroom at work. She had sat on the toilet, cradling the white stick in her hands, had stared at it and stared at it, as if staring could change the answer one way or another. Then, emerging from the mists, had come the single word. *Pregnant.*

From downstairs now came the sound of pans bumping hard against the counter, a cupboard door opening, closing, the beep of a timer. "You need to eat," Ramsey had said. "You look done in. I'll cook. You go and take a shower."

Isla stared at her reflection in the window.

I'm not the killer on the wall.

Heath had delivered the words to her softly, the way one might pass on news of a death. Had kept his eyes trained on her, trying to read her reaction. The guard at the door had turned toward them, all pretense gone now.

What? He was lying. There was no other explanation. Isla had recoiled. He was a psychopath.

They lied. That was what they did. They lied to get their own way. They lied to get out of trouble. They lied simply because it amused them to do so. Heath McGowan was lying. There was no other way to see it.

"You see," he'd said, his voice dropping low and becoming urgent, "I had issues back then. Lots of issues, drugs and such. I needed money. Now, that Kitty, I'd seen her in the post office, collecting her pension money. And I figured that it wouldn't be hard, go in there late one night, while she was asleep, and away we go, enough money to see me through a couple of days, have a bit of fun with. I was going to break in through the back door. I could get there over my grandmother's back wall. We were only a couple of houses down. No one would see me. I'd be in and out. But the thing is, when I got there, the house was empty, and the back door wide open. I must have touched it. I don't remember. I know I'd been drinking, so it wouldn't really surprise me. But the handbag, it was lying right there. So I took the money, went through the house, just having a scout around, found some other bits and pieces, and then I left."

Her face must have shown her blatant disbelief, because he reared back, raised one eyebrow. "See," he said, "I knew you wouldn't believe me."

"Frankly, Heath, I don't. It makes no sense to me that you would have taken the rap for something of this magnitude when all you had done was steal some money and some jewelry. Why let the world believe this for twenty years?"

He looked at her, and Isla felt a growing, shifting discomfort, like one who was being eyed up by a wolf. "But," he said, "that wasn't all I did. Was it?"

Then she remembered the small, curled-up figure of Lucy Tuckwell. He saw it, the realization in her, nodded slowly.

"You see, the shit hit the fan the next day. The old woman, that Flowers bloke"—he nodded at her—"your husband, and his brother, they were all found out by the wall, and I thought, *Well, shit, they're going to be looking at me.* So you know what I did?"

"What?"

"I went out, and I got high. I'm telling you, you got a problem you want to stop worrying about, it's the only way. I got high, and I pretty much stayed high for the next six weeks. Long enough for the two women to be murdered. And, to be honest, I wasn't worried. I was high. But then my grandmother started acting weird around me, started asking why I'd been asking her about Kitty back before it happened, and I started to think . . . I'd been in the house. If I'd made a mistake, if I'd left prints . . . So I packed up, went out to Lucy's." Heath looked down at his fingers, folded tight together. "Thing is, what you've got to know is, I never wanted things to go the way they went. But then, when I got there . . . she could see that I was high. That was how it started. She was angry with me, had been begging me to quit ever since she found out she was pregnant. And, I mean, all I wanted to do was go to sleep. But she kept on at me and on at me. And then she said it."

"Said what?"

"That I was no better than my own father." He shook his head. "So, I killed her."

There was no air left in the room.

"Afterward, when it was done . . . I sat there with her for a long time. I just sat with my hand on her big belly. I think I was waiting for the baby, for my baby, to move. See, I don't think I really got it, that she was gone, that the baby was gone too. But, eventually, I started to sober up, started to think cleaner. And then I realized what I'd done." He leaned in closer to Isla. "I didn't mean it. It was just . . . she made me so angry. And she shouldn't have said that. But I didn't want to hurt her. I didn't want to hurt my baby."

"What then?"

He shrugged. "What do you think? I found some money in her purse, and I went and scored with it. When they came for me, when your father came for me, I thought they were there about Lucy. Still away with the fairies, see. It was only later, when they were questioning me, that I got it. And"—he shrugged—"I don't know. I just, I never said it. I never said anything."

"Right," said Isla, "so it never occurred to you to say, 'I'm not the killer on the wall'?"

Heath looked down at his hands, frowning under the weight of the introspection. Finally, "The thing is . . . I . . . I think I almost wanted to be."

"What?"

"I mean, this guy, he's a predator, right? He's like a lion, hunting for food. He's looking for prey to fill this need. And that, I get that. He's doing these things, but he's doing them for a reason. But what happened with Lucy, well, there wasn't really

a reason for that, only I got angry. It felt better if
people believed that I was him. That I killed people because I had to. And . . ." He looked up then,
gave a grin that chilled Isla. "You get a lot of fan
mail when you're the killer on the wall. Lot of people want to talk to you. You get put on magazines,
on newspapers. You get respect." He jerked his
chin toward the door. "Respect is important in
here. The guys out there, they don't fuck with me.
Because they know what I'm capable of. What I've
done."

"So . . . why tell me now?"

Heath shrugged. "I like you."

"Okay, so what about the evidence, the items
they found on you from the other victims?"

At that, Heath merely looked up at her, gave her
a slow, creeping smile, which hung in empty air for
endless moments. Then he shook his head and
said, "I'm tired. I think I'm done for today. But it
was good to talk to you. Isla."

The rain had begun again, the roar of it cutting
through the wind. It bounced off the window,
making Isla's reflection shimmer, and she shivered, suddenly chilled. The day clung to her skin,
even after the shower, as if she could not wash it
off. She stared at her reflection and thought, *He
was lying. He is a psychopath. That is what they do.
There is no other explanation for this. I attempted to play
him, and instead I got played. He's lying.*

Isla pulled her gaze away from her own reflection and looked across to the corner of the room
where the thickly cushioned armchair and the coffee table stood. The box file was there, where she
had left it. She stood slowly, carefully, as if she were

on the deck of a bucking boat, and walked with bare feet over to the armchair. She sat carefully, tucking the dressing gown in around her, pulled the file toward her.

She had brought the fMRI results home, had thought that perhaps in a different environment, in a different frame of mind, she would find something there that she had missed before. Now she flipped the file open and pulled out the sheaf of glossy paper, studied the top image. The brain of a psychopath, with dark where there should be light, light where there should be dark. And beneath it another and another and another. *Heath McGowan is a psychopath. His brain functions differently from mine. He is lying to me. He is lying to me simply because he can. Because I made myself vulnerable and I allowed him to. That is all that is happening here.* She gazed at the colors, letting the shape soothe her. *It's a lie. That is all.*

Then in the rain and the wind came footsteps on the stairs. Isla rested the brain scan pictures on her lap and set her hand back against her belly, felt her breath quicken. It was time. It had been time for ever so long. And so she was waiting when Ramsey entered the room, his mouth open to tell her dinner was ready. She was sitting with her hand upon her belly, and the words thick on her tongue.

"Isl—"

"I'm pregnant."

Her husband stood in the doorway of their bedroom, and it seemed that he swayed. But it could simply have been the nausea, the spinning wrongness of the day. He opened his mouth, closed it again, took a step forward, one back.

"I . . . what?"

Isla smiled in spite of herself. "I'm pregnant." The shape of the words felt strange in her mouth, and beneath them lay those old familiar jagged edges of fear. But it was too late for that now. Time and life were marching on, and she would have to hurry to catch up.

"You're . . . oh my God. Oh my God." Ramsey seemed to have forgotten himself. Seemed confused about whether to go or stay or stand or sit. "Are you sure?"

Isla nodded, took a breath. "I . . . I've known for a while. I should have told you. I know that. But I was . . ." *What?* "I was trying to get it straight in my own head before I could say it. I'm sorry. I should have told you."

But Ramsey was already at her side, waving away the words. "It doesn't matter. I don't care. This . . . it's what I've always wanted. To be a real family. To be normal. We . . ." His face crumpled and then straightened out again, and he smiled, a smile that seemed to encompass the entire world. He pulled her into him, the brain scan images fluttering to the floor like so much confetti, and allowed her cheek to rest above his heart, and she could hear the thud of it, like the drum of a marching band. "Everything is going to be okay. Everything is going to be just fine now."

Isla breathed her husband in, could smell the garlic that clung to him, the cologne that always reminded her of their trip to Paris, the essential himness that lay beneath it all. And, for just a moment, she managed to push away Heath McGowan and his slow, deliberate smile and the body of the boy beneath the oak tree and was able to just be. They sat there for a lifetime. And then, finally, Ramsey drew back, stroking one hand along her cheek.

"Come on. You need to keep your strength up. Dinner!"

Isla smiled. "Yes." She was suddenly hungry for the first time in days.

But around her feet there lay a puddle of brain scan images. "Let me just get these." Isla crouched down, gathered the images together. The psychopaths, the controls . . . she was beginning to stack them together when one caught her eye. A psychopathy brain image had fallen farther than the others and become mixed together with the control group. Isla frowned, looking at the identity tag. There should only have been . . .

"What's wrong?"

"No . . . I'm confused. I must have miscounted the psychopath scans. I . . . I don't know where this one has come from."

"Baby brain." Ramsey grinned. "Is it labeled?"

"It . . . it has a number, but according to the number, this is a control-group scan." Isla's insides had begun to shimmy, whether from hunger or a sudden burst of fear, she couldn't tell. "I haven't had a chance to go through them yet. I don't . . . Wait, I have a table. Let me just . . ." From the bottom of the box file, she pulled out a sheet and cross-referenced the number with the scan identifier. But her hands had begun to tremble, and now nothing made sense.

"Whose is it?"

Isla checked the number, holding the scan up next to the name. Was aware that she had begun to feel faint.

"Isla?"

Isla sank back into the chair, the scan held tight in her fingers. "It's my father's."

Where the evidence leads – Mina

The tension in the room had become palpable. All conversations had ground to a stultifying halt. Two more dead. Two young men with their lives ahead of them. Chief Superintendent Clee had delivered the briefing, Superintendent Eric Bell standing to one side, his head down, gaze fixed firmly on his feet. The chief super had looked close to tears, whether from exhaustion or merely the overwhelming nature of what they were investigating. "There are search teams out at Vindolanda, attempting to find the body, but based on photographic evidence, it seems inevitable that the boy is dead. I'll update you when I can." Then he had spun on his heel with a hard look at Eric Bell, who followed behind him, the two of them marching from the room.

There had been little conversation in his wake, just a stunned sense of the world spinning out of control. Mina had pushed herself to her feet, the scrape of her chair dragging all eyes to her. "I just . . . I have to move," she had said lamely.

How could she explain that she seemed to be crawling out of her skin? Drowning in the notion that it still was not over, that perhaps it would never be over. Mina walked slowly to the office window, watched wild rain lash against the footpath below, turning its grassy sides into bog.

How long had he waited? How long had he watched? Was this why he was now in a frenzy, attempting to kill as many as he could before he was stopped again?

"You okay?"

Entirely absorbed, she had not heard Owen come up behind her. She had been thinking about Rachel being bludgeoned once again by this monster, who seemed determined to destroy any sense of safety that she had built. And the fear that had begun to swell up with the announcement of the DNA results, and had grown and grown with each subsequent death, began to give way to anger. *Fuck this man.*

"Yeah," she said quietly, aware that her voice was all but gone in the thunder of the relentless rain on the window. "You think people like this . . . I mean, what do you suppose happened to him in those twenty years?"

"You mean, assuming that this is the same guy."

"Assuming that, yes. I mean, how does it work?

Do they go cold turkey for twenty years and then just, I don't know, snap?"

Owen had positioned himself beside her, looking out into the rain. "I don't know. Maybe."

"Or . . ."

"Or what?"

Mina looked at him, the cold of the window harsh against her cheek. "Or maybe he never did stop?" She spun on her heel and walked quickly to her computer terminal. Twenty years. Twenty years was an awfully long time to stop killing. If he was driven by it, if he needed it—as presumably he did, given the past few days—how had he survived that long without satiating that need?

She sat there for hours, which felt more like weeks. She was dimly aware of Owen every now and again looking at her, his mouth opening as if he would speak, and yet each time thinking better of it. The lines of text had become blurry, and Mina's shoulders had begun to ache, and her mouth felt thick with cotton wool. There was an emptiness in the pit of her stomach that had little to do with hunger, but on and on she moved, from Briganton to Sheffield, to Edinburgh, to London and beyond.

At one point, perhaps about midnight, she became aware of the office door swinging open, of a breeze that tugged at the notepad on which she wrote, of a flurry of coats and heavy footsteps. The distant recognition of a name she knew—Toby Benedict.

Mina looked up. "What was that?"

Cain had the look of a drowned rat. He pulled off

his raincoat—ineffective, from what Mina could see—wincing at the shucking sound it made, and eased it onto the back of a chair, where it proceeded to drip puddles on to the floor. "I went to interview Toby Benedict, Ben Flowers's friend. Chief Super Clee is keen for us to look for any threads left hanging in the original investigation."

"And?"

Cain shrugged. "Same as before, really. He was drunk. He left Ben not far from the pub, and they went their separate ways. Although," he said and sank into the chair, wincing as his wet trousers pressed into his skin, "he did say that he remembers seeing some guy earlier in the evening, when they were on their way to the pub. Says he was across the street from them, that he didn't really get much of a look at him and thought of it only years later, once McGowan was already on the inside. Says he remembers that he thought he was watching Ben. They had a bit of a laugh about it, apparently."

"Okay," said Mina. "So no description . . ."

Cain pulled a face. "Average height, average build."

"Excellent," grunted Mina.

"He did say he saw the guy walk away. That he thought he was limping."

Mina turned her chair around to face him.

"I tracked down some of the other friends from that night. No one else saw him. No one else remembers anything other than what they've already said." Cain leaned back in the chair and closed his eyes. "Bloody hell."

"Are you okay?" asked Mina, suddenly aware that Zachary Aiken had had more than one brother. That it wasn't just Ramsey who had suffered in this.

Cain made a noise, a cross between a laugh and a sob. "Aye. Just keeping on keeping on."

Mina felt a weight settle on her, of an inevitable reckoning coming, then shook her head, turning back to the monitor. That was not the problem of this moment.

It was 1:30 a.m. by the time she finished. Her eyes were heavy; her hand was shaped into a claw from writing. Mina stopped, laid down the pen, and stared at the list she had compiled. She stared at it, then stared some more. "Fuck."

"What?" asked Owen.

Mina simply shook her head and handed the notepad across to him. "It's the unsolved murders nationwide. I've compiled a list of those that seem to relate to our killer's MO—attack pattern, use of manual strangulation, tendency to display the bodies in a naturalistic manner . . ."

Owen scanned the list, his mouth dropping open. "You are shitting me."

Mina said thickly, "Fourteen murders in twenty years. A series spread across the South of England—Poole, Southampton, Portsmouth—in the nineties, then a gap of six years, then seven spread across the North. There were murders in Sheffield, Newcastle, Sunderland, Edinburgh. Those ones were prostitutes mostly, and one young man who was known to be homeless. They match the MO. The bodies were, for the most part, positioned, although the display element was less obvious than we're seeing here." She leaned forward, put her head in her hands. "Maybe I'm wrong. Please God, I'm wrong. But if I'm not . . ."

"If you're not," said Cain, looking over Owen's shoulder, "then he has spent the past twenty years killing freely."

"Okay," said Owen. He sounded dazed or drunk or both. "Okay," he repeated, "so . . . so why now? If he transitioned to prostitutes in the North, he was clearly trying to keep things on the down low. He was trying to hide it. But here . . . there's been no hiding here. This is murder. In your face, 'Look what I just did' murder."

Mina looked up. "Maybe he just got sick of hiding."

The sound of footsteps, the bang of a door. Chief Superintendent Clee's steps were slower than normal; he was battered down by the exhaustion plaguing them all. "Right, guys, go home. Get some sleep." His voice sounded thick and unwieldy.

"Sir," said Mina, "I think you should see this."

Owen handed him the sheet of paper. His face turned pale.

"Are you sure?" he asked.

Mina shrugged. "I don't know that I can be sure, sir. Not yet. I wanted your permission to approach the various forces involved and have any forensic evidence forwarded to us."

The chief super pulled out a chair, sat down heavily. "Shit. Okay . . . this . . . Yeah, this just got a whole hell of a lot more complicated. We're going

to have to bring these forces in. Bugger." He
looked at his watch, scrubbed his hand across his
face. "Okay, I'll have to tell the chief constable.
Mina, well done. Now go home. Get a couple of
hours' sleep." He stood quickly, was gone in a flurry
of coat.

Mina sat. She had moved into a place far past
exhaustion, where her need for sleep was all con-
suming. She watched as the others began to shrug
coats on.

"You coming?" asked Owen.

"Yeah, you go on. Just one more thing I want to
take care of."

She watched as they filed out, with their heads
down and their shoulders pulled up tight against
the weather. Then she turned back to the computer. Because something didn't feel right, something no longer worked in the story of the killer
on the wall. What the hell was Heath McGowan's
involvement? Was he merely a shadow, following
along in the wake of a harder, darker man? The evidence against McGowan remained as it ever was—
damning. The fingerprints on Kitty's door, and
then the items, the mementos. Kitty's necklace
and Zach's key chain and Leila's wedding ring, all
found in his possession.

Mina logged back in to the evidence log. Perhaps it was the exhaustion, perhaps it was that she
had spent too long on the computer, but it seemed
that her actions were conducted by someone far,
far away, and she scrolled through the lists with an
uncomfortable sense of premonition.

There were three items in all that had been definitively proven to have belonged to the victims and were subsequently found in the possession of Heath McGowan.

And each of those three items was entered into evidence by Eric Bell.

Thursday, October 27

Someone to stop me – Isla

Isla closed the door behind her. She stood in their front garden, the wind whipping at her coat, her gaze fighting to move to the hedge through which the photograph had been taken, every survival instinct in revolt. But still Isla stood there beneath the gray sky.

"So what does this brain scan mean? I don't get it." Ramsey had stood in their study, examining the brain scan, turning it about in his hands, as if that way he would make sense of it.

"It means . . ." Isla had felt the words sticking, her mouth clumsy with the effort of creating them. "My father is showing a pattern of brain function that one would normally see in a psychopathic brain."

She had leaned over her husband's shoulder, had allowed her fingers to trace the shadowed image of the brain. "See? Here and here and here, this means that there's a deficit in the brain's functioning." She'd shaken her head. "His entire paralimbic system is compromised."

Ramsey had looked at her, as if he was trying to read her thoughts so that she wouldn't have to say them. "So . . . your father, he's a psychopath?"

On her front doorstep, Isla let her toes bounce in empty air and lifted her chin so that the wind that swept down from the Cheviots scored across her cheeks. She had slept little, two hours, maybe three. The accumulated exhaustion was weighing down her limbs, making her brain sluggish.

"Why don't you go back to bed?" Ramsey had asked, up early, dressed in suit and tie. "I have to go and meet the *Journal* editor. I'd put it off, but . . ."

"Don't put it off. Go. I'm going to try to get more sleep."

Ramsey had leaned in, kissed her, letting his hand rest on the shallow curve of her stomach. "Make sure you lock the door behind me, okay, Mama?"

Isla stepped away from the door now and walked with steady steps along the front path, through the low gate, onto the pavement. Allowed herself one moment of mercy, to scan from left to right, to check the hedge, to look for cars. There was nothing but a heady silence. The village had gone into hiding. Blitz spirit gone. Fear had taken hold now, driving all of Briganton indoors, behind chains and alarms and dead bolts. Isla walked down the hill, her footsteps unnaturally loud.

So . . . your father, he's a psychopath?

No. Because her life had pirouetted around this point and this man. And hadn't everyone always known that if you had a problem, you went to Eric Bell? Eric would sort it, would put the bad people away, would make all right again. Her entire child-hood, a collage of images of one sort of heroism or another. That time when the Mackenzie house burned, a fry pan catching alight, and most of the family making it out, but Libby, blond hair, blue eyes, the year below her in school, trapped in the rear bedroom. And her father, breaching the flames as if they were nothing, somehow, and no one knew quite how, getting to Libby, dragging her out, limp and smoke damaged. It had been on the news. He'd got an award for that one, not to mention a three-day stay in the hospital. That fight at the Dog & Bone where the fists had become knives, the pub emptying, her father wading in re-gardless, in spite of orders to stay back, receiving for his trouble a stab wound to the shoulder. Her father was a hero. The great Eric Bell.

She crossed the road, careful on the carpet of slick leaves. A police car had been parked on the corner, and another was just visible over the crest of the hill. A flash of yellow against the dull sky, PCSOs on patrol.

Her father was a hero. *And yet our physiology does not lie.* So she turned the recollections, shifting them so as to see them from new angles. Courage to the point of recklessness. A disdain for orders and for following rules. The village looking at him with an adoration that verged on the sycophantic.

So charm, then, the kind that can manipulate and control.

She passed the church, the large wooden doors shut tight. Her father, missing her sixth birthday, her seventh, her eighth, until in the end it had become a long-running family joke. But that was how the world looked when your father was a hero—you had to accept that tragedy came before cake. And then a new memory—of Isla crying when, on her ninth birthday, her father had once again failed to return home, had missed the party and the balloons, had drifted in some time after midnight. *Why are you crying? It's your birthday. You had a party.*

Yes, Isla had sniffed, *but you weren't there.* And her father looking at her with that curiously blank expression.

She knew that expression. The emptiness of it. Like when you asked a psychopath what guilt felt like, and their brain cast this way and that, trying to grip the tail of a concept they knew only in principle.

She pulled up outside the deathly quiet school and stared down the hill toward the wall and the moor beyond. Her father was a psychopath.

She slipped out of the car, tucking her handbag beneath her arm. Her steps quicker now, a few hundred meters to where the houses were smaller, lined up in the neatest of rows, with their small square windows making them look slightly surprised. She knocked hard on the door of number twelve. Waited. Knocked hard again.

She was just beginning to think that it was empty

and her trip had been in vain when a sound came
from within. The creak of stairs, shuffling footsteps on wood floors. Mina opened the door cautiously, her eyes heavy with sleep.

"Did I wake you?"

"Isla. I . . . No."

Yes.

Mina pushed the door open wider. Her hair
stood up, wild and bouffant; beneath her eyes were
the black remains of the previous day's mascara.
She wore pajamas with ducks on them. "Come in. I
was . . . I was just making coffee. You want one?"

Isla closed the door firmly behind her, followed
along in Mina's barefooted wake. "Sure. Thanks."

The living room was small, contained far more
furniture than it should. Isla hung there as from
the kitchen came the sounds of a kettle being
filled, a yawn suppressed. What Isla took to be yesterday's clothes had been slung haphazardly
across the sofa's arm. There was the faint smell of
cigarette smoke.

"So . . . you okay?" Mina pushed a cup of instant
coffee into Isla's hand, waved her toward the sofa.
She had made an attempt to tidy her hair, had
dragged it back into a high ponytail, which served
only to emphasize her exhaustion.

"Yes. I'm so sorry I woke you."

Mina shrugged and drank her own coffee with a
gulp. "Had to get up, anyway." A ping sounded
from the coffee table, and Mina sighed, leaned
over to pick up her phone, a lightening of her expression, an almost smile. She glanced at Isla.
"Sorry. It's Owen. You know Owen Darby? From
work? He grew up here too. Anyway." She shook

herself slightly. "You didn't come here to talk about any of this. What's up?"

"Are you investigating my father?"

The cup froze in midair, Mina's eyes large behind it. "Am I . . ."

"You see," said Isla, "a detective, Eve, I think her name was, came to see us last night. Was asking Ramsey about the time he was attacked. She did her best to be discreet, but I got the distinct impression that the powers that be think there was a problem with the original killer on the wall investigation. Eve mentioned she'd seen you, so I thought . . . You are, aren't you? You're investigating my father."

Mina sat silent for a moment, gathering herself. "No. Well, not strictly . . . Chief Superintendent Clee, he's ordered us to open up the investigation, to expand it to see what was missed in your father's original one. I know that sounds bad . . ."

Isla opened her handbag, pulled out the image of Eric's brain scan, and handed it to Mina. "This is my father's brain. His fMRI scan shows indications of psychopathic brain function."

One beat. Two.

"I genuinely have no idea what you just said." Mina cocked her head, frowning at her. "Isla, what are you asking me?"

Isla stared at her coffee. "Psychopaths often have trouble following the rules. They can be impulsive, do things that are extraordinarily self-serving. They can do things that they shouldn't do to meet their own ends. In their worldview, the ends will always justify the means. I . . . I know it's not fair to ask you this, but . . . in the original investigation, did my father do something that he shouldn't have done?"

Mina bit her lip. Then sighed heavily. "Isla, look . . ." She glanced at Isla. "We got the DNA back. From some of the original victims. It wasn't a match for Heath McGowan."

The coffee cup swayed in Isla's hands. *I'm not the killer on the wall.*

"Your father, I think, may have planted the evidence on McGowan, the pieces that connected him to the killings on the wall." Mina looked close to tears. She pulled at her long ponytail, tugged at the ends of it. "I . . . I found more. There have been more murders. The killings, they didn't stop after McGowan was arrested. They just moved. Whoever is doing this, they've been moving about the country, killing with impunity."

Isla wanted to get up, to run from this house and these words and Briganton itself. But following close behind the nausea came something else, a flutter low in her belly, as if a butterfly had gotten trapped there. Then the world collapsed into that minuscule movement, that tiny spark of electricity across her abdomen. She placed her hand on her stomach and waited for the flutter of her baby's heart. It came again, more certain this time. And Isla felt the fear moving backward, something else sliding into its place, harder and softer both. Because it wasn't about her or Ramsey or her father. Now it was about this child and the world that would surround it.

"How many?" Isla asked quietly.

"Fourteen. Not counting the Briganton ones.

For the past ten years, he appears to have been targeting prostitutes."

"Staying under the radar."

"Yes."

Isla set the coffee cup down on the table and allowed her head to sink into her hands. "It's because of my father. It's all because of him. If he hadn't planted the evidence . . . they would have kept looking. They would have found the actual murderer. And why? Why would he do that? What would be the point?"

"This case made him, Isla. He solved it single-handedly. He was on TV, for God's sakey," said Mina. "Okay, you want my theory? I think that Eric genuinely believed McGowan was guilty. I mean, you know yourself, McGowan is no angel. He was absolutely responsible for the murder of Lucy Tuckwell. I think he was in the wrong place at the wrong time, and that he did a lot of things that, to your father's mind, must have made him look pretty damn guilty." Mina shrugged. "I'm betting your father figured the odds of there being more than one murderer in a village like Briganton had to be pretty slim."

"So he shored up his case," said Isla softly.

"I think so. I think he took a gamble on it being McGowan. And that he made damn sure the rest of the world would bet the same way." She blew out a sigh. "Only trouble is, he was wrong. There was another killer all along," said Mina. "Isl, let me ask you something. Whoever this is, he's been killing for years. Quietly, discreetly. Why the change?"

Isla wrapped her arms around her knees and

considered. "It seems that the killer's motives are different now. These other murders, they were just enough to satisfy him. To satiate his need. But now the killing isn't enough. He needs the attention, the thrill that comes from people knowing what he's doing. He wants Briganton to know that he's hunting. He's looking for the fear."

"Why?" asked Mina.

Isla thought of Ramsey. Of him staring at her father's brain scan. "Why do they do it, Isla?" he'd asked. "Why would someone do this? Kill people the way he has?"

She had chosen her words carefully. "We don't fully understand it yet. The brain dysfunction, that's likely to be a part of it. Sometimes you see that people who do these things have a certain gene others don't. We call it the warrior gene. But whether they are born like that or whether it's created by the environment, we can't really say yet. Most serial killers, they've generally suffered extreme abuse as children. My money is on it being a combination of the two—genes and upbringing. Say, a genetic vulnerability to do terrible things, which can be avoided by a good childhood. But, once those two factors combine . . ."

"So, what are you saying?" Ramsey had asked, his voice almost fearful. "It's not their fault?"

Isla had looked at the scan, had considered. "These people may have urges—weaknesses that other people wouldn't have. But still, they know that they are wrong. They understand that much. And, in giving in to those urges, they are still making a choice."

Ramsey had held the brain scan tight and had slowly nodded.

Isla picked up her coffee again now and took a sip, the granules gritty in her mouth. Then she looked at Mina. "Perhaps the killer has experienced some kind of change in his life. Perhaps he feels that he's vanishing in some way, that he is no longer important or seen. This coming back here, killing so publicly, it may be a way for him to regain that sense of importance."

"But . . . why so many?" asked Mina. "So close together. It's like he's lost all control now."

Isla studied her. "Perhaps he is hoping someone will stop him."

The killing path – Mina

"He has killed two young men within the space of the past twenty-four hours." Superintendent Bell stood, his hands upon his hips, his expression grim.

Mina watched Eric Bell as his gaze swept the room, then settled finally on her. She felt herself color. It seemed inevitable to her that he knew—about her digging, about what she had found, about all of it.

"Parker MacDonald was killed first, between twelve noon and three p.m. yesterday. The twenty-year-old man was killed by manual strangulation." It appeared now that the superintendent was talking to her, his gaze locked on hers, his face flat.

"He also had a wound to the rear of his head. It is believed he was struck by a blunt object, presumably to incapacitate him."

Without wanting to, Mina dipped her head, breaking away from his gaze, and glanced sideways across the crowded room, close on a hundred people in there now. They stood and sat and perched, each one of their faces tight with tension. There was no chatter, no quietly held sense of excitement. No illusions left, everyone knowing now just how bad this thing could get.

"Jake Gilbert was killed between one p.m. and five p.m. Same scenario—blow to the head, which, in Mr. Gilbert's case, was sufficient to fracture his skull, followed by manual strangulation." Eric Bell shifted through his notes. "Interviews with acquaintances of the two young men have allowed us to determine the pattern of their day. Parker MacDonald attended a nine a.m. psychology lecture, had coffee with friends. He was seen around eleven a.m. in the psychology department. According to another student, he decided to return to his residence in order to collect an assignment he'd forgotten to bring with him."

On the screen behind Eric appeared an aerial photograph of the university and its surrounding areas. He pointed to a footpath connecting the campus to the student village, a line of gray in among a blur of green. "This path cuts through moorland. It's overgrown, trees on both sides. Students have been warned to avoid it. It's been the site of a number of sex attacks over the past couple of years. But it's considerably shorter than the route around the road, and students will be students."

The superintendent turned to Cain, who stood off to one side, arms folded. "Cain? You want to take it from here?"

Cain nodded, looking far older than he had before. But then, this had aged them all.

"Following on from the sexual assaults that happened in this area, CCTV was fitted along this path. Unfortunately, the system hasn't been updated, and as such, there have been a number of failures, creating blind spots along the path. The footage that we do have shows Parker MacDonald entering this path at eleven thirty-six a.m." Cain pressed a button, transforming the image into black-and-white footage.

The room fell silent as a lanky figure entered the screen, his hair swept unruly by the wind. He walked forward, hefting his bag up higher on his shoulder, and then vanished into the clambering trees.

Cain spoke softly. "Ninety seconds later, a second figure is seen entering the path behind Mac-Donald."

They waited. Then the figure appeared, a dark shape, thick padded jacket, baseball cap pulled low, and a quick step.

"Parker does not reappear. He is not picked up again by the cameras at the campus end, and there's no sign of him on the cameras that cover the student accommodation." Cain pressed a button, and the image changed to a new angle. "This is the student village." *Wait. Wait.* "And this is our mystery man." He clicked on a closer shot this time. "His face is shadowed by the baseball cap, as you can see. I think it's unlikely we'll be able to use this to identify him."

Cain sighed. "Now, Jake, on the other hand, attended lectures all morning. At around two p.m., he told friends he was going for a run." Another image, this one footage of a lithe, strong young man jogging onto the path and vanishing. "He entered the path at two eleven p.m. At two twelve p.m., what appears to be the same man followed him." He waited as the scene unfolded again. The hunter, the prey. "Again, we can't see his face, and there don't appear to be any identifying features that we can see."

Eric Bell stepped forward, pointing to the frozen image. "We have to identify this individual. I need house-to-house throughout the entire student village. This man was there at least twice. Someone must have seen him. I need another team on the university campus. Maybe someone saw him there." He glanced about the room. "I need someone to check the area for any additional CCTV, any ANPR."

"This guy," said Cain softly, "he's picking up his kill rate. It's only getting worse. Let's get going."

Words settled; glances were exchanged. A low rumbling mutter. Then, like a spell broken, came the scrape of chairs. Mina sat for a moment, watching the flurry of movement, watching Eric Bell standing just beyond it, head bent, in quiet conversation with Cain.

"Well, that was fun," muttered Owen.

"No shit," said Mina softly. The superintendent's gaze had fallen on her again, and she noticed, as he said something to Cain, the younger man's gaze drifting over to land on her too.

She pushed herself up to standing.

Cain separated himself off, weaved through the crowd toward her, spared a quick nod for Owen. "Mina. I'm going on out to the university. Come with me, yeah?"

It was the feeling of walking along a cliff's edge. Mina nodded, forcing her face into a smile. "Sure."

The university campus was quiet. The few students that were to be seen walked quickly, their heads down, shoulders pulled up, as if that way they could save themselves. Mina climbed slowly out of the car. It occurred to her that you would know it, even if you didn't know. You would be able to tell that death had been here.

"I'm guessing the kids are reevaluating the whole 'university is the best time of your life' thing," said Cain, slowing his pace so she could fall into step with him.

Mina snorted, watched as a woman spotted them. Detaching herself from a cluster of detectives, she strode quickly toward them.

"Eve. What have you got?"

She pursed her lips. "I was just about to call you. We found something on the path."

"Show me," said Cain.

She turned abruptly and, not waiting to see if

they followed, ducked beneath the police cordon and onto the path beyond. Mina and Cain followed in her wake, watching as her blond ponytail swung with the wind. The path led through a tunnel of trees, until the campus had disappeared behind them and it seemed that they could have been anywhere. After they had been walking for five minutes, Eve stopped, held up a hand to stay them.

"It's here." She pointed at the undergrowth. "If you look closely, you can see where it's been trampled down." Eve racked her ASP, used the metal baton to move tree branches aside and reveal a clearing. "I'm not sure if you can see it, but if you look closely, there's blood staining on the grass back there. CSIs are on their way. They're pretty busy," she added redundantly.

Mina shifted her position, peered through the undergrowth. "He left the bodies here." She pulled back, scanning the scene. "Pretty good position. They'd have been hidden from the view of anyone walking by."

"The question is," said Eve, "how did he transport Jake Gilbert's body to the wall?"

Mina stood up tall and pointed past the undergrowth. "The road is that way. Wouldn't be too far if you didn't mind fighting your way through the undergrowth. He could have had a car there, waiting. Moved them after dark."

Mina shook her head—it seemed that she could smell the death here, though that was probably little more than her imagination. Then a sound cut through the susurration of the trees. Cain glanced at his mobile, its ringing vibration harsh and unwelcome.

He answered, listened, and Mina knew. You could see it in the color of his cheeks, the emptiness in his eyes. She didn't need him to say it. But say it he did, the phone sinking from his ear.

"There's another one. Stephen Doyle is missing."

Getting what you want – Ramsey

They gathered on the moorland, the search team approaching fifty people, a shuffled together affair of uniforms and villagers. Ramsey looked out over their faces, tight with the cold and the fear of what they might find. Briganton had reemerged, had ventured from behind its locked doors onto the empty moor, drawn out of doors by a police appeal. *We're stretched too thin. We need help.* Off to one side stood a knot of police officers, faces Ramsey did not recognize.

"Mutual aid," Cain muttered, pulling Ramsey to him in a half hug. "We're drowning. Northwestern force has sent two dozen officers over." His brother looked afraid, stripped bare by where they were now. "I'm glad you're here, Rams."

"Ladies and gentlemen . . ." Eric Bell stood on a mound of earth, his voice taking on a screeching tone as he battled to make himself heard above the murmurs and the wind. "Thanks for coming out. I know it's not pleasant. We appreciate your help."

Ramsey pulled his beanie hat lower, shifted his sling so that it sat more easily. He shivered. He had been driving when Cain had called him, had for once not been thinking about death. Instead, his mind had become hooked on the notion of soft baby cheeks, dimpled hands, a mewling cry. Would it be a boy or a girl? He had imagined that soft puff of breath on his neck.

Then the call. Stephen Doyle was missing.

"Now, we've already searched along the wall and have come up empty. That's good. That gives us hope." Eric looked about them, not saying the one thing that was on everyone's mind. That no body on the wall did not mean no body at all. "So, what we're going to do is have you walk about an arm's length apart. We've got flashlights here for anyone who needs one. We're looking for anything, be it property, footprints. Anything seems out of place to you, shout out." He clapped his hands together. "Okay, people, let's get going."

They moved in a swarm, working outward from the rear of the modern housing estate—the home of Stephen Doyle's sister, Bronwen, and, more recently, of Stephen himself—that edged Briganton, up toward Bowman's Hill. Ramsey began to walk, his movements careful, measured, and glanced at Connor beside him. His jaw was tight with strain;

teeth ground together in a rhythm at odds with their footsteps.

"You okay?" asked Ramsey.

Connor shook his head. "Should have damn well stayed in London. None of this drama there."

Ramsey grinned, stepping carefully on the uneven ground.

"So, what do you think?" asked Connor quietly. "Is it . . . is he . . . another one? Or is it something else?"

They shared a glance, both thinking of Stephen Doyle on the edge of a roof. The plummeting drop below.

"I don't know," said Ramsey.

He thought of Bronwen Doyle standing on her front path as the searchers had gathered, her hands tucked into the sleeves of her sweater, tears bubbling up and over as she spoke. "Thing is, Rams, I thought he was okay. I mean, I took some time off after he tried to . . . you know . . . but I can't keep that up for ever, and he said . . . I mean, he's been living with me, just while he sorts himself out, and so you think, well, you'd see it, if he really meant it, if he was really going to do it. And today, see, I had to go into work today. The maternity ward, we've had this bug going round. All the midwives are going down with it, so they needed me to cover. And he said he'd be fine. That he felt much better. But then everything went mental at work. We had a shoulder dystocia, and then another one of the midwives threw up mid-shift, and I ended up staying on. I didn't get in until three last night. I should have checked on him."

She had twisted the hem of her sweater over and over again. "I should have gone into his room. But the house, everything looked right, so I just, I thought I shouldn't wake him. It was only when I woke up this morning that I realized he wasn't there."

"The grief of losing Leila, it's all been brought back up again by what's been happening here. It's tough for people to survive that," Ramsey had offered. "Maybe Stephen . . . Maybe it's been too much for him. Living all that again."

"You're kidding, right?" Cain said from the other side of Connor. It seemed as if he was ready to break, his voice uneven and fractured. "It's the killer on the wall again. It's always him. He's like a ghost."

Ramsey stared at his brother, startled.

"Sorry. Sorry, guys. Just . . . I want this whole thing to be over. That's all."

Connor looked uncomfortably from one brother to the other, then returned his gaze to the roughened ground. "Maybe Stephen's just gone off somewhere. Maybe he needed to be on his own for a bit, away from here. To forget about everything that's happening."

His words hovered in the air, a potent magic, like the mention of Christmas or laughter or the fierce grip of a newborn baby.

Cain shook his head, shivering in the bitter cold.

And then, from a small rise about a hundred meters away, came the call.

"We've got him."

Ramsey began to run, his damaged arm in a sling bouncing with the movement. He could hear Connor, Cain, their footsteps pounding behind him, while he fought to keep his balance as the ground became looser, boggier.

"No one touch him. No one touch him." A uniformed officer whom Ramsey did not recognize held his arms out, an unofficial barrier between them and what lay beyond, and Ramsey stopped sharp.

In a puddle of light lay the dead body of Stephen Doyle. His knees pulled up, hands folded together, he lay, a fetus in its mother's womb, face gray, the ground beneath him soaked black with blood.

"Oh God," muttered Cain. "His wrists. Look at his wrists."

In truth there was little left of them: the knife had sliced them open wide enough to expose the bone beneath.

Ramsey leaned forward, pressed his hands on his knees.

"I guess," said Connor, "he finally got his way."

Unmasked – Mina

Bronwen Doyle sat at the kitchen table and cried. Mina sat beside her, giving a tentative pat on the back every now and again, as if that could make any difference at all. Superintendent Bell stood off to the side, looking uncomfortable, letting his gaze wander over granite countertops, linoleum floors, anywhere to avoid the woman who wept before him. He opened his mouth, seemed as if he was about to speak, but then closed it again.

But, thought Mina, *what is there to say now? What is there that anyone would want to hear?*

It must have been suicide. That was what the guys out on the moor were saying. The MO didn't fit—Stephen Doyle's wrists were sliced open, no sign of strangulation, and the body had not been positioned like the others.

A coincidence, then. A grief-stricken man pushed too far.

Mina had heard one of the guys say that at least there was that—that at least Stephen Doyle wasn't another victim of the killer on the wall. But as she sat there, her useless palm laid limply against the heaving back of Bronwen, it occurred to Mina that that simply wasn't true. After all, what else had Stephen been but one more victim? It had just taken him far longer to die than the others.

"I need the bathroom."

Bronwen's voice shocked her, hoarse and broken, so different from what it had been before.

"Sure," said Mina. "Of course."

She watched Bronwen stand, her movements billowing, so that she seemed to be floating in space, and Mina stood, moved with her, one hand on her elbow. The woman stopped, pressed up against the kitchen table, and for a moment looked down at her feet, her forehead furrowed, as if she was trying to remember just what came next, how this whole walking thing worked.

Then, with huge effort, she began to move, and Mina followed her. They passed Superintendent Bell, Bronwen paying as little attention to him as if he were a cardboard cutout someone had left in her kitchen.

As Bronwen closed the bathroom door behind her, Mina let out a breath, searched for some oxygen in this airless house. The hallway was quiet. Beside the bathroom door, a bedroom, its door standing wide open, and Mina found herself moving almost in spite of herself, peering inside what was, it transpired, a ground-floor bedroom, with a neatly made double bed, a single wardrobe, an old-fashioned television on a narrow chest of drawers.

The bed had not been slept in. On the nightstand stood a single framed picture, of Stephen and his wife, Leila, the only sign that the room was inhabited. Mina eased her way into the center of the room, thinking it felt like a morgue, that the grief and the loss seemed to seep out of the very walls. She studied the photograph, thinking how handsome Stephen had been once, before his eyes became hollowed out with pain, before his cheeks sank inward, and his hair thinned away to nothing. He had his arms wrapped around Leila, was smiling the kind of smile that seemed to suggest they had forever. *How much longer had she lived after that?* Mina wondered. *How much time had they had left?*

It's perhaps best that you can't see the future, she thought. *Because who could bear knowing all that would come?*

The floorboards creaked, and in spite of herself, Mina started. Eric Bell stood in the doorway to the room. And yet it seemed to be a different Eric Bell, with fingers that twitched at his waist, a gaze that danced from wall to wall. Gone was the certainty, gone was the ever-present cool. Now, something different.

"Sir?" She hesitated. "Are you okay?"

He looked about the room and sighed. "Aye. Tough couple of days."

"Yes, sir," Mina allowed.

The superintendent leaned against the doorjamb. "I remember him back then. Stephen, I mean." He waved toward the photograph. "He'd just got into the fire service. He was so full of it. 'Course, then Leila died and . . . he didn't last too long after that. Seemed when she died, he died too. Only, he kept walking around for longer."

Mina reached over and picked up the framed photo. "It's so sad."

Then something seemed off; her fingertips hit on something that simply did not feel right, an unevenness where smoothness should be. Mina frowned, turned the frame over in her hands. An additional layer of card had been laid across the back. Thick, but not thick enough to disguise the shape that lay underneath.

"What's up?" asked the superintendent.

"I . . . There's something behind here." A feeling had settled on her, déjà vu . . . but not. Perhaps rather a premonition of the moments to come. Mina slid her fingernail beneath one edge of the card, lifted it up just a little, so that she could peer beneath it. There, in the darkness, came a glint of light. Mina's stomach turned over. She tugged at the cardboard.

"Mina . . ."

Taped to the rear of the picture frame was a slender gold chain, a heart-shaped locket dangling from it.

"That's . . ." Mina felt light-headed. "That's Victoria Prew's. It's the locket that was stolen from her house." She stared at the locket, at the superintendent, as the pieces slid into place for her. "He . . . No." She looked about the room wildly. "No, he couldn't be."

Eric Bell had stood up straighter, his face switching to cool control again. "We're going to need to do a full search. I'll get some people in."

Mina nodded, set the photograph back down. Her gaze darting this way and that, she tried to take in everything at once, to make sense of it. It landed on something meant to be hidden, a fabric edge that had nudged its way out from beneath the bed.

"Sir," she said quietly, "there's a bag under here."

The superintendent gave one small nod. "Check it."

Mina pulled gloves from her pocket, slid her fingers into them, trying to keep it together, to remember to breathe. *In, out, in, out.* She reached beneath the bed and tugged out a rucksack. Carefully, she slid the zipper open, peered into the darkness of it: a boxlike shape was just visible at the base of the bag.

She pulled out a digital camera.

Mina looked up at Eric. But it seemed that the superintendent was stuck, the carpet quicksand, and he could no more move closer than he could fly.

"Turn it on." His voice came out hoarse, raw.

She glanced down at the camera, took a quick breath, then toggled the switch, and the screen turned from black to blue. Then to something else. Mina stared at it. "Oh God."

The superintendent moved then, crossing the room to her in awkward steps. She turned the camera screen toward him silently.

Jake Gilbert seated dead at Vindolanda.

"That's the photo that was sent to Rachel Flowers," Mina said.

She toggled back.

And there they were, as they were always going to be. Jake and Parker, Isla and Ramsey kissing, and Maggie and Victoria.

Eric looked at her, face white as death. "Stephen Doyle was the killer on the wall."

Making everything okay again – Isla

Isla watched as Ramsey poured tea from the long-spouted teapot. Two cups, three, four. She felt Emilia's arm snake around her waist, her head resting upon her sister's shoulder the way it used to when they were children. Bonnie sat neatly on a kitchen stool, her hands folded into her lap, her face lit up from the inside.

"Honestly, I can't believe it's over. I wish your father could have come home, but he says there's lots of mopping up to do. They didn't want the press to get it so soon, but you know how they are. Still"—she accepted the cup from Ramsey with a grateful smile—"it's almost over now." She patted her son-in-law on the cheek. "Thank you, my love."

Ramsey gave her a swift smile, a glance to Isla.

She knew what he was thinking, had been married to him long enough to read it without the words ever being uttered. *How could I miss it? How could it have been under my nose the entire time?*

Ramsey had come home from the search, had sat down on the sofa, buried his face in his hands. *How could this have happened, Isla?* She had wrapped her arms around him, thinking that perhaps, of all the sins, hers was the greatest. Hadn't she gone into forensic psychology for this very reason? Hadn't the plan been to arm herself for the future, to learn all she could so that never again could a monster come near her without her knowledge? But then, Isla allowed, it was rarely that simple.

She had kissed her husband's head, had murmured that it was okay, that he couldn't have known. Had explored her own failure, a tongue probing a cavity. What it came down to was that Stephen Doyle had embodied his persona, that of the victim. He had suffered too well, had grieved too painfully, so that all about him had been blinded to the fact that it was make-believe. It was, after all, a human failing to accept that which was presented to you as truth. And even after arming yourself, even with all the knowing, sometimes it just wasn't enough.

Isla felt the brush of her sister's curls against her cheek, and the butterfly flutter low in her abdomen, and felt a flood of relief. It was over. And even though she had failed, it was a gentle failure. Because all that mattered was the end of it.

"Why didn't you bring the boys, Em?" Ramsey asked her sister, then sipped his own tea. "House feels bizarrely quiet without them."

Emilia snorted. "You can say that again. No, Adam has taken them swimming. Be good for him to have to control all three of them on his own for once."

Isla watched her sister catch the quick side glance and knew that she was lying. That it wasn't about paternal bonding or about marital revenge. That her sister had not brought her nephews here, to Briganton, to this house, because—in spite of the news, of the relief, of knowing that the killer on the wall was dead—Emilia remained afraid.

"So, Rams," Emilia hazarded, "must be weird for you. I mean, you knew him pretty well, yeah?"

Ramsey nodded slowly, setting his cup down on the kitchen counter. "Yes. Or . . . I thought I did. When I think back . . . to think that it was him, that it was Stephen, what he did to Zach, to me . . ." He shook his head. "Look, it's done. Let's talk about something else."

Stephen Doyle. In Isla's mind now that never-faded image of three dead bodies sitting at the wall. Had he picked them out, selected them ahead of time, or was it something different? He would have been young then, just at the beginning of his killing career, and yet, with three in one, clearly determined to make a name for himself.

Isla sipped her tea, wondered where her father was now and if this new discovery would seem like a reprieve for him or a hangman's noose. The final, incontrovertible proof that he had been wrong about Heath. Was he turning it, attempting to reshape this history into one in which his actions had merit? That, of course, would be the psychopath's way. The thought brought with it a flourish of guilt. And yet, she allowed, she, of all people, should know that biology was not destiny.

A knock on the door shook her from her reverie, and Isla disentangled herself from her sister, padded to the front door with slippered feet. Her hand upon the latch, she felt a brief thrill, a moment of daring, that it was over, that she could open this door without first checking through the peephole, without fear that what waited on the other side of it was death come to claim her. But then a little voice in her head said, *Always best to check. Just in case.* Isla smiled, pulled open the door, anyway.

Connor stood, shivering, on the doorstep, his light jacket zipped right up to his chin. He grinned. "Ta-dah."

"What are you doing here?"

He scuffed his feet against the path. "Well, I was going to go home, but I thought . . . I didn't know how you were—you and Ramsey, I mean—what with everything. And Stephen . . . I just thought I'd come check on you guys."

Isla smiled and pulled the door open wider. "Come on in." She watched as Connor slinked through, could sense the adrenaline, the fear. For despite all his protestations, Connor was not like her. He had not grown up in the shadow of the killer on the wall, had not built up the same kind of immunity. The events of today—tough to go home alone after that.

She shepherded him into the kitchen, then poured him a cup of tea. "Make yourself at home."

"Connor," said Ramsey, with a grin, "good to see you." Then he gave a little cough, caught Isla's gaze with a meaningful look. "Shall I?"

Isla smiled back. "Be my guest."

"Well"—Ramsey looked from her mother to her sister in the manner of one settling in to make a speech—"we were hoping that Eric and Cain could be here, but what with everything . . . I'm sure they'll understand." He nodded to Isla. "Isla and I . . . we're having a baby."

The room stilled for several long heartbeats; then Isla was engulfed in a flurry of sound.

Emilia squealing, wrapping her arms around her. "You'll love it. You'll love it. I know mine can be little sods, but they're fab, really."

Bonnie crying, hugging Ramsey, then Isla. "This . . . it will make your father so happy. Oh, this is it. This is just what we need to make everything okay again."

Spin of the wheel –
Mina

Mina sat at her desk. She stared straight ahead, even though she didn't see. The others had gone home, grateful for an end to a seemingly endless day. The major incident room was stripped back to a skeleton of itself. Just the low hum of the heating, the television barely audible against the sound of it, Superintendent Bell closed up in his office, his door shut, his blinds drawn. And Mina. Waiting. She sat and sat. Telling herself that she should leave, that what she was doing now would ultimately come to be seen as the greatest of her crimes, but still not able to get her feet to move.

And so she waited.

There came the sound of footsteps in the hallway beyond. The door swinging open. Chief Superintendent Clee walked in briskly, his face set, a cold fury pulsing at the edge of him. He afforded her a glance, and it contained what she had already told herself. *Go home. You've done enough.* Then he rapped sharply on Eric Bell's door, entered without waiting for a reply.

Mina had returned from the house of Stephen Doyle, her head still thick, as if the grief there had attached itself to her so that now she would carry it in the absence of Stephen. The numbers had circled in her head. Twenty years. Twenty years of freedom spanning fourteen deaths. Then Briganton, four more. Eighteen deaths that could have been prevented had Eric Bell not done what Eric Bell had needed to do to make himself great. Had he not needed quite so badly to be the one to solve the murders, the one whose name was stamped across the front page of national newspapers, who was asked to appear in documentaries under the tagline "The detective who stopped the killer on the wall." Stephen Doyle had killed because Eric Bell had allowed him to. There could be little other interpretation.

Mina had marched through the crowded incident room, where the detectives had been congratulating themselves on an end, had yanked open the drawer, and pulled out the file.

The chief superintendent had been on the phone. He had been smiling. The smile had not lasted long. As she'd run through Eric Bell's accumulation of missed leads and buried evidence and into the murky woods of the victims' items that had somehow found their way into the possession of Heath McGowan, his face had darkened.

Leave it with me.

The door to Eric Bell's office was closed tight again now, yet it was not enough to drown the voices within. At first the edge of them, the hint of anger, suggestion of a battle afoot, then the chief super's voice rising, the words achieving clarity.

"Did you plant evidence on Heath McGowan?"

Mina's breath caught in her throat. Would he admit to it? Surely, it made little sense not to at this stage.

Then that single word. *No.*

A silence that seeped beneath the closed door, then the chief super, his words unclear, tone anything but. Mina strained, picked out the shapes of words—*investigation, suspension, federation representative.*

The door flying open, the chief super stalking past her, not a glance in her direction, his body seeming tall with fury. Mina watched his long strides, her heart beating hard. She should leave. It would not do for her to be sitting there when Eric Bell emerged. The truth of what she had done would, she felt sure, be written across her face. He would know.

What was that feeling? Guilt? But surely that was not for her. It was as if she was picking up what Eric Bell had left free floating, taking on emotions he should have kept for himself. Her gaze fell on the television. A photograph of Stephen Doyle, the scrolling bar beneath: "The killer on the wall found."

For twenty years, Stephen Doyle had killed without notice. He had moved among the survivors, had been considered one of them, perhaps, she thought, because he had worn his vulnerability like a badge. The families had spoken of him in hushed tones as one broken by his lot in life. He was broken—he was damaged—so he could not be the predator. Mina thought of the eyewitness, the one who had been with Ben Flowers that night in the pub: *I saw a man. He was limping.* Perhaps for Stephen that had been as much of an MO as was strangulation, the placing of the bodies against the wall. Perhaps that was how he had got to them—by adopting a weakness and appearing to be safe, for long enough to get close to his victims, for them to let their guard down.

No. She would not accept guilt as her lot. Whatever she had done, it had been for the right.

She stood up, pulled her handbag toward her. It was time to go. She needed a shower. To sleep and, for once, not to dream. Mina slid her coat from the back of the chair and stuffed her arms into the sleeves. In her mind, she had already gone down the stairs, out into the chill night air, when the phone on her desk began to trill.

She answered it, not thinking. "Mina Arian."

"Mina? It's Zoe. I thought you'd all gone."

"You got something on my broom handle?" Mina said, an almost joke that now withered away.

"What . . . ? Oh . . . nearly." Zoe sounded ragged. "Look, is the super still there?"

Mina glanced over at Eric Bell's office, saw the door closed again. Heard a loud thump, as of something being thrown against the wall. "I . . . ah,

I think he's a bit busy . . . The chief super was just in here, though. Zoe? Is everything okay?"

A long breath in. "We finished with the hair found in Victoria Prew's house. We were able to develop a DNA profile on it. The results confirm that it was left by the same person whose DNA was found beneath the fingernails of Zach and Amelia."

Mina stared ahead of her, her brain trying to form Zoe's words into some kind of meaning. "Right?"

"But . . ." Zoe's voice cracked. "Mina, they compared the results to Stephen Doyle. It wasn't a match. It wasn't him."

An end and a beginning – Ramsey

Ramsey was drinking tea, the earthy, sweet taste of it still on his tongue, when the phone rang. He answered easily. This day was one of moving on.

"Rams—"

"Cain. Where are you, brother? You need to get over here. Me and Isla have some big news for you."

"Rams, listen to me." There was something in his brother's voice. "They have DNA. From the killer on the wall. It wasn't Stephen Doyle."

Ramsey felt his knees buckle, the room spin.

"Ramsey, it's not over."

Hanging up the phone without really meaning to, his hands on autopilot, disconnecting him from what he could not bear to hear.

Isla asking, "What? What's wrong?"

And Ramsey just standing, mute, his mouth working to form the words but somehow failing.

Connor's hand on his shoulder. "You okay, buddy? Here, sit down."

Then the words, "They have DNA. They have DNA from some of the victims. Stephen . . . he's not a match."

It was throwing a bomb into a room and watching the detonation. Long moments while they worked out what that meant.

Then Emilia, as if cut down in front of them, grabbing on to him. "No, no, no." Looking to her mother, her sister. "He's going to come for me. I know he's going to come for me. I said it. I always knew . . . I have to get out of here, Isla. I have to go. I can't stay here." Her voice shrill and uneven.

His wife looking like she was trying to figure out which of them to deal with first.

"Emilia. Breathe." Isla's voice was firm, calm. "Take a deep breath. Right. Now, it's okay. We're safe here. Adam will be coming to get you . . ."

"No, please, I can't wait that long. I can't. Please. If he, what if he comes and gets me? My boys, God, my boys would be left behind . . ."

There was little sense to her now, just fear. Pure, unadulterated fear.

Ramsey found his voice. "Emilia. Stop. You're with us. You're safe."

"Isla, take me home. Will you? Please."

"No." The strength of Ramsey's voice surprised even him as he fought to maintain calm. "Em, remember the photograph? If he's . . . if he's still out there, Isla is a target. She stays here. Where it's safe. Look, Adam won't be too much longer."

Emilia had begun to cry, had folded against Isla's shoulder, suddenly very much younger than her thirty-seven years.

"Rams, will you take her?" asked Isla. "Please? She's frightened, and she just needs to be at home with Adam and the boys. Will you take her home, wait with her until he gets there?"

Ramsey felt something race through him. "Isla. I can't just . . . What about you?"

"Connor will stay with me until you come back. Won't you?"

Ramsey refocused his gaze. Connor looked younger than he had ever seen him, as badly frightened as Emilia.

"Yeah," Connor said, attempting to sound like he had everything under control. "Yeah, of course."

Isla patted her sister on the back and moved closer to Ramsey, pulled him in for a kiss. "I'll be fine," she said quietly. "But Emmy's lost it now. Please, honey? Take her?"

Ramsey felt himself bow to the weight of the inevitable. "Sure."

"Rams, love, drop me off, too, would you?" asked Bonnie quietly. "I was going to walk, but . . . maybe best not." She looked to Isla. "Your dad will be home any minute. I want to be there when he gets in."

Ramsey looked from mother to daughter. "Yes, right. I'll go in with her, Isl. Check everything is secure. Yeah? Just make sure you lock the door behind me, okay?"

Isla looked up at him with her best approximation of a smile. "I'll be fine."

The right thing – Mina

They had returned; a small crowd was now gathered in the major incident room. Their heads were bowed. They looked, in a word, beaten.

"How is this possible?" asked Owen quietly.

Mina opened her mouth, then realized that words had escaped her. Because the truth was, it wasn't possible. It was over. And yet here they were again. She looked across at Cain, sitting with his head in his hands, the movement of his shoulders suggesting perhaps that he was crying. Mina felt her own eyes begin to fill.

"This is like a nightmare," she muttered.

She stared at the door of Eric Bell's office and remembered how his face went slack as she delivered the words *The DNA, it's not a match.* Then Chief Superintendent Clee, who looked as beaten down by recent events as it was possible to be. *Call them back in. As many of them as you can find. Mina, if you'll excuse us.*

Being ushered out of the office, dialing number after number. *Come back. It's not over.*

Then the super's door opening, the two men emerging, some kind of detente apparently reached, sufficient at least to allow them to survive this night.

"Guys?" The chief superintendent's voice had begun to fail, was raspy with exhaustion. "Listen, please." He sank down on a table edge, as if without that, he would have fallen down. Eric Bell stood a little behind him, to one side, his arms folded, face closed. "You all know why we've called you back in. The DNA for the killer was not a match for Stephen Doyle. I've just spoken to forensics. I asked them to do a fast turnaround on Stephen Doyle's toxicology report. Their findings indicate that there was a high level of benzodiazepine in Stephen's bloodstream."

The crowd remained silent.

Then Cain, lifting his head, said, "What does that mean?"

"Benzodiazepines can act as a sedative—"

"Okay," interrupted Cain, "so he sedated himself before slitting his wrists. Makes sense to me."

The chief super raised his head a little. "According to the sister, there were no benzodiazepines in the house. Forensic testing has found trace amounts of the crushed-up drug in a glass that was left in the kitchen."

Another silence, while people attempted to process what they were hearing.

"So," said Mina quietly, "you're saying you don't think Stephen Doyle took it deliberately? You think that someone laced his drink and then, when he was drugged, led him up onto the moor and slit his wrists? You're saying that Stephen Doyle is another victim?"

"Yes," said the chief super. "That's exactly what I'm saying." He paused a moment, to gather himself or to allow them to do the same, then pushed on. "I have at this point taken the decision to call in mutual aid. We are no longer able to cover this ourselves. We need help. Mina has uncovered a large number of other crimes that may also be related to our perpetrator and that fall under the jurisdiction of other force areas. Those forces will now be coming on board. I've already sent a search team out to Stephen Doyle's. I'm going to need people out there for a house-to-house." He looked down. "I'm sorry, guys. I had hoped this was over too."

He stood up and walked from the room without looking back.

Then Eric Bell. "Everyone, see Cain for your assignments. Arian, you're with me, please."

Mina balked. "Sir?"

"Come with me, please. Bring your coat."

Owen looked from Mina to Eric Bell and back again. "Sir? Anything I can do?"

The superintendent fixed him with a flat look. "I'm sure Mina is more than capable." He turned on his heel, walked from the room with an awkward step, Mina tugged along in his wake.

She walked behind him, thinking about Stephen Doyle. About the killer on the wall, still unknown. About Eric Bell's brain scan. Then about something else. About the limp.

Mina slowed, watching Bell in front of her, his gait lumbering, awkward, as he favored his left leg. *What had Isla said? A rugby injury?* She thought of the evidence, buried and planted, of twenty years' worth of killing. A case that made him the great Eric Bell. A chill raced through her, and she stopped right there in the hallway.

He must have sensed it, turned to face her. "Well?"

She shouldn't go with him. She should stay.

But it seemed that muscle memory had a greater sway over her than did good sense, and Mina found herself following behind him again. Because it couldn't be. Could it?

They got into his car, Mina in the passenger seat, and she watched as he drove her away from city lights, along winding country lanes, fast enough that the car slid on the damp tarmac.

She thought of Victoria and Maggie and Parker and Jake. And she wondered, *If death were to come for me now, would I be satisfied with what I have done with the time I have had?* She had an uncomfortable feeling that the answer to that would be no.

They plunged down into Briganton, its puddled lights spread out beneath them, past the church, the primary school, with its wrought-iron gates, down past the house of Victoria Prew, and then a hard left turn. The car skidded to a stop on Dray Lane.

And Mina just sat there. Thinking that this was where it had all begun, where Zach and Ramsey had been attacked, where life for the village had spiraled off into the unknown.

"Where are we going?"

For long moments he merely sat, staring ahead into the darkness. Then he shifted, tugged at his door handle, and said, "Come with me."

She could refuse to move. She could lock the door once he got out. She could get out and run.

But Mina did none of those things, merely slid into step behind him, as meek as a lamb, walked until finally pavement turned to boggy ground beneath her feet and she could see the wall up ahead, the curve in it where it followed the Whin Sill. Where the first victims had been left.

Mina stopped. "Why have you brought me here?"

Bell had walked a couple of paces on. He stopped, staring off into the distance, then turned back to her. "It was you, wasn't it? You found out about the photograph from Rachel Flowers. About the stuff on Heath McGowan. You found out. You gave it to the chief super."

She thought of Victoria and of Maggie. "Yes."

"You know I'll probably be fired?"

Mina's breath seemed to be too thin now. "Yes."

He studied her. "Why?"

"Sir?"

"Why did you do it?" Bell's voice almost sounded plaintive.

"Because . . . sir, it was the right thing to do. The

lies you told. They allowed a killer to go free for twenty years."

"Yes," agreed Bell distantly, "but McGowan was a killer too. And they put him behind bars."

Mina frowned, distracted by this trip through the looking glass. "Yes, but, sir, he wasn't responsible for *these* killings." She waved toward the wall. "You set him up. You made him take the fall. And yes, I get that he was not a good man. But Lucy, he would have paid for that. He would have been locked up, anyway. By doing this, you let someone far worse go free."

The superintendent turned to look at her, his head tilted slightly, as if her words had been spoken in Danish and he were trying to pick them apart. "That McGowan," he said, "he was a bad one. Rotten to the core. And if you'd seen what he did to that girlfriend of his. Any man who could do that to a pregnant girl would be capable of anything. It was him. It must have been him."

"Only it wasn't."

"But," he said, "I did what I was supposed to do. I put him away."

To Mina, it seemed that she was talking to a child, and she wondered if he simply did not understand the magnitude of what he had done. "Yes. But you could have done that without lying. He would have gone to prison simply for what he did to Lucy Tuckwell. You didn't have to turn him into the killer on the wall too. If you hadn't . . . we could have caught the real killer twenty years ago."

Now the superintendent frowned and looked toward Briganton. "This place. How the hell could I have imagined there would be two monsters here? I was just doing my job." He looked back at her. "He made me, you know."

"I . . . what?"

"The killer on the wall. Everything that came after that came because of him." His voice was flat, distant.

Mina suddenly became aware of the chill wind. Of the darkness.

The superintendent looked at her and yet didn't. "I didn't mean for it to happen."

Mina shifted. "What? Mean for what to happen?"

"All this. It just got away from me. You believe me, don't you? That it was never my intention that they would die?"

The missing one – Isla

Isla sat on the sofa, her legs pulled up beneath her, and sipped at her tea, watching the fire that Ramsey had set in the fireplace leaping and climbing. It felt like a dream. There were so many responses to this, so many ways in which one should move. Yet Isla had chosen none of them. After a lifetime of chasing monsters, she had finally stopped.

"I don't believe this." Connor sat with his head in his hands. The color had drained from his face, and he looked different now, no longer like the man she knew.

Isla did not respond, simply cradled the heat of her mug, watched the dance of the flames, and re-

membered to breathe. It was strange. Her entire
life had been defined by fear—of monsters, of this
very moment. Yet now that it had come, she was
not afraid. She felt the butterfly wing flutter in her
abdomen and wondered if that was why. If it was
the acceptance of something that for so long had
scared her so much, being a mother, if allowing
that in had driven the fear away. If she could face
that, then she could face anything. She took another sip of tea and allowed her mind to prod at
the alien quietude.

"The thing is," said Connor, "I never got it before. I mean, what the research we do means for
you. You've always . . . For you, it's like this mis-
sion. I mean, for me, yeah, it's fascinating and all
that, but I've never really understood this need
you have to get the answers." He looked up at her,
pulled a face. "I get it now."

She studied him, allowing the pieces to move
carefully in her mind. Kitty and Zach and Ben.
Amelia and Leila. Victoria and Maggie. Parker and
Jake. And Stephen Doyle. Stephen, a feint to the
left. An attempt to shut it down, to prevent the
hunt. Because deep down, the killer on the wall
knew it had gone too far, that he had done too
much, that with each death, the inevitability of
capture drew nearer. And he had panicked at the
last moment. Perhaps he had thought about the
reality of that capture, of prison walls, of a life that
would look very different from the life he had
known before, and perhaps he had balked. So,
Stephen Doyle. Poor sad Stephen. What better victim? What greater foil?

She studied the dance of the flames and felt the

movement in her abdomen, steadier now that she knew where to look for it. He hadn't known there was DNA. He had thought he had been smart enough, blinded by his own arrogance. So he had believed that, with Stephen Doyle, he would hand the world a suspect, that any suspect would do. And, she allowed, you couldn't really blame him. It had worked with Heath McGowan.

"You locked the front door, right?" Connor asked quietly.

Isla smiled. "Yes, Dad. We're locked up tight."

So much science. So many years. And the hunt had, in the end, turned on its head, so that all that was left for her to do was sit on her sofa, drink tea, and wait for the fox to come after the hound.

Connor stood up, walked to the window, tweaked the curtain aside, and peered out into the dark night. And in the pit of her stomach, Isla felt a familiar stirring. Fear. Abruptly, she stood, then walked with quick steps to the stairs.

"Where are you going?"

"I'll be right back." She hurried up the stairs, feeling the fear turn, crystallize. Because the thing was, sometimes you needed fear. Sometimes it was all that there was to drive you onward, to prevent you from simply sitting and waiting for your own death to arrive. She hurried along the landing, let herself into the study.

Connor was still standing when she reemerged, her arms full of box files. He frowned, pulled the curtain back down, careful to avoid any chinks, any lines of sight. "What the hell are you doing?" he asked. Then walked swiftly to her, reached out.

"You shouldn't be carrying those. Think of the baby." He took the boxes from Isla and carried them to the sofa. Looked down at them and over at her. "So . . . um . . . what, we're doing some statistics to pass the time?"

"No," said Isla. "I was just thinking. I know pretty much everyone in this village, right?"

"Right."

"So," she continued, "I have scanned pretty much everyone in this village at one point or another. I can't think of anyone who hasn't been a control subject at some time in the past ten years."

"Okay?"

"So, maybe there's something in there. Maybe there's a clue in among the fMRIs that we've never seen, simply because they were controls and because we weren't looking."

She had paused in her study to remove her father's scan. She smiled at Connor and hoped that the lie did not show in her face. Because, when you said it, the conclusions were inevitable. A murderer in the village, her father a psychopath, the planting of evidence. And yet a memory kept replaying around and around in Isla's mind. Of her father singing her to sleep. Climbing beneath her bed to search for the monsters she was insisting were there. It might have been denial, a refusal to see the truth, but no matter what she did, Isla could not equate that man with the monster. She lifted a box file, pulled free a sheaf of scan results. Besides, while you could say with some ease that most murderers had an excellent chance of being diagnosed as psychopaths, the reverse was not true. You could be a psychopath and a liar, and you could ignore all the rules that you chose to ignore, and still not be a murderer.

Right?

Isla sank to the living-room floor, crossed her legs before her, and began to separate the papers out. She would try to forget for a moment the other daughters, the other families that had been wrong before her. She would try to forget that sometimes, you could live with a monster and simply never know it. She would push forward, her fear driving her in search of another answer, a better answer. She would tell herself that biology was not in fact destiny.

Connor lowered himself down beside her. "So, what are we looking for?"

Isla handed him a pile of scans, a sheet containing a table of numbers. "I want to match up each scan with the subject name. They're all anonymous, but we do have the identification numbers. You can cross-reference back to this table here to find out which scan goes with which person."

He nodded "You want me to unanonymize them?"

"Yes."

Connor pursed his lips. "You know, I'm pretty sure this is a violation of participant confidentiality."

Isla looked at him and grinned. Perhaps her father wasn't the only one who cared little about rules.

"I'm looking for psychopathy?"

"Yes. Well, any dysfunction in the paralimbic system . . . Just see what you can find."

"God," muttered Connor, "this is an ethical nightmare."

Isla snorted. "Just get on with it."

They moved in a rhythm, working through each scan, so that in the end a pile had formed, of brain after brain, all of them operating as they should. Until in the end there were no scans left. Isla sat back, looked at the pile and at the empty space beside it, where there should have been an answer, and sighed heavily.

"Well, that went well."

The fear had turned in her now, had twisted into a low spoken chant that wormed its way through her brain. *There's always your father.* She covered her face with her hands, a child hiding from the dark.

"What? Isla, what is it?"

And so she told him. Even though she hadn't intended to, had meant to keep her father's secret safe. Still, the words tumbled out as Connor listened, his frown deepening. When she was done, it seemed that a plug had been pulled, that she had nothing left in her. Isla laid her head back against the sofa, closed her eyes.

"Look," said Connor, his voice coming from far away, "so your father shows psychopathy traits. Frankly, I'm not even vaguely surprised."

She opened her eyes. "You're not?"

He pulled a face. "Dude, have you met your father? That guy can be scary as hell."

"Oh, great."

"No, I don't mean it like that. I mean, he's tough.

You can see that. I think he's doubtful about me because, you know, I work with you. We spend so much time together, so he's protective. I get that. I think, given what we're dealing with here, I'd have been more concerned if I'd never had any vibes off him. It would have meant his persona was a bit more intact, that his ability to keep up a facade was better."

"Which would make him a better serial killer," said Isla quietly.

"And the thing is, yes, he's showing paralimbic dysfunction. But what isn't shown here, what we didn't test him for, because he was in the control group, was how much the other areas of his brain are taking over, how much he has learned to compensate for these failings. He may have a better level of functionality—of normality, then—than you are giving him credit for. You know this as well as I do. The brain is remarkably elastic. And with the right childhood and the right environment, your father may well have learned to compensate using other brain areas. It wouldn't be as easy for him to be empathic, to be compassionate, to be responsible, but it may well be the case that working harder means he is capable of it, anyway."

Isla closed her eyes again. The fear had grown now, had sprouted tentacles. Her armory had failed her. The knowledge that was meant to save her had proven suddenly defunct. What the hell was she going to do now?

She sat up again, grabbed the pile of papers.

"What now?"

"I'm not giving up. The answer is here. I know it is." She shuffled through the brain scans of her entire family, of everyone she knew, and then from somewhere in the back of her brain came a little voice, the nugget of an idea. That she was wrong. That what she had in her hands wasn't everyone she knew. That one was missing.

The fear roared.

The wall – Mina

The older parts of her brain screamed at her to run. Superintendent Bell stood beside the stones of the tumbledown wall, looking out over the moor. Mina thought of Isla, of the word *psychopath*, of all that the man before her had done and all that he was capable of. Of the words of Toby Benedict. *I saw a man. He was limping.* And she wondered what the hell she had just done.

They make themselves look vulnerable. They make themselves look weak.

She watched the superintendent, watched his hands. Were they the hands that had ended all those lives?

Mina took a step backward, reached into her pocket for her phone, in the same moment remembering that she had left it in her bag, that her bag was in the car, two hundred meters away, maybe more. The awareness was like a plunge into icy water.

"You know how you do something," said Bell, "and it's the work of a moment, and then it's done. And you think that life is just going to go back to normal. Only it doesn't. That thing you did, that one moment, it changes everything."

She should run. Her body screamed at her, and her feet twisted themselves away, as if they would flee with her or without her. But Mina had spent many years learning to walk forward when her brain screamed at her to run back, and so she did just that, walking nearer to the wall.

She took a deep breath. Plunged. "Is it you?" she asked.

"Is what me?"

"Are you the killer on the wall?"

The superintendent let loose a sound that startled her. He began to laugh. The laugh continued for what seemed to Mina to be an inappropriately long time. Then he looked at her, examined her, as if he had never quite seen her like before. "Sweet Jesus, no. I can be an arsehole, but I'm not that much of an arsehole." A thoughtful moment, and then the superintendent asked, "Did you really think I was?"

Mina's heart thudded. "Well," she said, venturing out onto paper-thin ice, "you framed Heath McGowan."

Another long moment of silence. Then the superintendent turned away. He let loose a low moan. "Mina," he said, his voice heavy, "what the hell have I done?"

The no longer great Eric Bell – Eric

To Eric, it seemed that he was walking underwater. There was a dullness to everything, a distance. He was not careful how he placed his feet on the rolling moor, so its unevenness sent shards of pain up through his knee, his hip. The girl walked beside him. No, not beside him. He could hear her footfalls in the darkness, to the side and a little behind. She was keeping him in front of her because, in spite of what he had said, she remained afraid of him. He looked out into the darkness. That was probably reasonable.

The great Eric Bell had a tendency to be a little blind to consequences. It was one of the things that had always vexed Bonnie the most, his tendency to dive into things without any thought as to what might be waiting below the surface. Yet now it seemed he could think of little else. He would be fired. That was inevitable. The girl, Mina, who was sheepdogging him now, being so gentle and so kind, she would testify against him in whatever disciplinary hearing emerged from the mists. That, too, was inevitable.

Eric walked, seeing not the undulating ground before him, but the body of Lucy Tuckwell. Seeing the blood and the brain matter and the arms that curled so instinctively around the mound of her stomach, a futile effort to protect the child that would never be. He felt the world still again, the way it had as he stood there in the doorway of that flat, so small and so neat. And just beyond the body on the living-room floor, an open door, a crib, already made up with a bright yellow duvet, a mobile hanging above it, which twisted in the breeze from the open window. Rabbits carrying umbrellas.

He had stood there for longer than would have seemed possible, had simply stood there and stared at the dead body of Lucy Tuckwell.

Had he felt sadness? Anger at two lives taken so unfairly?

Eric's foot sank into the loose ground, his heel slipping just enough to get the heart pumping. He wasn't one for introspection. He did not entirely understand what it was to stand over the dead body of an almost child, someone entirely unknown to him, and weep for her.

No, that wasn't it.

What he had felt was opportunity.

He had called it in, like any good little detective

sergeant would, had waited outside the flat, in that dismal hallway. He had greeted the forensic team, had exchanged some words that meant nothing, then had walked steadily down the stairs, out the front door to his parked car. The box had been tucked under the passenger seat. A random collection of trinkets from the victims. Later he would wonder why he had gathered them, whether he had had a purpose in mind, or if it was some macabre magpie urge that he simply didn't understand. He suspected the truth: That justice could be a mercurial woman. That sometimes it required good cops, willing to do what others would not, in order to lift the blindfold, help her to see. That the end would justify the means.

He had driven himself, and his little box, to the pub. The grandmother had said, "If he's not at Lucy's, he'll be in that White Star place. Terrible place. But then, you can't tell them what to do, can you? Not when they're adults." He'd found Heath slumped in a booth at the back, his head down, gaze hooked on a two-thirds drunk pint of bitter. Still with the blood of Lucy Tuckwell on his hands.

The boy had put up little resistance. Looked up at Eric in the manner of one who had been waiting, nodded once, drained his pint, stood, and placed his hands behind his back.

"The baby," Heath had muttered. "Is the baby okay?"

Perhaps that was the point when it would have appeared to onlookers that things had moved beyond his control. Eric had taken hold of Heath's hair, a straggling handful, had pushed his face down into the table, clamped handcuffs tight around his wrists. Had leaned in close. "The baby is fucking dead. Just like its mother."

He would later reflect on that moment, on the slip of his hand into Heath McGowan's pocket. The key chain, the wedding ring. That the smoothness of it, the ease, had made it all seem preordained somehow.

That this time justice would have her eyes open for once.

He remembered the booking in, the custody sergeant taking McGowan's details, the search, the reveal of the items that inextricably linked him to the deaths of Zachary Aiken, Leila Doyle. The look that had crossed McGowan's face, so fleetingly, of being bested, of having played and lost. That silent moment of communication that had passed between Eric and McGowan. *You win.*

And he had. He had caught the killer on the wall. He had become the great Eric Bell.

He should have retired. Years ago. But he'd been chancing his arm, pushing his luck. When you played roulette long enough without losing, you started to fool yourself that you knew the game, that your success was in some way connected to skill. When in fact it was luck all along. And luck always ran out.

They left the moor, boggy ground turning to pavement underfoot. Mina stopping at the car, retrieving her handbag with quick movements, careful always to keep him in her line of sight. Eric smiled. Then they turned, walked down the road toward Eric's house, he in front, Mina behind. His house didn't have a back gate that led onto the moor, hadn't had one for twenty years. Bonnie's idea, not his. Tonight, with the pain in his hip, he cursed that. But then his house came into view, with its creep of light from the gap in the window, and he remembered the other option and suddenly was glad that Bonnie was protected from the moor by a high wall.

The thing was, he could see consequences if he tried. He could work through repercussions. If, that was, he stopped long enough, if he really thought about it. Didn't rely on his instincts. Because, Eric would be the first to admit, when he relied on his instincts, he was an arsehole.

They turned into the driveway, Mina still a step or two behind him. Still cautious. They got to the front door as it was swung open from the inside. Bonnie, still in her coat, her eyes wide. "Oh, it's you. Thank God."

A spark of an emotion he couldn't identify. "The door should have been locked, Bonnie. Why wasn't it locked?"

She threw her arms up in the air, defiant. "I'm not a bloody caged animal, Eric. You can't expect me to just sit here behind a locked door, never knowing when you're coming home." Then she saw Mina and stopped. "Oh, Mina, love, sorry. Come in. Are you okay?"

Mina slipped into the house behind him and closed the door tight. "I'm okay. I just . . . I bumped into the super and . . . I thought it would be best to make sure he got home okay."

Eric, however, was studying his wife. "Where have you been? You haven't been out walking, have you?"

Bonnie pulled a face. "I was at Isla's. Remember? You were going to stop by? And no, I haven't been out walking. Your son-in-law was kind enough to bring me home. He was concerned about my safety." She gave Eric a pointed look. "Your elder daughter had a complete meltdown when she heard that Stephen wasn't the man they were looking for. Went completely hysterical. Poor Ramsey is having to drive her all the way home, while that useless husband of hers fannies about, doing God knows what. Mina, tea?"

"No, I—"

"Bonnie, I've done something." The words were out before he understood what it was he was going to say. He watched his wife's face, recognized the way she steeled herself, and had a sudden flash of awareness of just how many times he had seen his wife do that before.

"I should . . ." Mina began to inch toward the door.

"I planted evidence on Heath McGowan. I thought I had him. I thought there was no way the killer on the wall could be anyone else. So I . . . I made sure that they'd convict him. Only it wasn't him. The force knows about it. I think I'm going to get sacked. I may be prosecuted."

He ran out of words and air, felt a hollow silence settling all around him. Mina looked from him to his wife, who was suddenly paralyzed.

"Oh, Eric," Bonnie said quietly. "You really are an idiot."

"I did what I thought was right," he said.

"But that's the thing, isn't it? It's always about you. What you think is right. You never stop to consider that other people might have a view, that maybe your view isn't always the right one." Bonnie folded her arms across her chest and shook her head wearily. "Eric . . . I don't know what to say to you."

He should stop talking. That would be sensible. Unfortunately, his mouth did not agree. "Are you going to leave me?"

He saw Mina Arian, saw her head dip farther, as if she could make herself disappear into the parquet flooring.

Bonnie snorted. "Eric, love, you being a foolish man is not news to me. You've always been the same. So if I was going to leave you, I probably would have done it years ago, when I still had time to find myself a nice rich man to take care of me into my dotage. I'm pretty sure no one is going to be queuing up for that job now."

He looked at her, strangely uncertain.

"Eric . . . ," she said, enunciating carefully, "I'm not going to leave you. You're a fool, but unfortunately, you're my fool, so . . . I don't know, we'll figure it out." She sighed heavily, then pulled her coat off. "Well, I don't know about you, but I'm going to crack open that Baileys in the kitchen. Mina, you sure I can't tempt you?"

Mina, with a half smile, edged closer to the door. "No. I'd better head back to work. Super, is it okay if I take the car?"

"Yes. Right. Yes."

Bonnie nodded, waving Eric toward her. "Best walk her out, Eric. Make sure she gets there safe."

"Yes, sure." He patted his pockets, pulled out the car keys.

"There's no need."

"Aye, girl. Best do what she says. She's clearly in no mood to hear no."

They walked back out of the house and onto the drive. Eric pulled the door tight behind him and then stopped, breathing in the icy air. It tasted like snow. He followed close behind Mina, thinking of the next day. When he would wake up, get out of bed, and have nowhere to go. The great Eric Bell was no more. What would he be after this? What would be left? He stood on the driveway, looking at the plunging shadows from the hedges, listening as the wind tugged at the leaves and created a sound that reminded him of breathing. Someone else would have to find the killer on the wall now.

He raised the key fob to unlock Bonnie's car, then stopped. Mina had ducked down, was crouching near the hedge.

"What the hell are you doing?"

At first she didn't answer. Then she said a word which he thought sounded like *vulnerability*.

Eric frowned and moved closer. There, stuck on a twig toward the bottom of the hedge, was a flash of white. He frowned and, with care, reached down, then held it up so that the dim curtained glow from the house illuminated it. "What is that?"

A musical tone shattered the darkness, and Mina's hand flew to her handbag. She answered the phone with a "Yes."

She sounded different, thought Eric. She sounded like him.

"You got it? Okay. And the match . . ." Mina's voice faded away as she crouched there, phone held to her ear for absurdly long moments. Then she hung up without saying goodbye.

"Everything okay?" asked Eric.

Mina stood up abruptly. "That was Zoe from forensics. They got a fingerprint from the broom at Victoria Prew's."

Eric stared at her. "Who? And what the hell is that?"

The girl looked as though she would cry. "It's a sling," she said. "It's Ramsey's sling."

The killer on the wall

He stood where he had stood before. Twenty years ago and then today and so many times in between. He stood at the wall. Beyond lay nothing but empty moor. Above, pinpricks of starlight had broken through. A vivid cold wind tore at him. He didn't feel cold, though. Instead, that too-familiar sensation of having left his body for parts unknown. He watched his body from the outside, the movements that were so familiar now, a train on tracks. He watched as his hands moved as they were always meant to move. Because that was the thing, wasn't it? It was no more a choice for him than was the pumping of his heart, the inhaling, exhaling of his lungs. It was who he was always meant to be.

The body felt unspeakably heavy hung across his shoulder. But it was a good heaviness, familiar and whole. And, over the years, he had built up his skill with this part, with all parts. To do what he did, strength was necessary in so many different ways. He lowered the body to the ground, careful, careful, watched the chest rise and fall, rise and fall. Blood had begun to pool around the collarbone, and he felt in his pocket for a rag. He'd have to wipe that away before the finish. Because it always had to finish the same: with the pressure of his fingers. He could not have told you why, could not have explained what it was about this that made him feel whole again, only that it did.

But the thing was, he had fought against it. For so long he had lived a lie, trying to pretend that he was human, that he was normal. Only he wasn't.

It was coming to an end. He could feel it, as a book that had only a few pages left. He had hoped . . . what? That he could ride off into the sunset? That this need would suddenly disappear, leaving him exactly what he appeared to be? But it was too late for that. Time was almost up.

He sank to the grass, and the damp of it leached through his jeans onto his skin. In the past he would have taken more care. In the past he would have worried more about what he was picking up, what he was leaving behind. But it really didn't seem important now. Because in minutes or hours, they would begin to unpick his lies, and then they would come.

He looked back toward the lights of Briganton and felt something that was probably a distant relation of sadness. If only things could have been different. Then he saw something else, flashing blue lights in the distance, and he felt a spark of adrenaline, a spurt of fear.

And hadn't it been about the fear all along? To be in among it, that which you have created. It was like a scent, an unwashed bodily odor of terror. To walk among it, to see it reflected in the down-turned mouths, in the darting eyes. It was engrossing and addictive and so, so very dangerous.

He watched the blue lights, trying to place where they were, and to determine if they were coming for him. But, he found, he didn't really care anymore. His time was up, and he was tired of running.

He watched the shallow breaths, the chest rising and falling.

Then Ramsey stretched his fingers out, traced the outline of Emilia's jaw with tender care, and for a moment felt a wash of . . . what? He would call it grief, and yet he understood that the color of grief for him was probably very different from that seen by others. He thought of Isla, as he always did. She would be so sad. And yet he had never wanted to make Isla sad. She was home. She was the harbor to which he returned following each and every storm. She had given him the sliver of a chance to find something normal. The blue lights were coming closer now, and a sound broke into the silence of the moor: the wail of sirens. And here, at the end, Ramsey thought of Isla as he slipped his fingers around her sister's neck.

The man beside me – Isla

Isla ran. She was dimly aware of the sound of foot-steps behind her, all but drowned out by the thundering of her heart. The fMRI scan was missing. Ramsey had told her he had gone for it, had complained about how long it had taken, about the noise of the MRI, and all the while he had been lying. He had looked in her face, had lied to her. She ran past the school, her legs screaming, and off in the distance could hear sirens. She pulled hard left, plunged down the hill. She knew where he would be.

Connor had looked at her like she had lost her mind as she tore the pile of scans apart, searching for the missing one. "It must be there," she had screamed. "You ran it. Remember? I was away at that conference in Dublin? You said you were going to put Ramsey through the scanner, the PCL-R."

"He canceled, Isl. I'm sorry. I thought you knew."

She ran harder, thinking of her mother, of her sister. He wouldn't. But he would, wouldn't he? He had.

"Isl, come on. You cannot seriously believe that your husband would have killed all those people? He . . . I mean, his own brother? He was one of the original victims, for God's sake."

She had pushed herself up, hadn't been able to stop moving, around and around the living room, with that god-awful heat pumping from that too-hot fire, as if she could outrun this if she kept moving. It couldn't be. It couldn't be.

The trouble was, she knew it could.

"My father . . . ," she'd said, her voice high and strange, "he always said it looked like the killer on the wall was interrupted, that he never got the chance to finish Ramsey off properly, and that's why his head wound wasn't so serious, why he wasn't killed. But it wasn't that, was it? It was that he did it to himself."

"How? I mean, there was no weapon left—"

"The wall. He hit his own head on the wall. Just enough to make it bleed. Just enough to make us think . . ." She turned to Connor. "Just enough to create the persona of the victim."

Connor's knee was jumping; he, too, was unable to stay still. "Okay, then what about his arm? This guy, whoever he is, he is physically fit. I mean, he's taking down men, women. He's transporting the bodies across some distance. He would need to be physically capable of that. Ramsey has a bunch of torn ligaments in his shoulder. He couldn't—"

But Isla was remembering that day, the coming home, her husband sitting on the sofa, holding his shoulder. *I fell on my run. My shoulder really doesn't feel good.*

She remembered herself, car keys still in her hand, turning back around again. *Come on. Let's get you to A & E. Get that checked out.*

No, it'll be okay.

Ramsey, I really think . . .

It's fine, okay? A cold snap that had come from nowhere. And Isla, tired from work, tired from too much thinking, too much chasing monsters, simply not having the energy to fight, shrugging her shoulders, walking away.

"He went to A & E without me the next day—said he needed to wear a sling. I've never seen any hospital papers or a prescription . . . I have no idea if he really went."

"Jesus, Isl. This is mad."

She grabbed her phone. Dialed Mina, once, twice, three times, got nothing in return but an empty ringing. She shuffled through her options, finally called police headquarters, asked to be put through to Owen Darby. And she was vaguely surprised when he came on the line. She tumbled out a quick explanation, albeit not the real one. *Psychologist. Have an idea. Can you let me have a copy of the other murders, the ones that took place in the intervening twenty years? Well, I . . .* Then, the name drop. *I'm*

Superintendent Bell's daughter. Which of course changed everything, as it always had. She listened as he read it to her, scratching locations and dates with quick, rough writing. *Thank you. Great help.* Hung up and burst into tears.

"Isla, please." Connor pulled her into a hug. "Come on. You're . . . This isn't proof. None of this is proof. You're tired. You're frightened, and the hormones—"

"Would you fuck off! The hormones!" Isla waved the list in front of him. Jabbing at it with her pen. "Ramsey attended the University of Southhampton from nineteen ninety-six to nineteen ninety-nine. All the murders took place within a radius of sixty miles of there during that period. Then, for six years, there's nothing." She looked at him. "That's when we met. Remember Ethan Charles in Albany? Killed two, then met his wife and stayed clean for ten years, before falling off the wagon and going after those four sorority girls."

Six years. The honeymoon years, in which they'd been one another's everything. Then things had shifted. She had begun her postdoctoral research, had plunged herself into it, so rarely surfacing for air. And Ramsey . . . That was when the baby stuff had begun, when he had begun suggesting, cajoling, at times begging, for them to have a child. And she had said no, that she wasn't ready, that she was too busy with work. Was that it? That he had been looking for something to ground him, something to keep him clean?

"The killing begins again in two thousand five. Newcastle, Sunderland, Edinburgh." She felt nausea

rise and remembered the interview her husband
had conducted in Sunderland, the stag weekend in
Edinburgh, that receipt that she had found stuffed
into the pocket of his jeans, had shrugged off as
being nothing, a coffee shop in Newcastle.

It had been there, in front of her. There had
been that trail of bread crumbs, hints that something wasn't right. And yet she, like so many others
before her, had chosen to look away. She was no
better. In spite of all she had done, all the myriad
ways in which she had fought to protect herself,
she remained just as easy prey as the next person.

She ran through the Briganton streets now at a
flat-out pace, could hear the footsteps behind her,
Connor struggling to keep up, growing more and
more distant, her name being called and flung
into the wind. She ducked onto Dray Lane, running and running, footsteps uneven as pavement
turned to moor, and then she saw him.

Ramsey stood beside the wall, as if he was waiting for her. Her breath caught in her chest. Knees
waiting to buckle. And she slowed. But she did not
stop. Isla walked slowly, could dimly make out a
shape at his feet. The fear leapt in her belly. She
walked on. Ramsey was no longer wearing his sling.
He had no coat. His sleeves were rolled up. The expression on his face . . . It was as if her husband
had left. As if he was gone and the man who stood
before her was someone else, a different person
inhabiting the same body.

"Ramsey?"

He looked at her for long moments and then
slowly nodded, the acknowledgment of a stranger.

Then he looked down toward the shape at his feet. Isla's gaze followed his, and she gave a low moan. Her sister lay sprawled beneath him, her blond curls thrown carelessly above her head, the line of blood that traced its way from her forehead down to her chin and beyond, dark and bitter.

"She . . ."

"She's not dead," he said quietly.

Isla moved closer, three quick strides, dropped to her knees beside her husband, the prone form of her sister. And for dark moments, she thought that he was lying. That this was one final cruel twist of the knife. Then she felt a movement beneath her fingers, her sister's chest rising and falling.

"I could have," said Ramsey quietly, "but I didn't. I thought about you. And"—he glanced away—"the baby. I thought about that too. So I didn't. I mean, Emilia, she will be its auntie, after all."

Isla pulled her gaze from her sister and looked up at him. It seemed that she did not recognize his features. That his eyes were farther apart, lips thinner, nose more crooked. "You killed Zach." It was not a question.

"Yes."

"The others. You killed them too."

"Yes."

"Why?" The single word escaped her as a wail, shattering the silence. She stared at him, trying to find her beautiful, kind, gentle husband, but seeing only the blood on his hands, the emptiness in his face.

"I don't know why. I just . . . I had to. That day . . . You don't understand what it's like. I had to know what it would be like to feel someone die, to put my fingers around their throat and squeeze and squeeze until they were . . . gone. It was just, it was all I thought about. I wasn't sleeping. I couldn't eat. It was like this thing had invaded my head, and I just couldn't shake it free." He wasn't looking at her, appeared to be talking to the inert form of her sister. "I wanted it to be my father. It was going to be my father. I had it all planned out. And then . . . I don't know what happened. I saw Kitty leaving the church. I saw her go home. And I just knew how easily I could do it. I knew it would be nothing at all. I got in over the back fence. She'd left the back door wide open. I think she was feeding her cat. I don't know that she ever saw me. I knocked her down, I think I knocked her out, and then . . . I did it." He nodded toward the dark glass of the Prew house. "I hid her there. Remember that old bungalow? Every time I pass that house, I think about that old bungalow."

Isla gripped hold of her sister's hand and fought back a rising urge to vomit.

"Once I'd done it, I needed to do it again. You don't get it. You don't understand. It's like the most amazing high . . . I hit Ben Flowers with a baseball bat. He was so drunk, I could probably have attacked him with a sponge and he'd have gone down. And the thing is, I kind of regretted it once I'd done it. He was a big lump of a guy, and for a while I didn't think I'd be able to . . . but I did," he finished quietly.

"And Zach," added Isla.

"And Zach," agreed Ramsey.

"Why?"

For a moment he seemed to be casting about for an answer. Then he shrugged. "He was there. I mean, I didn't mind the kid. But it was so obvious that he was the favorite. The things my father, what he did to me, to Cain, he'd never think of doing to Zach. I don't know. Maybe I was punishing my father by taking his favorite away from him."

Isla tried to breathe, tried to focus. Best to forget where she was and whom she was talking to, because if she didn't, then she would crack in two, right here on the moor. So, she sat up straighter, her voice shifted, so that it bore in it the soothing tones of the psychologist at work. As if in this persona, she could survive. "What did your father do to you, Ramsey?"

He looked away. "I don't think you want to ask me that." He glanced down at Emilia. "Or maybe, then again, you do. You are always the scientist." He dropped his voice low. "He molested me. Time and time again."

That nausea again, the heat racing through her.

"He never did it to Zach. Cain, he got it a couple of times, but never as bad as me. I always wondered why that was. Maybe he was punishing me for whatever evil he could see in me." He looked down at her then. "I never told anyone before. But then," he allowed, "there are lots of things no one knew about me before today. You know, Isl, I did try to stop. And I did for a really long time."

"Six years," said Isla softly.

"Six years," Ramsey agreed. "Only, the need, it kept getting stronger and stronger. So in the end, I thought, *Well, just one. One won't hurt.* It would get it out of my system. Would make it stop. But it didn't."

"Why come back to Briganton? Why not just carry on, under the radar?" She watched him, this man she used to know. "Was it me?" she asked quietly. "Was it because of my work with Heath?"

He gave a little laugh. "I don't know . . . You were never there. You were always with him. And you were so determined you were going to get underneath the skin of the killer on the wall that I—"

"You were jealous?"

He shrugged. "Maybe. Or maybe it was that this is who I've always been, and I just got tired of hiding it."

"But Stephen Doyle?" Isla's voice cracked. "He trusted you, Ramsey, and he was so sad."

Ramsey looked at her with the empty blankness of one asked to describe the smell of purple. "He wanted to die. He said so, that day on the roof. And you were pregnant, and I thought it would be a chance for us, for me, to start again."

"So, you killed him. And you framed him."

He shrugged. "Yes. I thought it would make things better."

Isla wanted to run, wanted to turn and bolt. But there was her sister, unconscious before her, and this was on her, wasn't it? There was no running. She had lived with this. She had been blind. She had allowed this. She forced herself to breathe, to look at the man that had once been her husband, and there, in the corner of her vision, came the slightest impression of movement. Isla ignored it, kept her gaze fixed on her husband, on the killer on the wall.

"The photograph of us? The letters that came to the house?" she asked. "They were all you?"

He nodded slowly. "The camera was set on a timer. I put it in the hedge."

"Why?"

"So you would be afraid. So you would want to leave. Because I thought, if we left, then I could stop it. I wouldn't have this place, this bloody village, with its constant reminders. I thought if we went somewhere else, then things would be different. I'd be different."

"Like you were in Southampton? Like you were in Scotland?" A fracture in the facade, the grief breaking through, and Isla was shouting now. But the sensation of movement was growing larger, and there, if you listened hard enough, was the sound of footsteps, so she no longer cared.

Ramsey stared at her and opened his mouth, as if there could possibly be any more to say. But the sound of footsteps had become clearer now and undeniable, even to him. Isla watched as he turned toward them, her gaze following his, the dim figures taking shape, of her father, of Mina, of Connor, of uniformed police officers she had never seen before.

Ramsey looked across at the approaching figures and back at Isla, and Isla moved, placed her hand flat across her belly, bracing for what would come. But he merely stood there, looking at her sadly. "Guess that's the posse." He smiled. "It's okay, Isl. It needs to end. It's time." Then a low sigh. "It's finally over."

Isla looked down at her sister, at the flutter of her eyelashes, and pressed her hand against the movement in her own belly, and there she clung.

Tears bubbled up and spilled over. She did not look up.

Then, her father's voice rolling across the moor. He sounded like he was crying. "Ramsey Aiken, I am arresting you on suspicion of murder."

Thursday, November 3

One week later – Mina

Mina ran her fingers across the stones of the wall as she walked, her steps slow, measured. The first sprinkling of snow had fallen. Nothing much, a light dusting. But sufficient to bathe the village in a pearlescent glow, to allow them to believe, however briefly, that everything could be made new again. She walked steadily, with no particular destination in mind, merely to be in this place, to bear witness. And yet, in spite of that, her feet took her where she was always going to go. To where it started.

There at the stretch of wall that ran behind Victoria Prew's house stood Superintendent Bell. Although whether he would continue to be called that remained to be seen. Scuttlebutt abounded that he had handed in his resignation. Whether that would be sufficient to protect him from a criminal prosecution was doubtful. Eric Bell stood, looking out over the moor, his thick coat collar pulled up high around his chin. He turned with the sound of footsteps, and it seemed almost that he had been expecting her.

"Sir."

Eric waved her away. "You don't need to call me that anymore. Eric will do."

Mina found herself smiling. "Eric, then. How are you?"

He shrugged, his gaze still off into the distance. "Have been better. Could have been worse."

Mina tucked herself into position beside him, rested her arm against the cold old stones. "Emilia?"

"She's fine." Eric shrugged. "She had a concussion. They kept her in for a day or two but say she's on the mend now."

Mina, watching him, found herself smiling. "She's fine?"

He turned, his gaze finding her, assessing. Then a low snort. "You sound like Bonnie. Okay, Bonnie says she's far from fine. That what happened the first time, she never really got over that. And now this. To know that it was someone she trusted, loved as a brother . . ." He cast about, perhaps looking for the words, perhaps trying to pick his way through the emotions behind them. "Still, we could have been burying her, so there's that."

"And Isla? I wanted to call, wanted to see if she's okay, but . . ."

Eric shifted his weight, gave a slight wince. "What can I say about Isla? You know she's back at work, right? Bonnie's worried about her, but I don't know . . . Isla, she's got more of me in her than she'd ever admit to. She'll get past this, given time. And she's got the baby." His face took on a lightness that Mina had never seen before. "That'll help."

Mina nodded and scuffed at the snow beneath her feet with the toe of her boot. It was a strange sensation, that feeling that it had finally come to an end. It left the entire world feeling like the snow out on the moor, pristine and untouched, that anything could come next.

"Sir? Eric, I mean?"

"Yes?"

"How did we not see it?" She very carefully did not say, *you*, how did *you* not see it? "How did we pass by him every single day and still never know?"

Eric gave a low grunt. "Because, lass, he didn't want us to know. We were his cover. Us and that whole victim thing he had created for himself. That boy, he was able to slip our impression of him on and off like an old overcoat. And the thing is, we're people. Generally speaking, people are stupid. We look for whatever we expect to see. And not one of us here expected to see that boy as he really was. Isla says that his dad did terrible things to him. She says that if someone is vulnerable, if their brain isn't working quite right, they may still not turn out to be evil. Just . . ." He coughed. "A little bit foolish. But if they have all that brain stuff working against them, and then you add in a bastard of a parent, someone who tortures you and hurts you, sometimes all that can add up to murder."

Eric reached into his coat pocket and pulled out a small metal hip flask. He raised it and took a long swallow, then handed it to Mina.

Mina took it, looked up at him, eyebrow raised.

"You've earned it."

She raised the flask, took a pull. The liquid burned her throat, the heat spread along her limbs, and her head suddenly became a little lighter. Then she handed it back, tucked her hands inside her pockets, and turned to watch as the sun set beyond the wall.

Leah and Finn delve into each case, untangling the secrets and betrayals—large and small—that can lie just beneath the surface of a life, yet unprepared for where both trails will lead.

With engrossing characters, devilish twists, and evocative prose, *The Missing Hours* is that rare page-turner—as satisfying and complex as it is unpredictable.

Connect with  Us

Visit us online at
KensingtonBooks.com
to read more from your favorite authors, see books
by series, view reading group guides, and more.

Join us on social media

for sneak peeks, chances to win books and prize packs,
and to share your thoughts with other readers.

facebook.com/kensingtonpublishing
twitter.com/kensingtonbooks

Tell us what you think!

To share your thoughts, submit a review,
or sign up for our eNewsletters, please visit:
KensingtonBooks.com/TellUs.